praise

"*Tazia and Gemma* is the story of a mother's fierce determination to raise her daughter on her own terms, and a daughter's determination to discover and understand those terms. This is compulsively readable fiction: vivid, curious, and moving. It's also an intimate chronicle of early twentieth-century American history that needs to be remembered right now. The daily lives of working-class people, immigrants, minorities, and women—Epstein tells their stories with the attentiveness and dignity they deserve. You deserve to pick up this novel, for its lessons and its pleasures."

POLLY ROSENWAIKE, AUTHOR OF *LOOK HOW HAPPY I'M MAKING YOU*

"In *Tazia and Gemma*, Ann S. Epstein has created a novel of two complementary odysseys, one urgently looking forward, seeking a home, and one yearningly looking backwards, seeking origins. The two title characters are mother and daughter, and in Epstein's wonderful rendering, we follow the mother Tazia's journey across America over the course of several decades, from the Triangle Shirtwaist Fire early in the century to the wartime boom in California in the 1940s and 50s. Throughout her journeys, what shines through is Tazia's fierce sense of justice and her equally fierce love for her daughter. Gemma's journey, backwards in time, is more of a detective story, as she tracks down the people and places where she and her mother lived and worked when she was an infant and young girl. As Gemma pieces together an understanding of her mother's past lives, she comes to unexpected insights that take her beyond her original goals to a new sense of the meaning of home. Epstein's work shows a deep affection for her many memorable characters, and Tazia's dramatic encounters across the landscape of America over fifty years encapsulates our history from new and seldom-heard-from perspectives. A deeply-researched, deeply-felt, and deeply enjoyable novel."

LAWRENCE COATES, AUTHOR OF *THE GOODBYE HOUSE* AND *THE BLOSSOM FESTIVAL*

about the author

Ann S. Epstein writes novels, short stories, memoir, craft articles, and book reviews. She is the author of *On the Shore* (Vine Leaves Press, 2017) and *A Brain. A Heart. The Nerve.* (Alternative Book Press, 2018). Her other work appears in *Sewanee Review* (winner, Walter Sullivan Prize), *PRISM International, Ascent, The Long Story, Saranac Review, The Madison Review, Passages North, Red Rock Review, William and Mary Review, Tahoma Literary Review, The Copperfield Review, The Normal School, Carbon Culture Review, Earth's Daughters, The Offbeat, Wilderness House Literary Review,* and other journals. In addition to writing, she has a Ph.D. in developmental psychology and M.F.A. in textiles. Her historical works mix fact and fiction, and she is gratified to have forgotten what is and is not real by the time a story is finished.

To learn more about her work, visit her website: *asewovenwords.com* and follow **Ann S. Epstein Writer** on Facebook and Twitter.

Ann S. Epstein

Tazia and Gemma

ANN S. EPSTEIN

Vine Leaves Press
Melbourne, Vic, Australia

Print Edition
ISBN: 978-1-925417-72-2
Published by Vine Leaves Press 2018
Melbourne, Victoria, Australia

Cover design by Jessica Bell
Interior design by Amie McCracken

A catalogue record for this book is available from the National Library of Australia

NATIONAL LIBRARY OF AUSTRALIA

To mothers and daughters

table of contents

part one
Tazia, New York, 1911
chapter 1

One hundred minutes before the Triangle Waist Company will erupt in flames, Tazia Gatti pauses her foot above the sewing machine's treadle and lifts her throbbing eyes to the broken clock face on the grimy factory wall. *Two more hours.* Thank God it's Saturday, when she's out at five. On weekdays, she works seven to seven, later if she hasn't finished the allotted number of pieces.

Tazia studies the other immigrant women around her, pale from lack of sunlight with dark shadows underneath bloodshot eyes. They stitch with such haste that sometimes the needle goes through their fingers, but they're dead to the pain. They simply bind the wound in cotton and sew on. She sets a cotton sleeve in the armhole of the shirtwaist and stitches where the fabric puffs from shoulder to elbow, then tapers to the wrist. It's rumored that this popular new style will make Triangle the largest blouse manufacturer in New York. Tazia is awed that she works here, that sitting at her little machine connects her to something so big.

The foreman yells at them to speed up, but Tazia is already the fastest worker. Unlike the other girls, she doesn't need to pin the cloth in place to keep it from bunching. Feel alone lets her distribute the gathers evenly, saving a step. This skill got her moved from stitching hems on the ninth floor, to setting sleeves on the eighth. That was six months ago, a week before her seventeenth birthday and two weeks after she arrived from Italy to begin life in America.

The deafening clatter of hundreds of machines pounds in Tazia's ears and the smell of sweat and oil in the airless room makes her sway on the high wooden bench. Spring is only four days old, but already it's unseasonably warm. If her machine were in the front row, beneath the windows, she might see buds swelling on the oak trees in Washington Square. She's hot and tired and, unusual for her, hungry. Once fatigue sets in this late in the day, her stomach is as unsettled as when she wakes up. It's been two hours since she ate lunch—the heel of dark bread she tucked into her pocket at five this morning before taking two horse cars and the electric trolley to work. Mr and Mrs Campo, the couple she lives with in Brooklyn, had wrapped two olives as a snack, but like a greedy child, she'd wolfed them down with the bread. Little did they know how the salty olives quelled the queasiness and exhaustion that overtook her as the day wore on.

Ayal Gabay from Allegro Printers won't be back until Monday, with flyers advertising the new blouses. Saturday is the Jewish Sabbath, when he doesn't work. Tazia has mixed feelings about not seeing him today.

On one hand, a stolen half hour would relieve the tedium. When Ayal is here, Tazia feels alive. He calls her his *succosa shiksa*, his juicy non-Jew, and she fancies herself his *vietato frutta*, forbidden fruit that tastes sweeter than his arranged marriage. She nurtures the hope that his cleverness will allow her to escape life in a factory.

On the other hand, Ayal's absence today means she will be spared his urging to make a choice—his choice—and take care of the problem growing inside her.

"You'll have to come in tomorrow, girls," announces Mr Lemke, the floor foreman. "We're behind and the shipment has to go out by the end of Monday."

A groan escapes Tazia. Sunday is her Sabbath, the one morning she sleeps late, before the Campos wake her for Mass. "You got a problem?" Mr Lemke sneers. He points to a sign above the girls' heads. Most, like her, are only beginning to read English. Tazia barely reads Italian, having left school in third grade to help raise her younger siblings. But no one needs to read to know what the sign says: "If you don't come in on Sunday, don't show up on Monday."

***

Tazia's craving for sleep grows with each passing day. This morning, as she boiled coffee on the oil stove and willed her stomach to keep it down, she had looked forward to not setting the alarm clock when she went to bed tonight. Grigio, the gray cat Anna and Luigi keep to kill mice, would snooze beside her. It was during this fantasy that she'd discovered the precious olives and felt unworthy of the Campos' kindness. They'd promised her parents, back in Loro Piceno, to look after her. It was their way of repaying the Gattis for taking them in when fire destroyed their olive grove, forcing them to start anew in America. The Campos, who call Anastazia by her full name, are eager to introduce her to Luigi's nephew. Tazia is curious to meet the young man, but her situation makes this impossible. She doesn't know how, or how long, she can hide her condition.

Worry and guilt had stayed with Tazia on the two-hour trip to work. Her parents were so proud when she was promoted from hems to sleeves, how can she disappoint them? When she thinks of their shame, Ayal's solution makes sense. He already has the money, from his in-laws. He told them his boss was replacing linotype with monotype machines and would sell him an old model. Excited about Ayal's plan to open his own business making fanciful note cards, his wife's parents were happy to help. They consider Ayal, who came here at age ten and graduated college, a good match for their daughter. Tazia wants to know more about Ayal's wife, but he shushes her with kisses when she asks. He gave Tazia the cash to hold onto, perhaps thinking she'd be more likely to go through with the plan, but looking inside the envelope makes her feel more confused.

What she did with Ayal is a sin, but surely what he's asking of her is worse. And yet it would spare everyone pain. For now. She could continue to send the money her family counted on, and later Ayal, pleased that she'd seen things his way, would honour his promise to marry her. His wife would be hurt, but with her father's wealth, her parents could arrange another marriage.

Tazia's mind had still been in a muddle when she arrived at the Asch Building, where Triangle occupied the top three floors. As it did every morning, the light brown and terra cotta facade of the ten-storey structure reminded her of the stonework in the low buildings dotting her village's sunny hillsides as they sloped gently down to the Adriatic. Otherwise, the two worlds could not be more different. The red brick of the Campos' apartment building was so sooty it might as well be coal, while the sky above Greenwich Village, slumbering at that hour, was dishwater gray. Tazia misses bathing in the short rivers that line the gullies between Loro Piceno's hills, after a day picking olives. Because they must reposition the ladders up to a dozen times, it takes two hours to pick each of her family's five hundred and eighty-three trees. For two weeks, they work dawn to dusk to catch the fruit at the peak of ripeness. The labour is backbreaking, but less tiring, in Tazia's memory, than an equally long day hunched over a clattering sewing machine.

The clock had read 6:45 when Joe Zitto, one of the two elevator opera-
tors, dropped Tazia off on her floor. He'd teased her for being late because
even though work didn't start for fifteen minutes, several girls were already
busy, hoping to finish extra pieces that day. Tazia hung her things on the
uneven row of hooks. The girls had asked the foreman for a curtained
dressing room in the corner, but he said using the space would mean
a dozen fewer machines, ten dozen fewer pieces an hour, and fifteen
hundred fewer blouses a day. "If you'll take fifty cents less an hour," he'd
said with a laugh, "I'll give you your damned dressing room." So they
continue to hang their tattered coats and raveled sweaters beside the crisp
cotton blouses they make, but can't afford to buy.

Most of them are paid six dollars a week. Since moving down to the
eighth floor, Tazia earns a dollar more. Already her parents have used the
money she sends to buy a new wood stove and get medicine for her baby
brother, Zito, who was born with weak lungs. Men, who can work as
cutters or pressers, are paid up to two dollars more. Asking why will get
the women fired, so they keep their mouths shut and their hands and feet
moving.

The ones most taken advantage of work in the children's corner, girls
under the legal limit of fourteen, doing simple chores like trimming
thread. When inspectors visit, they hide inside packing crates and can't so
much as jiggle or whisper. They're paid only two dollars a week and if they
work on Sunday, get a slice of apple pie for lunch instead of money. Tazia's
favourite, Paulie, is an eleven-year-old from Hungary, whose tinkling
laugh reminds Tazia of her younger sister, Bianca. Last week, Paulie had
offered her pie to Tazia and was surprised when she turned it down. She
couldn't say she was nauseous, so she claimed she was too tired to eat.
Paulie had danced around singing, "I'd rather sleep than eat." Then the
imp had snuck into a cardboard case for a nap before the foreman blew
his whistle and ordered the children back to work.

Sometimes, when she's overwhelmed with worry and remorse, Tazia
makes herself smile thinking of Paulie's spunk. She's happy the child is
still playful, when girls a couple of years older than her are already listless
and discouraged. She knows Paulie's future will be the same as theirs, the
same as hers. If Tazia has any hope of making a better life, she must act
soon, yet confusion and lethargy prevent her. It will take an outside force
to propel her to move.

chapter 2

Now, to distract herself from the hunger pangs, Tazia does the one thing she knows will not take her mind off the bigger problem. While Mr Lemke inspects stations at the other end of the floor, she feels in the scrap bin beneath her table for the pieces of fabric she's been setting aside. Stealing, really. Because of her speed, the foreman isn't suspicious when she asks for extra material. The bins haven't been emptied in months, so she's not afraid her stash will be found. And the fine cotton is perfect for a layette. She even swipes some lace, which she attaches with tiny hand stitches as she imagines holding the infant to her breast. A girl. The old lady was certain.

Four weeks ago, telling the Campos she had to work on Sunday, Tazia instead went to Little Italy where the woman, wearing a black shawl that reminded Tazia of her nonna, beckoned her inside a damp basement apartment. Smoke from an oil lamp filled the room, and Tazia thought she would have to flee or gag up the breakfast she'd forced herself to eat in front of Mrs Campo. She lay on a bed covered with embroidered pillows which, if there had been enough light to see by, might have brightened the room with their colourful birds and flowers.

"Are you sure?" the woman asked, running her hand over Tazia's barely swollen belly.

"Is it too early to tell if I'm not showing yet?"

"No *cara*." The old lady stroked Tazia's cheek. "I can tell its sex from the moment the little one is planted inside you. Just relax and let the needle do its work." She inserted a foot-long piece of thread into a sewing needle and, holding the end of the thread, dangled the needle six inches above Tazia's stomach. "You see how it goes in a circle instead of swinging back and forth?" she said. "It will be a *bambina*!" The woman's intent face lit up in a wrinkled smile.

Feeling dizzy, Tazia let herself be helped to a sitting position. Unclasping her purse with her right hand, she took a few coins with her left and held them out. The old lady's smile turned into a deep frown as she stroked Tazia's bare ring finger and put the money back in her bag.

"Over there," she said, pointing to a chair beside the stove.

Tazia sat in silence as the woman boiled water and gave her a cup of tea smelling like the camphor balls in the drawers where her mother stowed woolens. "Tansy," the woman said. "One cup, brewed strong, four times a day for a week." Tazia pushed it away. Not that she hadn't eyed the Lysol under the Campos' sink, but she'd heard the whispered horror stories at work. She'd never have come here if all she wanted was to flush a bloody rag-wrapped ball down the toilet.

The old woman poured out the tea and wrote down an address. "If you change your mind. Twenty-five dollars. More if you don't decide soon." Ayal had given her sixty-five dollars.

Tazia lost her breakfast in the gutter. With hours to kill before going home, she slipped into a church for morning Mass, circled the block innumerable times, and returned for afternoon services. Still, with two hours to fill, a heavy sleet drove her back to Brooklyn. "The foreman's wife just had a baby boy," she lied to the Campos. "So, he dismissed us for the rest of the day."

"How nice!" Anna said. "Let's celebrate the new *bambino*." She cooked the spicy fish stew traditional in their village and insisted Tazia wash it down with Luigi's home-brewed Chianti. To calm her stomach, Tazia remembered another family celebration the day before she set sail. They'd brought the perfectly ripened olives to the mill and applauded as the yellow-green oil flowed from the press. Then they'd driven donkey carts to the river to picnic on ciauscolo salami, soft taleggio cheese, roasted chestnuts, a jar of preserved plums, and many bottles of Vino Cotto.

***

Tearing up at the memory now, Tazia wipes her eyes and lowers her head to the tiny gown. She could use ordinary stitches, like those she'd seen on the old woman's pillows last month, but she does Assisi embroidery, an ancient technique her nonna taught her in which images are outlined in black and surrounded in decorative scrollwork. On the billowy skirt, she sews Loro Piceno's birds and olive tree blossoms, small white feathery flowers in loose clusters, encircled by lance-shaped leaves that are dark green on top with silvery undersides. It is impractical to take such care with garments that will get stained, or not used at all, but she treasures the secret joy of making them.

Well, not totally secret.

Olga had caught her stitching a gown two weeks ago and her eyes widened in alarm. Tazia froze, afraid she'd report her to Mr Lemke, but instead, the big peasant girl from Poland put her fingers to her lips and smiled. Besides little Paulie, Olga is Tazia's only friend at Triangle. The others resent her for moving down to the eighth floor after two weeks when it took them years. Also, she and Olga are the only ones who don't smoke. It's forbidden, so the workers exhale into their collars to avoid detection. Tazia has always found the smell nauseating, but the other women think she is being stuck up. Now she's glad she never developed the habit.

Tazia wishes she could talk about her predicament with Olga, four years her senior, but that requires conversational skills and a level of trust neither yet possesses. In limited English, with gestures and small treasures, they guardedly trade information. Both are the oldest in their families, sent here while their brothers stayed home to tend the crops—olives in Italy, hops in Poland. Olga has a younger sister named Anastasia, big and blonde like her, from whom she's transferred a sense of protectiveness to the small, dark Tazia. Olga has also shown her a picture of her older cousin Veronika Nowicki, who works at a meat packing plant in Chicago.

Olga catches her eye now to let her know the foreman is heading her way. Tazia buries her needlework deep inside the scrap bin. She hasn't yet figured out how to get the layette past him and out of the factory. Mr Lemke inspects the girls' pockets and purses every day when they leave to make sure no fabric or thread has been pilfered. Lately, Tazia wonders whether being found out would be a sign from God to do what Ayal wants. Clever Ayal could devise a scheme for sneaking out the layette, but of course, she can hardly ask him.

His cleverness was what seduced her in the first place. Last fall, when the print shop owner was busy, he sent Ayal in his place. Ayal went in search of Triangle's assistant manager, whose office was blocked off a corner of the eighth floor, and found him admiring Tazia's sleeve-setting speed. Ayal stood, admiring Tazia. His attention made her self-conscious, yet she was flattered. Ayal showed off a new flyer he'd designed. Underneath his sketch of an attractive but wholesome female, he'd written: "Admired by suitors and spouses, today's modern women wear Triangle blouses." The enthusiastic assistant doubled the usual order, and Ayal's boss happily turned over the production and distribution of the brochures to him.

Ayal began coming to the factory twice a week, always stopping at Tazia's machine. He left little drawings and poems for her: "Ayal is Hebrew for deer/Anastazia Italian for reborn/The day I met you my angel/My night-time brightened to morn." The notes were on Allegro Printers stationery, and like the company name, dashed off quickly. It embarrassed Tazia that she often had to ask Ayal to read and explain the English words. He kept his visits brief to avoid getting her in trouble with Mr Lemke, but since the foreman was rungs below the assistant manager, he couldn't object when Ayal brought Tazia to the corner office. The assistant would find an errand to take him away for twenty or thirty minutes, and so their romance began. Ayal's lovemaking was as inventive as his note cards, and he made Tazia feel as pretty as the women on their covers.

By the time Tazia found out Ayal was married, she cared too much to pull away. Doubts about his trustworthiness nagged at her, but she dismissed them along with her guilt. Later, when she looked in vain for the predictable bloodstain on her panties, she could no longer deny her sins. Tazia believed Ayal loved her, but worried he was more entranced by his own success. He was smug about stringing his in-laws along to achieve his dreams. Tazia had to remind herself that what was good for him was also good for her.

chapter 3

Mr Lemke drops a big pile of sleeves and bodices to the left of Tazia's machine. He examines the completed blouses on her right and rips apart more than half, claiming the gathers aren't evenly spaced. They are as perfect as her other blouses, but he's still annoyed at her for groaning when he ordered everyone to work tomorrow. She'll have to sew even faster to finish her allotment by five, now only an hour away. A few minutes later, Olga gives her a questioning look. She's seen Tazia squirming and senses she has to go to the bathroom, an urge that happens more frequently lately. Being let out to go the ladies room means another inspection from the foreman before he will open the steel exit door, which is locked, and relinquish the lavatory key. But Tazia is afraid that if her mind is preoccupied by discomfort, her hands will be too slow to complete the blouses.

"If you're gone more than three minutes," Mr Lemke tells her, "I'll dock you fifty cents."

That's ten trolley tickets, a week's worth, Tazia calculates. "The ladies room is on the first floor," she says. "It takes longer than that just to get there and back."

"Sass me again and I'll dock you whether you go or not." The foreman eyes her stomach and snickers. Tazia decides to hold it in another hour and stop on her way out. She'll miss the first trolley home, but since so many factories let out at the same time, another will follow close behind. If only she could count on a back-up plan as reliable as the next trolley.

***

At 4:40, the girls who are finished pack up to leave. Tazia waves goodbye to Olga who lifts the corners of her mouth with her fingers, a gesture they use whenever one intuits the other is in a despairing mood. Tazia forces herself to smile and for a brief moment, she really is happy. Soon she will be outside, smelling the arrival of spring in the air. Instead, a moment later, she smells smoke. It is not the stench of forbidden cigarettes, but more acrid, like singed material.

"Fire!" screams one of the cutters, as flames shoot from the overflowing wicker scrap bin under his work table. Tazia's stomach lurches, only this time it is with fear rather than the usual nausea. Workers run to get pails of water from the small sink at the other end of the floor, but the bolts of cloth, tissue paper patterns, and wooden benches are already ablaze. Dinah, the Jewish bookkeeper who works outside the assistant manager's office, telephones the tenth floor to warn them. "Somebody run up to nine," she yells, "there's no phone there." People rush for the door, but as always, it is locked. Tazia's feet are frozen to the treadle.

"The hoses," another cutter hollers. Three men drag the nozzle toward the source of the fire, but when a fourth turns the valve, nothing comes out. Sirens approach from down below, then moments later firemen bang with crowbars outside the locked doors. Because the doors swing inward, they tell everybody to back away, but the crush of bodies makes this impossible.

Tazia wills her legs to move and races to the windows facing Greene Street. She sees people on the tenth floor escaping to the roof of New York University's law school next door. Students lower a ladder to help them climb up and across. Others crowd onto the fire escape. Tazia counts twenty, dreading how many more will try to clamber on, when the platform twists under the heat and weight, plunging everyone to the sidewalk below, where they are crushed like olives at the mill. She waits to hear herself cry out, but now she is oddly calm.

Workers begin to gather at the windows of the ninth floor too. They must have smelt or seen the fire, since no one was able to warn them. Women climb onto the ledge. Firemen from a truck emblazoned Company 20 raise a ladder. People on the street cheer them on. Four, five, six they count as the ladder scales each floor. Then the counting stops; the ladder does not reach higher. Other firemen wrestle with the hoses but the horses pulling the hose cart resist, spooked by the falling bodies. When at last the hose is connected and water bursts skyward, it too falls short.

More bodies sail past, people jumping off the ledge. Some cross themselves first. Tazia lifts the corners of her mouth, signaling them not to despair, but even if they could see her, they wouldn't understand the secret communication she's developed with Olga. Besides, they've made a devil's choice to leap to their death rather than be burnt alive. A man pushes a woman before jumping himself. He waves his hat, in a gesture of what? Triumph? Self-determination after a life obeying orders? And what of the woman he pushed; is it his decision or hers? The priests of Tazia's child-hood cautioned against doing cruel things in the name of humanity, but they never taught her that hell could precede death.

Now girls on her own floor race past, flying to their deaths. Tazia does not watch their descent but she remains standing at the window, debating whether she too should take flight. She pivots toward the oncoming rush. Behind the stampede, two elevators are operating. Visible through their glass doors is a crush of people, more than the cars are supposed to hold. Tazia wonders if they will break away and plunge like the fire escape. Men and women on her floor curse in a multitude of languages as the elevators bypass them heading up to ten, and again as they descend to the street. There is a peal of shattering glass as the mob breaks the elevator doors and people force themselves inside. Others jump down the shaft onto the car's roof as it creaks its way down.

Caught between the window and the elevator, Tazia cannot move. The Church considers suicide a sin, but if she does nothing, she will die anyway. Is it a worse sin to actively jump or to take no action to try and save herself? Either way would solve her dilemma, bringing her family grief, but not dishonour. "I can't," someone at Tazia's back shrieks in horror, and a retreating crowd sweeps her away from the window, past her row of work stations, and toward the elevators, where Tazia is pushed inside. Barely breathing, she bends over to protect her stomach and falls, face-down, on the gritty floor. Feet stomp on her back like it's the treadle of a sewing machine.

Tazia looks up in time to see Olga trying to clear a small space around her. Then she passes out.

chapter 4

Tazia wakes in a hospital ward with her right leg in a cast. Without windows, she can't tell the time. Families crowd around the other beds, talking in a polyglot of tongues. She needn't speak their languages to understand that they are thanking God for sparing a loved one's life.

A tired looking doctor moves from bed to bed. When he stops at Tazia's, she is surprised at how young he is, and relieved that the corners of his drooping eyes crinkle with kindness.

"Your leg is broken," he says in English, and gestures to be sure she understands. She nods. "Also, some bruises." He touches her arm, ribs, and thigh, very lightly to minimize any pain. "They will heal." He strokes the bare ring finger on her left hand and pats her stomach. "A bit of bleeding, but otherwise it is okay. Capisci?" Tears leak from Tazia's eyes. He gives her his handkerchief to wipe them away and, when she tries to give it back, shakes his head. He stands and Tazia expects him to leave, but he reaches under her pillow and brings out a wrinkled paper sack. "You were clutching these when they pulled you from the elevator. A nurse put them in this bag."

Tazia wants to know more, but now the doctor does move on. She opens the bag. Inside is a picture poem from Ayal, the paper slightly creased, and three gowns from the layette. She has no memory of grabbing them. The tiny garments smell of smoke but are otherwise as unblemished as when she stitched them, the silken threads of olive blossoms turning their heads toward the sun. She stows the bag under her pillow, although she no longer needs to hide the tiny dresses from the foreman's lecherous, prying eyes.

She dozes and when she wakes again, Ayal is sitting in a chair beside her. It must be past sundown, after his Sabbath has ended. Tazia does not ask what excuse he gave his wife to sneak away. He brings no note card tonight, but traces flowers and love letters in the palm of her hand. Then he takes a newspaper from his lap—*The New York Times*, which he's told her is read by those who want to get ahead—and reads aloud.

One hundred and forty-six died in the fire, mostly Jewish and Italian immigrant girls like herself. The two youngest were only fourteen. Tazia crosses herself. It means Paulie made it out alive. Triangle's owners fled to safety on the roof, but after twenty trips, the elevators gave out. Some were killed jumping down the empty shaft. The Fire Marshall blamed an unextinguished match or cigarette butt thrown into a scrap bin, but *The Times* said it could have been the overheated engines that ran the sewing machines non-stop.

His voice suddenly choking, Ayal sets aside the paper. "I was afraid I had lost you," he says. "First I searched outside the factory where the bodies were spread out on a dark red canvas. Then a policeman said to check the morgue at Bellevue, but the patrol wagons were slow to get there because it took so long to remove the remains. It was nearly eight before I checked the hospitals."

Tazia wonders, but does not ask, why Ayal searched for her among the dead before the living. Was he hoping to be rid of her? "I'm here. You found me," she says, pulling the pale green blanket tighter across her middle. Ayal raises his eyebrows. Tazia clutches her stomach and grimaces, as if it hurts down there when she moves.

Ayal breaks into a relieved smile, then quickly substitutes a solicitous expression. "Are you bleeding a lot? Should I get a nurse?" Tazia shakes her head no but rubs her belly so Ayal will think her pain is real. "It's *bashert,*" he says, "how God means it to be. For now. Until we're together." He checks his pocket watch, a wedding gift from his wife, and says he must go, but that he'll come visit her if she tells him where in Brooklyn the Campos live. "I'll say I'm the son of one of the factory owners, who insists I visit the survivors to see how my father can help."

Tazia smiles in spite of herself. Ayal will always be a schemer. She says the Campos are too smart to believe slave drivers would be so considerate of their workers, and that his visit would arouse suspicion. After all, he's not a nice Italian boy. She knows where to find him, and when her leg heals, she'll come to Allegro Printers and tell him where she has found another job.

"Until then, I will find another place where we can be alone," Ayal says. He strokes her stomach a final time and turns down his lips in a mock frown, before kissing her cheek, folding his newspaper, and exiting through the wide open doors of the hospital ward.

***

Tazia lies awake, pondering where to go. She cannot stay in New York. When she does not show up at his print shop, Ayal will track her down, assuming the Campos let her remain with them in her condition. They will feel guilty for having failed her family. Nor can she go back to Italy to face her parents' shame or the baby brother whose life depends on her help. Better to let the Campos think she was burnt beyond recognition and write to her family, who can then forever honour her as a dutiful daughter. Meanwhile, Tazia will escape into America's heartland. Another big city, another factory. Her new boss can assume she's a young widow with a baby on the way, her husband killed in an accident on the docks or loading a freight train, as happens so often.

The question still remains: Where?

Then Tazia remembers Olga's cousin, Veronika, in Chicago. She'll use Ayal's money to pay for a train ticket and lodging until she finds work. First, she'll buy a ring at the five-and-dime, and white cotton and embroidery thread to keep her mind and hands busy on the trip west. Stealing his money is the least of her sins. He lied to get it, with bad intentions. Tazia vows to use it for good. God is giving her a chance to make amends, buying her daughter's life and a better future.

"*Bashert*" was the word Ayal used. *Meant to be.*

part two

Gemma, Aguanga, 1961

chapter 5

This is Gemma Kane, speaking with my mother Tazia Gatti, at her home in Aguanga, California. Today is Sunday, May 7, 1961, and the time is 3:00 PM.

Gemma: Relax, Mama. I've used a tape recorder before.

Tazia: As a reporter for the *San Diego Union*. Not to interview me. (Frowns) Why can't you write by hand?

Gemma: Because I can't write fast enough. Not that I expect you to tell me much, but I drove all the way up here when I should be home making place cards for the wedding. You're not going to back out, are you?

Tazia: I wish you'd drop this whole idea, but I know better than to try talking you out of something once your mind is made up. (Stands) Do you want some espresso? Wine? Bruschetta?

Gemma: Sit. You know why I have to go on this trip.

Tazia: (Sighs, taps foot) To find your father.

Gemma: In three months, I'll be fifty. I long ago stopped asking you who he is for my sake, but this time I'm doing it for Frankie. When he gets married in six weeks, I intend to deliver his grandfather's name, even better the man in person—if he's still alive—as a wedding present.

Tazia: Won't Frankie be upset that you're not here to help him and Julia get ready? When are you coming back?

Gemma: Around June 10th or 11th.

Tazia: That's just a week before the wedding!

Gemma: You and Mrs Lonski can handle everything. It's a small affair. Julia is an only child, like Frankie, and he just has me, Todd and his parents, and you. Plus all the kids' friends, but they don't need much to be happy. They'll do those crazy dances under the tent that the Benedettis are setting up next door.

Tazia: (Laughs) You mean the twist and the mashed potatoes? I'm glad the crowd will be small, although it's odd that with an Italian-Irish groom and a Polish bride there won't be more people.

Gemma: (Laughs too) Father O'Brien said as much, but he likes the idea of a simple outdoor wedding instead of a fancy to-do at church. Mid-June is a perfect time of year, before it gets too hot, and the Benedetti's olive farm is the perfect setting.

Tazia: (Nods, leans forward) Suppose you do make this grand discovery in the next few weeks, which I hope you don't, how will Frankie deal with it? Just getting married is a big adjustment. Remember, you didn't have it easy at first.

Gemma: Well, Mama. It's not as if I had a role model to follow.

Tazia: (Grimaces) I did my best. There weren't many single parents when you were growing up.

Gemma: Even if there had been, you wouldn't have sought them out. Just like you weren't eager for me to get to know the other kids. Besides, it was hard to make friends when we kept moving. Were you afraid my father would find us?

Tazia: I didn't have time for friends. I was too busy raising you.

Gemma: For which I'm grateful. But ...

Tazia: What about Frankie's reaction if you find your father?

Gemma: He'll be fine. Todd and I ended up with a good marriage and Julia's parents seem happy enough. Two kids from stable homes. Whatever I turn up from the past won't derail them.

Tazia: How can you be sure? (Folds arms across chest) I think you're being selfish.

Gemma: Look. This isn't *your* inquisition. Can we get to *my* questions?

Tazia: (Snorts) I've told you everything I'm willing to. But, you drove seventy-five miles north, so go ahead and ask, before you turn around and go back.

Gemma: (Grits teeth) Please state your name, when and where were you born, and where you've lived since then.

Tazia: You already know that.

Gemma: Mama. For goodness sake. I need it on the record.

Tazia: Why? Is this a courtroom?

Gemma: You're not on trial, but I learnt on the job that it's dangerous to depend on memory.

Tazia: My first name is Tazia, which is Italian for born again, and my last name is Gatti, which means cat. I was born in Loro Piceno, in Italy, in

September 1893. I came to America, to New York, in 1910. From there I went to Chicago, where you were born in August 1911, then I moved to Topeka and Las Vegas before I settled in San Diego in 1927. Two years ago, after my heart attack, I retired to the town of Aguanga. This is where I'll die. People grow olives in Aguanga, like the village where I grew up. In a way, I've come back to where I started.

Gemma: Thank you. Now, let's begin with New York. What do you remember?

Tazia: The fire, and the horrible working conditions that led to it. But you know that story. You said it was why you became a labour journalist.

Gemma: Yes, because of Triangle and the awful places you worked after that. I hated how you were treated. I sometimes wished we could move back to Loro Piceno to harvest olives in your family's orchard. You said the work there was hard, but honourable.

Tazia: The difference wasn't so much between Italy and America as between towns and cities, farms and factories.

Gemma: What else do you remember about New York?

Tazia: Nothing.

Gemma: Come on. The street where you lived? Your neighbours? People at the factory?

Tazia: I blotted it all out after the fire. I left to escape the memories.

Gemma: And to escape from my father?

Tazia: You're assuming I knew I was pregnant when I left, but maybe I didn't know until I got to Chicago.

Gemma: Touché! Okay, let's talk about Chicago. You were there when?

Tazia: I came in 1911 and we stayed until 1914.

Gemma: You lived in Little Italy?

Tazia: No. There were lots of Italians, but neighbourhoods were mixed back then. Poles, Russians, Irish, Germans, Greeks. Everyone together. Only the Negroes lived separate, on the South Side.

Gemma: So, who were your neighbours?

Tazia: Like I said, lots of different people.

Gemma: I vaguely remember you and I shared a bed, and a big blonde lady played with me when you had to work at night. She lived with us or we lived with her. Am I right or am I imagining it?

Tazia: You were three when we moved away. Children's memories are fuzzy.

Gemma: I'm sure I remember cuts on your hands and arms and blood stains on your clothes.

Tazia: That's real. From working at the meat-packing plant.

Gemma: What was the name of it?

Tazia: There were scores in Chicago. You worked a week here, a month there. It's not like you made a career at one place and moved up the ladder.

Gemma: Did being pregnant and unmarried make it hard for you to get work?

Tazia: I wore a wedding band, but I said I had no husband to support me, which was true. Some bosses figured a woman like that was abandoned. Mine assumed my husband had died. It wasn't uncommon for immigrants to lose their lives in industrial accidents or from TB or other diseases.

Gemma: Why didn't you make up a story to tell me about my father dying? I might have stopped pestering you with questions.

Tazia: I thought about it, but I decided not to. Lying like that would have been a sin.

Gemma: But you told other lies. You let your family think you were dead, for God's sake.

Tazia: It's worse to lie by what you say than what you don't say. Let people think what they want, but don't put the idea in their heads.

Gemma: So, you let me think I had a father somewhere. Did it occur to you that I might think he would come to look for me some day and be forever disappointed and hurt that he didn't?

Tazia: You said this interview was about what happened in my life, not yours.

Gemma: Back to your life, then. Topeka. We lived there ...

Tazia: From 1914 to 1917.

Gemma: And you worked ...

Tazia: On a farm.

Gemma: Where they grew what?

Tazia: Crops.

Gemma: Oh, holy mother of God! Kansas is the wheat belt. Was it a wheat farm?

Tazia: Why not? And watch your language.

Gemma: Where did we live? I remember having Negro children in my kindergarten class. Not a lot of snow, but the teacher herded us inside during a hailstorm. And once I huddled in a closet with you during a tornado. When *The Wizard of Oz* came out, Frankie was a year old. For some reason you couldn't babysit, so Todd and I snuck Frankie into the movie theatre under my coat. The tornado scene brought back such a scary memory that I made us leave. Todd got mad at me.

Tazia: But my wonderful son-in-law forgave you. (Smiles)

Gemma: He always does. Todd's a good Catholic. (Laughs) Speaking of which, we always joined a church. Which one did we belong to in Topeka? I read in my background research that it's the home of Pentecostalism. Were you ever tempted to join one of their churches?

Tazia: (Wags finger) I know you're teasing. But seriously …

Gemma: (Leans forward) I can't believe you're about to tell me something. Go on.

Tazia: Those people spoke in tongues. Glossolalia I learnt it was called. Members of our church were horrified, and you and the other children sometimes imitated and made fun of them. I insisted you stop. I raised you to believe it was wrong to mock people for their beliefs.

Gemma: It's one of the things I admire most about you and I'm thankful you passed it on to me. Maybe it comes from your being an immigrant, an outsider. When I interview people of different backgrounds and they sense I won't judge them, they open up to me more than to other reporters.

Tazia: So why can't you respect that I don't wish to talk about my background?

Gemma: Because it belongs to me too.

Tazia: Children think that what belongs to them is theirs alone, but what belongs to their parents also belongs to them. Private property is for grown-ups too. Sometimes you act like I'm a boss and you're a worker and I'm violating your rights. We're a family, not a business.

Gemma: Agreed. But families are partnerships.

Tazia: I already gave you more than half of everything I earned.

Gemma: Everything but the other half of my identity.

Tazia: That you'll have to earn on your own.

Gemma: I'm trying, but it's hard without a union rep to help me. Let's go on. (Checks watch) Wait. It's almost an hour. I have to change the tape reel. Can I have that glass of wine now?

Tazia: It's from the Benedettis. They invited me over last night. We drank most of the bottle but … (Gets two glasses of wine while tape is switched)

Gemma: All set. Why did you leave Topeka?

Tazia: Hailstorms. Tornados. Who wants to live under such weather?

Gemma: So, you moved us to sunny Las Vegas.

Tazia: We lived there ten years, from 1917 to 1927.

Gemma: The photo album. Can I see it? (Gets album) Here's the snapshot I'm looking for.

Tazia: The two of us together.

Gemma: It's the *only* picture like that. All the others are of me, alone, with no date or identifying landmarks around me. It's like you planned the photos that way to keep me in the dark.

Tazia: You're about fifteen here. How pretty you look.

Gemma: You look pretty too, all dressed up.

Tazia: I'm wearing a sun dress. What else would I wear on a hot day?

Gemma: There's a bench behind us so maybe we're in a park. Oh, I never noticed this before. There's a sign with the letters " zi" at the end. Ring a bell?

Tazia: It's so long ago. Who remembers?

Gemma: Who took the picture?

Tazia: A stranger passing by? I handed some person the Brownie and voila!

Gemma: (Gulps wine) You worked in a laundry, right?

Tazia: Yes, which made things twice as hot. No air conditioning back then. I couldn't afford child care so I brought you there after school to do your homework and when you got tired, you napped in a canvas laundry hamper. I felt terrible, but I didn't have a choice. When you turned eight, I let you persuade me you were old enough to be a latchkey kid.

Gemma: I'm surprised, since you're Italian, that you couldn't get a better job. Even in those days, organized crime was active in Las Vegas, running underground casinos and speakeasies.

Tazia: True. I went there because it was a boom town. Only Nevada had outlawed gambling a few years earlier, so the city went bust and the Mafia moved in. Working for them would have set a bad example for you, so I sweated it out in the laundry for ten years. Four years after I gave up and came to California, Nevada legalized gambling again. I arrived too late and I left too early.

Gemma: Poor Mama. You've had your share of bad luck.

Tazia: I had you. That's all that mattered to me.

Gemma: (Chuckles) And I had my first boyfriend in Vegas, and no one at home to supervise me. That would have been a year after that picture was taken. Did we move because you were afraid I'd become pregnant like you did?

Tazia: (Stiffens) I raised you to be a good Catholic girl.

Gemma: Weren't you raised the same way?

Tazia: My situation was different. I didn't have a mother looking out for me.

Gemma: Or a father. Just like I didn't.

Tazia: It wasn't the same. (Rubs temples) I'm tired. Can we finish up? You were sixteen when we moved to San Diego, so you should remember what happened from then on without my help.

Gemma: You lived in San Diego for thirty-two years, in the same place.

Tazia: Wasn't that stable enough to satisfy you? You were the one who moved, not me.

Gemma: Sure. When Todd and I got married, although we lived near you. We stayed there until Frankie started junior high, then we moved so he could go to a better school.

Tazia: I loved living near you when Frankie was young. We saw each other every day. It was hard to let go when you moved across town. But children grow up, life changes.

Gemma: Yes. Especially now that Frankie's getting married. When he was in college, he'd still come home to visit. But with him and Julia setting up house, I know my baby is gone for real.

Tazia: Frankie will always be your baby. (Smiles)

Gemma: (Smiles back) Just like I'll always be yours.

Tazia: (Blinks back tears; sips wine) You didn't ask me about Italy.

Gemma: I don't need to. The search for my father only goes back as far as New York.

Tazia: Harvest time was my favourite. We played music in the groves, and the whole family and all our friends came to help. And visit. The fragrance of fresh olives and olive oil was everywhere.

Gemma: Reminiscing about Loro Piceno is a diversion from telling me what I want to know.

Tazia: Then let me talk about Aguanga, where my journey ends. I'm happy here. Don't you want to hear about that?

Gemma: I want more than anything for you to be happy.

Tazia: More than finding your father? (Tilts head, winks)

Gemma: After all your hard work, and everything you sacrificed to raise me, you deserve to take it easy. I know you love Aguanga because it reminds you of Loro Piceno.

Tazia: The climate is like the Mediterranean. All the cultivars the Benedettis grow are Italian—Frantoio, Leccino, Maurino. In fact, Emilio and Donatella began with a grove of Seville olives planted by the old missionaries. Do you know what else I like about living in Aguanga?

Gemma: (Laughs) The free wine they give you?

Tazia: Having my own cat. All my life, I loved cats but they belonged to someone else, or to no one. Years ago, people kept cats to catch mice. Later none of the apartments where we lived permitted them. I would put food outside for the friendly strays who let me pet them.

Gemma: Sometimes I think you love Lucy more than me, or Frankie. (Pretends to pout)

Tazia: Are you jealous of a cat?"

Gemma: Do you talk about your past to the cat?

Tazia: What I say to Lucy is between her and me.

Gemma: What about the Benedettis? Does your tongue loosen with wine? Do they know your secrets?

Tazia: I have no secrets anymore. The trail is cold.

Gemma: Aren't you even a little curious about what happened to my father?

Tazia: Absolutely not. You and Todd and Frankie are the only family I need.

Gemma: And Lucy.

Tazia: So, you're leaving for New York tomorrow?

Gemma: I'm not starting in New York. Other than the fire, which is public knowledge, you haven't given me anything personal to go on.

Tazia: So where will you start?

Gemma: At the end, in San Diego. A journalist learns two things. One, start with the evidence at hand and follow the trail back to the beginning. Two, what you're looking for is sometimes hiding right under your nose.

Tazia: You think I told your husband and son things I wouldn't tell you?

Gemma: Todd, maybe. Frankie, for sure. (Smiles) You and that boy are as close as two peas in a pod. I admit I'm jealous. But I won't only talk to them. I'll interview the people I've known since high school, when we moved there. Also, one or two from college.

Tazia: I can't imagine what you hope to learn poking around with your old high school friends.

Gemma: (Nudges Tazia) What friends? You never let me have any. Until Yolanda, when I was too old for you to stop me.

Tazia: (Humph) Stop exaggerating. Even if you do find some "acquaintances," all they're likely to remember is what music was popular and who dated who and wore what to the prom.

Gemma: Superficial memories can be a good start. You know the eight years I was a diver in high school and college?

Tazia: Of course. It's what got you the scholarship to UCLA.

Gemma: That taught me an important lesson too. You have to break the surface, slicing it just the right way, before you can go deep. (Moves to turn off tape recorder)

Tazia: Wait. I have a question for you. Have you thought about the effect that tracking down your father will have on *me*? It could be another shock to my heart.

Gemma: Naturally I thought about it. But if you'd told me all the times I asked—as a child, a teenager, before my own wedding, when Frankie was born—there'd be no risk to your health now. It was your choice to keep silent when all I wanted was to know myself. I won't do to my son what you did to me. I should have tracked down my father twenty-three years ago when he was born. Todd urged me to, but it was too much to take on as a new mom trying to establish my career. I have the time now, in these weeks before Frankie's wedding, and I intend to succeed.

Tazia: Can't you be content knowing you're a wonderful wife and mother? With a job that lets you speak out for the poor people sweating in factories and fields? I couldn't be prouder of you or feel better about everything I did to raise you on my own. Wasn't I enough?

Gemma: I love you, Mama. (Stands to hug her) I'll call you from the road so you won't worry. Do you want me to tell you what I find out along the way?

Tazia: No.

The interview ended at 4:50 PM.

chapter 6

This is Gemma Kane, speaking with Emilio and Donatella Benedetti at their home, on their olive tree farm in Aguanga, California. Today is Sunday, May 7, 1961, and the time is 5:30 PM.

Gemma: I hope you don't mind that I stopped by without calling first. I was visiting my mother.

Emilio: Of course not. I'm sure you're anxious about the wedding. We've taken care of the tent and the tables and chairs. Mrs Lonski called Donatella about the flowers. What else?

Gemma: Actually, I'm here to talk to you about my mother.

Donatella: (Sets down a tray of wine glasses and bowls with three types of olives) Is Tazia alright? These affairs can be stressful, even a small one like this.

Gemma: She's fine. But I have another wedding project, a present for Frankie, that you might be able to help me with. I'm putting together a family history and while Mama's memory is as sharp as ever, there may be things she has neglected to tell me.

Emilio: What sorts of things? Family secrets? (Looks doubtful)

Gemma: (Smiles) Nothing like that. Just things she didn't think to mention. Don't worry. Mama knows I'm here so I'm not going behind her back.

Emilio: (Sighs with relief) All right then. (Looks toward wife)

Donatella: We really don't know much about Tazia. Your mother is private, keeps to herself. But she loves being at the farm. It reminds her of where she grew up.

Emilio: She was here every day in early spring, when we pruned the trees. She was thrilled to see we use the old Italian-style vase shape, not the Christmas tree shape that's popular now. Pruning is my favourite time of year because you shape the future of each tree for centuries to come.

Gemma: I remember Mama saying that a well-pruned olive tree is a thing of beauty.

Donatella: Your mother has a good eye. Pruning is more art than science.

Gemma: I think the artistry she learnt in the olive grove transferred to her embroidery skills. Have you ever seen her needlework? She tried to teach me, but I never developed the knack.

Emilio: Sewing and farming both take infinite patience. Your mother strikes me as a patient person.

Gemma: Not when I was growing up. She was restless. We moved a lot. But when Frankie was born, Mama was the most patient grandmother in the world. Often better with him than I was. She seemed unsettled again when he became a teenager, but she's mellowed since moving here.

Donatella: After your son grew up, Tazia may have felt she was no longer needed. We're the same as you, around fifty? (I nod) Our parents are gone, so I think she enjoys being like a mother to us. Sometimes I sense she wishes your father was still alive to share old age with.

Gemma: What has she told you about my father?

Donatella: Nothing. We don't like to pry, but we assume she was widowed. Like her, we're old-style Catholics who don't believe in divorce. (Puts hand over mouth) I hope I haven't offended you. Most people our age are less religious than our parents, and you may hold different views.

Gemma: No offense at all. (Leans forward) The thing is, my father wasn't even here to see Frankie grow up. That's why I'm doing this wedding project, to tell him about his grandfather.

Emilio: I'm sorry we can't be of much help. Your mother likes to lend a hand with the work, but as we said, she doesn't share much about herself. Or your father.

Donatella: (Chews olive pit) Although she once said something that surprised me. Maybe it was how she said it.

Gemma: (Swallows) Yes?

Donatella: I asked if she met her husband in Loro Piceno and if they came to America together. And she said, "The man knew *nothing* about growing olives." Her exact words, and tone of voice.

Gemma: Did she say anything else about him?

Emilio: Her generation is more reserved than ours. (Gazes out window at orchard.) Although sometimes mouths, like blossoms, open up. The trees are just starting to flower, so your mother might not reveal anything in time for the wedding. Should we call you if we learn something?

Gemma: I hope to have all the information I need by then, but it's never too late to learn more.

The interview ended at 6:10 PM.

part three

Tazia, Chicago, 1911-1914

chapter 7

"The baby is breech," the midwife says in Polish-accented English. Tazia understands "baby" but before she can ask what the other word means, a contraction clamps her mouth shut. Veronika Nowicki, Olga's cousin, explains. She's been in this country long enough to speak good English and has picked up some Italian in the five months since Tazia moved in with her. "Backwards, *all'indietro*." Veronika points to her pelvis, taps her head, and nods. Then she thrusts a foot forward and shakes her head. "The baby is turned around. Its feet are coming out first."

Rivulets of perspiration trickle down Tazia's temples, stinging her eyes. Her armpits are lakes. "Open the window," she begs. It's mid-August, late afternoon. She's been in labour since before dinner yesterday.

"Sorry, *Cara*, we can't. *Insetto*, insects." Veronika mops Tazia's face and neck.

The closed window keeps out the flies, but Tazia still smells blood and guts, and hears the rumble of trains carrying livestock to the meat packing plants where she and Veronika work, along with thousands of other immigrants and Negroes. They rent two rooms in Packingtown, the area behind the Union Stock Yards. The front room, with a stove, washbasin, and splintered cabinet, is the kitchen. The back room has a bed and a dresser with three drawers, one each for Veronika, Tazia, and the embroidered baby clothes under which Ayal's note is buried.

Veronika had insisted Tazia and the baby take the bedroom; she sleeps on a folding cot beside the stove with Felix, her cat. Tazia had wanted her own place, and cat, but earning nine dollars a week at Armour, she can't afford even a single room. Besides, Veronika had persuaded her that if they worked different shifts, they could trade off taking care of the baby. It was better than leaving the child with a stranger, plus Veronika had refused Tazia's offer to pay her. "A child in the house is payment enough," she'd said. "It will help me miss my brothers and sisters less."

Tazia nods off between contractions, until they come so quickly there is not even time to blink. She is too tired to see anyway, and the surge of blood in her ears renders her deaf as well. She feels herself rise and hover above the two women as they work on her body, like a seamstress bending over a sewing machine to align the fabric just so.

"Flip her on her hands and knees," the midwife tells Veronika. "It's better for a breech delivery." Magically, Tazia understands these words, as if she and the midwife are themselves connected by an umbilical cord. She turns herself over. Seeing the tangle of dirty, crumpled sheets beneath her, she momentarily regrets her decision to flee to Chicago instead of returning to Italy. At a time like this, a daughter, even one who has shamed her family, needs her mother.

"Can't you give her something to relieve the pain?" Veronika asks. "Like the doctors do?"

"That poison makes women too stupid to talk and too numb to push," the midwife says. "The babies are born so drowsy they can't suck. Sometimes they're too woozy to breathe."

"No medicine," Tazia says, gasping, afraid of becoming unconscious, like in the elevator during the fire. And anyway, the pain is the punishment she deserves as she awaits the blessing God is about to deliver. The midwife says she is a good girl for not complaining or begging to be put to sleep.

It doesn't seem possible, but the contractions get stronger and more frequent. Still, another hour passes before the midwife thrusts a hand inside her and explains that she wants to make sure the cervix is open before she lets Tazia push. Sometimes in a breech delivery, it clamps shut. Tazia is finally allowed to bear down. She lowers her head to look under her body and see what is happening. At the first push, the amniotic sac balloons out and the midwife breaks it to reveal a foot with tiny toes. Two more pushes and the other foot pops out.

"Ooh." Veronika reaches out to touch them. The midwife slaps her hand away, saying it's the worst thing she can do. It will startle the baby and make it raise its arms so it's even harder for it to get out. "Can't you pull it out?" Veronika asks. Tazia hears the anxiety in her voice.

"That's the second worse thing to do. Pulling is only a last resort, if the baby is stuck."

Nothing happens for fifteen minutes.

"I'm getting a doctor," Veronika announces. "Mr Armour will pay."

It's true. He fancies himself a philanthropist and pays for medical care, kindergartens, trade schools, and libraries.

"No!" Tazia raises her head and bellows like a bull being led to slaughter. Suppose the plant keeps records of those who avail themselves of these charities and Ayal uses them to track her down? Not that he'd be looking for anything to do with a baby after she convinced him she'd miscarried, but Tazia clings to the hope that his love is strong enough to search for her.

At last, there is another gush of water. The baby spirals out partway, surrounded by a tiny skirt of amniotic sac. Next comes black tarry stuff. The midwife calls it meconium but says there's no need to worry over a small amount. Just then, however, the baby's butt emerges, along with a huge squirt of the black goo and the midwife yells at Veronika to hand her every sterile cloth boiling on the stove. "If we don't wipe away the meconium before the head comes out, the baby will breathe it into its lungs." Tazia hears Veronika race across the warped floorboards and Felix's claws skitter out of her way, followed by a hesitant knock at the front door. Veronika runs back into the bedroom with the scalding towels.

"Who is it?" Tazia calls out, imagining in her delirium that God has sent her mother.

"Probably a neighbour complaining about the noise. Pipe down," Veronika jokes in an attempt to give Tazia courage. The midwife tells her to send whoever it is away. "A woman in labour has the right to scream her head off." Veronika agrees and goes the door.

"Does Tazia live here?" It's a man's voice with a twang that Tazia recognizes.

"What if she does?" Veronika speaks with a mixture of suspicion and scorn.

"We work the same shift at the plant. When she didn't show up for two days, I figured the baby had come. I'm here to help."

"Get out of here, nigger. We don't need your help." The door slams shut.

"Elvan," Tazia whimpers, knowing he cannot hear her. Veronika and the midwife are busy wiping away the meconium. Tazia wishes she could see their faces. "Was he missing a finger?" she asks Veronika, although it seems half the men on the killing gangs have lost digits.

"Yes. And whatever good sense God gives his kind. If he ever bothers you again, I'll grab one of the knives he uses to slit the animals' throats and cut off more than his finger."

A momentary surge of joy replaces the pain as Tazia realizes Elvan meant it when he said he wanted to take care of her and the baby. Yet she says nothing, afraid of angering Veronika. She's learnt that whites don't like Negroes, but she's never heard her friend use such language. How can she treat a sinner like Tazia with such kindness, yet be so mean to innocent people just because their skin is coloured?

When the women stop wiping, Tazia looks down between her legs again. The baby has continued to rotate and slide down the birth canal. Two chubby legs emerge. Now she's halfway out and turned, so that her back is towards Tazia's back, an even more dangerous position. The umbilical cord is wedged between the baby and Tazia's pubic bone, threatening to cut off the blood supply.

"Stop pushing," the midwife orders. With one hand, she presses on Tazia from the front, with the other she raises her bottom. Tazia shoves her away. She's had enough of being touched. But the midwife explains she is trying to tug the cord to the side. Once it comes out, she'll have to deliver the rest of the baby quickly because of the pressure. The cord won't budge. She waits for the baby to move down farther. "I've got it," she cries at last, freeing the baby's right arm and pulling it down, followed by the left. She tells Tazia to start pushing again.

Seconds later, a perfect girl is born, and the cord is cut. The girl belts out a mighty cry. The midwife says it's proof that the baby didn't inhale meconium. Tazia knows she was right to refuse painkillers. Veronika kisses mother and child, then unwraps a white swaddling cloth, free of the grime of Packingtown. Tazia accepts the gift with gratitude but can't wait to wrap her daughter in the blanket that she embroidered with olive blossoms and the birds of home. She nuzzles the baby's soft crown, strokes her velvety cheek, and outlines her rosebud lips. Then she puts the infant to her breast, where she latches on and tries to focus on her mother's face.

Veronika asks what she will name the child. Tazia looks down into the eyes that glisten like emeralds. Her own are brown. What colour are Ayal's? She cannot remember, but it does not matter. Her daughter's eyes are as green as the summer hills of Loro Piceno. Were Ayal to see this miraculous baby, he would change his mind and want to claim her as his after all. Tazia will never let this happen. "Gemma," she answers. This jewel of a child will be Tazia's alone.

chapter 8

Tazia has been back at work two weeks when Elvan Wright shows up at her work station.

"You should have waited until break time." She wants to scold him, gently, but she has to hiss loudly to be heard over the clanking line. Her swollen fingers shove pork scraps, the rotten ones dyed red, into the sausage grinder. She worries that the foreman, Miloslav Mucha, will see them talking. If she falls behind, Mucha will dock her pay. Worse, if she hurries to catch up, she could lose a finger in the churning machine. It happens all the time, but the line never stops. The finger, along with rat shit, sawdust, and human hair and sweat, is simply ground into the meat.

"I couldn't hold off seeing you any longer." Elvan, over six feet tall and the brawniest ripper on his killing team, crouches in a vain attempt to be less visible. The women on either side of Tazia take their eyes off their work just long enough to glare. They don't want to lose anything either, especially on account of a Negro with no business hanging around a white woman. Thank goodness Mucha is nowhere in sight. He's either forcing children to shove their hands inside the clogged grinder one line over, or in the toilet drinking his mid-morning beer.

"Besides," Elvan adds, "you're busy feeding the baby during break and I aim to steer clear of your friend Veronika. She scares me." He covers his crotch with his four-fingered right hand. The thought of Elvan afraid of a woman, even one as big as Veronika, makes them both laugh.

Tazia stops first. Laughing makes her breasts ache. She nurses Gemma before work and pumps enough milk to last her until noon, when Veronika brings Gemma to the break room for another feeding and collects more milk to tide her over until Tazia comes home. By then, Tazia is as hungry for a sight of Gemma as Gemma is for milk. From her breast, not a bottle. Snuggling with the baby on the bed while Veronika makes dinner, before leaving for the night shift, is her favourite time of day. The break room, by contrast, is filthy, and so far from the single toilet that men piss in the corner and don't even pretend to wipe their hands on their pants before eating or returning to work. Tazia is afraid Gemma will get sick from the germs, but she's already gained so much weight that she'll soon outgrow the tiny gowns Tazia embroidered on the train.

"Swing low, sweet chariot," Elvan sings softly from his crouch, until he coaxes a smile. His deep voice, carrying over the bellowing livestock, was what had drawn Tazia to him in the first place. It was a warm day last spring, and along with the flies swarming through the window, came this marvelous sound. Tazia had taken her lunch outside to watch the man who produced it. The kicking inside her belly made it plain the baby liked the music too. Tazia had never before heard the mournful yet hopeful melodies of Negro spirituals, and it reawakened her yearning to be back in church, hearing the Latin hymns she'd grown up with.

She soon learnt that Elvan's heart was as big as the man himself. One day, the foreman had called him inside to move some heavy machinery. At the end of the line closer to Tazia, the grinder was churning erratically because of a buildup of gristle. Mucha ordered a three-year-old girl to clean it out. He'd threatened to fire the child's mother unless she let her daughter work. Mucha set down a stool for the child to climb on, but when she hung back, he grabbed her arm and yanked her up. The little girl teetered and tipped forward. Her mother screamed. Just as the child's head was about to disappear, Elvan rushed up, reached in, and pulled her out. Everyone stopped breathing but the grinder kept churning, taking Elvan's finger in place of the child's head.

Mucha fired the sobbing mother on the spot. No one spoke for fear of losing their jobs too. He thrust a dirty rag at Elvan. "Patch yourself up, boy. I'd send you back to Mississippi if I didn't need you on the line. Instead, I'm moving you up." Elvan had been a breaker, separating legs from carcasses. Now he'd be a ripper, slitting live throats, the worst job on the killing gang.

Days later, meeting in a secluded place behind where the stock cars were repaired, Tazia had gingerly touched the jagged hole where Elvan's right pointer finger had been. "You paid a high price to save that child," she said. Her white hand looked as small as a child's next to his huge black paw. She was glad the day's heat excused the blush spreading across her cheeks.

"My Mama told me, with a name like Wright, you gotta do right."

"All you got for your trouble is a worse job than before."

Elvan laughed. "Those songs I sing about salvation? Working in this here place of death, the men can't get enough of them." He touched Tazia's belly, a gesture that felt natural to her, not at all improper. "Now, bringing life into this world. That beats singing about the one to come after." He bent down to look into Tazia's eyes. She looked up into his. Wordlessly, they kissed.

"I'd like to do right by you and your little one," he said. "I ain't never gonna be rich, but I don't drink, I seldom cuss, and I'm clean." He winked. "Also, I cook a tasty spicy barbecue, Delta style." Tazia knew that if it was as warm and smoky as his voice, she'd like it. Over the next few months, they continued to meet by the repair sheds, away from prying eyes. He brought her food and serenaded her. She used the American words she was learning, and gestures, to tell him about Loro Piceno. They left behind Chicago's blood-filled yards for the warm greenery of their homes.

Now, hunkered down beside Tazia, Elvan repeats his offer. His words sound genuine, but she doesn't trust her English enough to be sure. Much as she's tried to blot out Ayal, she cannot forget his empty vows. "What are you saying?" she asks, wishing she could look Elvan in the eye, but afraid to remove her gaze from the grinder. He stands and takes over so she can watch his lips. "I'm asking you to marry me." He emphasizes the word "marry," so there can be no doubt.

She nudges him aside and shoves scraps into the relentless churning maw. "Why? Do you think I'm so *disperata* I'd accept a proposal from anyone?" Instantly she regrets the words.

Elvan winces. "My sister got pregnant at fifteen. The man who did it ran off, and she killed herself before the baby was born. I followed that man to Chicago, planning my revenge. I couldn't find him, thank the Lord, but I stayed because I couldn't go home and face my family. I ain't never stopped feeling guilty for not protecting my sister or seeing Mama through her sorrow."

It's the longest speech Elvan has ever made. Tazia understands enough to say, "That's not a good reason to marry me. I don't need anyone's protection."

He smiles. "It's true. You're the strongest woman I know, including Mama. And I love you for it. Is that a good enough reason?"

Tazia laughs at the thought of running from the arms of a Jew into those of a Negro. Ayal's magical world was seductive, but Elvan's practicality is better for bringing up a child. She quickly dismisses the idea. A white woman marrying a black man is a greater liability than Gemma growing up with only a mother for a parent. Elvan mistakes Tazia's secret smile for acquiescence. He pulls a small package, wrapped in a clean bandana, from his bloodied overalls and opens it where she can see without taking her eyes off her work. Inside is a hand-carved wooden rattle.

Tazia marvels at the delicate ridges. "How can you carve with only four fingers?"

The rattle makes a crisp but soothing sound. Elvan replaces Tazia's right hand with his left. Together they feed the grinder, while their free hands trade the rattle back and forth. Elvan sings, "... coming for to carry me home," and they shake the rattle to the hymn's stately beat.

"What the hell are you doing?" Mucha appears behind them. Tazia slips the rattle inside her smock and takes over stuffing the machine with both hands. "Get the fuck back to your station, darkie, and stay there, or next time, I'll kick your black ass South for sure." He spits in Elvan's face, then into the grinder. Elvan glares and clenches his fists, but swivels and leaves. Mucha snorts with satisfaction, then turns toward Tazia. "That baby of yours a nigger too?" Tazia shakes her head. "You want to keep your job, prove it." Mucha slaps her buttocks so hard, she almost loses her balance. "Bring me the kid so I can see it's white."

***

"You look upset," Veronika says when Tazia gets home that evening. "A touch of home will cheer you up. See, I made the noodles with tomato sauce, not creamy dill." They cook dishes from each other's countries, although Tazia hopes that when Gemma eats solids, she'll prefer Italian food to Polish. She accepts tea with lump sugar and lets Veronika tuck her inside a nest of pillows. She treasures Veronika's kindness, yet envies her time with Gemma. Much as Tazia loves nursing, she is eager to wean Gemma so the women can switch shifts and she can spend daytimes with her daughter. She'll take her to the park, splash in the lake, and show her the Italian masters at the art museum. Gemma will speak fluent English but grow up proud of her heritage too.

"Mucha pushes too hard," Tazia sighs, rocking to the rhythm of Gemma's sucking. "He speeds up the line after lunch to keep us awake." Veronika sets steaming bowls and coarse bread on the rickety table. "That crazy Bohemian is worse than the Russian who lords it over my shift. He slows the machines so he won't have to wake up from his nap if a hand lands in the sausage."

Veronika is right about the tomato sauce. Tazia soaks it up with bread, then sucks on the crust, like a hungry baby at the breast. She looks away when Veronika feeds Felix scraps of meat from the factory. Not too many, or they'll kill his appetite for mice. Tazia once brought scraps home too, hoping to ingratiate herself with the cat, but he only accepts food from Veronika.

"I still don't understand why you want to work at the plant." Veronika ladles what is left in the pot into Tazia's bowl. She insists Tazia have seconds as long as she's nursing and eating for two. "There's plenty of piecework for a skilled seamstress and you could do it at home, at night." They've had this conversation before. In fact, Tazia had tried piecework after she got to Chicago, but her fingers were clumsy. "It reminds me of the fire. Smoke, screams, silent bodies floating through the air." Several times, coming home near dawn, Veronika has rushed into the bedroom to awaken Tazia from a nightmare. "From now on, I sew only for my family." She smiles to show that she includes Veronika in this category. "*Capisco*," Veronika says. "I won't ask again." She points to the bowl, nods toward Gemma. "*Mangiare.*" And Tazia does.

While Veronika washes the dishes, Tazia turns on the radio, their one luxury. Veronika bought it to help herself learn English. Now Tazia listens to do the same. "Protests continued months after the owners of the Triangle Waist Company were charged with first and second-degree manslaughter," the announcer says. "Their trial begins in December, but demonstrators fear they'll be acquitted. Meanwhile, the Joint Relief Committee has collected tens of thousands for victims' families and Tammany Hall is behind a law mandating a fifty-four-hour work week."

Tazia bolts from the table to turn it off, waking Gemma. Veronika circles the room with the child, singing a Polish lullaby, until mother and baby calm down. Then she ushers them into the bedroom. Tazia listens to her clean up, feigning sleep, then strains to hear as Veronika turns the radio back on. " ... continue to look for the cause of the blaze that killed nearly a hundred and fifty." By the time Tazia tiptoes across the floor and presses her ear to the door, the announcer is onto last month's theft of the Mona Lisa. Veronika turns off the radio, locks the door, and leaves for work. Tazia lies awake, fearing that, like the famous painting, her smile will never be seen again.

***

"I'm waiting," Mucha reminds Tazia that Friday, as he turns over her pay envelope. She counts the nine dollars inside as soon as she leaves the plant, relieved he hasn't docked her. At lunchtime on Monday, when Veronika hands her Gemma to be fed, Tazia tells her to find the foreman and bring him to the break room. "He wants to see the baby."

Veronika laughs without humour. "You said the man was a monster. Is he going soft?"

Tazia shrugs and says Veronika will recognize Mucha by his vest, white on top and red on bottom, like the Bohemian flag. He refuses to cover it with a butcher's apron, and it looks like it's never been washed. While Veronika searches, Elvan, seeing Tazia alone, comes from behind and taps her on the shoulder. Startled, Tazia jerks and Gemma, losing hold of the nipple, starts to cry. Tazia tries to soothe her while hissing at Elvan to get out of there. Neither attempt works.

Elvan swoops up Gemma and sings, "There is a balm in Gilead to make the wounded whole." At the sound of a hymn she heard in the womb, the baby quiets. She looks up and waves her arms. Elvan makes funny faces back but keeps singing until her tiny body relaxes into sleep.

"By God if she ain't white after all," Mucha bellows, cuffing Elvan's ear. "How'd you manage that, nigger boy?" Gemma awakens and starts bawling again, until Tazia takes her back and hooks the child onto her breast. Frantic at first, Gemma finally establishes a sucking rhythm.

"You feed her good, little *matka*," Mucha tells Tazia. "And when she turns three, bring her to me and I'll put her to work cleaning out the machines." He turns to Elvan. "As for you ... "

"He's a dead man!" Veronika rushes at Elvan, brandishing a hook used to hang carcasses while they're disemboweled. Mucha roars with laughter and disarms her. "Sausages are seasoned with plenty of white blood. Mr Armour don't fancy nigger blood in there too." He turns back to Elvan. "Don't want no nigger babies neither. I don't care if you are my best ripper, if I catch you hanging around a white girl again, I'll pitch you into the grinder myself, prick, balls, and all."

***

Elvan is waiting at the gate that evening. Tazia's breasts drip and she longs to run home, but he draws her into an empty stock car. "Mucha's bluffing," he says. "He won't fire me because every knocker, ripper, breaker, and gutter on my gang would quit too. Lots of other jobs in the Yards."

"He could make you have an accident. You'd lose more than your job." Tazia touches the space where Elvan's finger used to be. She turns to leave but he grabs her wrist. "Marry me," he pleads. "I'll work a double shift and you can stay home with Gemma." He crosses himself. "I'll even join your church and learn your hymns." He smiles. "Long as I can still sing mine at home."

Tazia looks at the darkening sky and takes a deep breath. She pictures a clean apartment outside Packingtown where her hands, supple again, stitch clothes for Gemma and embroider a vest for Elvan to wear to Mass. At night, as she makes dinner, Elvan and Gemma play with the little dolls and animals he's carved for her. "You're a fool," she says, shaking off his hand.

"So they tell me." Elvan sings, "Beams of heaven," quietly at first, but finishes, "I shall be free someday," in his strong voice. "With the Lord's help, we can make a good life together."

Tazia is tempted. Elvan is kind and gentle. Gemma would learn not to hate people who looked or spoke differently. Didn't they share the same God? She closes her eyes and beseeches the Heavenly Father who forgave her for Ayal and blessed her with Gemma. Can He accept Elvan too? The cattle car is silent. "I have to get home," she whispers. "Gemma is waiting for me."

chapter 9

"Gemma, stay on Mama's lap." Sitting in a back pew of the old stone church, Tazia enfolds the squirming two-year-old in her arms. "Here, have a biscuit." She fetches a biscotti from her bag. Gemma tries instead to feed it to her, and when it falls, goes after it headfirst. Tazia grabs her around the waist to keep her from crashing onto the floor. This child dives after things. Veronika calls her a "daredevil." Gemma is indeed daring, but too sweet-tempered to be a devil. Restless and full of energy, like Ayal, Tazia thinks. Also naughty as an imp, and good at getting her way.

Tazia is grateful for Sundays, not only because it is her day off, but because it is a comfort to be in a sanctuary, observing familiar rituals. Veronika goes to a Polish church near their house, while Tazia takes Gemma an hour each way on the elevated train to Holy Guardian Angel, the Italian church on Arthington Street, far from Packingtown. The organ and stained-glass windows are fancier than the village church of her childhood, but the music and liturgy remind her of home.

"*Dòminus vobìscum.* The Lord be with you," Father Xavier says now, bringing Tazia back from wistful memories of Loro Piceno to the harsh reality of Chicago.

"*Et cum spìritu tuo.* And also with you," Tazia chants. The communion service is ending, and the hymns that come next will quiet Gemma down. Sometimes, when her daughter is too worked up to nap, Tazia sings her snatches of Elvan's spirituals. Two years on, she occasionally misses him, but she no longer sees him since Mucha demoted him to the lowest position on the opposite side of the Yards. Meanwhile, Gemma is growing up happy in the family she and Veronika have created. The women are exquisitely attuned to each another. Except for Gemma's occasional tantrums, home is peaceful. Having seen the brutality of men, neither regrets their absence. Elvan was the lone exception, but Tazia dares not speak his name in front of Veronika. It is best that she forget it herself.

"*Ite, missa est.* The Mass is ended, go in peace." Father Xavier finally dismisses them.

"*Deo gràtias.* Thanks be to God." The congregation files out.

Tazia tugs Gemma toward the El station, anxious to begin the long ride home. Gemma wrests her hand free and runs back up the church steps. Tazia hurries after her.

"Mrs Gatti, *un minuto.*" Father Xavier beckons Tazia and grabs hold of Gemma. When she bites his thumb to get away, he raises his arm. Tazia flinches, afraid he'll strike her daughter, but the priest pulls back and glares at Tazia instead. "The child needs a firm hand."

"She's really a good little girl, Father." Tazia smiles, embarrassed. "Just restless after the service." Gemma continues to climb up and down but doesn't seem in danger of running off. She checks in every few steps with Tazia, content to play while her mother talks with the priest.

"All the same, she'd do well to have a guiding male presence at home. A growing number of suitable young men are joining our church. Perhaps you would allow me to make the proper introductions?" Father Xavier nods toward a cluster of men whom Tazia judges to be in their twenties, with slicked-back hair, clean-shaven cheeks, and stiff collars irritating their pink necks.

"That's very kind of you, Father." Tazia averts her eyes. "But I'm not ready yet."

"Ah, you must have loved Mr Gatti very much," the priest says. Tazia lets him think what he wants. He beckons Gemma, who approaches cautiously. "Would you like to have a daddy?" he asks. Confused, she looks toward her mother.

"We don't want to be late for lunch with Auntie Veronika," Tazia says and pulls Gemma toward her. "Auntie Vonka," the child shouts, suddenly eager to leave. Tazia shakes the priest's hand. "If we don't move along, we'll miss our train. They run so infrequently on Sunday."

As Tazia instructs, Gemma waves goodbye and takes Tazia's hand. "What's inquently?"

"It means that if we miss our train, we'll have to wait a long time for the next one."

Gemma lets go and skips ahead. "Can I feed the pigeons?"

"Sorry, I didn't bring any peanuts today."

Gemma runs back. "Can I have a daddy?"

Tazia halts. She's been waiting for this question, yet she's never rehearsed an answer. Half a block behind her, the train approaches. If they hurry, they'll make it. Gemma hears the rumbling too. She tugs her mother's skirt. "Inquently," she reminds her, but Tazia cannot move.

***

Back home, Gemma flops down in the middle of the kitchen, crying and flailing her arms. Felix escapes to the back room. Tazia wishes she could follow. How nice it would be to crawl under the covers with the cat purring alongside her. But Felix snuggles only with Veronika.

Veronika covers the stew and plunks herself down beside Gemma, stroking the child's trembling back. "Is something wrong?"

"She's cranky because she's tired and hungry."

Veronika rises, hands Gemma a piece of bread, and settles her in a chair. "I still don't understand why you don't come with me to St. Nicholas," she says, bringing the food to the table. "It's a few blocks away and you wouldn't have to drag her on the train. I'd even go to late Mass and stay home with her while you went to the early one. Or the other way around. You could sleep later."

"I don't feel comfortable going to a Polish church." Tazia reaches for Veronika's hand. She doesn't want to hurt her feelings.

"It's the same Mass," Veronika protests, but squeezes Tazia's fingers and jokes. "Latin. Your old tongue." Tazia smiles, but she can't explain that being surrounded by her own kind connects her to her spiritual roots, like returning home.

"You could join one of the new Italian churches closer to here," Veronika suggests.

"Too small." Tazia wipes the front of Gemma's dress. She's getting good with a spoon, but when money is short and meals are diluted, she can't scoop up the watery liquid without dribbling.

"No! Me do!" Gemma pushes away her mother's hand, spilling more. She rubs her bread in the puddle, then mashes and smears it on the table. She looks at the two women with defiance.

Tazia sets her on the floor with Elvan's rattle and the rag doll Veronika made for her. "I want a big church where I'll fade into the crowd and people won't pry. I don't want to be found."

"Then join a big Polish church. It's the last place Gemma's father would look for you."

"I wouldn't feel connected to God there," Tazia says. She doesn't want to imply Poles are second-class Catholics, but her faith grew on Italian soil, as surely as her family's olive trees.

Veronika shoves back from the table. Felix curls around her legs, mewing for scraps, but she ignores him and dumps what's left of the stew into the sink. "Gemma's father hasn't turned up in two years. He's given up by now. *If* he ever tried to find you in the first place."

"Just because he hasn't found me doesn't mean he isn't looking." Tazia knows Veronika is lashing out from hurt, but the words sting. By now, the idea that she's fleeing from Ayal sounds ridiculous to her own ears, yet she can't bear to think he wanted to be rid of her as much as the baby. "He loved me."

Veronika returns to the table. "*Cara*, you are worth pursuing across an entire continent." The women embrace and join Gemma on the floor. Tazia makes the doll dance and sings "Plynie Wisla," a Polish folk tune Veronika taught them about a river near the town where she grew up. "Pinee Wissa," Gemma warbles. Veronika, with a look of distaste, lifts the rattle with a thumb and forefinger and shakes it to the music. Tazia gently takes it from her. "Gemma's growing. There's no need for this anymore." She slips the rattle into her pocket. "*Dziękuję*," Veronika murmurs.

Taking Gemma's hands, Tazia and Veronika together lift her to her feet and circle slowly, trading songs from their homelands. As the late afternoon sun sinks, Gemma's eyelids droop too. She leans towards Veronika, then slumps against her mother. Veronika kisses her on the forehead and Tazia carries her to bed. Before closing the door to rejoin Veronika, Tazia puts the rattle beneath Gemma's baby clothes, where Ayal's note is also hidden. "Out of sight, out of mind," she thinks, hoping Gemma will not ask for her old toy.

If only her own mind worked like a child's.

chapter 10

A year later, eager to feed her daughter's curiosity, Tazia takes Gemma to the annual Electrical Show. "What's that Mama?" Gemma asks, leaving a nose print on the glass case.

Tazia reads the sign. "A Time-a-Phone. It's a kind of clock."

"But there aren't any numbers." Already Gemma knows her numbers and letters. Tazia dreams of being able to send her to college someday. "How does it work, Mama?"

"If you wake up at night and want to know the time without turning on the light, you push the red button and the clock chimes the hour, gongs the quarter-hour, and rings the minutes."

Gemma bounces on the balls of her feet. "Will you buy us one?"

Tazia laughs. Tired workers don't wake up in the middle of the night. They sleep, dead to the world, until their wind-up alarms go off. "We don't need one. Besides it's too expensive."

"You bought a camera. Why can't I have a clock-a-ring?"

Gemma is fascinated by the Brownie box camera Tazia bought with money she was saving for shoes. How can she explain that as memories of her own past fade, she wants to preserve this time for her daughter? The day she got the camera, Tazia snapped Gemma in front of a cathedral built by Italian stonemasons. Next came a picture beside the grape trellis in an Italian-designed garden. She is passing down her heritage to Gemma. The photos are taken in public places that could be found in any city, never in the squalor of home, or with Tazia in them. She's aware of the absurdity, hiding from a man she simultaneously longs for, but she won't leave any evidence for Ayal to find her. "Clocks break," she says, "but pictures last forever."

Gemma pouts and refuses to pose in front of the display case. Just as well, Tazia thinks, the exhibit's location is traceable. "Let's go to Marshall Field," Tazia offers. "Looking is free." Instantly, Gemma recovers her good humour. Soon they are gazing up at the Tiffany dome and watching models wearing jewels and furs strut past mahogany cabinets filled with leather and silk.

"The Narcissus Tea Room," Gemma says when she tires of looking at things she can't touch. "I want to eat crettes." Weeks ago, Tazia had treated them to chicken croquettes. Gemma had spooned up the crème sauce without spilling a drop. Today Tazia is hesitant to spend the forty-five cents, but reluctant to use money yet again as the reason to say no. Instead she tells her daughter that eating now will ruin her appetite for the nice dinner Veronika is cooking for them.

"I don't care." Gemma kicks the base of the cabinets. Tazia frowns. "Veronika's feelings will be hurt. She may not bake you a birthday cake next week." The child brightens. "I'm going to be three." She holds up three fingers. Tazia twirls her around. "Let's pretend you're a princess and we're buying you an outfit for the royal party." They skip to the girls' dress department.

"Mama, look." Gemma stands beside a pink tulle dress with a rose velvet collar and green sequins, shining like her eyes. Tazia fingers her child's summer shift, tiny birds embroidered with an ornate filigree border, which now barely covers Gemma's knees. "Please? For my birthday?" Gemma whispers, her face buried in Tazia's own threadbare skirt. Tears fall on her daughter's dark curls. Looking isn't free after all. Then Tazia spots the tiny music box. A china ballerina on top, striking an arabesque, wears a tutu the same colour and fabric as the princess dress. She steers Gemma to the toy counter, where the saleslady nods permission for the little girl to wind the key. Music from *Sleeping Beauty* begins to play; the doll slowly turns. Gemma is rapt.

The toy is less than half the price of the dress. Tazia smooths out the bills on the counter. The woman wraps the music box in pink floral paper and makes an elabourate bow. On the train, Gemma's fingers twitch to tear it off, but she slips them into the bow's loops to contain herself. "You don't have to wait until your birthday to open it," Tazia says. "Just until we get home."

"Auntie Veronika," Gemma cries, as soon as they walk in the door. "Look what Mama bought me for my birthday." The bow and wrapping paper are soon on the floor. Gemma turns the key and shoves aside plates to make room for the music box on the table.

The spoon in Veronika's hand pauses mid-stir. "How much?" she asks.

"Less than most other things at the store," Tazia answers, resetting the table.

Veronika stands over her. "You need shoes. The child needs clothes. The landlord is raising the rent. And Armour says that if we don't keep up with Swift, the plant will be forced to cut our wages."

Gemma wraps the ribbons around her legs in imitation of the ballerina's toe shoes and spins around the room, holding out her hands for the women to dance with her. Tazia takes her left hand. Veronika returns to the stove. "No pork tonight," she says, "just plain cabbage soup." The music winds down. Tazia carries the music box to the back room. Gemma looks from her mother to Veronika. She is afraid she's done something naughty but doesn't know what. "We'll play it again and dance after dinner," Tazia tells her, "until it's time for me to go to work."

Gemma stands on a stool to wash her hands and the three of them sit. Tazia says grace and thanks Veronika for making dinner while she and Gemma went off for a day of fun.

"Save your thanks for God," Veronika says. "But as Father Banik at St. Nicholas reminds us every Sunday, accept that His bounty is not endless."

chapter 11

That evening, Tazia arrives at the plant a half hour late. The women who work on either side of her have been standing close together so Mucha won't notice her absence. Now they separate seamlessly, like dance partners, so she can slip into place without disrupting the line's flow.

"Is anything the matter?" asks Sophie, the woman on her right.

"Gemma wouldn't go to bed." Tazia sighs. "She kept taking things out of the cabinets and counting them." Sophie laughs. "When my children refuse to go to bed, it's because they want to jump off the cabinets." She has five boys, the youngest of whom is three years older than Gemma. "You're lucky your daughter won't go to sleep because she's busy learning," Sophie says.

She's right but tonight Tazia feels cheated. Veronika finally put Gemma to bed while she rushed off to work. Tazia missed that final cuddle under the covers, which gets her through the long night shift. They talk about the day and Tazia sings an Italian lullaby, "Ninnananna," until the lids close over Gemma's eyes and her breathing fades to a soft snore. Maybe it was just as well they hadn't talked tonight. Gemma's been asking again about her father and the only answer Tazia has been able to come up with is that they have enough people in their family.

Barely two hours into her shift, Tazia is so busy worrying about Gemma that she doesn't see Mucha come up behind her, demanding to know why she was late. "My daughter," she blurts out. "You know children. They don't always do what you tell them to." She gasps at her own words. Using her child as an excuse might anger the foreman. Suppose he thinks it will happen again. Mucha just smiles. Tazia breathes. When he asks her daughter's name, she tells him.

His smile broadens, showing rotten teeth. "Gemma must be about three years old now."

Tazia nods. "She knows more than most five years olds."

"Then it's time she came to work." Mucha points to Sophie. "Her kids' fingers are getting too big to unclog the machines. I could use a set of smaller hands."

Tazia own hands freeze. Sophie kicks her under the table to get them moving again.

"You bring your little girl with you tomorrow and I won't dock you for being late today." Mucha's smile becomes a sneer. He ratchets up the speed of the line before leaving.

***

Ten hours later, when Tazia leaves the plant, the late autumn wind is drowned out by voices chanting, "A-M-C-B-W, let the union speak for you." Organizers for the Amalgamated Meat Cutters and Butcher Workmen swarm the exit, twice as many as yesterday morning. A burly man accosts Tazia. "Tell the men to join up," he says. "Power lies in numbers." But she doesn't want trouble, and the union doesn't want women. She tries to step around him; he thrusts a brochure at her. They begin a reverse tug of war, each pushing the pamphlet toward the other.

More workers stream past. Mucha's shift ends too. He pulls something from his pocket, but Tazia doesn't wait to see what it is. She drops the brochure, shoves past the union organizer and races the wind home. For the next few days, she dreads Mucha's approach, but he just nags her to speed up. Maybe he was drunk and has forgotten. Near the end of the week, however, he inserts himself between Tazia and Sophie. "Where's little Gemma?" he hisses.

"I won't let her work here. You can dock my wages." Tazia doesn't dare remove her eyes from the machine's gears to see his reaction, but when Mucha pulls something from his vest pocket, she takes a quick look. It's a Brownie camera, like her own. From his other pocket, he extracts a stack of photos. Beckoning Sophie to fill in, he tugs Tazia off the line. She watches him flip through the pictures, shot after shot of people marching for the union. "I'm showing these to Mr Armour," he says, "newspapers too. No other plant owners will hire these agitators." Tazia recognizes men from the shop floor and killing gangs. Thank goodness, Elvan isn't among them.

"Here's my favourite." Mucha holds out the last photo. Tazia wipes her hands on her smock before taking it. It's of her and the burly protester. "Of course, if you change your mind about Gemma, I can rip this up."

She wonders if he is bluffing. There are innocent workers in these pictures, heading home like she was. Most have their heads down, however, so the agitators stand out from those rushing past. Tazia's photo, on the other hand, can be misconstrued. It's impossible to tell whether she is accepting or rejecting the brochure. Her stomach clenches at the thought of losing her job. Then another worry comes to mind. Suppose Ayal saw her picture. A big labour story might make it into the *New York Times*. She tells herself she's being foolish. The sole threat is to Gemma.

And there is only one solution. Tazia will have to take her daughter and flee Chicago.

chapter 12

The second her break starts, Tazia rushes to the end of the Yards where the killing gangs work. It's been three years since she saw Elvan, but she recognizes his tall, broad frame from afar. She knows he's spotted her too when his pig ripper stops mid-swing. He steps through ankle-deep blood to reach her. Wordlessly, they walk beneath the gauzy moonlight to the empty stockcars.

Elvan reaches out. Tazia holds back, though her body reawakens to the tug of his desire. He lowers his arms but moves closer and cocks his head.

Tazia hugs herself. "I'm leaving, Elvan."

"You already left me. No need to tell me again."

"I mean, I'm leaving Chicago. Mucha wants Gemma to work on the line, picking gristle out of the grinder. If I don't let her, he'll put out the word that I'm a union agitator."

"All you gotta do is leave the plant, not the city."

"No one else will hire me. I have to work."

"Not if we get married." Elvan shrugs; it's hopeless. "So why did you come to find me?"

Tazia says she is going to Topeka. A radio announcer described it as a town in the middle of nowhere, a safe place to raise Gemma. She doesn't add that Ayal is unlikely to look for her there. "It's abolitionist history makes it safe for Negroes too. Doesn't your brother live there?"

"Yes, but Denton's already married," Elvan jokes, "and he doesn't sing as well as me." He begins softly, "I sing because I'm happy, I sing because I'm free." A break in the clouds reveals a pulsing star. Elvan's voice expands. "His eye is on the sparrow, and I know He watches me."

For the first time in weeks, Tazia's neck muscles relax. She looks up at Elvan and smiles. "I don't want your little brother to sing to me, I just want him to help me find a job."

"Topeka ain't nothing like Chicago. Everyone there's a farmer."

"I worked on the land in Italy. It would feel good to do that again."

"Growing wheat on flat land is different than growing olives on hills."

"The landscape is different," Tazia agrees, "but the backbreaking work is the same."

Elvan gently squeezes Tazia's upper arms. "If any woman is strong enough to do it, it's you. I'll write my brother tonight and tell him to expect you ... when?"

"How long does the train take to get there?" Tazia plans to leave the next day.

Elvan shakes his head. "Might as well just give you the letter to carry in person. I'll write it when I get home and bring it to your house first thing tomorrow."

"Wait until after seven, when Veronika goes to work." Tazia's neck stiffens again. How will she tell Veronika she's going, or prepare Gemma to never see her "Auntie" again? She'll wait until the last minute, so Veronika won't have time to try talking her out of it. As for Gemma, let her think they're taking the train for a day in the city. With so many new things to see and do, Gemma will soon forget Veronika. As long as she has Tazia, she'll be fine.

"You'll like Denton's wife, Lula Mae. She'll fatten up Gemma and smother you with love, but I'll warn Denton to respect your independence. I know you won't be beholden to anyone."

Tazia *is* beholden, to Veronika. But if Elvan needs to think it's why she turned him down, she lets it be. She takes his hand. "Elvan, you're missing another finger!"

He chuckles. "Another mother beholden to me for saving her child. Don't worry, I can still write that letter."

"Can you still carve?"

Elvan looks up at the sky where the opening in the clouds is growing bigger, revealing more stars. "As long as I can sing, I can carve."

***

"Why are you home in the middle of the night? Are you sick?" Veronika closes the bedroom door behind her and whispers, so she doesn't wake Gemma. Tazia should tell Veronika right now that she is leaving, explain it's to protect the child. But she can neither say the words, nor make up a lie. So, she tells a bit of truth and lets Veronika fill in the rest herself. "Mucha wanted to clean out a gristle build-up in the machine. The line should be fine when you get to work in the morning." She pulls out a chair to sit at the table. The scraping noise is followed by Gemma, whimpering in the back room. Although Tazia hadn't planned on waking her, the distraction is perfectly timed.

Gemma comes into the kitchen, rubbing her eyes and frowning. They brace themselves for a cranky outburst. Instead, Gemma laughs to see her mother sitting in the kitchen at this strange hour. "Mama, Auntie, play!" she commands, and opens her eyes and arms wide.

Veronika should go back to sleep; her shift starts in a few hours. Meanwhile, Tazia should secretly pack and wrap food for the train, so she and Gemma can hurry off as soon as Veronika is gone. The women smile at each other, unable to resist Gemma's giddy demand. Like mischievous children, they get out pots and pans and compete to see who can build the tallest tower. When they come crashing down, they pretend to shush them so they don't wake up the neighbours.

At 6:00, someone knocks on the door. Tazia answers, ready to apologize for the racket. Instead, it's Elvan, holding out the letter with his three-fingered hand. She tries to block Veronika's view, but he fills the doorway. Gemma peeks out from behind Veronika's skirt. "I told you to wait until seven," Tazia snaps.

"I got called to work the day shift. Two men walked off to march with the union." Elvan peers over Tazia's head. "Besides, I got no reason to be afraid of your friend anymore."

Tazia slips her fingers into the empty sockets of Elvan's hand and gently squeezes a thank you. He kisses the top of her head. "Your daughter is beautiful." He sighs. "Take good care of the little sparrow." A gentle kiss, this time on Tazia's lips, and then Elvan is gone.

Veronika follows Tazia into the bedroom and wordlessly watches her pack a battered leather satchel. The embroidered baby clothes go on the bottom. Not that Tazia will need them again, but she can't bear to throw them out. Next, she packs the things Gemma wears now, setting aside one of her two dresses for the train. Last come her own few clothes. She feels for Ayal's note and Elvan's rattle hidden inside her old shawl, glad that Veronika cannot see them.

"Where?" Veronika asks.

"West." Before closing the latch, Tazia spreads over the clothes the white receiving blanket that Veronika gave her minutes after Gemma was born. A peace offering.

"You're lucky you didn't get pregnant again and have a nigger baby this time."

The words burn. Does Veronika think Tazia's been seeing Elvan behind her back? Or is it hurt at the breakup of their family that makes her talk mean? Either way, Veronika's anger serves its purpose. It makes it easier for them to part ways.

Veronika grabs her own clothes from the middle drawer, dresses in the kitchen, and storms out the door. Gemma, her outstretched arms anticipating Veronika's goodbye hug, bursts into tears. Tazia kneels to console her, but her own sobs are louder than the child's. She leads Gemma back to bed, hoping she'll nap while she finishes packing. Instead, Gemma follows her into the kitchen, clinging and fretful. It's just as well. She'll sleep soundly on the train.

At last, daylight penetrates the murky windows. Tazia takes the satchel in one hand and Gemma by the other. The cat, impassive, watches them leave. From now on, Tazia will be more careful not to get close to anyone else. She can flee the Muchas in this world, but she'll also have to protect her daughter from losing another Veronika. Or her own friends, once she starts school.

It will be hard, but Tazia knows what she must do. She will remain the most important person in Gemma's life. As long as it is just the two of them, they can travel light. Mother and daughter walk rapidly toward the El. Thankfully, the satchel does not weigh much.

part four

Gemma, San Diego, 1961

chapter 13

This is Gemma Kane, speaking with my husband, Todd Kane, at our home in San Diego, California. Today is Monday, May 8, 1961, and the time is 7:30 PM.

Todd: This feels a little weird. You haven't given me the third degree since I proposed. (Laughs)

Gemma: Relax, sweetie. You know it's not about you, it's about Mama. I'm picking your brain in case she told you things she kept from me or something I've forgotten.

Todd: Forgotten? Your mind is a steel trap.

Gemma: (Smiles) And my mother's mouth has a steel lock over it. So, back to the beginning. What do you remember about Mama?

Todd: She was relieved I wasn't a sailor.

Gemma: Funny how Mama never wanted me to date anyone from the Navy base.

Todd: Do you suppose she was afraid he'd ship out and leave you, like your father left her?

Gemma: That assumes he was the one to leave. I used to wonder if my father was an Italian sailor. America and Europe traded a lot before the First World War. My parents could have met on the docks in New York.

Todd: An Italian longshoreman with green eyes? (Flutters his lashes)

Gemma: (Flutters back) Not necessarily. It's a recessive gene. Emerald eyes are somewhere in my history, but it could be generations back.

Todd: Odds are your father's Italian, though. Heritage matters a lot to your mother. She never came out and said it, but I know she worried when you married an Irishman that our children would lose touch with their Italian roots.

Gemma: You told her you loved me so much you'd learn Italian. Which was laughable, because I hardly speak it.

Todd: And Tazia said (mimics Italian accent), "No! No! In America we speak English. It's the magnificent culture, not the language, I want to pass down."

Gemma: Ah yes. The magnificent culture of San Diego's Little Italy, the tuna fishing and canning capital of the United States. (Holds nose)

Todd: And yet you never lived in Little Italy. Anywhere. (Snaps fingers) It might help narrow your search, knowing your mother never stayed in Italian neighbourhoods. Although it seems odd.

Gemma: Maybe she figured that was the first place my father would look for her.

Todd: So, when she moved to California, she picked a city where the buildings are Spanish and the people are from Mexico. (Shakes head.) You've always liked Spanish architecture.

Gemma: Blame Yolanda. When we met, my first week of school here, I was so grateful to have a friend that I'd have sworn allegiance to a pagoda if she'd been Chinese. I was captivated when she took me to see the mission style buildings at Balboa Park. If Mama had raised a ruckus, I'd have argued that they were built by the Catholic church and deserved her respect.

Todd: And she'd have told you that Italian churches were nevertheless more beautiful. And older.

Gemma: I also loved *corridos*. When Mama caught me listening to Mexican ballads on the radio, she huffed that Italian operas had better stories with better music. Actually, I liked them too, but I didn't want to give her the satisfaction by admitting it.

Todd: And you complain your mother withholds information. (Wags finger) I may not be Italian, but your mother was also relieved I was Catholic. In high school, you snuck off with Jewish boys.

Gemma: (Alarmed) How do you know about that?

Todd: Tazia told me. It worried her sick.

Gemma: I had no idea she knew. What else did she tell you about me?

Todd: This interview concerns what I know about your mother, not what she—or I—know about you. *Non è così?*

Gemma: (Grimaces, but concedes the point)

Todd: I remember meeting Tazia. It was 1931, our freshman year at UCLA, and you brought me home to go to a protest rally outside Lemon Grove Grammar School.

Gemma: The first successful school desegregation case, more than twenty years before *Brown v. Board of Education*. Mexican parents angry about their kids being sent to a separate building.

Todd: I was impressed that your mother wanted to march alongside Mexican parents.

Gemma: She wasn't anti-Spanish about civil rights, just culture.

Todd: (Frowns, thoughtful) I don't remember seeing Yolanda at the rally.

Gemma: (Laughs) She was there, but she didn't march with us.

Todd: She wanted to march with her own people?

Gemma: No, she just wanted to avoid my mother.

Todd: (Chuckles) Tazia can be formidable. I was afraid of her too until I proved myself. After twenty-five years of our marriage, she's finally convinced I'm not going to leave you. Or Frankie.

Gemma: She's protective. I just wish I knew what it is about my father she's protecting me from.

Todd: Maybe what she's keeping from you isn't about your father.

Gemma: What do you mean?

Todd: Maybe she's the one with the big dark secret. She was a gangster's moll and extorted money not to turn him in. Or she was a woman of ill repute and doesn't know who your father is.

Gemma: Todd! You're talking about my mother. (Long pause until sees his eyes twinkle) Are you sure there isn't something she told you about her past that you're not telling me?

Todd: Really, honey, there's nothing. Tazia focused on the present and future, never the past. Speaking of which, who or what's up next for you on this search?

Gemma: Interviewing Frankie and Yolanda, of course, then other people in San Diego before I head to Las Vegas next week. (Wrings hands) The farther back in time I go, the shakier my own memories get, until I hit a blank. Suppose I come back with nothing?

Todd: (Hugs me) You won't be coming back *to* nothing. You have me, and Frankie, and Julia is going to be a wonderful addition to our family. Plus, you've always got your mother.

Gemma: I couldn't erase her from my life if I wanted to. (Sits up abruptly) Todd, what if you're right and there isn't any big secret about my father? Suppose Mama hides his identity to keep me for herself. Maybe she's afraid I'll want a relationship with him and is too selfish to share me.

Todd: Like a mother cat. With a litter of one.

Gemma: Sometimes she makes me feel like a helpless kitten. If I had nine lives, she'd give birth to me every time. No Papa cat in sight. Before I'm reborn as a mother-in-law, I'm changing that.

Todd: Journalists don't change events. They just record them.

Gemma: Not me. Beat reporters write because we're convinced we do have an influence.

The interview ended at 8:10 PM.

chapter 14

This is Gemma Kane, speaking with my son, Frankie Kane, at his apartment in San Diego, California. Today is Tuesday, May 9, 1961, and the time is 7:50 AM.

Gemma: Thanks for getting up early. I promise we'll be done before you have to leave for work.

Frankie No problem. I used to get jealous when you interviewed other people, now I finally get my turn. Thanks for bringing the espresso and biscotti. (Inhales and smiles) Smells like mornings at Nonna's house.

Gemma: You spent lots of time with Nonna as a child. Did she ever talk about her early days in America?

Frankie: No, only about Italy. Growing olives, helping her big family. I think she felt sorry for me, being an only child. I once asked why she didn't stay in touch with her sister and brothers.

Gemma: Me too. I wonder if she gave us the same excuse. (Laughs) You go first.

Frankie: She said there weren't phones then and she didn't have the same chance I did to learn to read and write. When people left the old country, they said goodbye forever. Is that what she told you?

Gemma: (Nods) Close enough. Only she made it sound like I was lucky to be an only child. I suppose since Nonna was responsible for that, she could hardly criticize herself.

Frankie: Nonna never criticizes herself.

Gemma: (Laughs) True. You have to have regrets to do that. And if she has any regrets, she won't admit them. So, tell me what you remember about your time with Nonna growing up.

Frankie: Not much when I was little, but I have vivid memories of our seeing the Guardian of Water statue at the Civic Center. It must have been 1948, because it was my tenth birthday and she said the statue was the same age as me. It was monumental, and I was impressed by it, until Nonna said it couldn't compare to Italian Renaissance fountains that were hundreds of years old.

Gemma: That sounds like my proud Italian mother. What else?

Frankie: A year later, Nonna and I rode the last electric street car when it left Union Station. I said I was going to miss them, they were so much fun. Nonna said she rode the street car for hours between Brooklyn and Greenwich Village and it was no fun at all. I wanted to hear more, but she clammed up. Said there was no point spoiling the day with stories from the dirty, cold distant past. She bought me an ice cream cone and a box of Cracker Jacks, I think to shut me up.

Gemma: Mmm. The Triangle factory was in Greenwich Village, so Mama must have lived in Brooklyn. You're sure she didn't say more about where she lived or who she lived with?

Frankie: (Shakes head) My next clear memory is when I was thirteen, the day we moved into our second house. It felt strange not to live down the block from Nonna anymore. While you and Dad unpacked, she took me to Jack in the Box, the first ever drive-through restaurant. It struck me that she was the only grandmother I knew who could drive. I realize now how independent she was. Maybe because she had to raise you alone. It must have been hard for her. And you.

Gemma: She had a steady civilian job as a janitor at the Navy base. It didn't pay great, but it was better than the jobs she had before. Also, a lot safer.

Frankie: When kids at my school joined the Navy, she was terrified I would too. She had a thing against sailors, even though she worked at the base. Something to do with your father, you think?

Gemma: Possibly. Or, after working for the Navy so many years, she knew what that life was like. Moving all the time, living under the threat of war. You graduated high school just a couple of years after Korea. I was glad you chose college instead of the military too.

Frankie: (Snaps fingers) There *was* one time Nonna talked about her first year in America. We were at Mission Beach Amusement Center, riding the carousel, and I dared her to go on the Giant Dipper roller coaster. She'd gone on other scary rides with me, so I was surprised when she refused. When I teased her and asked why, she said something about bodies flying off the window ledges of the factory where she worked. As soon as I pushed for more details, she pressed her lips together and I could tell she was sorry that she'd said anything.

Gemma: Ah, a rare instance of regret.

Frankie: A year later, my class went on a field trip to the Center, after it was renamed Belmont Park. The guys teased me because I was the only one who refused to go on the roller coaster too.

Gemma: It wasn't like you to be scared.

Frankie: I think I did it out of solidarity with Nonna. It was the first time I'd seen her shaken.

Gemma: (Half talks to self) Knowing how the fire traumatized Mama, I used to wonder if my father died in it. But most of the dead were young women, and if he were gone, she wouldn't be worried about him finding her. Unless she was afraid his family would and try to take me away.

Frankie: There was one other time I remember Nonna being scared. Five years ago, my last year in high school, right after the glass elevator was installed outside the El Cortez Hotel. You gave me money to take her to dinner at the rooftop Starlight Restaurant for her birthday, but I couldn't persuade her to ride up. She wouldn't say why, but we walked the whole way. Twelve floors.

Gemma: You never told me. (Laughs) You did confess Nonna let you drink most of her Chianti that night. Thankfully, she insisted on driving you home in our car, and then Todd had to drive her home. She said you had a bit of a stomach ache, not that you were tipsy.

Frankie: Nonna knows lots of things about me that you don't. I trusted her to keep my secrets.

Gemma: (Hurt) I know. I always felt bad that you confided more in her than in me, but I suppose that's natural. (Leans forward) Are you sure she didn't trust you to keep any of her secrets?

Frankie: Honest, Mom. I wish I did know more about Nonna. It's as much my history as yours. But I guess it'll go the grave with her.

Gemma: (Superstitious; flaps hands to shoo away bird of death) Not if I use all my wiles as a reporter to dig up the past.

Frankie: I know you're doing this for me, but I don't really care about my grandfather. That may change when Julia and I have kids but for now, satisfy your own curiosity. I'm not sure how much you'll learn about your father, but you may learn more about your mother. And yourself.

Gemma: How did I raise such a wise child?

Frankie: (Smirks) It must be my maternal grandfather's genes.

The interview ended at 8:30 AM.

chapter 15

This is Gemma Kane, speaking with my best friend, Yolanda Soto Garcia, at her home in San Diego, California. Today is Tuesday, May 9, 1961 and the time is 2:00 PM.

Gemma: Thanks for lunch. Your gorditas are even better than your mother's, and goodness knows I devoured hers in high school.

Yolanda: You devoured everything Mexican, even the crappy tacos from the taqueria where we hung out after school. You carried a toothbrush so your mom wouldn't smell the chili peppers on your breath when you got home.

Gemma: (Hand over mouth) I forgot about that. You pestered me to take you home to my house so you could taste my mother's great Italian cooking. I felt bad that I couldn't.

Yolanda: At first, I thought it was because your mom didn't like Mexicans.

Gemma: You didn't believe me when I said she wasn't prejudiced. Although she was partial to Catholics. (Laughs) She just didn't want anyone getting close to us and poking into our past.

Yolanda: No doubt she's thrilled about you poking into the past now. (Playfully slaps my knee) I'm not sure how I can help you, though.

Gemma: You may remember something I forgot because it didn't seem important to me at the time. Start with when we met.

Yolanda: We were sixteen, it was the first week of school, and you looked like a twerp. Your top was tucked in when the style was dropped waists with over blouses. When it rained, you buckled your galoshes. (Snorts) Here, look at you. (Pulls out a picture of us with Mr and Mrs Soto)

Gemma: (Groans) I knew what was fashionable, but Mama didn't let me dress that way because she was afraid I'd look like a hooker. Where was this photo of us with your parents taken?

Yolanda: At Rockwell Field, the day Lindbergh took off for New York before flying nonstop to Paris. (Turns picture over to show me the date, exactly thirty-four years ago)

Gemma: Your dad worked for the company that built the Spirit of St. Louis and we got to stand behind the VIP section, right?

Yolanda: (Nods) I remember asking what kind of your work your father did.

Gemma: I had two or three pat answers to that question. Which did I tell you?

Yolanda: You said, "We lost him before I was born." I figured he died. You didn't sound sad, but something told me not to push it. Besides, I was more interested in hearing about Darius.

Gemma: Darius Ignatius. The boy I left behind in Las Vegas.

Yolanda: I thought his name was so romantic compared to Pedro or Juan. We talked about how far we'd gone with boys. I think it's a litmus test when girls are deciding whether to be friends.

Gemma: Mama was convinced I was into heavy petting, so she spirited me away to San Diego.

Yolanda: You insisted you never got past kissing, mouth only "half open." (Half-opens mouth)

Gemma: Not more until here, senior year of high school, when we'd go out to Inspiration Point.

Yolanda: (Laughs) Before we got too busy looking into boys' eyes, we'd look past Mission Valley and share our dreams about heading out into the world, far away from home.

Gemma: We were both American-born children of immigrants. Is that what bound us?

Yolanda: Not for me. There were plenty of other Mexican kids. In fact, you said how different we were. My folks came a short distance by land to get here. Your mom crossed an ocean alone.

Gemma: Are you sure I said she came alone? That means I thought she didn't know my father before she got to New York.

Yolanda: Or that he came over first with the intention that she'd follow.

Gemma: However, I got the impression that she sailed alone, it might be worth something. Can you remember any other places we went in high school or anything else revealing I said?

Yolanda: We went to the grand opening of the Fox Theater our senior year, that would have been fall of 1929. I can't remember what movie we saw. Do you?

Gemma: No, but the pink marble lobby had a carved ceiling and Italian Renaissance fountain. I took Mama to see it later. She has a photo of me under the chandelier. I'm tall, but I look tiny.

Yolanda: We also went to the San Diego Zoo.

Gemma: You dragged me to the gorillas and elephants, but I wanted to hang out with the lions.

Yolanda: You said the only way you resembled your mother was that you both loved cats.

Gemma: Except I like big jungle ones and Mama prefers small ones curled up in her lap. So, the theatre, zoo, make-out spots. How did I manage to go there? Mama watched me like a hawk.

Yolanda: After we joined the competitive diving team, practice became an excuse to sneak off. God, sometimes we were dumb. Remember when Miguel Martinez threw a my-parents-are-gone-and-there's-booze-in-the-cabinet party and you told your mom there was a late-night practice before the state championship?

Gemma: I was afraid she'd give Coach Brooks a piece of her mind that practice was interfering with my doing homework, and then I'd be caught out and locked up like Rapunzel.

Yolanda: To her credit, your mother looked out for your interests. And the rights of others. I guess you get that from her.

Gemma: Mama wanted me to have the chances she didn't. Like most immigrant parents, she saw education as the way for that to happen.

Yolanda: Mine too. It's good we both got into UCLA and you got the diving scholarship. Our friendship was much easier once you escaped her clutches.

Gemma: I also stopped hiding it when we came home for vacations.

Yolanda: Because you got braver, or because you knew she'd like me when she found out I was studying Italian renaissance art?

Gemma: Because by then she worried more about my relationship with Todd than with you. (Laughs; pauses) Do you ever regret that you got married and had kids right out of college and never had a career? (Afraid to offend her) I mean, besides volunteering as a docent?

Yolanda: I'm happy with my choices, but I admit I admired your ability to be a journalist and a mother.

Gemma: It helped that Todd was so supportive, but it was never easy. Especially when I decided to have only one child. Everyone said Frankie would grow up spoilt.

Yolanda: You retorted you were an only child and weren't spoilt, which raised a few eyebrows.

Gemma: (Slaps Yolanda's knee) I am *not* spoilt! I just don't take no for an answer.

Yolanda: Actually, you care about other people more than anyone I know. Except for your mom.

Gemma: (Kneels) Confession: I take after Mama in two ways. One, I like cats, though a little less. Two, I defend the rights of the poor and minorities, as much as, if not more than her.

Yolanda: (Pulls me up to standing) Most people object to the group but make exceptions for individuals. Your mom fought for the rights of groups; she just objected to me as an individual.

Gemma: Nothing personal. She was afraid of our getting close. It took her a few decades, but she finally admitted she admired my ability to make and keep friends.

Yolanda: Agreed. Your mom wasn't a racist. Just a clucking mother hen. So, baby chick, did I tell you anything that helps explain why she protected you from your father?

Gemma: Maybe *he* was a racist.

Yolanda: Or he was rich, and she wanted no part of his ill-gotten gains. Not even to send to her poor family back home. (Cocks head and grins)

Gemma: Or she's been blackmailing him and secretly sending her family money for fifty years.

Yolanda: Now that would be an interesting discovery.

Gemma: (Sighs) The only discovery that interests me is finding out who my father is.

The interview ended at 2:55 PM.

chapter 16

This is Gemma Kane, speaking with Reginald (Reggie) Brooks, my high school diving coach, at his nursing home in Clairemont Mesa, California. Today is Wednesday, May 10, 1961, and the time is 9:15 AM.

Gemma: What a breathtaking view of Mission Bay you have from these bluffs.

Mr Brooks: Beats watching students thrash around the pool.

Gemma: So, you're enjoying retirement?

Mr Brooks: Immensely. Don't get me wrong, though. I loved coaching. When San Diego won the state championship your senior year, it was the highlight of my career. Your reverse three and a half somersault with a half twist was the best 5371D a student of mine ever did.

Gemma: It's what got me the diving scholarship to UCLA. I have you to thank for that.

Mr Brooks: (Bald head blushes) You had good grades too, but you owe me thanks for another reason.

Gemma: (Frowns) You pulled strings?

Mr Brooks: Nothing of the sort. That's bad sportsmanship. But after you got the letter, your mother came to see me. Absolutely furious. Apparently you never told her you'd applied.

Gemma: And she never told me she spoke to you! (Thinks back) I didn't want to tell her unless I got in or got a scholarship. It was the only way I could afford to go.

Mr Brooks: Your mother was angry because she wanted you to stay closer to home.

Gemma: San Diego State Teachers College. What did you say when she turned up at your office?

Mr Brooks: That I sensed you didn't want to be a teacher.

Gemma: No offense to your profession; it just wasn't me.

Mr Brooks: No offense taken. Teaching wasn't my first choice either, although I turned out to love it. There was more at stake for you, though. You needed to get away from home.

Gemma: How did you know? I never said anything to you.

Mr Brooks: Every young person wants to escape. But your situation was extreme. You had to sneak off with Yolanda to places other parents *encouraged* their kids go to. (Winks) Like the time you left practice early when the Junipero Serra Museum opened. With that giant cross out front.

Gemma: Yolanda and I pretended to be nuns walking down the colonnade, weaving in and out of the columns. Only we couldn't keep straight faces because the boys chanted dirty limericks, in Latin. (Laughs uneasily) How did you find out we went there?

Mr Brooks: Teachers have their ways. (Winks) I also knew about the shenanigans at Inspiration Point and hidden corners of the zoo. I never reported you kids to your parents or to the principal, though. I kept what I knew to myself.

Gemma: What else did you know about me?

Mr Brooks: That you felt different because you didn't have a father. San Diego is a Catholic town. Families stick together. I tried to keep an eye on you without being too obvious, but your mother resented it. She accused me of putting you up to applying to UCLA ...

Gemma: Well, you did.

Mr Brooks: ... with the intention of stealing you away from her.

Gemma: (Hand over mouth) Oh God. What did you say?

Mr Brooks: The wrong thing. That I thought you could use a father figure in your life.

Gemma: And she probably said something like I had her and didn't need another parent.

Mr Brooks: Exactly.

Gemma: I don't suppose she said anything about my actual father?

Mr Brooks: Not then. But after I apologized, I steered the conversation around to what a great opportunity UCLA offered. I've never known parents who didn't want their child to succeed, and your mother was no different. I told her you were one of my brightest students and, to appease her further, said you no doubt got your cleverness from her. Your mother turned pale. She didn't say anything, but I could swear her mind was thinking you got your smarts from him.

Gemma: I wondered about that growing up. My mother got after me to study and do homework, but she couldn't help. I once said she was stupid and that if I had a daddy, he could help me. She left the room, I think to stop herself from slapping me. Of course, later I realized my mother was very smart, she just didn't have the education.

Mr Brooks: Getting her daughter the best education possible was the argument I used to talk your mother into letting you go to UCLA.

Gemma: Here I thought I was the one who convinced her. (Shrugs) I suppose it doesn't matter. Mama signed the forms and off I went. I wouldn't have gone though, without her blessing.

Mr Brooks: (Pats my arm) It was hard for her. You were her whole life. Instead of being angry at her for resisting, admire her courage in letting you go, even if it meant leaving her behind.

Gemma: And alone.

Mr Brooks: She's not alone now. She has you, your husband, and son. Plus a granddaughter-in-law very soon. Congratulations to you and your family.

Gemma: (Nods thank you) But she left me and my son and his children missing a family member.

Mr Brooks: (Rests arms on knees, leans forward) When you were diving, your biggest problem was learning not to splash when you entered the water. Judges deduct nearly a third of your score for that. I taught you to hit the surface straight, not from an angle, to barely create a ripple. Now you're trying every angle to find your father. I'm not your coach anymore. You're on your own. So be careful how you hit deep water to avoid making a big splash. Life will mark you down.

The interview ended at 9:50 AM.

chapter 17

This is Gemma Kane, speaking with Dr Morton Stein, my college journalism professor, at his home in Los Angeles, California. Today is Wednesday, May 10, 1961, and the time is 2:15 PM.

Gemma: You're looking robust. Are you still teaching?

Dr Stein: No, but I still write angry letters to the editor. How was the drive up the Pacific Coast Highway? People use route numbers nowadays, but I like the old names.

Gemma: I was a bit rushed. I had another interview in San Diego this morning. Luckily, driving along the ocean clears my head.

Dr Stein: (Grins) I'll do my best to re-muddle it. You can clear it again on the drive home.

Gemma: (Smiles wryly) I was pretty muddled when I started your class. Hard to believe that was over thirty years ago. The parents of most students in the class weren't born in California so our first assignment was to interview them about where they were from and what brought them here.

Dr Stein: I used that assignment up until I retired. The stories never ceased to be interesting.

Gemma: I got a bad grade because my mother was so vague about herself and had absolutely nothing to say about my father. You scribbled "Probe for details!" in red at the top of my paper.

Dr Stein: Funny, I don't remember that. What sticks in my memory is how tenacious you were about gathering information and tracking down sources. For years I used your paper on the 1932 Norris-LaGuardia Act, giving workers the right to join unions, as a model for other students.

Gemma: That exercise became a model for my own future work on labour issues.

Dr Stein: (Grins) I've followed your career. Your articles on using the Taft-Hartley Act to break the steel strike were especially impressive. I'm proud to claim you as my student.

Gemma: (Blushes) Can I be your student again today? As I said on the phone, I'd appreciate any advice you can give me on how to go about finding my father.

Dr Stein: Let me turn the question back on you, like I used to do in class. (Adjusts eyeglasses, laces fingers in front of chest) What do you think has made you a good investigative journalist?

Gemma: Being pugnacious. Sticking my nose where folks don't want me to go.

Dr Stein: Okay. Think about what your mother was afraid of and go there.

Gemma: She was afraid of people, men especially, stealing me away from her. (Laughs) Do you suppose that means my father was a thief?

Dr Stein: What does your gut tell you?

Gemma: That she was a poor young woman, alone in this country, and she wanted something to call her own. Gemma, gem. I was her precious possession.

Dr Stein: Thieves don't just steal money or possessions.

Gemma: (Ruminative) They steal hearts.

Dr Stein: So, assume your father stole your mother's heart. He wasn't a casual tryst.

Gemma: That should make me feel better, knowing I was a love child, but I was still a mistake.

Dr Stein: Don't think emotionally. Think analytically. What other qualities do thieves have?

Gemma: They're secretive, dishonest, manipulative, out for themselves, possibly violent ...

Dr Stein: Whoa, you're painting your father as a very bad man. You'll talk yourself out of finding him for fear he'll be someone whose paternity you don't want to acknowledge. Revise your statement. Do thieves have any positive traits that might help you track him down?

Gemma: (Smiles) He could be clever, smart, charming, and seductive.

Dr Stein: That's more like it.

Gemma: But it doesn't narrow the field. Lots of men my father's age have those qualities.

Dr Stein: Not most immigrants, circa 1910. Their lives were limited. Home and work, work and home. Odds are your father was a poor immigrant like your mother, or the son of immigrants.

Gemma: (Despairing) There were millions of them.

Dr Stein: One thing you do know is that your mother was in the

Triangle fire. Nose around—find other survivors, remaining family members. True, most were nameless, but there was enough hubbub and outrage to leave some records.

Gemma: (Excited) I'll revisit my earlier notes. Check out the burial societies that raised money, and the witnesses interviewed by reporters. There are bound to be court records too.

Dr Stein: (Thumbs up) As I said, you're dogged and persistent.

Gemma: You taught me well.

Dr Stein: I suspect you also learnt more from your mother than you give her credit for. After all, I had you for a few years in college, but your mother influenced you your whole life.

Gemma: I suppose my father, by his mere absence, influenced me too.

Dr Stein: Half your genes are his. Look inside yourself for clues to his identity.

The interview ended at 2:40 PM.

chapter 18

This is Gemma Kane, speaking with Captain Robert Morris, my mother's first supervisor at the U.S. Naval Base, at his home in San Diego, California. Today is Thursday, May 11, 1961, and the time is 1:30 PM.

Gemma: I wasn't sure you'd remember my mother. After all, you hired her thirty-four years ago.

Captain Morris: Mrs Gatti—you won't mind if I use the more familiar Tazia?—was unforgettable. Back then, we called women "cleaning ladies" and men "janitors," but Tazia wanted a job like the men. They got paid fourteen dollars a week, women earned twelve.

Gemma: Either amount sounds paltry today, but I suppose they were decent wages at the time. How did my mother propose to earn higher pay?

Captain Morris: She learnt to drive. Women didn't in those days. So I could assign her tasks reserved for men like picking up cleaning supplies from central depot or fetching spare parts for equipment. Even a few maintenance jobs, vacuuming air vents and cleaning and oiling fan blades.

Gemma: So you paid her the same wages as the men?

Captain Morris: I wanted to, but Navy rules forbid it. All I could manage was an extra fifty cents a week, now and then a dollar. When I was reassigned after four years and Captain Nimitz took over—this was long before he became fleet admiral—he cut her wages back.

Gemma: Some things never change. (Sighs) Other than needing the money, did my mother say if having a man's job, or earning a man's pay, was important to her in other ways?

Captain Morris: She never said anything about your father not being around, if that's where you're going. Several ladies who worked on base lost husbands in the war, most in the Navy. I assumed that's what happened to her, although later, when I learnt she'd come here from Las Vegas, that didn't fit. I just figured Tazia was poor and wanted to give you the best life she could.

Gemma: My mother was proud. She wouldn't have admitted to being needy.

Captain Morris: True. But I misjudged her. Once, checking inventory, I discovered tinned meat was missing. I assumed she was taking it home to feed you.

Gemma: That's horrible. I never knew I was eating stolen food.

Captain Morris: (Laughs) You weren't. It turns out she was giving it to Sailor Boy, the base cat. We kept him around because he was a good mouser, but he wasn't particularly friendly. If any of the men tried to touch him, he'd arch his back and growl. Except with Tazia, he'd flop on his back and expose his belly for her to rub. Frankly, I hated the darned cat, but I worried that the more your mother fed him, the fewer mice he'd want to catch. So I confronted her.

Gemma: Goodness. What did she say?

Captain Morris: Tazia had integrity. She'd never deliberately lie. (Smiles) Without batting an eye, she said she was "redistributing" food among Navy personnel, the cat being an "employee."

Gemma: (Tsking) My mother draws a fine distinction between lies of commission and omission. This is the first I've heard of her telling lies of ... derision, flouting the rules. What did you do?

Captain Morris: Nothing. Sailor Boy *was* underpaid. If Tazia could fight to bring about justice for herself, she had every right to pursue it for the cat too. (Grins)

Gemma: (Grins back) My mother tried hard to keep me from feeling that we were poor. I knew we couldn't afford many of the things my schoolmates had, but I never felt deprived.

Captain Morris: It helped that Tazia earned extra doing personal laundry for me and the other family men on base. It paid for your swim suits and travel to diving meets. (Scratches chin) I remember a strange conversation about how much she'd charge for the service. She wanted more than I was willing to pay, fifteen cents instead of ten a garment, and twenty not fifteen a sheet. I said since she wasn't a laundry expert, I didn't see why I should pay more.

Gemma: Did she make up a story of omission to convince you she had the expertise?

Captain Morris: The opposite. In a rare instance of admission, Tazia protested she had ten years of laundry experience in Las Vegas. She spoke with such fervor, I had no doubt it was the truth.

Gemma: (Nods) It was. So, you capitulated?

Captain Morris: I would have, except right after she spoke, she pulled back, as if withdrawing what she'd said. She looked so uncomfortable, that I made a joke about her trying to cover up her Mafia connections. That's when gambling was still illegal in Nevada. Your mother turned pale.

Gemma: (Leaning forward) What did she say?

Captain Morris: She said that ten cents a shirt would be fine.

Gemma: I mean, what did she say about the Mafia?

Captain Morris: Not a word and I didn't dare crack another joke. In the end, Tazia did such an excellent job doing the laundry that we gladly paid her the higher rate after all.

Gemma: (Disappointed, but laughing) I can't imagine my mother toting bottles or guns as a bootlegger's moll. Or counting chips at an underground casino. Her hands were too slippery with sweat after a twelve-hour shift at the laundry. I guess that was the only work she could find there.

Captain Morris: No offense, but Tazia was an attractive woman. She could have gotten ... other jobs. My guess, pardon the pun, is that she worked in a laundry to make a cleaner life for you.

Gemma: I didn't make it easy for her once I hit my teens. I wish I hadn't been so caught up in myself and paid more attention to what was going on in her life. It would come in handy now.

Captain Morris: What I know isn't likely to help you find your father, but if it makes you feel better, your mother was one of the best workers I ever supervised. If she hadn't been a civilian, or a woman, she could have gone far in the Navy. I'd be proud to salute her.

Gemma: (Saluting) Thank you Captain.

Captain Morris: You said on the phone that she continued working at the base long after I left.

Gemma: Thirty-two years in all. A heart attack two years ago forced her to retire. No pension, but she was able to save once I got settled. She won't accept help from me and my husband.

Captain Morris: I'm not surprised. (Gestures at waterfront outside apartment window) I always loved this area. I was happy to come back here after I retired. Is Tazia happy in retirement?

Gemma: Yes, maybe for the first time in her life. Or, more accurately, for the first time since she was a child. Aguanga, the place where she lives, reminds her of Italy.

Captain Morris: I'm glad, but tell her it's important as we get older to look to the future, not just fixate on the past. We can't redo what's already happened, but we can try to undo any lasting damage we've caused. In the Navy, it's called starting each watch with a clean slate.

Gemma: Any other nautical advice for me as I set sail, so to speak?

Captain Morris: I wish you well in your quest, but since you're diving deep into the past, sail close to the edge of the wind, not directly into it. And if you find the father you're looking for, be prepared not to like the cut of his jib. It's your mother who cuts a fine feather in my logbook.

The interview ended at 2:25 PM.

part five

Tazia, Topeka, 1914-1917

chapter 19

"Dear Denton," Elvan's brother reads, standing inside his doorway while Tazia, Gemma clutching at her skirt, waits on the sagging porch. "The woman who handed you this letter is my good friend, Tazia Gatti." His voice is gruff, unlike Elvan's smooth cadences. Tazia's empty stomach contracts. Perhaps coming here was a mistake. Denton plods on, his calloused finger pointing to each word as he sounds it out. "My friend needs work and she and her little girl, Gemma, need a place to live. I pray that you and Lula Mae can assist them, and may the good Lord bless you."

As Denton stumbles through the letter, Lula Mae and six children, the oldest near ten and the youngest crawling, gather behind him in the front room of their two-room shack. Lula Mae taps her foot, waiting for her husband to finish. At last, he tells Tazia, "I don't ... We barely get by ... a white lady ... " Lula Mae nudges him aside with her hip, and pulls Tazia and Gemma inside.

"Where are your manners?" she clucks. "Making them stand in the cold instead of inviting them in for a meal." She smiles at Denton. "And today the Sabbath." He grins sheepishly.

The children stare. Tazia wonders if this is the first time a white person has been in their home. "Sorry, Ma'am." Denton bows his head. "I get so nervous when I read, everything flies out of my head. Like I'm waiting for the teacher to whip me for saying the words wrong. I didn't get as much learning as Elvan. After he left, us older kids quit school to help Mama with the little ones." Denton's eyes, unlike his voice, are kind and gentle. Maybe things will work out after all.

Lula Mae takes their satchel and shows Tazia where she and Gemma can wash up out back. Two of the Wright children follow them.

"You and your little girl, no one else?" asks Lula Mae, priming the rusty pump.

Tazia nods, wincing as the icy water washes away the grime of the long train trip.

Lula Mae hands Tazia a thin towel, patched in several places. "Your man done run off?"

"It's just me and Gemma."

Lula Mae nods briskly and thrusts Gemma's hands under the gushing water. Gemma gasps at the cold, and her directness, but doesn't pull away.

"Mama." One of the Wright children, a girl about Gemma's age, steps closer to the pump. "Her skin's getting more white!"

"Her skin ain't changing colour," Lula Mae replies. "Just the dirt coming off." Sceptical, the child puts her own hand under the water and rubs vigourously. "Mirlee Bee," Lula Mae says, "all the washing in the world ain't gonna turn your skin white. Besides, it's fine as it is."

"What about her hair, Mama," asks a boy, a couple of years older. "It gonna wash out lighter too?" He pats Gemma's head. "It soft," he marvels. Gemma holds her breath.

"Her hair dark, same as yours, and curly, just not so much." Lula Mae gently removes her son's hand and smiles at Gemma, who lets out her breath. "Now you two stop being so nosy." She shoos her children inside and says to Tazia, "Least we know Elvan ain't your girl's father." She raises her eyebrows, waiting for an explanation of how Tazia knows Denton's brother.

Tazia dries herself and Gemma. "I feel like I washed away the blood from the meat packing plant too." She rests a clean white hand on Lula Mae's brown forearm. "Elvan said you'd be kind. He was right." She says nothing more about Elvan. They head inside.

The family sits around the table, smaller children squeezed on a bench to free two chairs for their guests. Denton says grace. Lula Mae dishes out the food. "Cornmeal mush and greens," says, with apology. "We eat our big meal midday, after church. I figure on leftovers for supper, but ain't never none with this crowd." She wags a finger; the children poke one another and giggle. "No matter." Lula Mae ladles deep into the pot. "We can always feed another couple of mouths."

After filling Denton's plate, Lula Mae doles out the next biggest portion to Tazia, then heaps Gemma's dish too. Tazia worries her daughter will balk at this unfamiliar food, but the hungry child lifts the bowl to her mouth and scoops up every bite, silently watching the other children over the rim. When Gemma's plate is clean, Lula Mae winks and gives her a sugar cube.

"Aw, Mama," the oldest child protests. "How come we ain't getting no sugar tonight?"

"You done had your treat today. This poor child travelled a long way to our table."

Gemma holds the sugar cube, uncertain what to do with it. "Put it in your mouth and suck it," says Mirlee Bee. Still, Gemma hesitates.

Lula Mae laughs and hands each child a piece of sugar. "Here, show her how it's done." The children pop the cubes between their lips, followed by Gemma. Tazia reminds her to say thank you, which she does, drooling sugary saliva. The Wright children titter. Gemma covers her mouth, but dimples betray a smile. The others grin back. Soon she is laughing with them, sated and happy. Tazia, too, relaxes. Packingtown seems long ago and far away.

***

When she'd gotten off the train late that afternoon, and shown the station master the address she was looking for, his eyebrows had shot up. "What do you want in that part of town?" he'd asked, before directing her to the trolley. She and Gemma were the only ones to get on board, and the trolley conductor, grateful for the company, had been friendlier. When Tazia asked about the huge copper-domed building they passed, she got a tour guide's description of the Kansas State Capitol. "Took thirty-seven years to build," he bragged, "and cost over three million dollars." Tazia asked whether Italian artisans had worked on the Renaissance-style structure. "Indeed," he said. "Italian marble all over and hand-hammered copper columns with the state's native wild flowers." Tazia planned to take Gemma to see the building once they were settled.

They passed shops, closed on Sunday but with bright window displays. Then Smoky Row, where the conductor said no respectable woman ventured. Soon the faces on the street changed from white to black, and multistorey brick buildings gave way to squat wooden structures. Tazia saw a hodgepodge of salvaged barn boards, tin, and tar paper, with newspaper stuffed into the chinks. "How do they keep out the snow?" she'd asked, thinking of Chicago blizzards.

"Topeka's below the snow line so our winter is pretty dry. Wind is the real problem. Cuts through you like a plow blade. Then summer's so hot and sticky, even the atheists pity the poor ministers who have to wear collars around their necks."

"You must be grateful for fall and spring," Tazia had mused.

"Fall's pretty. But spring…" The conductor hooted. "…is the worst. Thunderstorms, tornadoes. Scariest are the hailstorms. We get some as big as baseballs."

Instinctively, Tazia's hand had covered Gemma's head, but the sleeping child, slumped against her, didn't stir. After trying to keep her amused on the train, Tazia was grateful to talk to another adult. She missed Veronika and was sorry when the trolley stopped to let them off. "You be careful now," the conductor said, before clanging the bell and turning back toward downtown.

Tazia had stood in the middle of the desolate street, amid a swirl of dried leaves, until she spotted a Negro man and approached to ask directions. He'd looked at her as suspiciously as the white station master had but pointed to a house with a tangle of tacked-on rooms. Then she'd led Gemma, fully awakened by the bell and her curiosity, to the Wrights' porch.

***

Now, sitting at their table, Tazia twice thanks Lula Mae for the meal, uncertain where their next one will come from. "Elvan doing all right?" Denton asks. She can't admit she's hardly seen him the past three years, not if she wants the Wrights' help. So she answers, "As well as someone in that job can be."

"Foreman still got it in for him?"

"Mucha's got it in for everyone," Tazia says, shuddering.

Denton frowns. "Harder for a dark man. People like that foreman are scared of us."

"Lately he's more scared of union organizers. If Elvan steers clear of them, he'll be fine."

Denton splays his fingers. "Union's right to protest working conditions at the plant. We ain't got it easy here, but it beats ripping open a hundred and fifty hogs a day."

Tazia sees her opening. "Elvan said you worked on a wheat farm. Can you help me get a job there too?"

"Only women there are the wife and daughter of Mr Tapper, the Swede who owns the place. They cook for us farmhands, do barnyard chores." Denton frowns. "Mr Tapper's near as poor as us. Don't reckon he needs another woman in the kitchen or the henhouse."

"I want to work in the fields," Tazia says.

Denton grips the arms of his chair. "You don't understand how it is, Mrs Gatti."

"Please, call me Tazia." After Veronika, being called by her last name sounds so lonely.

"Mr Tapper can't afford large teams of horses, let alone steam-powered tractors like the rich farmers use. We break sod by hand, clear two or three acres a day. Machines do five times that. Same with planting. We ain't got no broadcast seeders to drag behind the plow. It's hard work, and it ain't fit for a woman."

"It's what I did on my family's olive tree farm in Italy. Every step by hand. Backbreaking work, but an honest day's labour." So different, Tazia thinks, from mixing unspeakable things into the sausage and finding any excuse to dock your pay. "I can do it." She flexes her muscles.

Denton squirms. "But Mrs ... I mean Tazia. The farmhands ain't only men. We're all of us Negroes too. Mr Tapper is the only one who'll hire us."

"In Chicago, your skin colour mattered less than whether you were tough enough to do the job. It ought to be the same here."

"Ought to be, but it ain't. White farmers and farmhands ..." Denton trails off. "Let's just say there's been trouble."

"Have you been hurt?" Tazia is alarmed. She expected Topeka to be safer than Chicago.

"Mr Tapper got threatened a time or two in town, at the general store, but nothing's happened." Denton looks at the children, who have stopped fidgeting and are listening closely.

Tazia takes a deep breath. "Mucha threatened Elvan," she says. "But he always backed down because your brother was too good a worker. I'm a hard worker too, and I know farming."

"I just don't think Mr Tapper is going to like the idea of a white lady in his fields."

Lula Mae stands. The children's eyes follow her. "Now, husband. You let that farmer decide for himself."

He grins. "Just like you let me decide for myself, wife?"

She grins back. "Yes." She taps her foot. "So, what will it be?"

Denton nods and says to Tazia, "Mr Tapper's son comes in a wagon to fetch us by sunup. Parks right down the street. You can come along tomorrow."

"Meanwhile, you'll stay with us until you're settled." Lula Mae ignores

Denton's gaping mouth. "Gemma will sleep with Mirlee Bee; Tazia next to the stove, where it's warmest."

"Plenty of places for you to rent in the poor white part of town, two trolley stops back," Denton informs Tazia. "You would have passed it on your way here."

"I'm not riding the trolley in the dark to get here by sunup every day," she tells him. "I'll find a place near here."

Denton explodes. "You're asking for real trouble. More for us than for you. Just cause this ain't the South, don't mean white folks aren't afraid to burn and lynch Negroes."

"Nonsense," Lula Mae shoots back. "Topeka was the heart of the abolitionist movement. Lots of freemen came to Kansas to start a new life. We got a regular land of opportunity here."

Tazia looks from one to the other. She doesn't know who to believe. Denton and Lula Mae glare at each other, then break into peals of laughter. All Tazia can figure is that both are right.

Lula Mae says the Mabley place, on the corner, has been empty since the old woman died, and her sons are eager to rent it before hooligans turn it into a bawdy house. It's only two rooms, but they're big, plenty of space for Tazia and Gemma. The house is also half brick and keeps out the wind. It needs a few repairs, but Denton will fix it up after work this week and they can move in next Sunday. "I'll watch Gemma every day while you're at the farm," Lula Mae says.

"*If* Tazia gets the job," Denton says.

"I should pay you," Tazia says, knowing she has nothing to give.

Lula Mae waves away the idea. "The Lord put us here to do for each other. Besides, in a couple of years, she and Mirlee Bee will be off to school." Tazia looks at her daughter, no longer a baby. With a pang, she realizes that Gemma will soon leave the cocoon she has spun.

"Now, if you insist on helping," Lula Mae says to Tazia, "let's get these dishes washed."

The children race outside, the oldest carrying the youngest on her hip. Denton follows and sits on the porch, lighting a corncob pipe. Soon the women join him, Lula Mae taking the rocking chair next to his, Tazia perched on the top step. Their neighbours rock, smoke, and talk too. The wind has died down, and while the air is chilly, no one wants to waste this fall evening inside.

One by one, porch conversations cease as people notice Tazia. "Evening

Denton, Lula Mae," the man next door calls over. He looks pointedly at Tazia and frowns, then at Denton.

"Lady knew my brother Elvan, back in Chicago," Denton says. Tazia is silent. Opening her mouth will only make matters worse. "She just wants a place to settle down, raise her little girl," Lula Mae says, looking straight into the neighbour's eyes, and those of the people rocking across the street. Some suspend their pipes in the air, others puff faster. No one speaks.

"Didn't you never play leap frog?" Mirlee Bee crouches next to Gemma, who shakes her head and startles as a bigger Wright child vaults over his little sister. Nonetheless, when told it's her turn to get down, Gemma obeys. She pokes up her head after Mirlee Bee clears the jump. "Now you leap over me," Mirlee Bee orders, tucking herself into a tight ball.

Instead, Gemma gingerly steps over her, but her back foot catches Mirlee Bee's shoulder and she tumbles sideways onto the hard-packed earth. Tazia bolts from the porch, ready to rescue her, but Lula Mae pulls her back. Tazia waits for her daughter to cry.

"Rest a hand on my sister's back for balance," says an older child, helping Gemma stand. "First-timers can cheat." Gemma brushes herself off, palms Mirlee Bee's head, and eases herself over the top. The Wright children clap. Mirlee Bee pops up and she and Gemma spin in a circle.

Children descend from the other porches, forming leap frog lines up and down the street. Their parents glower, but the children ignore them. Soon they are deliberately falling and rolling in the dirt. Next, they crumble dried leaves on one another's heads. Gemma sticks close to Mirlee Bee, but in the fading light, her pale skins becomes indistinguishable from the dark ones.

"Look Mama," she calls. "I'm playing."

Tazia smiles, but when the parents continue to glare, Lula Mae's dinner backs up in her throat. She and Gemma don't belong here. In Packingtown, they blended in, another immigrant family seeking a better life. These Negroes are more American than she is. On the other hand, Ayal would never look for her here. Topeka is not ideal, but it's the best Tazia can do. For now.

The children play until the outlines of their bodies merge with the night. Their elders rock in silence, the glow of the men's pipes the only sign of their presence. Lula Mae ushers everyone into the house. She casts an evil eye on her neighbours, even though they cannot see her curse. By the time she closes the door, the Kansas wind has again picked up and it is downright cold.

***

In the wagon next morning, the others stand back, creating an island around Tazia and Denton. It's too early, as they roll through the white part of town, for them to be seen, yet the men glance nervously around. Denton deserts Tazia too, riding midway between her and the other Negroes.

The farmer's eyes bug open when Tazia gets down from the rig, but he extends his hand. "Hampus Birger Tapper. Birger is Swedish for one who helps. What can I do for you?" Tazia tells him she wants a job. Not in the house, in the field. "Well, Ma'am. I've always hired Negroes. I admire their work ethic. But a woman ..." He repeats what Denton said about the work being physically demanding. "I'm afraid ladies don't have that kind of stamina."

Tazia describes the exertions on the olive farm where she was used to working long hot days and chilly moonlit nights. For the past three years, she shoved bloody meat through a grinder in the Chicago yards. She is fully capable of breaking sod and pushing seeds into the ground. The farmer turns to Denton, who shuffles and says his brother swears she's a good worker. The other men glare at Tapper's leathery face. He looks out at his fields, then at her.

"Ma'am, I've never even hired *their* wives. I don't see how mixing black and white, and men and women, can work."

Panic washes over Tazia. She hates to beg, would rather let her work speak for itself, but she remembers Gemma greedily eating Lula Mae's food last night. So, swallowing hard, she tells Tapper she has a young child to feed and doesn't want to work in a factory where bosses will take advantage of her. "You strike me as a good man, sir. I trust you to treat me well."

He reddens at the praise, then looks at the men's implacable faces. Denton steps forward. "I can't testify to the lady's stamina, but I can account for my brother's character, and I've never known him to speak an untrue word." Tapper shifts from foot to foot. As daylight peeks over the horizon, he stands firm, having made up his mind. "I ain't sending the wagon back to town until this evening," he tells Tazia, "so I might as well give you a try for today. We're planting winter wheat and I can use an extra hand." He orders Denton to fetch Tazia a hoe and a sack of seeds, then adds, "She can work alongside you, Cyrus, and Willie in the southeast quarter field."

With the memory of the farm in her muscles, Tazia soon establishes an easy rhythm with the tools and seeds. When the sun is high in the sky, Nellie, the farmer's daughter brings a pot of stew and tin plates to the field. The men will not eat with Tazia. However, the barn cat, who has followed the smell of the meat, wraps himself around her legs. Nellie says his name is Alvar, Swedish for elf warrior. Tazia is hungry, but nevertheless she first offers a piece of meat to the cat. Without hesitation, he gobbles it up and his coarse tongue wipes the gravy from her fingers.

"I'll be," declares Nellie. "I've never seen him eat from anyone's hand, let alone lick it." She clicks for the cat to follow her back to the barn, but he yawns and curls up beside Tazia. "He's supposed to eat varmints," Nellie warns her, "so don't feed him too much."

By late afternoon, Tazia has helped the men clear and plant a quarter-acre more than any other team. When the sun sinks level with the top of the barn door, Tapper's daughter brings a water bucket. The others continue to sit apart from her, but after they finish drinking, they set the bucket next to her and wipe the ladle clean with dry leaves. Tazia nods her thanks. Still, none of the men look at her when they climb into the wagon to go home. Only the farmer gives her a hand up. He also says she can come back tomorrow and, if she keeps up this pace all week, he'll take her on permanently to help with the spring crop too. He shakes his head at his own decision, but explains to the wagon load, "A good worker is a good worker, regardless."

***

That weekend, Tazia moves with Gemma into the Mabley house. She is grateful for a week of Lula Mae's hospitality, but glad to escape the questions and her habit of ordering people around. Denton has fixed the roof, taped windows, and filled in cracks between the bricks. His wife teases he's made the place nicer than theirs. Tazia sews curtains from a worn-out dress of Lula Mae's. The dead woman has left behind all the furniture they need, including a dresser. Tazia hides Ayal's note and Elvan's rattle, both still wrapped in her nonna's shawl, in the back of the top drawer.

Mother and daughter settle into a routine. Having declined Lula Mae's invitation to eat with the Wrights, Tazia and Gemma have breakfast at home. Then they walk down the street, where Gemma plays with the younger children while the older ones do chores and get ready for school. Tazia and Denton board the wagon. She gets used to riding by herself and watching the rising sun burnish the Capitol dome in the early morning silence. At day's end, she thanks Lula Mae, who often hands her a pot of beans or greens, scoops up Gemma, and returns with her to their private cocoon. Once Gemma asked to spend the night at Mirlee Bee's, but Tazia cannot bear the thought of sleeping alone. To cushion her disappointment, Tazia tells stories when they go to bed each night, about cats who perform magic tricks and birds who fly in patterns like embroidery stitches around the sun. Gemma, transfixed, never asks to sleep at her friend's again.

Sundays are solely for Tazia and Gemma too. They take the trolley to Most Pure Heart of Mary Church. It is one of only two Italian Catholic churches in Topeka; all the rest are German. Afterwards they play in the park where Tazia photographs Gemma on the swings with naked trees as the only backdrop. Come winter, when it is too cold to play outside, they'll have to go home after church. Tazia hopes to teach Gemma to sew but worries her child is too impatient. Gemma, who is tall like her father, prefers to run and jump, pumping her long and sturdy legs.

"Why not come to church with us?" Lula Mae had asked Tazia on her third Sunday in Kansas. "It's one street over, no need to take that child and yourself all the way downtown."

Denton knocked ashes from his pipe. "What would they do in a Baptist congregation?"

"Pray and sing," his wife had retorted. "God hears better through thin clapboard walls than thick stone ones."

"Lula Mae, you don't believe that." Denton chuckled. "You could whisper from under a boulder and the good Lord would hear you." He turned to Tazia. "But in this town, you'll need God's protection whether you're Catholic or Baptist."

Tazia frowned. Was she about to hear again that Topeka wasn't as safe as she thought?

"Town's overrun with Germans," Denton had explained. "Mostly Lutherans. Protestants can't abide Negroes but they're no friends of Catholics either."

"And everyone hates Pentecostals," Lula Mae had added, at which the oldest child began babbling nonsense. The younger ones copied her, and Gemma joined in too. Lula Mae tittered but admonished them to stop. They shuffled their feet, embarrassed. Tazia was confused.

"Speaking in tongues. Glossolalia. Folks think it's weird, especially if they're looking to pick on someone who ain't one of their own. Guess even we're guilty of shutting folks out." It was as close as Denton came to apologizing for the Negroes giving Tazia the cold shoulder. At least now the men nodded with grudging respect when Tapper paid her the same wages as them.

***

The first morning a dusting of snow covers the ground, the horses step gingerly and the wagon arrives at the farm late. White men cluster outside the farmhouse, carrying signs. The sky, although overcast, is by now light enough for Tazia to read them: NIGGER LOVER, NO COLOURED IN KANSAS, NO SLAVES FOR HIRE. The marchers swig from jugs of whiskey.

"Looks like trouble's moved from the town store to the farm," Denton says. He and the other men grip the sides of the wagon.

"What the hell, is that a white woman riding with them?" one of the white men yells.

Too late, Tazia ducks behind Denton.

Thrusting their signs like battering rams, the men storm the wagon, shouting "String up them niggers" and "Lynch the coons."

Tapper's son yanks the reins and tries to turn the horses. They balk and the wagon almost tips over. Two farmhands jump out, grab their harnesses, and lead them in a tight circle until they are facing back toward town. Hands reach down to pull the men in just as the mob arrives. The driver cracks his whip and the horses tear over roads that they'd minced along minutes ago. White men stumble into their rigs and follow. The Negroes reach town in half the time it took to get to the farm. Amid their silence, Tazia's heart thumps louder than the clattering wheels.

When they reach town, the Negroes dash to their houses to grab shovels, rakes, hoes, and anything else long and sharp. Tazia jumps from the wagon before Tapper's son screeches around the corner, turns the horses, and hightails it home. She runs inside the Wrights' front door just as Denton exits. He joins the other men in a defensive line down the middle of the street.

"What's going on?" Lula Mae demands, trying to follow her husband outside.

Tazia stops her. "Out the back way," she says, "to my place." She prays her bricks will withstand battering better than the Wrights' flimsy boards. It is also a few houses down from where the centre of battle is taking shape. Together, she and Lula Mae herd the children through the rear door. They're too scared to exclaim over the first snowfall. At Tazia's, they hover next to the stove. Even the older ones hold onto their mother's skirt. When Tazia goes back out, Gemma follows. Tazia tells her to stay with Lula Mae, but Gemma clings to her, refusing to be left behind. Tazia takes her daughter's arm and runs to the back of the next house. She bangs on the door.

A frightened woman opens it, children hiding behind her skirts as well.

"Hurry," Tazia says, panting. "Everyone to my place." The woman looks at her like she's crazy. Tazia kneels down. "Gemma, tell the children they're invited to our house for a party."

"Is it my birthday again?" her daughter asks, puzzled.

"Today we're going to celebrate every child's birthday!"

Gemma hesitates, but after Tazia gives her a big smile, she invites the children to come home with her. They clap and follow her out. Tazia turns to their mother, who tosses her head but follows too. After they are safely inside, Tazia and Gemma repeat this scene with all the other mothers and children. Back at their house, there is not much food to offer them, but fortunately Tazia has baked biscotti that Sunday. Gemma tells the children a story about tiny fairies and they compete to see who can nibble the tiniest bite of cookie. Their mothers look on nervously.

In the front room, Tazia draws aside the curtain. Snow dampens the sound, but she sees a line of Negro men facing an angry white mob. Everyone is still standing but blood spatters the mounting drifts of white. Before she can close the curtain, a white man spots her and within five seconds, he's banging on the front door. She steps outside and closes the door firmly behind her. Two men are on the porch. One brandishes a cracked bat, speckled with blood, the other a log wrapped in kerosene-soaked rags. He pulls a box of matches from his pocket. "Turn those nigger ladies and kids outta there or I'll set your house afire," he says with a woozy grin.

Visions of flames with no exit flash before Tazia's eyes. "There's a white child in there," she says, clearing her head of the frightening memory. "You planning on killing her too?"

"Get her out first," he demands.

Tazia refuses. She must protect her own child, but she cannot let the others face the flames either. The man lights the torch. Tazia steps up to the fire and stares down the drunken animal. "You'll have to kill this white woman first," she snarls into his reddened face. He squirms.

"Come on, Nigel," the other man says. "Them niggers is gonna whip our boys if we don't get back to help 'em out."

"I ain't moving til this nigger-loving lady clears out the premises."

"I'm not moving until you clear off my porch."

The bat-wielding man snickers. "She's a tough one. You ain't gonna best her. Come on." Reluctantly, Nigel throws his torch into the snow, where it sizzles but continues to flicker. Tazia marches down the steps and stomps it out. The two men return to the street fight.

An hour later, it is over. The Negroes have driven off the whites, for now, but there is no telling when or where they will strike again. Denton bleeds heavily from a gash on his forehead, Cyrus has a broken arm, and Willie's nose is battered. The others sustain breaks and bruises too. Tazia's house becomes a field hospital. Men lie shoulder to shoulder on the floor, while children clamber for space in their mothers' laps. Tazia fetches Nigel's log and tosses it on the stove.

A man called Preacher leads everyone in prayer. "Dear Father, thank you for the strength in our arms that allows us to defend our families and the strength in our necks that allows us to hold our heads high." They sing the hymns Elvan used to serenade Tazia with. When they get to "His eye is on the sparrow," she thinks of the magic sewing bird in the nighttime stories she tells Gemma. This morning, God has stitched a protective border around her neighbours.

The women briefly go home and return with sheets torn into bandages, and food. The men eat with Tazia, while the wives hold the children, Gemma included, on their laps. Denton and Lula Mae hold tightly to each other. Tazia longs for Elvan's arms, but also feels embraced by those around her. She will never be one *of* them, but she can be one *with* them. For now, that is enough.

chapter 20

Gemma is now old enough to attend Sunday preschool in the basement of Most Pure Heart of Mary Church. For the first time in years, Tazia is free to lose herself in the service, led by Father Leon. Unlike Father Xavier in Chicago, he cares only about her spiritual life. Not having been to Confession since she became pregnant, Tazia cannot receive Communion. Yet, closing her eyes during the silent prayer that follows, she is so at peace that she lingers in communion with the Divine, not bothering to listen to the deacon's recital of the week's upcoming activities.

One windswept Sunday in February, Tazia and Gemma walk past the foundation and first-floor of a building under construction down the street from Heart of Mary. Only a week ago, the lot had been flat and empty. A handwritten sign says, "Home of Lighthouse on the Rock Apostolic Church." The Pentecostals, housed in a small church across town, are moving to larger quarters here. During services, the deacon cuts short his remarks to announce a meeting about Lighthouse right after Mass. "Fueled by fanatical faith," he spits, "they are burning through frozen ground to erect an alien temple upon our sacred land." Father Leon squirms, but says nothing.

Sunday school hours are extended so parents can attend the meeting. The congregants on either side of Tazia encourage her to come. She declines, as eager to get home for a quiet meal with her daughter as she is to avoid their ugly words. Rushing downstairs to get Gemma, listening for the familiar sounds of bible stories, she instead hears "Goola, uba, michee, gooli." The teacher is leading the children in a mockery of glossolalia. She wants to grab her daughter and run, but Gemma will grow up with the same prejudice as the other children if she doesn't act. And so, Tazia decides to go to the meeting where perhaps, quietly, she can change one or two minds.

When Gemma hears she can stay later at Sunday school, she claps for joy.

"But," Tazia adds, "you may not talk any more gibberish." Her daughter sulks. "Why? It's just a silly game." Tazia searches for an explanation a three-year-old can understand. "It's mean to make fun of others for being different. It's nicer to include them, like when Mirlee Bee taught you to play leap frog." Gemma considers, then asks, "Like when Pharaoh's daughter was nice to Moses even though her father wanted to be mean to the Hebrews?" Tazia smiles. "Yes, exactly like that."

The meeting is packed. Father Leon is nowhere in sight. The deacon stands up front. Tazia takes a seat in the back. "Why do they have to build here?" a man starts off.

"Because it's right on the trolley line," another answers. "Easy for poor folks to get to."

"There's plenty of land near the Negro district. That's on the line too."

"Lighthouse ain't gonna stop. They already invested in the foundation and lower level."

"Suppose we bought the land for them and reimbursed their costs so far. Heart of Mary ain't rich but we got more than the Pentecostals. It'd be worth it to get them out of here."

"I'm not spending a penny on godless folks."

Tazia hears a chorus of "Amens," including, for the first time, the voices of women.

"I say we burn them down," shouts a man in the front row.

"I hear they dance naked. Fornicate too. Our kinfolk ain't safe around them."

"That nonsense they babble is the Devil himself speaking." Men shake their fists, women fan themselves with hymnals. People stand and demand they destroy what Lighthouse has built.

Tazia is on her feet, unable to listen to more. She speaks calmly so as not to inflame them further. "This church is named for Mary, Blessed Mother, who was told there was no room at the inn. Do you propose to tell God's creatures there's no room for them here?"

A few people sit, but most stare, eyes ablaze and lips pursed. Tazia has no more words to answer their silence. Plans resume to burn down the new church the following Sunday.

Tazia slips downstairs. Her daughter is not happy about leaving early. "I'm not ready to go," she says. Tazia pushes Gemma's stiff arms into her coat sleeves. "I am."

***

The following Sunday, Tazia goes to the old Lighthouse church across town instead of Heart of Mary. She takes Gemma with her. She doesn't want her at Sunday school, but if she leaves her with the Wrights and tells the truth about why, they'll try to talk her out of her mission. She arrives at Lighthouse early to speak to the pastor. Paint flakes litter the cracked path to the listing clapboard building. On either side are a livery and a barbershop, closed on the Sabbath, but obviously not busy during the week either. Tazia can understand why the Pentecostals want to move. Not that Heart of Mary is in a prosperous neighbourhood, but it is better kempt than this section of Topeka.

A sign states the name of the pastor, Alonzo Jesse Balter, times for Sunday and midweek services, and the words ALL ARE WELCOME TO BE BORN AGAIN IN THE FOURSQUARE GOSPEL. PRAISE JESUS THE HEALER. Gemma, already beginning to read, recognizes the "Gs," "ALL," and "JESUS." She asks if they have Sunday school here too.

The service starts in forty-five minutes. Cautiously, Tazia pushes open the creaking door while Gemma peeks under her arm. Given the church's gloomy exterior, it is surprisingly bright inside. Immediately, a man walks down the centre aisle from the altar and introduces himself as the pastor. He bends down to shake Gemma's hand first before shaking Tazia's.

"All God's gifts are welcome at the Lighthouse. How may I help you?"

Tazia says she is there to help him, or so she hopes. "I belong to Heart of Mary," she explains, "and they are not happy about having you as their neighbour." She warns him of the plan to knock down, possibly even burn, Lighthouse after Mass that day.

To Tazia's surprise, Alonzo Jesse Balter chuckles. "We're known as the church of 'good news,' but I daresay even Christ Our Lord and Savior would not rejoice as such tidings. Please, come and sit." He leads them to a pew at the front and extracts a small carved Baby Jesus from the pocket of his robe. Handing it to Gemma, he says, "I made it for my daughter. She likes me to hold it during the sermon, but I'm sure she'd want me to share with you while I speak with your mother." Gemma busies herself wrapping the doll in her scarf and making up a lullaby.

Tazia apologizes for not coming during the week, but she could not miss work without arousing suspicion. She hopes the pastor can amass enough people today to defend Lighthouse. "If only prayer could turn Heart of Mary back," she adds, "before they resort to violence."

Pastor Balter thanks Tazia, regretful but not angry. "Hatred saddens me. Our religion has a tradition of being open to all, including Negroes, yet many are closed to us. Apparently you feel differently. Why do you suppose that is so?"

Tazia finds herself making excuses. "Catholics are good people, but what they don't know scares them. Like you, we believe in the Light of God. Yet many live in the shadow of fear."

"Praise the Lord who has granted you the gift of light," declares Alonzo Jesse Balter.

If only that were true, Tazia thinks. With Gemma, she basks in light, but she also lives in the shadows, eluding Ayal. Next to her, Gemma sings a lullaby about scaring off goblins who want to steal the baby. How can Tazia enlighten others when she keeps her own child in the dark?

Pastor Balter tells her about another Pentecostal gift, the Word of Wisdom, whereby the Holy Spirit reveals how to solve a problem by applying scripture. "We will pray this morning for the Word of Wisdom that we may avoid violence." He holds out both hands. "Will you join us?"

Gemma's ears perk up, and when the pastor says children participate in the service along with parents, she begs to stay. Soon the hall overflows with people praying, singing, testifying. Tazia sees why they want a bigger church. Words bubble up; some speak English, others in tongues. In this context, it sounds like a real language. Gemma is enraptured. She asks Tazia's permission to try. Her ear is uncanny, reproducing the musical sounds. "Mama, can I teach Mirlee Bee how to do it?" she asks. When Tazia says it is only allowed in the Pentecostal church, Gemma asks if they can bring Mirlee Bee next week. Tazia can't bear to dim her excitement. "We'll see," she murmurs, hoping Gemma will forget, yet knowing how tenacious the child's memory can be.

Except for words of welcome, Pastor Balter lets his congregants lead the service. Tazia prefers the orderly conduct of the Catholic Mass, yet the ecstasy of the Pentecostals draws her close to God too. Certainly Gemma pays more attention than she ever did at their church. After a healing rite, and rituals called "running the aisles" and "dancing the spirit," everyone sits again for the pastor's sermon. He sets it aside, however, and talks spontaneously to the upturned faces.

"God has presented us with a challenge. While we welcome Jesus into our hearts, those at Most Pure Heart of Mary do not welcome Lighthouse into their neighbourhood. They plan to take us down, by force or flame, this afternoon." He asks them to kneel. "Let us pray for the Word of Wisdom to respond to this earthly threat according to the heavenly Father's wishes." Then he lays out a plan. With himself in the lead, the men will ride to the new church. They'll carry no obvious weapons, only construction tools, to show they intend no harm. Women will stay behind with the children and continue to ask Jesus to send mercy and understanding into the Catholics' hearts.

The women gather the children in the centre of the sanctuary. Men move toward the door. Tazia walks up to Pastor Balter. "I'm going too," she says.

For the first time that day, he looks rattled. "It's not safe. You belong here."

"I belong with the people at Heart of Mary. My prayers are theirs. God willing, I can turn them around." She failed last week but today's service has renewed her resolve.

Belying his call to avoid violence, Pastor Balter says, "Sometimes words of prayer are not enough." Tazia, remembering the battle in Negro town, responds, "Words can deter as much as threats. And some prayers are better uttered by women than by men." Pastor Balter, anxious to leave, comes to a quick decision. "I can't stop you, but you'll have to get there on your own."

"As soon as I leave my daughter with friends, I will meet you at Heart of Mary." Tazia buttons their coats and heads for the door. Gemma turns back. "Thank you for letting me play with Baby Jesus," she says, returning the doll to Pastor Balter. He lays his hand upon her head.

Once home, Tazia heads for the Wrights and asks if Gemma can spend the afternoon with them. "You mean I can stay here and play?" Gemma and Mirlee Bee hold their breath. Never before has Tazia allowed them to spend Sunday together; it is reserved for mother-daughter time.

Denton asks if something is wrong. Lula Mae sets out an extra plate while her eyes probe Tazia's face for an explanation. Tazia speaks quickly. "I promised to do something at Heart of Mary and it would be easier if Gemma weren't tagging along." It skirts the truth, but it's not a lie.

Lula Mae nudges Denton. "The Lord's house is a good place to meet people." He winks at his wife. "Now, woman, ain't you glad she's praying with the Catholics, not us Baptists?" Tazia blushes, thanks them for watching Gemma, and leaves. She can't help it if they wait in vain to hear about a new man in her life. She races to the corner where the trolley has reached the end of the line and jumps aboard, just as the conductor turns it around and heads back to town.

***

In front of the new Lighthouse Church, two lines of men draw closer to each other. The Catholics from Heart of Mary wield clubs, axes, and unlit torches; the Pentecostals grip hammers and saws. Unsure where to stand, Tazia stops midway between them but off to the side, where afternoon shadows obscure her from view. The men's voices get louder, shouting over the wind, until the pastor and deacon raise their hands for quiet, and address one another. Speaking first, the deacon says, "For thirty years, since 1883, Heart of Mary has dwelt peacefully in this neighbourhood. "

"The Lighthouse comes in peace too," says Pastor Balter.

"In Beatitudes, Jesus says, 'Blessed are the peacemakers, for they shall be called sons of God.'" The deacon jabs an accusatory finger. "You do not follow this teaching."

Pastor Balter speaks softly. Everyone leans forward to hear. "The Holy Spirit preaches pacifism to us too. In the Sermon on Mount, He commands all to practice peace, not violence."

Someone from Heart of Mary yells, "You want our country to fight the Germans. They're our brethren, and that ain't practicing peace." The crowd surges forward, torches aloft.

Tazia smells sulphur, first one match, then another. Her head tells her to run but her feet move toward the men from her church. They step back, but keep their torches raised. "Does not Paul write that Christians shall do whatever is possible to live peaceably with all men?" she asks and is met with silence. She tries again, louder. "Where does the Bible say there is room for but one house of worship on earth? Is a church built of wood and stone, or the company of the faithful?"

The deacon thunders, "The Bible says there is but one way to worship Christ the Lord and it is not *their* way." He throws a clod of frozen dirt at the pastor. Tazia is pushed aside as the two lines charge each other. Fleeing the cries and grunts, the heat and smoke of fire at her back, Tazia runs blindly toward the trolley stop. She longs for the peace of holding her child in her arms.

***

As soon as she enters the Wrights' house, Tazia sees the consternation on their faces. "We heard there was trouble between Heart of Mary and Lighthouse." Denton yanks her into the middle of the front room and Lula Mae pushes her toward the stove. Gemma stops playing with Mirlee Bee, her eyes suddenly wide with fright when she senses the fear in the grownups' voices.

Tazia's body floods with relief as well as warmth. "How did you hear about it?"

"Word gets around," Lula Mae says. She and Denton exchange a look Tazia has seen before when Negroes are alert to the threat of violence. "You didn't happen to have something to do with that, did you?" Lula Mae thrusts a cup of marrow broth into Tazia's trembling hands.

Tazia raises it to her mouth. "I tried to convince them we were all people of peace, but ... "

"A woman can't sway men's minds when they're up to no good." Lula Mae wraps an arm around Tazia's slumped shoulders. Then she turns to Gemma and pulls her close too. "Your mama done tried to do a good thing."

Gemma snuggles up to her mother. "Me and Mirlee Bee danced the spirit," she whispers. Tazia strokes her hair. What good is faith, any faith, when it is overpowered by fear and anger?

***

The following day after work, Tazia asks Tapper's son to drop her off in town, telling Denton she has to run an errand. He raises his eyebrows but says he and Lula Mae will feed Gemma supper. As soon as the wagon is out of sight, Tazia takes the trolley to Lighthouse Church.

Pastor Balter kneels in the unlit sanctuary. A white bandage around his head gleams in near-dark; his right arm is in a sling. Tazia lowers herself and they pray in silence. With his good arm, the pastor lifts her up and answers her unspoken question. "Burnt to the ground. We won't rebuild. The livery owner next door wants to sell the property, so we'll add on here instead."

"Maybe you can try again in a few years. People change." Tazia doesn't believe her own words.

"The new church was *our* mistake," the pastor says. "We got above ourselves. It wasn't God telling us we needed a bigger space, it was us inflating our own importance. You were right when you said a church is its people, not a building."

And yet, a beautiful building can also show one's love for the Almighty. Tazia thinks of Italy's magnificent cathedrals. Surely her God approves of those. Perhaps the deacon was right; the Catholic and Pentecostal religions are too divergent to ever come together.

The pastor turns toward Tazia, wincing in pain. "I haven't thanked you for yesterday. You were very brave to help us."

"I did it for my daughter as much as you," she admits.

Pastor Balter nods. "That only adds to its importance. I still believe our religions are not so far apart. We share a faith in Jesus and His resurrection. If you are open to being born again, you and your daughter are welcome to join us at Lighthouse on the Rock."

Tazia laughs. "Gemma would enjoy that." She closes her eyes and steps through the ritual of the Mass, hears the Gloria, tastes the Communion wafer and wine on her tongue. I did it for my fellow Catholics too, she realizes. She is responsible for saving their souls as well as her own. She bows her head and prays. "Dear God, forgive me for abandoning my faith." She knows she must return to Heart of Mary. She can run from people and cities, but not from God's Holy Kingdom.

***

The following Sunday, when they board the trolley, Gemma asks whether they are going to "the play church or the dancing church." Tazia says they're going to Heart of Mary, their church.

"Why? I liked the other one." Gemma's kicks the empty seat in front of her.

"Because they do things differently at Lighthouse. It's a good way, but it's not our way."

Gemma seems satisfied with this explanation, but she's not done. "Mama, the father at that place ..." It takes Tazia a second to realize she means the pastor. "What's his whole name?"

"Alonzo Jesse Balter."

"Alonzo *Jesse* Balter," Gemma repeats. "Mirlee *Bee* Wright, Lula *Mae* Wright," she chants. "Do you have a name in the middle?"

Tazia is relieved the theological discussion is over but puzzled about where Gemma is headed. "Catherine," she says. "I took it at Confirmation, after Saint Catherine of Siena. She lived over five hundred years ago, in Italy, and is the patron saint of firefighters." Tazia catches her breath. Not until now has she connected her saint's name with surviving the Triangle fire.

"Can I have another name in the middle of mine?" Gemma asks.

Tazia is relieved that this is all she wants. She says Gemma can choose a saint's name when she gets confirmed, after she takes her first Communion. Gemma, happy with this answer, swings her legs back and forth. "Mama, is there a saint for children who don't have fathers?"

Tazia stiffens. "The Church gives fathers to everyone. You have Father Leon."

Gemma brightens. "Then I'm glad we go to Heart of Mary. If we went to Lighthouse, I would only have a pastor." She is silent for a minute and Tazia, grateful, leans back in her seat again. Gemma, however, has one more question. "Is there a saint for mothers?"

"Yes, Monica, the mother of Saint Augustine. She was born fifteen hundred years ago, in a faraway place called Africa."

Gemma, satisfied at last, squeezes Tazia's hand. "When I get big, my whole name will be Gemma *Monica* Gatti."

chapter 21

A month after Gemma turns five, she and Mirlee Bee go to the one-room schoolhouse that Lula Mae says started out as a tool shed. "Our oldest went to kindergarten there, and the Board of Education acted like they was doing us a favour adding a room for each grade, up to eighth. They stopped at fifth until us parents threatened to sue." Tazia says she's seen two-storey brick schools downtown, many brand new, and asks why Negroes can't go there. Lula Mae tosses her head. "Ain't no rule says they can't, but it's understood children are supposed to learn close to home."

Gemma is one of only three white students at Harrison School. The other two, twin girls a year older, are orphans and rumored to have "nigger blood" in the family. There are two hundred desks for three hundred students and the books are twenty or more years out of date. On the first day, when Tazia goes to meet the teacher, she can barely read the chalkboard. A hole in the slate swallows the second "L" in "HELLO" and cracks divide "CHILDREN" into three words.

The second week, when Tazia picks up Gemma at the Wrights' after work, the child bursts into tears. Tazia cups her soft chin in calloused hands. "What's wrong, *Cara*?" she asks.

"No one will play with her," Lula Mae says.

"Mirlee Bee ..." Gemma's sobs increase, and she cannot finish the thought.

Lula Mae completes it for her. "Even my daughter sided with the other children." Mirlee Bee stares at the floor and draws small circles with her foot. "I told her that she was not to treat Gemma different at school than at home." Lula Mae waits for Mirlee Bee to look at her. "Mirlee Bee is a natural born leader. If she plays with Gemma, the others will too." Lula Mae slams the lid on the pot. "If Mirlee Bee refuses, she can also play by herself from now on."

Mirlee Bee fetches a doll and tentatively holds it out to Gemma who, still sniffling, accepts it. The girls sit on the couch and make doll clothes from fabric scraps. Mirlee Bee brushes a piece of flannel across Gemma's tear-stained cheeks. Tazia watches a moment, then thanks Lula Mae.

Lula Mae doesn't accept her thanks. "I don't see why you won't send that child to a white school."

"How would I get her there?" Tazia says. "I can't take her on the wagon because we leave too early, and if I wait to take her on the trolley, I have no way to get to the farm. Besides, you yourself said that children have to live near the school they attend."

"Exactly." Lula Mae shoots her a look that says it's about time Tazia moved to live with white folks, and work with them too. Tazia can't tell her why she wants to stay here; she doesn't fully understand it herself. But she does want Gemma to get a better education. Her dreams won't come true if her daughter attends a school where children aren't expected to go past fifth grade.

"Maybe I should talk to the teacher, or the other parents, about helping the Negro children get along with Gemma. Adults set the example. Our neighbours already know I'm on their side."

"Do you really think they give a goddamn about a poor little white girl?" Lula Mae's skin burns the colour of hot bricks. "All they care about is that their children are going to leave school after a few years barely able to read or add. You can walk out of this mess. We can't."

The girls' eyes dart between their mothers. Tazia folds her weary body into a chair. Lula Mae comes over and kneads her shoulders. "I ain't got nothing against *you*, although there's days I want to shake some sense into that stubborn Italian head. And you know I love Gemma like my own." Tazia does. Lula Mae returns to the stove and says again, "Negro lives are a struggle. It makes no sense why a white woman would choose to make things harder than they need to be."

The reason eludes Tazia too. Whether she fears the past will catch up to her or wants to be part of a future where people don't judge one another, she can only do what feels right at the moment. Sometimes that means running away; at other times, like now, it means staying in place.

***

Hoeing and weeding the next summer, Gemma's schooling weighs even heavier on Tazia's mind. In the fall, her daughter will start first grade, when serious learning begins. One afternoon, while Tazia ponders what to do, Nellie, trailed by Alvar, appears with water for the farmhands. As the men step aside and pull out their pipes, the women pack down a flat place on the ground to sit.

Nellie is a schoolteacher during the winter, which gives Tazia an idea. She could bring Gemma to the farm two mornings a week and pay Nellie to teach her reading and arithmetic. What better way to spend the little money she's saved during her three years in Topeka? Tapper's son could bring Gemma back to the Wrights' at midday, when he ran errands in town. Alvar insinuates himself into Tazia's lap as if to reward her for her good idea. She rewards herself with a gulp of cold water. Nellie asks where Gemma goes to school and what she's learnt so far.

"Harrison," Tazia says, at once defiant and guilty. "She's learnt almost nothing there, but I've been teaching her letters and numbers at home, and she can write her name."

"Do you read books to her?"

"Only the Bible. I can't afford to buy other books, especially ones she'll soon outgrow."

"If she can write her name, she can get a library card," Nellie explains. "The public library, near the State House, is free. Let her pick out some books, like the *Bobbsey Twins*, to bring here. We'll start next week. A dollar a lesson?" Tazia nods. Alvar's motor vibrates against her thighs.

At first, Gemma is reluctant to leave Mirlee Bee, but she soon enjoys the early morning wagon ride. Even the men, groggy at that hour, smile at her patter. In the evening, Gemma reads aloud from the Bobbsey books. "I wish I had a twin brother like Freddie," she says with a sigh. At least, Tazia thinks, she's stopped asking for a father. One morning however, Gemma startles Tazia by asking, "Is it because Mirlee Bee is dark that you don't want me to play with her so much?"

Tazia's heart lurches along with the wagon. "No, *Cara*. It has nothing to do with the colour of her skin. It's because you're so smart that Mama arranged these extra lessons over the summer. Aren't you happy that Nellie is teaching you?"

Gemma clutches the book to her chest. "Mirlee Bee is smart too. If she came with me in the morning, we could practice reading to each other in the afternoon. And race to see who adds numbers faster." She's right, Tazia realizes. Mirlee Bee is as clever as her daughter and deserves the same opportunity. The Wrights can't spare the money, but Tazia could offer to pay as a way to compensate Lula Mae for babysitting the rest of the time. "I'm sure it would be all right with Nellie," Tazia tells her daughter, "but I'm not sure Lula Mae will give her permission."

Gemma regards her mother with hope, and trust. "But you'll ask?"

Tazia promises and is surprised when Lula Mae agrees. "Not because I expect to be paid for watching Gemma," she hastens to explain, "but to make a better life for Mirlee Bee."

chapter 22

Summer passes, then most of the next school year, and soon it is another spring planting season. Conditions at Harrison School are not much better, but Tazia and Lula Mae have persuaded the first-grade teacher to assign the girls extra reading and arithmetic to do at home. When Tazia comes to pick up her daughter, she finds them "playing school," with Mirlee Bee as the teacher and Gemma as her star pupil. She and Lula Mae exchange looks of motherly pride.

The hailstorm that demolishes this routine arrives late one April afternoon as Tazia, hoeing around the newly sprouted grain, knots a bandana around her dripping forehead. "Wind's picking up. Temperature's dropping fast," Denton calls out to their crew.

"Thanks goodness," Tazia says. "I could use a breath of cold air."

But Denton sniffs and scans the western sky. Nellie, school over for the day, approaches with the water bucket. Tazia wonders why she's walking funny until she sees her skirt tied around her calves to keep it down against the updraft. Right after Nellie starts back to the farmhouse, the skies darken, followed by thunder and a downpour. But before the rain can soak Tazia's clothes, the drops turn to apple-size hailstones, pelting the farmhands and flattening the tender shoots.

Tazia reaches for her hoe. "Leave it," Denton cries. "Make a run for it." Just as he grabs her hand, an ice ball hits the back of the head. Unconscious, he falls face down, his arms and legs splayed. Tazia puts her hands under his shoulders, but strong as she is, she cannot budge his dead weight. Tapper and his son come running, and with two other men, lift him and head toward the house, slipping in the mud. Cows and horses, likewise heading for shelter, stumble too, their moos and neighs an apocalyptic cry. The farmhouse, hard to see through the icy veil, seems miles away.

"We won't make it to the house before someone else gets conked," says one of the men. "The small barn," Tapper's son orders, and they veer toward a weathered building only half as far away. Tazia doesn't race there, but trudges beside Denton to cover his bruised face with her bandana, as if the hailstones will bounce off it. When she finally reaches the barn and bolts the door, the men are praying that the ramshackle structure holds up. "*Dio, salvaci,*" Tazia joins in.

Tapper peeks between crooked slats toward the house where his wife and Nellie hover in the tornado shelter beneath the kitchen. They hear two loud cracks from the sky, the deafening rat-a-tat of hail on the roof, and then a roar as the farmhouse collapses. Tapper falls to his knees, clawing his scalp. Tazia presses her eye to a knothole and sees that only the kitchen wing still stands. She gently lifts Tapper by his elbows. "Your women are safe," she says. "God is merciful."

Miraculously, the small barn is erect too, as is the big barn, where equipment and seeds are stored. It is early enough in the season to replant. The hailstones shrink to the size of olives. Tazia kneels beside Denton, who awakens, jumps up, and staggers toward the door. Two men restrain him. "Not yet," Tazia says, as another cascade strikes the roof. Twelve minutes later, as suddenly as it started, the storm ends. They wade across a field of ice balls, glinting in the sun, and scoop hailstones off the wagon floor. Tapper's son gently guides the skittering horses toward town. Other farms have been hit worse. Almost every home and outbuilding has been leveled.

As they pass through downtown, Tazia sees water from the flooded river sluice through debris-filled streets. Stores lie flattened, the splintered lumber carried helter skelter by mud slides. Farther along, the Capitol dome is dented, while the white children's school is reduced to a pile of bricks under uprooted trees. The farmhands are quiet as they near the Negro section of town. To their surprise, it is largely intact. The hailstones are thinly spread, and women are already sweeping them off the porch, yelling at the children to stop throwing them before someone gets hurt.

Denton leaps from the wagon and races to his porch, where he lifts Lula Mae and swings her around. She pulls his head toward her and plants a big kiss on his lips, whereupon her hand touches the knot on his scalp. "I got beaned," he says sheepishly. She grabs a hailstone, presses it to his head, and leads him inside. Meanwhile, Tazia sees Gemma down the street, counting ice balls with Mirlee Bee. She scoops her up and runs home, only to find their house has not been spared. Like Tapper's, the front half with the kitchen is intact, but the back is gone. Only the chest of drawers with Tazia's hidden treasures stands; their bed looks like a mad axman has cleaved the head from the foot. Tazia thanks God for not sending the storm in the middle of the night.

Relief gives way to despair, however, when she and Gemma have to move back with the Wrights. The girls are thrilled, and Lula Mae accepts them as easily as when they first arrived, but Tazia is disheartened about living again under Lula Mae's watchful eyes. This time escape will take longer. She has little money for repairs, having spent her savings on Nellie.

That Sunday, Tazia kneels as Father Leon leads Mass in the one room of their church that wasn't flattened. Its fourth wall is a mud-encrusted tarp. When the congregants emerge at noon, blinking into a bright sun that seems to mock their gloom, they face an assembly from Lighthouse. The Pentecostal men bear tools and leftover lumber from the aborted expansion two years earlier. Their wives carry blankets, food-laden picnic baskets, and toys for the children.

Reverend Balter addresses Father Leon. "Our church was spared. When we sought the Word of Wisdom, God told us to help you rebuild." Before the priest can answer, the deacon steps forward. He spreads his arms and summons the other men to do likewise, keeping the women and children behind them.

Tazia slips out from underneath. "We thank you for your help, Reverend Balter." She hands a doll to Gemma and spreads a blanket on the ground. Then, facing the Catholic women, she makes eye contact with the mother of Gemma's favourite Sunday school playmate. The woman takes a breath and ducks out from behind her husband, towing her daughter. By ones and twos, other women come forward to set up the picnic lunch. Father Leon removes his robe and accepts a board, hammer, and nails from the reverend. Other Heart of Mary men follow suit, except for the deacon and his group who hustle their families into carriages and teeter down the rutted roads.

Similar standoffs occur the following week when Tapper leads his Negro field hands to help the white farmers. Unlike at the church, only a few accept the offer, but Tazia sees it is as a first step and is grateful. She is also glad when the Negro farmhands take it for granted that she will join their building crew. Denton teaches her to hammer and saw. "Measure twice, cut once," he instructs, making her think of embroidery. She can now also help Denton fix her house, but the work goes slowly. Impatience makes Tazia testy. Three months after the hailstorm, when Lula Mae invites her and Gemma to Sunday dinner for what feels like the hundredth time, she snaps, "Must I tell you again that I'd rather pack a picnic lunch for the two of us to eat at the park?"

"Of course, if our food ain't good enough for you ..." Lula Mae hitches her shoulders but blinks away tears. Tazia apologizes but won't back down. Sundays are the only private moments that she and her daughter have these days. Tazia's moodiness affects Gemma too. She spurns the extra homework the teacher assigned her over the summer and when Mirlee Bee begs her to play school, runs off with the other children. Mirlee Bee comes crying to her mother.

"You and Gemma are welcome to stay as long as you need," Lula Mae tells Tazia one hot evening, "but if it's making my little girl cry, we got to find a quicker way out." Tazia agrees but can't afford the building materials she needs. Lula Mae continues. "Years ago, when Denton got hurt, Elvan sent money until he was back on his feet. Ain't you got no family can help you out?"

Tazia feels her face turn to stone.

"I'm not talking about Gemma's daddy. There's plenty of no-accounts around and Lord knows, he ain't none of my business. But maybe you got parents or siblings you can call on?"

Tazia shakes her head.

Lula Mae plows on. "They still in Italy or did any kin come with you to America? I know you're too proud to ask, but I ain't afraid to ask for you. That's why God made families. Unless..." Pity clouds her face. "They did something bad to you or you did something ... to hurt them?"

Angry tears fill Tazia's eyes. How dare she ask such a question? When Lula Mae puts a sympathetic arm around Tazia's shoulder, her body stiffens.

"Ain't no shame in bringing a baby into this world," Lula Mae says. "Only shame is in not loving it. You love that child, but you ain't giving her grandparents a chance to love her too."

Tazia's fury mounts. Not only is she homeless, with a defiant daughter on her hands, now this woman is reviving her guilt over the family that she hasn't let herself think of in six years.

That night, after Gemma is asleep, Tazia appeals for a divine message. Toward dawn, it comes. God tells her she should not rebuild in Topeka, but start fresh someplace else. Two years ago, when Lula Mae hinted it was time for Tazia to move back with her own kind, she was right, but for the wrong reason. Race has little to do with it. Rather, people who are like you don't need to ask questions. They simply assume you're like them. The way to end prying from Lula Mae and her kind is for Tazia to go where she and Gemma will blend in and not arouse curiosity.

Tazia finds the map Nellie used to play a reading game with the girls. They'd close their eyes, point to a spot, and sound out the name. Once, Gemma's finger landed on Las Vegas, which Nellie said was Spanish for "The Meadows." Tazia pictures something green and lush, if less hilly than Loro Piceno. She's had enough of the dry, searing winds of the Midwest and Plains states. Also enough cold. Spaniards, like Italians, are warm-weather people. She will feel at home there.

She wastes no time telling Gemma. That Sunday, eating lunch at the park, Tazia says they are moving to that warm place on Nellie's map. Gemma frowns. "Is Mirlee Bee coming too?"

"No, *Cara*. Just you and me. The Wrights are fine here, but it will take too long for us to fix our house. In Las Vegas, the weather is always nice, and we won't ever lose our home again."

Gemma throws her lunch to the ground, sobbing. "I don't want to go. I'll never see Mirlee Bee again. Or have another friend. Why, why, why do we have to move away?"

Tazia repeats that the storm took everything they had. It was an act of God, she explains, and they must accept His will. Slowly, Gemma calms down. She's still unhappy, but if God is the reason they must leave, she accepts her mother's word that it is the right thing to do.

Two days later, the Wrights wait with Tazia and Gemma for the trolley that will take them to the train depot. Denton presses a few dollars on Tazia "for the sake of the child." Lula Mae silently hands her a basket of food, then turns her face in the direction the trolley will come from.

The girls cling to each other, cheeks glistening with tears and snot. Seeing them, Tazia is no longer sure she understood God's message. By doing what feels right to her, is she doing what is wrong for her child? She reaches for Lula Mae as the trolley comes into view but withdraws before making contact. Gemma wrenches herself from Mirlee Bee and jumps on the runner. Tazia hefts their satchel and follows her on board. The half-rebuilt city gradually recedes from view.

part six

Gemma, Las Vegas, 1961

chapter 23

This is Gemma Kane, speaking with my high school boyfriend, Darius Ignatius, at The Lucky Cherry Diner in Las Vegas, Nevada. Today is Tuesday, May 16, 1961, and the time is 1:00 AM.

Gemma: (Accepts cup of coffee) It's strange to see you after thirty-four years. This is my first time back in Vegas.

Darius: You made it to the diner in one piece. Didn't get mugged in the parking lot? (Chortles)

Gemma: Truthfully, I was afraid to drive the rental car at this hour, in this neighbourhood. I took a cab. How long are you on break? I'd have gladly come to your place before or after your shift.

Darius: This *is* my place.

Gemma: Oh, you own it? (Looks around greasy spoon; four hung-over gamblers at counter)

Darius: No. Fred, the owner lets me sleep here (points behind kitchen) and use the telephone.

Gemma: You're a short-order cook? I remember when you made me scrambled eggs in olive oil, with tomato sauce and Parmesan on top. We called them "Italian Eggs." My Irish husband Todd won't touch them, but my son Frankie loves them. I taught his fiancée how to make them.

Darius: Nah, I'm not a cook, just a dishwasher, but Fred says he'll try me at the grill once I've been sober for a year. Lucky Cherry's an okay place to start over, although the success rate ain't high. (Nods toward men at counter) Worse odds than the slots. (Studies me) You look successful.

Gemma: (Chooses words carefully) I've been lucky. My mother pushed me to do well in school, and between Todd and me, we earn a decent living.

Darius: It might have been that way for me if my dad hadn't been too drunk to care. (Snorts) Like father, like son. Did you ever think that maybe you were better off without a father?

Gemma: (Taken aback) Honestly no, but I suppose there are more ways than one to grow up fatherless. (Hesitates) You never said your father drank, but I guessed from your silence that things weren't great at home.

Darius: My mom meant well, but she was too busy making ends meet to pay attention to me. I cooked at your house to impress you, but mostly to eat a free meal. (Eyes sweep room) Still looking for a handout.

Gemma: Don't lose hope. How long since you stopped drinking?

Darius: Six months.

Gemma: See. You're halfway there. Odds are fifty-fifty you'll make it to a year.

Darius: (Blushes? Hard to tell in this light) Hey, you know why the symbols on slot machines are fruits? (Pours himself more coffee; holds out pot to me)

Gemma: Tell me. (Puts hand over cup)

Darius: The machines paid winners with fruit-flavoured chewing gum, not cash. It's how they got around "no gambling" laws back in the late 1800s.

Gemma: You were always good at history.

Darius: (Shrugs) Not much history to be proud of now. But, speaking of history (smiles slyly) I'm surprised you don't recognize this place.

Gemma: (Looks around blankly)

Darius: It used to be a Chinese laundry. This is where your mother worked.

Gemma: Wow. It looks completely different. Poor Mama, slaving away for twelve-hours, six days a week. (Smiles) It gave us lots of time to hang out at our apartment after school, alone.

Darius: (Smiles back) And fool around, but only up to a point. (Pours a third cup, hand shakes) Sorry. It's not the caffeine; it's the quitting.

Gemma: (Nods, touches his wrist)

Darius: (Gently squeezes my fingers) You didn't mind my sneaking in booze. You'd even take a nip with me, although you brushed your teeth and aired out the place before your mom got home.

Gemma: Oh, God. Remember the time we thought we heard her coming back early and hid a half bottle of rum inside the toilet tank? Only it turned out to be the plumber fixing a leak upstairs. He wanted to make sure it wasn't dripping down into our apartment. (Shakes head). I remembered the bottle a few days later, but by then it was gone. My mother never said a word about it.

Darius: She didn't trust me after that.

Gemma: She never trusted you before. But it wasn't personal. She didn't trust any of my friends.

Darius: She was right not to trust me, but she should have had more faith in you. You wouldn't let me get to second base. All the same, I felt bad when we broke up.

Gemma: (Puzzled) But you were the one who ended it.

Darius: (Puts down his cup) Your mom never told you what she did?

Gemma: (Shakes head)

Darius: She waited outside my house one morning, before I left for school. Threatened to report my drinking to the principal and have me expelled if I didn't break up with you.

Gemma: (Mouth agape) She didn't have to do that! I told her I had no intention of making the same stupid mistake she did and ending up a single parent with a string of lousy jobs. (Swallows) That sounds awful now. I don't know if hearing it made her feel more hurt or relieved.

Darius: I'd have married you if you did get pregnant.

Gemma: (Snorts) That's probably what my father told my mother. (Swipes hand to erase comment) Sorry, that was unfair. This interview isn't about you, or us. I'm just frustrated trying to find out who the man is. (Smiles) Put your history hat back on. Can you recall *anything* my mother said about him?

Darius: She barely talked to me, remember?

Gemma: Well, was there something in our apartment, a postcard, knickknack, even a matchbook that could be a lead? (Grins) I know you used to snoop when you thought I wasn't looking. I told myself you were trying to find out more about me. The illusions of youthful love.

Darius: (Shamefaced) Once while you were in the bathroom, I peeked in your mom's dresser, hoping I'd find cash or something worth pawning. I needed money for booze. There was a little jewellery box, but it was locked. No key in sight. I didn't want to break the lock, so I put it back.

Gemma: I don't remember the box, but I doubt it held anything valuable. We were too poor. (Stares at greasy cobwebs on ceiling) Do you suppose there was a keepsake from my father inside? Damn, I was such a good girl, I never poked around in my mother's things. (Sighs) If there was a clue in there, it's too late now.

Darius: (Thoughtful) Suppose your mom did know what a good girl you were, and the reason she threatened me wasn't sex, but because she was afraid that if we got too close, I'd nose around about your father.

Gemma: That would fit with her trying to stifle all my other friendships. (Long silence) Thanks, Darius. Even though you can't help me find my father, I feel better about my broken heart in high school. (Laughs) Do you by any chance remember the name of the owner of the Chinese laundry?

Darius: No. We just called him "The Chink."

Gemma: (Shudders) I hope my mother didn't hear us. That would have upset her almost as much as our fooling around.

Darius: (Jams hands in pockets) You look good, Gemma. It makes me want to try harder, to find that lucky streak in my life. I hope you find what you're looking for too.

The interview ended at 1:35 AM.

chapter 24

This is Gemma Kane, speaking with Ju-long Pan, former owner of Star Chinese Laundry, at the Howard Cannon Nursing Home in Las Vegas, Nevada. Today is Wednesday, May 17, 1961, and the time is 2:45 PM.

Gemma: The nurse said you usually take a nap at 4:00. I promise we'll be done by then. Do I call you Mr Pan? Mr Ju-long? (Laughs apologetically) I'm never sure with Chinese names.

Ju-long: (Lights cigarette, coughs) Ju-long fine, mean "powerful as a dragon." (Smiles) "Pan" mean water you wash rice in, not so good. Ju-long what your mother call me and I call her Tazia. She nice lady. Not prejudiced.

Gemma: Tell me how the Chinese were treated back then.

Ju-Long: Only can work in laundry. People call us names, throw rocks. Once, teacher at your school beat boy so bad he no longer can walk. Newspapers not report, but Chinese community small. Word travel fast.

Gemma: It's still a small community. I was surprised there wasn't a Chinatown in Las Vegas, but it made it easy to find you.

Ju-long: How you do it?

Gemma: I looked up old tax records for the address where your laundry used to be, 53 Ogden Street, then checked the telephone book. It's not like California, where big cities have thousands of Chinese with the same last name.

Ju-long: Too bad you have mother's last name, cannot use it to look up father. Unless Gatti his name too?

Gemma: I have no reason to think she took his last name. She was raising me alone so to her it made sense that I share her name.

Ju-long: Tazia good mother and hard worker. She deserve take all credit. But I not pry about your father. I respect her privacy; she respect mine. Because of jobs I did, that important. (Winks)

Gemma: My mother is a private person. Still, I'm hoping she let something slip, any clue about her past. It's a long time ago but I'd be most grateful if you'd tell me whatever you remember.

Ju-long: (Lights another cigarette) Tazia bring you to laundry after school. You outgoing girl, not reserved like your mother or "inscrutable" Chinese. (Chuckles) Customers like you, even tough guys. They help you with homework, especially arithmetic. (Moves fingers across palm like beads on abacus.) Those men good at numbers, always busy do accounts.

Gemma: What kind of accounts? (Leans forward) Do you mean selling opium?

Ju-long: (Laughs) No. Wong family do that. I not deal with Chinese businessmen or customers. But having you at laundry good for my business. Like I say, you popular. Sometimes grown men get down on floor, play jacks with you. Clothes get dirty, mean more work for me.

Gemma: (Wags finger) You didn't spread dirt on the floor just to make sure?

Ju-long: (Giggles, coughs) No, I run clean business. (Puts hand on chin) Clean *laundry* business.

Gemma: (Notices patchy, discoloured skin) Goodness, your hands. Can't the nursing home give you medicine for the rash?

Ju-long: Not rash. Skin sick from hands so many years in hot water, harsh soap. Many gallons bleach. (Looks worried) Tazia, her hands okay?

Gemma: Yes. She only worked here a decade. You ran the laundry for what, forty years?

Ju-long: (Nods) Happy Tazia go in time to save hands. She have nice hands, do fine needlework. Customers bring clothes, ask we fix before we clean. (Frowns) Feel bad now. Tazia do all the extra work but I keep most of extra pay.

Gemma: My mother was used to being short changed. (Touches his hand) I don't blame you. A labour reporter learns that poor people often cheat each other worse than rich people cheat them. It's not out of cruelty or disrespect; they're just struggling to survive.

Ju-long: Thank you, you forgive me. You nice lady, like Tazia. Not judge people.

Gemma: My mother still sews. When she slowed down after her heart attack, she took up the embroidery she learnt as a child. Fortunately, there's no sign of arthritis in her hands. Yet.

Ju-long: You sew too?

Gemma: I haven't the patience. Maybe I inherited restlessness from my father. (Pauses) Getting back to the chemicals at the laundry. I should have thought of this before, given what I know about occupational hazards. Do you think it's possible my father was hurt in an industrial accident and it was actually my mother who left him?

Ju-long: That not sound like your mother. Tazia a devout Catholic.

Gemma: True. She's so devout, the guilt would have killed her. Even so, did she ever make a reference to people getting hurt on one of her jobs?

Ju-long: No. (Squirms) But she maybe heard people here talk about getting hurt when they bring in things with bad stains.

Gemma: (Frowns) What kind of stains?

Ju-long: Blood. Lots of it. On shirts, pants, sheets, blankets. Even on socks and underwear. Too expensive to throw away, so clean instead. (Squares shoulders) Don't look so surprise. Mafia pay good money. I not ask questions. Just wash, wrap nice, and give back.

Gemma: I can't believe my mother did work for the Mafia.

Ju-long: Tazia not ask, she not know. Maybe she think from hospital, I do laundry for them too. (Grins) Oh, the names I could spill to FBI, but Mafia trust me to keep quiet. Remember, Chinese not talk. (Throws back head and laughs until starts coughing again)

Gemma: (Composes face; tries to look matter-of-fact) Tell me some names.

Ju-long: (Shakes head) I old but I not wish to die yet.

Gemma: (Conspiratorial) I remember one—Virgil. He was my mother's boyfriend. But I don't know his last name. Can you just give me that one surname?

Ju-long: (Lights another cigarette; leans back)

Gemma: Please. I'll buy you a carton at the commissary on the way out.

Ju-long: Virgil Capello.

Gemma: (Excited; writes name)

Ju-long: (Hesitates) I think Tazia wrong to date him. Bad idea get friendly with customers. He dangerous. You forgive I say this, but Tazia bad mother to go out with this man. Could get hurt, then what will happen to you? Tazia selfish, only time I not like her. (Stares at cigarette smoke) But understand she lonely. (Flicks ash) I only spill last name because maybe he your father. I hope not so, but you come long way here, I not want you leave empty-handed.

Gemma: Oh, I don't think he was my father. I was already six when we moved to Las Vegas.

Ju-long: Maybe Tazia know him where she live before and follow him here later when he make enough money. Chinese families do that all the time, sometimes twenty or thirty years pass before they come to America. Unless too late by then. (Looks sad, maybe applies to him?)

Gemma: It's taken me fifty years to make the trip in reverse. I hope I'm not too late.

Ju-long: (Grins) Fortune cookie say, "When you travel back in time, return to where you started and then move forward." (Stretches) Nap time. Please, you tell Tazia I wish her long life.

The interview ended at 3:30 PM.

chapter 25

This is Gemma Kane, speaking with Virgil Capello, my mother's one-time beau, at The Golden Mint Casino in Las Vegas, Nevada. Today is Thursday, May 18, 1961, and the time is 9:00 PM.

Gemma: Swanky place.

Virgil: Help yourself to the all-you-can-eat buffet before we start talking. Golden Mint was the first place to open one, fifteen years ago. Folks come in thinking they're getting a freebie, but they spend more on the slots than we do on food. After one plateful, they're glued to their "lucky seat" and don't hit the buffet again.

Gemma: Thanks, but no thanks.

Virgil: I can see you're not the gambling type. For you, the buffet really would be a good deal.

Gemma: Maybe I'll sample it on the way out. Right now, it's "food for thought" I'm after. As I recall, you began dating my mother when I was fourteen, so that would be 1925?

Virgil: Your mother was very proper. I was six years older and a bit of a fast guy, so it took a while to convince her to go out with me. (Flexes muscles, smooths hair) Surprised I'm seventy-three? Not slowing down either.

Gemma: (Smiles) You and my mother met at the Chinese laundry where she worked?

Virgil: Yeah. I used to bring in my boss's dirty laundry. (Snickers) I got Tazia to warm up to me by talking about us both being Italian. My parents came from Sicily in 1885, with my older sister. I was born in New York but moved to Chicago in my teens.

Gemma: Mmm. My mother moved there not long after. But you didn't know her then?

Virgil: Not unless she hung around with my gang, Lizard Legs Lagorio and Tommy Marmo the Marble. Head as bald and hard as a Steely. (We laugh imagining my mother as a gang girl.) Tazia talked about the village where she grew up, though she never named it. It reminded me of my parents' stories, how life was ruled by the rhythm of planting and harvesting, yet they still found time to relax, feast out in the countryside. Here, everything is a hustle. Tazia made me stop to look and listen, breathe and taste. She was like no other woman I knew. Am I embarrassing you?

Gemma: Not at all. I like hearing what my mother was like when she was younger. When did you find out she had a daughter? Did she say anything else about her past?

Virgil: Not really. The other thing I liked about her was she didn't go on about herself, like other broads. Even when I got curious, the most she'd say is that she lived different places, wherever she found work. The only city she named was Topeka, before she moved here, and that only came up because she missed farmwork. She said she could plant the seeds of her sorrow and something new and better would grow. Your mother was quite a poet.

Gemma: You're the one who's named after a poet. Virgil.

Virgil: My last name, Capello, means trickster. My parents hoped that by giving me a respectable first name it would cancel out the second. (Smirks) They were disappointed.

Gemma: What did my mother say about having me?

Virgil: That you were a seed she expected to grow up and be better than her. (Waves one of the dealers over to our table) Drago, give the guy in the red vest a taste. (Drago bows and leaves)

Gemma: You give out free booze too?

Virgil: (Laughs) We'd lose money if we did that. A "taste" is a small amount we pay out so a player will stay in his seat and keep betting. The slots do it automatically; the dealers at their—or more often at *my*—discretion. (Points to the red-vested man) He'll spend big if we get him to stay at least one hour. At that point he's "in" and he'll stay ten more trying to recoup his losses.

Gemma: I know casinos win by playing the odds. I never dreamt psychology was involved too.

Virgil: Big time. Vegas was bankrupt when I first got here. Nevada had outlawed gambling seven years earlier; Prohibition hit us two years later. Yet, after moving all the way from Chicago, I was already "in" so I invested in staying. In my case, the gamble paid off.

Gemma: (Sweeps hand around casino) All this is yours?

Virgil: (Thrusts out chest) I began as an errand boy. The Mafia ran casinos and speakeasies, so there was plenty of work. I made myself indispensable. By the time gambling was legalized again in 1931, the Mafia was rooted in the city. A few years later, I was made part owner of this place.

Gemma: Why do you think my mother stayed?

Virgil: (Grins) I'd say on account of me, except it was eight years before we met and she only stayed two more. I think Tazia stuck around because she had faith that God brought her here and would make things work out. If she'd had enough faith to wait another four years, it might have.

Gemma: I don't think I've ever seen my mother lose faith, although I don't suppose there's a person who hasn't questioned his belief in God at some point.

Virgil: (Rubs fingers together) The only God I believe in is money and for prayers to come true, you gotta supplement faith with cheating. Not Tazia, though. She wouldn't even tell a lie.

Gemma: You're right my mother doesn't lie, but she doesn't tell the whole truth either. There's more in what she doesn't say than in what she does.

Virgil: Just like the Mafia; it pays to keep your mouth shut.

Gemma: I still find it hard to believe that my mother worked for the Mafia, even indirectly. Did she know you were connected? The owner of the Chinese laundry said you used to bring in bloody sheets. Can you tell me what they were from? Were you just the carrier, or did you ... ?

Virgil: (Covers mouth with hand and shakes head theatrically) No can say.

Gemma: Well, what did my mother say? Didn't she ask?

Virgil: I told her I worked for an abortion doctor and she believed me. Or wanted me to believe she did. I never figured out what she really thought, but I didn't care as long as she kept quiet.

Gemma: (Hesitates) Did my mother ever say anything about wanting to have an abortion when she was pregnant with me?

Virgil: I doubt she would have even considered it. Despite our affair, your mother was a good Catholic. (Looks thoughtful) Now that I think of it though, Tazia was pretty tolerant. There wasn't much about human behaviour that shocked her. In fact, she was more likely to shock me.

Gemma: What on earth did my mother do that shocked you?

Virgil: She told me that on the farm in Topeka, not only was she the only woman, she was also the only white person. Other than the farmer himself. He was Norwegian or Swedish or something, and he actually employed niggers. I can't imagine working with those animals.

Gemma: (Scribbling down this clue just in case tape recorder fails) Why do you suppose my mother told you about working with Negroes? It seems like a big piece of history to share.

Virgil: I don't think she thought about my reaction. It was just the way she romanticized working in the fields, with everybody equal. (Makes a disgusted face) Ugh. Ask me a different question.

Gemma: Tell me what you and my mother did on her days off. Did you ever include me?

Virgil: Your mother waited a long time before introducing us, and by then you were usually too busy with your own boyfriend to tag along. Except one day, I'll never forget, when I took you both to the grand opening of Lorenzi Lake Park. That would have been in 1926.

Gemma: So that's where this old picture I found was taken. (Fishes inside pocketbook) Now I remember. There was a dance pavilion where you taught me how to do the Charleston.

Virgil: (Laughs) I told your mother she should let you dress like a flapper and bob your hair.

Gemma: Then I made a joke about skinny dipping in the swimming pool. My mother shot daggers at you when you said we should all do it.

Virgil: (Chuckles) We both had fun provoking your mother. What she liked best about the park was the fruit orchards around the lake. She'd have been happy spending the whole day walking through the trees, but I wanted to be where the action was. You too. We hit it off right away.

Gemma: I always was an active child. I assume I got that trait from my father. (Raises eyebrows)

Virgil: I am *not* your father. Do we look alike?

Gemma: We both have thick, curly hair.

Virgil: And mine was dark like yours before it turned gray. Big deal.

Gemma: You're right, we're nothing alike. (He: Brown eyes, medium height, muscular. Me: Green eyes, long and lean)

Virgil: (Laughs) I don't blame you for hoping. If people didn't hope, I'd be broke. (Closes eyes) I can still picture what the two of you wore that day. Your mother's yellow sun dress had straps that crossed in the back, pretty revealing for her. (Opens eyes to make sure I'm not embarrassed; I nod he should go on) You wore a pink skirt and white blouse, which she made you tuck in, but you were most excited about your new open-toed sandals.

Gemma: Here it is. (Pulls out photo) Mama's facing front and it's black and white, but you can tell that's what we're wearing. And see the "zi" at the end of the sign. Did you take the picture?

Virgil: (Snatches photo) Yes, with your mother's Brownie. Look how young she is. (Eyes tear) She said to make sure the sign wasn't in the photo. I missed those two letters in the viewfinder.

Gemma: My mother looks so happy, like she's having fun and not worrying for a change.

Virgil: She helped me relax. I'd like to think I did the same for her, even if it was only for a day.

Gemma: What else do you remember about that day?

Virgil: I'd just done a messy job for the boss ...

Gemma: A hit?

Virgil: (Wags finger) I told you, young lady, I ain't saying, but I was moving up to being a "made man" and the boss paid me a wad of money. I wanted to spend big and show off my girl, and when Tazia asked if she could bring you along, I thought "*Two* girls, why not?" You were every bit as pretty as your mother and I liked your rambunctiousness. (Frowns) Maybe too much.

Gemma: What do you mean?

Virgil: (Takes a deep breath) I think your mother ...

Gemma: Damn. Hold on a second, I have to change the tape. (Inserts new reel). You were saying you liked me and that my mother ...

Virgil: (Silently watches tape spin for a minute before speaking again) Maybe your mother thought I liked you too much, you know, that I was ... interested in you.

Gemma: (Scowls) Were you?

Virgil: Of course not. I did some bad things in my time, but nothing that sick. Still, Tazia was young when she got pregnant, so I thought maybe she was a little crazy when it came to sex stuff with you. We never took you with us again, and a year later, you and your mother were gone.

Gemma: Did you ever talk to her about her suspicions?

Virgil: Nah. It was just a hunch I had. Gamblers live on hunches.

Gemma: (Yawns) Sorry. I'm not bored (laughs), just tired.

Virgil: Already? The night's still young. Things won't get hopping for another few hours yet.

Gemma: I'm not a night person. As a labour reporter, I interview people on the night shift now and then, but most of my work is during the day, in corporate board rooms and courtrooms.

Virgil: Tazia wasn't a night person either. She worked long hours and then came home to take care of you. Like I said, she was different from all the other broads I knew. She was my daylight girl, my sunshine. She opened me up to a whole different world.

Gemma: Why do you suppose she was attracted to you?

Virgil: Maybe I did the opposite for her. You know, let her brush up against the underworld. You'd be amazed how many good girls like the thrill, as long as they can keep a safe distance.

Gemma: That doesn't sound like my mother, but you can never tell. I'm learning things about her on this trip that I never knew before. (Starts to pack up)

Virgil: Don't forget to try the all-you-can-eat buffet on your way out. Shrimp, egg rolls, ravioli.

Gemma: Thanks again, but I'll pass.

Virgil: (Grins) Lost your appetite?

Gemma: (Smiles back) No. Just ready for some fresh farm food.

The interview ended at 10:20 PM.

part seven
Tazia, Las Vegas, 1917-1927
chapter 26

Adolfo, the owner of Mancini's Market, takes Tazia's grocery items off the shelves as she reads from her list. When she asks for tomatoes, however, he goes to the back of the store where he keeps the best ones. "Because you make tomato sauce like my mama's." He kisses his fingertips, then fetches an anise cookie, baked by his wife, from the jar on the counter. "For Gemma."

Having arrived in Las Vegas a week ago, Tazia marvels at how easily she finds the foods she couldn't get in Topeka. Garlic. Olive oil. Eggplant. There is no Little Italy to hide her here, but there are plenty of Italians. Most work in the mines or railroads, transplants from northern Nevada, where Italian immigrants settled fifty years ago. The rest run the small businesses that serve them, like this store. Tazia found an apartment a block away. She and Gemma each have a bedroom, along with a parlor and a sunny kitchen where Tazia can cook them nice dinners after Sunday Mass at St. Viator. The rent is cheap, but she will soon run out of money.

"You helped me find a church, maybe you can help me find a job too," she says to Adolfo. "Preferably working for Italians. So far, all I've come across are bars."

"Have you tried a boarding house? You might even get free rent."

"I tried one, two streets over, with a big vegetable garden out front."

"Elda Abbruzo's place. I buy zucchini from her. Her place is packed with boarders"

"Yes, all dirty. And drunk." Tazia shivers, remembering how their red-rimmed eyes stared at her. "Mrs Abruzzo offered me a job, but it's not where I want to work. Or live with Gemma."

Adolfo rearranges the peppers. "An Italian restaurant, with a little after-hours gambling?" He winks. Tazia chuckles. She's not opposed to the idea. Her father and uncles used to bet over which tree would yield the most olives. "I know just the place," Adolfo continues. "They serve the best Italian food and wine in Clark County." He points behind him. "They buy my tomatoes."

Tazia salivates, remembering the tastes of home. She tells Adolfo she's very interested.

"Go to the Ten Spot Roadhouse on Highway 91. See Mr Salvatore Vannozzi, Sal V, and tell him his associate, Mr Mancini, sent you." Adolfo bows when Tazia thanks him. "One thing, though. You gotta wear something a little classier to the interview."

"Why do I have to dress nice to cook?"

"Appearances matter to these guys."

Tazia doesn't care about her own clothes, but she wants to afford nice ones for Gemma. Adolfo reaches under the counter and brings out a plaid jumper and white blouse with a lace collar. "My niece outgrew it. I hope Gemma doesn't mind hand-me-downs."

"She'll be thrilled. At her age, she doesn't know the difference."

"She will soon enough," Adolfo says, shaking his head. "But when you get this position, you can buy her brand-new clothes." He walks Tazia outside. "And stylish outfits for yourself."

***

"I'm hoping you'll have a job for me at the Ten Spot, Mr Vanozzi." Tazia has covered up the holes in her dress with her nonna's lace shawl. Too late, she sees where the fringe has frayed.

"Call me Mr V." He twirls his diamond pinky ring. "We serve Italian specialties, drinks. A little roulette, craps, blackjack. Whatever diners like, provided they're discreet."

"I'm good at keeping secrets," Tazia says. She names the dishes her mother taught her to cook: smoked sausage, lasagna with wide egg noodles, spaghettini and meat sauce.

"Old country. Our clientele will appreciate that." Mr V lights a cigar. "But a pretty young woman like you shouldn't slave away in the kitchen. What do you say to being a waitress?"

Tazia leans forward. "Does it pay more?"

"A bit. You can also be a table dealer." Mr V eyes her above the curling smoke. When she nods eagerly, he puffs and says, "But if you really want to increase your tips, you can provide extra services to clients who are looking for more than Chianti and craps."

Tazia stands so abruptly her knee whacks the table leg. She limps on the way out, but her head is held high. Even if word gets back to Adolfo and he stops saving his best tomatoes for her, she will find a more respectable place to work. She doesn't care if the owner isn't Italian.

***

In fact, when Tazia blushes in response to his question about the job interview, Adolfo stammers an apology and gives her a bag filled with tomatoes, eggplants, and melons. She promises to pay him as soon as she finds work and asks if he has any other suggestions.

"What about the Chinese laundry a few blocks up? The Chink does good work." He points to his spotless, starched apron and grins. "Not a big talker. Inscrutable, but honest."

Tazia ignores the slur, thanks Adolfo, and finds her way to the Star Chinese Laundry and its proprietor Ju-Long Pan. Assaulted by steam and chemical smells, she focuses on his wrinkled hands and instinctively trusts him. He shows her around the shop.

"Here, mix soap." Tazia sees a huge bowl, scoops, and wooden churn. "Lye ash and fat, add bleach for very bad stains. Let soak." Next is a perforated double tub with a crank. "No can afford electric washing machine." Tazia watches him turn the crank to rotate a set of paddles that agitate the clothes and linens. Beside that is another tub for rinsing and spinning out excess water, with thicker paddles. After further manual ringing, the laundry goes into a hand-cranked mangle for another squeezing and is draped over racks to dry. Finally, the items are pressed with heavy irons heated on the stove, then bundled and marked with the customer's number.

"Numbers easier than names. Fewer mistakes." Ju-long Pan smiles for the first time. "Hard work. You think you can do, Missy?"

"Yes, I can do it. How much?"

"Two dollar a day, six day a week."

Less than Tazia had hoped, but prices are cheaper than in Chicago and she won't have to pay for heat and warm clothes here.

"Work twelve hour a day, sometimes fourteen if very busy. Okay? You not have family?" Ju-long Pan looks at Tazia's bare left hand.

Tazia hesitates. It's been a while since Ayal's absence caught her unawares. "A young daughter. Can I bring her here after school and on Saturdays?" The owner raises his eyebrows. Tazia reassures him. "She won't be any

Ann S. Epstein

trouble. She can do her homework in the corner and she likes to read and
draw. No noise, no running around."

"You make sure she keep fingers away from mangle? She not splash in
bleach?"

Tazia promises. Ju-long Pan extends a wrinkled hand. They shake.
"Cannot call each other numbers." He smiles. "Okay I call you Tazia?
You call me Ju-long?" Again, Tazia agrees. If they are to spend that many
hours together, first names are good. She begins tomorrow at six. Living
so close, she and Gemma can walk to the laundry early, then Gemma can
get herself to the nearby school at eight and return after three. The two of
them can walk home together at dinnertime.

***

Tazia welcomes the routine, but the days are long and hot. The windows
have to stay closed, not only to keep out dust, but also because the shop
must be above room temperature for the soap to dissolve stains and the
chemicals to kill germs. Tazia's hands soon look like Ju-long's. At home in
the evening, her fingers snag the material when she tries to embroider. No
matter, she's hasn't the time or energy for fancy stitching. The only sewing
she does now is mending clothes.

The one creature immune to the laundry's heat is Chlora, the white
cat named for chlorine bleach, who sleeps in the sunlight that streams
into the front window. Even the normally energetic Gemma wilts after
finishing her homework. Sometimes she naps in a hamper of clean clothes.
It reminds Tazia of little Paulie hiding in the scrap bins at Triangle. She
wonders what became of the mischievous girl, who would be seventeen
now, the same age as Tazia when she had Gemma.

Two months into the job, as he cranks the mangle, Ju-long says, "You
right, Gemma no trouble. She quiet, also smart. Like ..." his voice trails
off and he looks away, turning faster.

Tazia waits for him to continue, then asks, "A child you know?"

"Knew." Ju-long stops cranking. "A boy ... so long ago." He sighs.

"You left him in China?" Tazia watches him wipe his face. She does not
think it is sweat. "I left family behind too," she whispers, her hoarse voice
unaccustomed to such revelations.

Ju-long sits beside the hamper where Gemma sleeps. His shoulders
droop, the first time Tazia has ever seen him look tired. "Will he—your
son—ever come here?" she asks.

"Too late." Ju-long peers at the snoring Gemma. "You lucky have her." He gently strokes the child's wild hair. "I like she come here." So do his customers, men in dark suits with pressed cuffs. When Gemma is awake, she amuses them with stories of playground turf wars. She cajoles them into helping her with her homework, especially arithmetic. "They businessmen. Good with numbers," Ju-long tells Tazia with a finger to his lips. Like him, she knows not to ask questions.

Gemma soon has them on the floor, playing jacks. "They think it's a form of gambling," Tazia jokes to Ju-long. "Look, Mama, a lucky seven," Gemma sings one afternoon. Tazia peers around a laundry tub to discover that these men have not only been throwing jacks, they've been teaching her daughter to throw dice. Next Gemma rolls a two. "Snake eyes. Crap!"

"No more games." Tazia grabs the dice; Gemma pouts and stamps her foot. Guilt gnaws at Tazia. It's her fault the child is stuck in this steamy environment. She returns the dice. "Okay, but no more curse words." Gemma looks contrite and apologizes, then brightens. "Mama, if I roll a two, three, or twelve, can I use a word that means something bad but isn't naughty?"

Tazia, trying not to smile, waits to hear what her daughter comes up with.

Gemma thinks. "How about 'wormy tomatoes'?"

Tazia laughs. From the far end of the drying racks, she hears Ju-long tee-hee too.

***

The laundry does well, but things pick up when word gets out that Tazia can do repairs. It starts one day after she hears ripping, followed by a deep voice crying, "Wormy tomatoes!" Tazia finds that Beppe "the Bulldog," while crouching to play jacks, has caught a heel on his trouser cuff.

"Brand new," he says with dismay. "Ottavia is gonna kill me."

"I can fix it," Tazia offers. It's funny how these tough men fear their wives. Their children too. No wonder they'd rather hang out here. "Once they're cleaned, they'll look better than new."

"How much?" asks Beppo, trembling.

Tazia makes up a number. "Twenty-five cents. I'll have them for you tomorrow."

"Sold!" Beppo says. Ju-Long gives him a spare pair of trousers, one of the many garments that people, inexplicably, fail to pick up. Beppo pats Gemma's head and slinks on home.

"I keep twenty, give you five," Ju-Long tells Tazia. She decides not to protest. If not for him, who knows what she'd be doing. Certainly not earning extra nickels for respectable work.

A day after picking up his trousers, Beppo comes back. "When I came home in the wrong pants, Ottavia accused me of messing around, so I confessed what happened. She still got mad, but you fixed the pants so good, she made me bring you these." He gives Tazia two torn dresses. Then, looking sheepish, he hands her a jacket with a slashed lapel. "Ssh. Ottavia hasn't seen this."

Word spreads and soon other clients bring in mending. The wives' clothes have torn hems or seams; the men's are ripped and often bloodied. Neither Tazia nor Ju-long asks how they got that way, but between them they marvel at how finely these garments are tailored. Pleased to discover they both care about such things, Tazia shows Ju-long the traditional Assisi designs she embroidered on Gemma's baby clothes. He shows her his wedding jacket, decorated by his wife-to-be with classic Shu embroidery. Both techniques feature a profusion of blossoms and soaring birds from their respective countries. They look out at the dusty Nevada landscape and sigh.

They rarely talk about their pasts, however. Like their customers, they don't name people or places, but over time they stop masking the feelings associated with them. Tazia concludes she needn't hide among people who look like her, only those who share her desire for privacy. She thinks this absentmindedly one day as she pets Chlora. The cat rolls on her back, exposing her soft belly. There, amid the pure white coat, Tazia spots a patch of dark, matted hairs. She flips the cat back on her stomach. As with clients at Star Chinese Laundry, it is best not to look underneath.

chapter 27

Two years later, when Gemma turns eight, she begs to go to a friend's house after school, instead of the laundry. "I'm bored," she complains. "Nobody here plays with me anymore." It's true; the men no longer have time. Business has boomed since Prohibition. The clients now deal in illegal speakeasies as well as casinos. Blood-soaked garments pile up on the counter.

Tazia turns down her daughter's request. "Not when I haven't met their parents."

Gemma pouts. "How can you when you work all the time? And we spend every Sunday together?" Tazia flinches but does not budge. "What if I go back to the apartment?" Gemma asks.

It's tempting. Tazia is working longer hours. When they finally get home, Gemma is too tired to eat dinner. Tazia also worries she'll start to ask questions about the things the men bring in. "We'll try," she says, "but alone means alone. No friends and you stay put until I get home."

Gemma gloats over her victory in the war for independence. Tazia blinks back tears. One battle at a time, she will lose her daughter.

***

This arrangement works well for six years. By then, Tazia has lived in Las Vegas for eight, longer than any place save Loro Piceno. Gemma excels in school, especially arithmetic and social studies, so Tazia loosens the reins, provided her daughter doesn't get too close to any one friend. Gemma takes her First Communion and at Confirmation, as promised, chooses the name Monica, Patron Saint of Mothers. Tazia recalls her own rite of passage, followed by a feast in the Gattis' orchard, and wishes someone other than Ju-long were there to celebrate with her and Gemma.

Meanwhile, she and her boss continue to open up to each other. They still withhold many details but release first names and cherished memories. "Bianca was next oldest after me," Tazia tells Ju-long. "It fell to her to take care of the boys after I left." For a moment, memories of her shimmering laugh drown out the laundry's sloshing water and hissing steam. "Bianca was a daydreamer. I worried she'd forget to change Zito, the baby, or keep track of what Fino and Fredo, the twins, were up to."

"She sound like my brother Yan," Ju-long says, chuckling. "His name mean bird, so fit him. Yan head off for village to trade rice for oil, next thing climbing mountain to chase cloud. My mother start sending youngest boy, Kun, along on errands. His name mean earth and Kun down to earth, so he keep Yan on ground." Ju-long sighs. "No sisters. No aunts. Poor Mother, she only woman."

"I don't know if my sister finally settled down. Mama never said in the letters she asked our neighbour to write for her. She was worried about little Zito, who was born with bad lungs. I sent money to pay for a doctor and medicine."

"The baby okay after that?" Ju-long asks.

"I don't know. I ... moved and lost touch." Tazia shakes with silent sobs. Ju-long puts a wrinkled hand on her shoulder.

"My son Bao—it mean gem, like Gemma—he healthy. Loved fly kites. His mother Li send me kite string." Ju-long opens the top of his shirt to reveal a threadbare necklace of faded red ribbon with a dozen frayed bows of indeterminate colour. He quickly pulls his collar closed. Tazia always wondered why, in the heat, Ju-long never loosened his shirt. She suspected he had a scar or ugly birthmark. Now she understands that he hides a different kind of disfigurement.

Tazia's eyes ask the question she cannot voice. Ju-long answers. "Too hard find work here, too many years before can save enough. By then, too late for Li and Bao to come."

What was it like for Bao growing up with no father, Tazia wonders. How did Li raise him alone? She thinks it must be harder for a single mother with a son, although now that Gemma is fourteen, Tazia feels increasingly unsure of herself. Her daughter chafes at restrictions. The battles inevitably centre around Gemma's freedom to do things after school with her classmates.

"I'm not asking to hang out with boys," she argues. "Just Helen and her girlfriends."

"Helen is a year older than you. She was held back." Tazia senses something wild in that girl. And she's not very bright, especially compared to Gemma.

"You're wrong, Mama. When her parents moved here two years ago, Helen lost a grade."

"Helen's friends are also a year older."

"Well, yeah. She wants to be with kids her own age."

"Then why does she want to be friends with you?"

"She says I'm more mature than the other girls in our class."

This is exactly what terrifies Tazia. Her daughter's body is developing at a normal rate, but her mind races ahead. She wonders if years of secretly trying to puzzle out the mystery of her father has sharpened Gemma's thinking. Whatever the cause, she has no time to ponder that now. With a war on her hands, she tells her daughter that Helen and her crowd are off limits.

"Then," Gemma says, "what about Mildred and Francine? They're the same age as me."

Oh, her child is clever. "I don't want you spending that many hours with friends without a grownup around." Tazia attempts a compromise. "Invite your friends here on Sunday, after we go to Mass and have dinner. I'll bake a special dessert. Tiramisu? Torta Caprese?"

The bribe doesn't work. "Great," Gemma says and snorts. "Just what teenagers want to do, get together and gab with someone's mother lurking in the background."

"I'll visit with Adolfo and his wife," Tazia offers. "For an hour or so."

"Thanks for nothing." Gemma stomps to her room. These arguments repeat every week. They go around like linked coils, one bent on pulling away, the other on entangling. Tazia can't decide whether loosening her grip will coax Gemma back or spring her into space, where she will orbit a new star and her mother will cease to be the centre of her universe.

***

Then, without warning, these arguments stop. Even the pettier fights, about Gemma's messiness, cease. Tazia comes home to a spotless apartment and dinner on the table. She believes a crisis has been averted until, one Sunday, with Gemma at an after-church activity, Tazia sweeps under her desk and finds a slip of paper with the name, Darius Ignatius, underlined. Three times, in red ink. Rather than asking who he is, she puts the paper next to Gemma's plate and waits for her to talk.

Gemma waves it in the air and kisses Tazia. "Where did you find this? My paper on him is due Thursday. Surely you've heard about the great Italian war hero who fought with the Allies? I remembered his last name, cause it's like the Saint, but not his first. You saved me, Mama."

The hero's name is not familiar to Tazia, but she was too busy raising Gemma to pay attention to the Great War. Three months later, she's forgotten the incident, when Gemma admits that she lied. "I'm tired of skulking around, Mama. Darius is a boy in my class and I like him. A lot. He's really cute. And nice." She blushes and awaits her penance.

The confession disarms Tazia. Also the boy is Italian and presumably Catholic. Her arms tremble as she hugs Gemma and tells her to invite Darius for dinner that Sunday. He arrives on time, is well groomed, and praises the food before they even eat, adding that he cooks too. Yet, for some reason, Tazia dislikes him. The way he jams his hands in pockets and rattles the change reminds her of Remo "the Rat," a laundry customer who makes even the tranquil Ju-long jumpy. Questions that would pass for polite conversation sound like prying when Darius asks them.

"I spent my whole life in Las Vegas," he says, unfolding his napkin. "I'm third generation. I like history, but my parents never talk about my ancestors in Italy. What was it like there?"

"Warm like here. Rainier. Would you like more tomato sauce?" Tazia holds up the ladle.

"Where in Italy did you live? Calf, toe, or heel?" He laughs. "Plenty of heels in this town."

Tazia doesn't answer. She heaps more sauce on his plate and eats, a sign for him to do the same. But Darius keeps talking, twirling spaghetti on his fork. Gemma, who usually has a good appetite, doesn't eat either. Her eyes dart back and forth between her mother and her boyfriend.

Darius looks only at Tazia. "Gemma says you used to work on a farm. Is it hard?"

"Any job is as hard as you work at it." Tazia forces down another mouthful.

"My dad's always after me to work harder. Maybe I should be a farmer." Darius seems not to notice Gemma's alarmed look. "What did you grow?" he persists.

"Farmers grow what's right for where they live."

"So tell me again, where did you live?"

Tazia clears the table and brings out coffee and dessert. Darius nibbles cannoli with one hand, the other jammed and jingling in his pocket. He again thanks Tazia for a wonderful dinner before he leaves. Afterwards, as they wash the dishes, Tazia waits in vain for Gemma to ask what she thinks of him. She would have answered that he's nice looking, but doesn't know when to let go of things. She wouldn't have said she worries he will try to hold Gemma back when she is ready to move on. Tazia herself wonders how long she'll continue to let Ayal hold onto her.

Gemma continues to get top grades and keep the apartment clean. With no evidence that her daughter and Darius spend time alone there while she's at work, Tazia nevertheless locks up Ayal's note and the baby rattle from Elvan in a small enameled jewelry box she finds at a second-hand store. She wears the key around her neck, hidden like Ju-long's kite string, and checks the box nightly for signs of tampering but sees none. Gemma asks for permission to spend part of Sunday afternoons with Darius. Without a good reason to say no, Tazia consents.

"Just be careful," she warns her daughter.

"Relax, Mama. *I* won't do anything stupid." She pales. "I'm sorry. I didn't mean ..."

"I don't mind if you use me as an example of what not to do. That's what parents are for." Tazia takes a deep breath. "I meant be careful that your heart isn't broken."

Tazia tells herself that is indeed the danger she has in mind, until the evening she finds a bottle of rum in the toilet tank. Instead of confronting Darius the following Sunday, she buries it under a pile of blankets and waits for the day it will be most helpful. The deception, like that of Ju-long's clients, haunts her, but she reasons that God allows secrets meant to protect her child.

chapter 28

A new customer appears at work, younger and cockier than the other men. Virgil Capello lets his dark curls grow past his collar. He wears tight shirts and jackets that show off his muscles, and his deep brown eyes regard the world as if he owns it, Tazia included. "Dashing," she thinks, same as Ayal. Also, like her long-ago lover, Virgil projects excitement and danger. Tazia thinks he must be important. "No," Ju-long tells her, "He errand boy for big capos, but his type move up fast."

One day Virgil swaggers in with a bigger load of sheets than usual. Tazia winces at the dark brown stains oozing from the package he sets on the counter. "Sorry to upset your delicate sensibilities," Virgil says, smirking. "The doc had more patients than usual this week."

Tazia has never heard any of the bosses referred to this way. "The doc?"

Virgil puts his lips close to Tazia's ear. She thinks he's about to nibble it and tries to quell the wave in her belly. "The abortion doctor," he whispers, "a kind man who performs a service from the goodness of his heart." He backs away and looks Tazia in the eye. "He's clean, not like some back-alley creep. The girls he helps wish it hadn't come to this, but they're grateful."

Tazia sweeps up the package as smoothly as a gambler scooping up dice and dumps it in a scalding bath of bleach. She nods as if she believes Virgil. He looks pleased at having convinced her, but when his grin widens, Tazia suspects he knows she knows he's spinning a tale to seduce her. Before long, he's entertaining her with Mafia talk and she's drawn into a den of intrigue that she's purposefully avoided until now. She slips into his world as her daughter slips out of hers.

"Benny Eggs," he jokes, the next time he delivers a package. "We had to break him."

"It looks like someone did more than break him." Tazia mixes a strong batch of bleach.

Virgil laughs. "Breaking means you demote an associate for getting out of line. Usually it doesn't go this far. But in Benny's case, we had to call in a button to carry out a contract." He explains a button is a family member who performs an execution. Contract, she already knows.

Tazia wonders what Benny Eggs did, but Virgil says only that he tried to "muscle in" on Fat Dominic's territory to up the percentage of his "vigourish." These terms are self-explanatory too. "Too bad," Virgil continues, "because the guy was close to being made. Joey Dove was in charge of the induction committee." He lights a cigar. "Unused refreshments from the ceremony."

Tazia puts it out. "It's hot and smelly enough in here. You can leave but poor crumbs like Ju-long and me can't." Virgil smiles. He enjoys hearing Tazia say the words he taught her, like "crumb" for a legitimate working man. He's also tickled when she repeats the more outrageous nicknames the men are given, Louie Lump Lump, No Nose, and Ripe Charlie. "You haven't told me what you're called," she teases after knowing him a few months, "or are you ashamed of it?"

"The Poet," he says proudly. "Not just because of my first name, but because I have my own way with words." A silver tongue, Tazia thinks, as he polishes the many words for killing: bump, burn, hit, knock off, pop, rub out, whack. Still, she resists his enticements to go out. So, Virgil changes tactics. He gets her to talk about Italy, where his parents, like her, came from.

Tazia won't name places, but is free with sights, sounds, tastes, and smells she hasn't even shared with Ju-long. Mostly she talks about olives. "The trees were like looms with pale green fruit woven among their branches. They made a canopy above us, a feast spread below. We never added salt to the food. The air was salty enough. Breathing it was all the seasoning you needed."

Virgil tells Tazia that she is the true poet.

Next she remembers the feel of freshly pressed olive oil. "First the smoothness coats the inside of your mouth, then it slides along your tongue, and last it makes a slightly scratchy journey down your throat. My Papa said a good wine lasts one meal, but a good olive oil lasts for many."

"Mine said bread is good for a day, oil for a month, wine for a year." Virgil circles Tazia's wrist. "To that I add, a beautiful woman is good forever." She blushes but does not withdraw her hand. "I wish we could bottle Italy's sunlight. It's so much softer than the glare of Las Vegas."

"I'm raising my daughter to appreciate her Italian heritage." Tazia's hand breaks free.

"You have a child?"

Tazia busies herself bundling shirts and blouses. "It's not a secret. Her name is Gemma, my jewel." She looks up. "My daughter is fifteen, smart but a handful."

Virgil seems to take this news in stride. "I'd like to meet her. You're right to want Gemma to know about her ancestry. I wish I'd asked my parents more questions before I left home."

"You're not in touch with them anymore?"

He smiles. "I chose a different path than they had in mind for me."

Tazia doesn't ask what that was. She knows what Italian parents want for their children.

***

A few weeks later, Virgil comes in empty-handed, but waving excitedly. "I can't promise you the Italian countryside," he tells Tazia, "but a new park just opened with lakes and orchards, also a pool and dance pavilion. It's even named for a *connazionale*, Lorenzi. Come with me on Sunday."

"How many lakes? What kind of orchards?"

"We'll see when we get there." Virgil gets down on one knee. "The boss gave me a bonus. I want to celebrate. *Per favore*." Tazia's defences tumble. "Bring your daughter," he adds. "I deserve a beautiful girl on each arm."

Gemma balks at giving up Sunday afternoon with Darius to visit a park with her mother.

Tazia misses the days when her child loved such outings as much as she did. "There's someone who wants to meet you," she says quietly.

Gemma draws a sharp breath. "Is this something to do with my father?"

Tazia, taken aback, stutters. "Of course not. Another man, though, a customer from the laundry. A ... nice man. I think you'll like him."

"Mama! You have a boyfriend too?" Gemma grins. "What did you tell him about me?"

"That you were smart. And test my patience. You promise to behave yourself? And not ask too many questions?" Tazia can't tell if she's more nervous about going out with Virgil or Gemma nosing into his business. She's both relieved and anxious her daughter will come along.

As giddy as a teenager, Tazia wears a lemon-yellow sun dress with spaghetti straps that cross in the back. She would never buy something like that, but it's been unclaimed at the laundry for over a year and Ju-long has been urging her to take it. She doubts he had in mind her wearing it on an occasion like this. Gemma puts on a rose-coloured skirt with a white over blouse.

"Tuck it in," Tazia orders.

"All the girls wear it his way. Do you want your boyfriend to think I'm unfashionable?"

"I want him to think I'm raising my daughter to be a proper young lady." When Gemma angrily shoves in her blouse, Tazia worries that she's setting the wrong mood for the day. "Here," she says, "I bought you these." Gemma's eyes light up at the open-toed pink sandals. The blouse is soon forgotten as she dashes to the bathroom to paint her toenails. Tazia does not object.

Virgil comes for them in a Model T, on loan, he says, from the capo himself. Neither Tazia nor Gemma has ridden in a car before. Virgil whistles when he sees Tazia's dress. "My beautiful goomah," he says, using the Mafia word for mistress. Tazia looks at him as if he's just called her a queen. Gemma looks at her mother as if she were indeed a royal stranger.

Lorenzi Park has two lakes, each with a small island. To Tazia's disappointment, there are no olive trees or grape vines, but there's a working farm with beans and tomatoes, and orchards filled with ripening apples, pears, and plums. Shade trees border the interlocking paths.

"Let's go boating," Gemma says. Tazia, remembering a seasick voyage across the ocean, demurs, but Virgil is already in line for tickets. She's queasy in the boat, but not so much that she can't appreciate the muscles in Virgil's arms as he rows them to and from one of the tiny islands. Gemma kicks off her new shoes, hikes her skirt, and dangles her toes in the water.

Tazia pulls her daughter's bare legs back in the boat. Virgil releases one oar long enough to swing them back out. "My celebration and I say it's Lady's Day. Women may do whatever they want." Gemma flashes her mother a defiant grin. "Men too," says Virgil, making as if to grab the oar but instead planting a kiss on Tazia's lips. She gasps and looks at him, but he's exchanging a mischievous look with her daughter. It's two against one and that's how the day continues.

Back on the dock, they hear music coming from the band shell. Virgil and Gemma make a run for it; Tazia has no choice but to follow. Beside the musicians is a polished dance floor.

"Dance?" Virgil asks, extending his hand. Tazia shakes her head, so he reaches for Gemma and before Tazia can react, they're doing the Charleston and slapping their backsides to the Black Bottom. Tazia can't help but admire what a graceful dancer Gemma is, her long limbs as fluid as the branches of a young olive tree waving in a gentle wind. Her daughter looks so happy that she gives up any thought of reining her in. In fact, she feels nothing but pride in her child, and herself too, for having found a man who attracts the eyes of every other woman on the floor.

"You two have fun," she calls out. "I'm heading for the trees." And for the rest of the afternoon, as Virgil and Gemma dance and play a new game called table tennis, Tazia wanders through the orchards and strolls the winding trails, as if she were a young girl roaming the hills of Loro Piceno. She stops often to lift her chin to the sun. With her trusted Brownie, Tazia shoots pictures of the geese, herons, mourning doves, and hummingbirds that fill the park with colour and song. The camera is still in her hand when they meet at the park entrance to head home.

"A picture of my ladies to remember this glorious day at Lorenzi Park." Virgil reaches for the Brownie. Tazia pulls it away. He laughs and says, "Don't be so modest. Here," handing her a comb. "You can spruce up first. Although the windswept look becomes you."

Before Tazia can protest, Gemma grabs the comb, smooths Tazia's hair, and then touches up her own. Standing in front of the sign with the park's name, she pulls her mother close for the picture. Tazia claims the sun is in her eyes and moves so they're standing to the left of the sign. Virgil makes them say "salami" before clicking the shutter. Only after the picture is developed does Tazia see the "zi" in the corner. She keeps it anyway. It doesn't seem like much of a clue.

chapter 29

Tazia does not mind when, a year later, Virgil announces he is not the marrying kind. "In my line of work, we don't usually give out warnings," he says, "but I don't want you to get hurt." In fact, Tazia likes being single. She may feel differently when Gemma is grown, but for now, raising her and having fun with Virgil is enough. She's also less bothered by the laundry's heat and long hours and is reassured when her daughter makes honour roll. Smart, like her father, and hard working, like her mother. Moreover, there are no further signs of mischief at the apartment, although Gemma makes sure it is spotless by the time Tazia gets home.

Her first premonition that things are about to change is a sharp increase in the number of bloody packages. Then Virgil truncates their Sundays to take care of "jobs" for the new capo. "Al Capone himself sent Frank Detra here," he confides, twisting her curls in his fingers. "I trust you not to tell. You keep your own secrets too." Tazia is pleased but grows wary when he hints at "our ways of getting information from people. A little pressure on them can be worth a lot to us."

Then one day Virgil brings along a new young man he calls Sonny Red and says that from now on Red will be the delivery boy. Virgil sports a pinky ring with three small diamonds and struts around the shop like a peacock. Ju-long calmly takes the package to the bleaching cauldron, but after the men leave, Tazia can feel him studying her for a reaction.

"The ring," he says, when she remains silent. "It mean your boyfriend a made man now."

"He's working for the over boss," Tazia acknowledges, "but his hands are still clean."

Ju-long snorts. "No can be a made man without making a hit. Your boyfriend a button."

Furious, Tazia cranks two loads through the mangle before looking up. "Not so."

"You wanna bet?" Ju-long tosses imaginary dice in the air. "You be careful. Not want to lose best worker. Or friend." He fingers his necklace.

"Like losing family." Reluctantly, as the evidence mounts, Tazia admits he is right. Still, she cannot decide what to do without pinpointing any obvious danger to herself. Then, one Sunday in Virgil's arms, her fear takes shape.

It begins with a kiss, which stirs memories of Ayal. As New York's Jewish Mafia has grown, Ayal, the schemer, could have wormed his way into that "family" the same way Virgil has in Las Vegas. Suppose he uses that connection to track her down. Granted, Ayal knows nothing of Gemma, but he could still be rankled that she ran off with the money he gave her for the doctor. His Mafia cronies could have convinced Ayal that no one, let alone a goomah, should get away with stealing from him. Her imagination let loose, Tazia decides Darius is a weak link in the chain that leads to her. The boy is not above being bribed to probe Gemma for information about her mother. Now Tazia has a reason to use the hidden liquor bottle against him. At the same time, if she doesn't want to lose her daughter, she must make it appear that it is Darius, not she, who is responsible for rubbing out—bumping, popping, whacking, knocking off—their relationship.

"*Amante*. I miss you." Tazia snuggles in Virgil's embrace. Everything in her lover's room—sheets, pillow cases, bedspread, and curtains—is as white as she and Ju-long can bleach them. "If I tell you my secret, will you tell me yours?" Virgil raises himself on one elbow and gazes down at her, curious yet cautious. "When I'm with you," Tazia purrs, "I feel like a naughty girl."

Virgil's laugh roils the air. "And when I'm with you, I feel like a well-behaved man."

***

Monday morning, Tazia waits outside the Ignatius's apartment and waylays Darius as he leaves for school. She wastes no time stating her mission. "I'm here to talk to you about Gemma."

He plunges his hands in his pockets, scans the empty street. "Did she put you up to this?"

"Do you think my daughter is the type to make others do her work?"

Darius shakes his head. "No, Gemma's too honest. A real straight arrow."

Tazia pulls the bottle, still half full, from her satchel. Darius's eyes widen.

"So?" Darius takes his hands out of his pockets. "What does a bottle of rum prove?"

"That a sixteen-year-old is buying alcohol, which is illegal at any age. And," Tazia gives the bottle a little shake, "that I can take this to the principal and have you expelled."

"I don't have the money to pay you off, if that's what you want." Darius wipes his nose.

Tazia gives him a pitying look. "You know what I want. Break up with Gemma."

Darius sneers. "I'm not gonna get her pregnant, if that's what you're worried about."

Tazia lets him believe that protecting her daughter's virtue rather than safeguarding family secrets is in fact her concern. She folds her arms and waits. Darius will get in more trouble being late to school than she will at work.

"What should I say to her?" the boy finally asks.

"You're clever with questions. Ask one Gemma can't answer to your satisfaction, then use that as the excuse to call it off."

Darius nods and reaches for the bottle. Tazia whisks it away. "Not until the deed is done." She's learnt by now not to give away the goods ahead of time.

***

Tazia's relief at having Darius out of the way is soon dispelt. First, Gemma's misery makes her feel guilty. Her once confident child now castigates herself for being ugly, stupid, and selfish. What on earth did the boy say to her? Second is the escalating violence over who will control the casinos and speakeasies. Even Ju-long comments that he wouldn't mind a little less business.

As predictable as the change of season, Tazia feels impelled to flee. Unlike the urgency of past escapes, however, she has more time to decide where. She prays it will be the last move and asks God to send a signal when she's made the right choice. One possibility is California. Ju-long often wonders if he should have settled there, like so many of his countrymen. Tazia wouldn't mind living among them, but a bigger draw is that California is at the opposite end of the country from New York, and Ayal. Also, as far as she knows, the Mafia hasn't spread that far west.

One night, after Gemma cries herself to sleep, Tazia sits with her daughter's geography book. California is long and skinny, like Italy. Repeating Nellie's game, Tazia closes her eyes and points to ... Sacramento. Not the first pick, she reminds herself. Take it slow. She decides to live on the ocean where gazing at the endless water means she will never again feel trapped. Next she moves her finger halfway down the coast, because Loro Piceno is in the middle of Italy. She stops at Monterey and smiles when she reads that it is hilly. Also, alas, sandy as well. After dry plains and desert, Tazia craves moisture. Plus, Monterey is foggy. She's grown accustomed to sunshine.

Tazia slides her finger farther south. Los Angeles is too risky. People from there come to Las Vegas to gamble and drink. Suppose she lived near the border where, if need be, she could flee to Mexico. As if drawn by a magnet, she lands on San Diego. The textbook says the climate is mild year-round. Good, she thinks, no more extreme weather. There are hills and a river runs through the city. More touches of home. Now, where would she work? Tazia will accept anything other than a factory or sweatshop. She learns that the U.S. Navy has a big base there and employs civilians. Tazia nods at the thought of being around boats without actually having to board one.

Gemma stirs and Tazia hides the book before she shuffles into the kitchen. Like a child, she sits on the floor and puts her head in Tazia's lap, which is soon soaked with tears. Silently, Gemma lets her mother rub her back. They stay like this for an hour, maybe more, then Tazia leads Gemma back to bed, tucks her in, and sings *Ninnananna*, the lullaby she rocked her to sleep with in Chicago. "I love you, Mama," Gemma says, drifting off. Tazia smiles. God has spoken.

Two weeks later, Tazia announces they are moving to San Diego. Gemma, demanding to know why, collapses on a chair littered with cookie crumbs. She no longer cleans the apartment.

"The work is getting too dirty for me," Tazia answers. Technically, she is telling the truth. "For God's sake. You work in a laundry." Gemma wails that now she'll never get Darius back. "What about Virgil?" Tazia hasn't anticipated this question, but Gemma answers it herself. "You don't love him as much as I love Darius." Her child is right, Tazia realizes. There's something about a first love that you never let you go of, or that never lets go of you.

***

"Westward ho to the sea!" Virgil jokes when Tazia tells him she is picking up stakes. They are at Lorenzi Park, just the two of them, strolling around one of the lakes. Tazia doesn't say where she is going, nor does Virgil ask.

"It's lovely here," she sighs, watching a heron take flight, "but it's not enough."

"What about me? Not enough either?"

"You made me happy," Tazia answers, and means it. "But soon I won't be enough for you. You're going places too."

"And you don't want to follow?" Virgil pulls her head to his chest. "I'll miss you," he says simply. "You're the most interesting woman I've ever been with."

"You brought excitement to my life." Tazia's cheek rests against Virgil's muscles. They're bigger, which simultaneously thrills and frightens her. She is less afraid than when she came here ten years ago. Although she is still on the run, her head spins with the freedom that awaits.

"If I were a real poet," Virgil muses. "I'd pen you a farewell ode." He circles Tazia's waist, but she twirls beyond his grasp. "Stop," he begs. "Let me take a picture."

But Tazia has not brought her camera. Some memories are best preserved in the mind.

***

Ju-long locks the door and hangs a crudely lettered sign in the window: "Emergency. Back one hour." Tazia cannot remember him ever closing the laundry before.

"So, I teach you to like Chinese people," he says, grinning. "Now you go be with more of them."

"I'm not sure who I'll find." Tazia shrugs. "Spanish? Irish? Maybe even some Italians?"

Ju-long gets two paper fans and hands one to Tazia. "I hear California have good schools. Better for Gemma." Tazia nods in agreement. "She will like swimming in ocean too," he adds.

They fan their faces. Despite the heat, it is important to remain cool. Otherwise they'd both dissolve into tears. They sit in silence, listening to the ticking clock. Occasionally there's a knock on the door, sometimes followed by swearing, then retreating steps. Ju-long goes into the back room and returns with a medium-size bundle that he tells her to open later. After an hour, he says, "Time re-open." They wipe their hands on a towel, shake, and briefly hug before Tazia flees.

When she gets home, she sees that Ju-long has packed up all the unclaimed white dresses that customers have left over the years. The folds are still ironed crisp. The material is spotless. But it will take more than chemicals and California sunshine to bleach the sadness out of her heart.

part eight

Gemma, Topeka, 1961

chapter 30

This is Gemma Kane, speaking with Hampus Birger Tapper, the Swedish farmer who employed my mother, at his house in Topeka, Kansas. Today is Tuesday, May 23, 1961, and the time is 7:30 AM.

Gemma: For a private person, you were surprisingly easy to track down.

Hampus: I don't seek attention, but if a man needs something, he knows where to find me.

Gemma: (Smiles) You know I need something. I found you through the article in *The Topeka Daily Capital* from 1938 about the local NAACP honouring you on their twenty-fifth anniversary. (Reads) "White farmer, Hampus Birger Tapper, has been hiring Negroes for as long as the NAACP has been fighting for their dignity."

Hampus: (Looks at his hands) *Det är inget.* It's nothing. I'm not the first white person to be honoured by the Topeka NAACP. Arthur Capper, their first president, was a white man too.

Gemma: Really? How did that happen?

Hampus: White men often led local units in the early days, not just here but around the country. Capper also happened to be the governor of Kansas and later a senator. Our names rhyme, but the resemblance ends there. (Chuckles) He was certainly more distinguished. Plus he owned the paper at the time. Died ten years ago. Employees own it now and they're not interested in an old farmer like me.

Gemma: I am, but I won't write an article or make you famous again. I do plan to transcribe our interview though, so how should I refer to you?

Hampus: (Laughs) My great grandchildren call me by my first name and you've known me since you were their age, so you might as well call me Hampus too.

Gemma: (Makes note; sips strong coffee; chooses a couple of cookies from hand-painted platter) They look homemade. And so many different kinds.

Hampus: It's a Swedish tradition to serve seven types of cookies. A reminder of good fortune, like the seven colours in the rainbow after a storm. When we ran the farm, my wife only had time to bake more than one or two kinds on special occasions. After my son and grandson took over, she returned to the tradition. I kept it up when she died. Luckily, I'd asked her to write down the recipes.

Gemma: You must miss her.

Hampus: (Wipes eyes) We were partners, in everything. That's how it is with farm families.

Gemma: It was that way in my mother's family, but she had to work and raise me on her own.

Hampus: I'm sure it was hard on Tazia, having her family and her job in two different places.

Gemma: I think she wanted to be in both places at once. (Takes another cookie) What are these? They remind me of thumb print cookies.

Hampus: *Hallongrottor* or raspberry caves. A family favourite, the one kind we always had in the house. My daughter Nellie cajoled you and Mirlee Bee with them whenever you two got restless during lessons. She didn't have to bribe you often, though. You were both eager students.

Gemma: Nellie was a good teacher. She came up with interesting ways for us to learn.

Hampus: (Laughs) You could say she ran the first integrated school in Topeka, almost forty years before the Supreme Court ruled on *Brown v. the Board of Education.*

Gemma: (Smiles) Now there's a newspaper story worth writing.

Hampus: (Pours us more coffee) I hope you don't mind my asking you to come this early. Even though I've turned over running the farm, I can't sleep past dawn. I still like to help out. (Grins) The children pretend to tolerate me.

Gemma: I don't mind. I'm still an eager student, ready to learn any time of the day.

Hampus: It's the same with me. Farming is always changing. My son and grandson got degrees in agriculture at Washburn University, here in Topeka. Now they learn about experimental wheat varieties and crop care through Kansas State's extension courses.

Gemma: It sounds more like science than farming.

Hampus: (Nods) Except when it comes to buying equipment, when loyalty to your brand comes first. Ours is International Harvester. (Looks out window at tractor crossing fields) Of course, when I started out, I couldn't afford fancy machinery. We did everything by hand.

Gemma: My mother remembers long days on the olive farm too, especially at harvest time. Some smaller farms in California are reverting to the old methods, but it's tough to make a go of it.

Hampus: I was sceptical about whether Tazia could do the work, but she was as strong as any man. Maybe that's why she thought she could do it all on her own with you. In a sense, she could.

Gemma: True, although I'm learning that she found people to stand behind her. Plus, she relied on her faith. Speaking of learning (brushes crumbs off fingers), I'd like to know whether, in the three years my mother worked for you, she dropped any hints about my father, or her own past.

Hampus: Only that she grew up on a farm, I assumed in Italy. Farmers don't need to ask about someone's background. The work speaks for itself. (Smiles) Tazia also had a good history with cats. Nellie and my wife marveled that hers was the only lap Alvar, the barn cat, would curl up in. I think they were jealous.

Gemma: (Chews inside of cheek) I was hoping you could tell me more about her.

Hampus: Only that she was a woman of deep faith, which you already know. I'll never forget that terrible day after the hailstorm, huddled in the small barn, when Tazia led people from three religions together in prayer.

Gemma: Hailstorm?

Hampus: You were too young to remember, but I'm surprised she didn't tell you about it. The storm of 1917. None like it before or since. Flattened almost every farm and most of the city. We came through okay, although our house, except the kitchen, was destroyed. Same with yours. I think that's why Tazia left. Too painful and expensive to rebuild. Oddly, the rest of Negrotown was hardly damaged. Maybe your mother she saw it as a message from God to move on.

Gemma: Do you know why we didn't live out in the country? Or in the poor white part of town?

Hampus: It wasn't my business, but I was grateful. That's how Tazia ended up working for me. Denton Wright, my best field hand, brought her here one day and, against my better judgment, I agreed to give her a try. Darned if she didn't out-clear, out-hoe, and out-sow every man on the team. (Chuckles) They were more resentful than my wife and daughter were about the cat.

Gemma: (Writes down name of Denton Wright; important clue) That must have made it doubly hard for her to come to work. Sometimes the people I report on threaten to sue me, but if my co-workers treated me with hostility, I don't know that I'd have the strength to face them every day.

Hampus: If you're anything like your mother, and I expect you are more than you realize, the challenge would make you dig in. And, if you're like Tazia, you'd succeed in winning them over.

Gemma: I never thought of my mother as trying to win people over. Not that she isn't liked, but she holds herself apart.

Hampus: Nellie would come back with the water bucket, feeling bad that the men wouldn't eat or drink with Tazia. But your mother worked hard, and didn't hog the credit, so she eventually earned their respect. In the end, she also gained their trust.

Gemma: Hard work. That sounds like my mother. She's also trustworthy, especially if you count her keeping her mouth shut.

Hampus: In this case, it was the opposite. Not long after I hired her, a mob rode up screaming that I was a nigger lover. When they saw a white woman here, they went crazy. Chased the field hands back home, started a war in the street. Later I heard Tazia protected the wives and children and stood her ground when drunken ruffians threatened her. She scared or shamed them off.

Gemma: I've known my mother to stand up for others, but I had no idea she took physical risks to do so. God, she was brave.

Hampus: (Frowns) Yes, but I thought she was foolish as well. She should have stayed out of it.

Gemma: But you put yourself in the middle, hiring Negroes.

Hampus: It was dangerous enough for a man, but downright reckless for a woman. It put you at risk too.

Gemma: I think she wanted to teach me a lesson I couldn't get from books. I learnt well.

Hampus: She didn't stop with defending Negroes. Other religions too. The Pentecostal Church. I can't recall the pastor's name, but the church was something like Beacon or Lighthouse.

Gemma: (Writes down names; more leads) I read that Topeka is home to the Apostolic faith. Hopefully, the church is still around, or the pastor, or some older congregants. What happened?

Hampus: My son came back from town one day and said it was buzzing about a bloody fight between Pentecostals and one of the Catholic churches. We heard later that Tazia tried to stop it. I expect anyone who was around then would remember her.

Gemma: "*Tried* to stop it." Sounds like she failed. Maybe I'll find another article in *The Capital.*

Hampus: If you do, mail me a copy. I'd rather read a story about her than about myself. (Stands) If you don't mind, I'm anxious to head out to the fields. My grandson just bought some new kind of manufactured fertilizer and the latest IH spreader. I'm going to badger him to let me drive it.

Gemma: I see what you mean about farming not being the same as the old days.

Hampus: (Hitches overalls) Farming has changed a lot. Unfortunately, attitudes haven't.

The interview ended at 8:20 AM.

chapter 31

This is Gemma Kane, speaking with Alonzo Jesse Balter, the pastor at Lighthouse on the Rock Apostolic Church, in Topeka, Kansas. Today is Wednesday, May 24, 1961, and the time is 1:30 PM.

Gemma: What a lovely church. Catholic cathedrals are beautiful, but I can see how you feel closer to God in a smaller place like this.

Pastor Balter: We believe in a personal connection to Jesus. An intimate space is conducive to that.

Gemma: I'm surprised that you're still the pastor after all these years.

Pastor Balter: (Chuckles) My wife has been urging me to retire for the last ten, but you never retire from serving the Almighty.

Gemma: What brought my mother to your church?

Pastor Balter: Anger at her own. Lighthouse had outgrown this place—it was even smaller then—so we started to build a new church down the street from Heart of Mary, where Tazia was a member. Imbued with the Lord's power, we never considered that our faith wasn't welcomed by others. People at your mother's church threatened to burn ours down. She came here to warn me.

Gemma: (Shakes head) Seems like folks in Topeka often threaten to burn things down.

Pastor Balter: The Plains are dry, so it's a surefire means of destruction. (Ducks) Sorry, my wife threatens to clip my tongue if I don't stop making puns. I've prayed to change my ways, but, so far, the Lord has been silent on the matter.

Gemma: (Grins) So what happened between the churches?

Pastor Balter: We faced off. Us with construction tools, them with sticks and torches. I told your mother to stay away, but she was stubborn. Worse than that, reckless. She should have worried what would become of you if something happened to her. I told her she was being irresponsible.

Gemma: What did she say?

Pastor Balter: Nothing. She took you to a safe place, then showed up alone at Heart of Mary.

Gemma: Mmm. It seems she didn't fear physical confrontations, even if she avoided emotional ones.

Pastor Balter: To be frank, it was wrong of your mother to sacrifice your wellbeing for her own moral principles. That's *not* what God asks of us. I assume that goes for Catholicism too. (Frowns) I won't deny she was brave, though, standing up to the deacon and his men at her church. I don't know who your father was, or how to help you find him, but the inheritance you get from your mother alone is enough to bless you in this world and welcome you into the next.

Gemma: Thank you for your kind words. Back to the two churches, did my mother succeed?

Pastor Balter: Not at first. We abandoned the new building, or things would have gotten uglier. That defeat turned out to be our salvation, though, because it restored our humility. Instead of erecting a grand structure, we added on to this one without getting too full of ourselves again.

Gemma: How did my mother take her failure?

Pastor Balter: I prefer to call it a temporary setback. A few years later, after hail destroyed Heart of Mary, Tazia convinced the Catholics to let us help them rebuild. (Laughs) She knew enough to give up on the men and instead rallied the women, for the sake of the children. Our churches remained friendly for a long time after that. We stood with the Negroes when they battled to get their children a decent education. Held a big social together when the Brown decision came down.

Gemma: My mother would be pleased to know the Catholics were on the right side of that cause.

Pastor Balter: Her faith went deep. I told her she was filled with the Word of Wisdom, a bridge between Heaven and Earth. (Rubs upper lip) I was struck by her curiosity about our religious beliefs and practices. Not that she was looking to convert, but I think she had her doubts.

Gemma: (Astonished) My mother had doubts?

Pastor Balter: Doesn't everyone? In my experience, the deeper the faith, the more probing the questions. Tazia was searching, not deserting. (Smiles) You on the other hand would have gladly come over to our side. Ours is a joyful service. You were infatuated with the laying on of hands.

Gemma: (Blushes) I guess many people are intrigued with the ... unusual parts of your practice.

Pastor Balter: No need to apologize. The difference is that children don't judge the way adults do. Except for your mother. She was the most tolerant, and courageous, woman I ever knew.

Gemma: I'm beginning to see how extraordinary she was for her time. Truth be told, I always saw something cowardly in her taking flight, but now I appreciate her gutsiness not budging in the face of prejudice. (Puzzled) Running, but also staying. How would you explain the paradox?

Pastor Balter: In both cases, Tazia was defending something.

Gemma: I can see the stakes when she stayed, but what was she defending when she ran?

Pastor Balter: You. (Looks at beatific picture of Jesus above our heads) Your mother never backed away from a fight, but ultimately, I believe she desired peace. Kansas has always been a battleground state. Perhaps she ran in search of a more serene life. (Smiles) I hope she found it?

Gemma: I think she finally has, these last two years.

Pastor Balter: I'm glad, and I trust that, whatever your own search reveals, you'll respect it.

Gemma: (Reluctant to make a hard-to-keep promise, especially in a House of God) I'll try.

Pastor Balter: (Nods) Good enough. You know, Heart of Mary Church closed a few years ago. Membership dwindled until they had to be absorbed into another congregation. We don't have a relationship with that other church, but you're welcome to come to Lighthouse on Sunday.

Gemma: Thank you for the invitation. I like to think I'd attend with the same childhood openness as I did forty-five years ago, but I'm afraid I'd bring an adult sense of irreligious curiosity.

Pastor Balter: (Spread hands) Either way, we'd love to have you. If it weren't for your mother, this building that's been our home for seventy-five years wouldn't exist. Older worshipers still talk about her. (Smiles) Perhaps the laying on of hands will heal whatever sits uneasy upon your soul.

The interview ended at 2:00 PM.

chapter 32

This is Gemma Kane, speaking with husband and wife, Denton and Lula Mae Wright, friends of my mother, at their home in Kiro, Kansas, a suburb northwest of Topeka. Today is Friday, May 26, 1961, and the time is 7:45 PM.

Gemma: (Pushes back from table) What a fantastic meal. Those collard greens were delicious.

Denton: Home grown. Gardening keeps me busy since I retired.

Lula Mae: (Gently boxes his ear) Even better, it keeps him out of my hair. You brought us up to date on your mother over dinner. Now, how about you?

Gemma: I'm a labour reporter for the *San Diego Union*. My husband Todd is a lawyer, a public defender. (Laughs) I guess you could say we're both do-gooders. And our son Frankie finished college last year, majoring in architecture. You can imagine how proud Tazia is, another Italian carrying on the great tradition. He's getting married next month to a wonderful girl named Julia, which, as I mentioned on the phone, is the reason I'm on this "quest" to find his grandfather.

Lula Mae: (Raises eyebrows) You're doing this for him, not yourself?

Gemma: (Holds up hands) Okay, there's a little self-interest. Not that I'm being very successful.

Lula Mae: Did you ever think you were asking the wrong questions?

Gemma: (Defensive) I'm a reporter.

Lula Mae: Maybe you're trying to find your daddy when you should be looking for your mama.

Gemma: (Reluctant) I'm beginning to think so too, but I'm not ready to abandon my search for him. (Looks at photographs of children, grandchildren, and great grandchildren on mantel) Tell me about Mirlee Bee and her family.

Lula Mae: Her husband Thomas works for the post office. Those four children there are theirs. The oldest one is expecting this fall. Mirlee Bee's been teaching almost a quarter century now.

Gemma: Good for her. I remember when the two of us played school, Mirlee Bee was always the teacher and I was her "star" pupil. (Laughs) We both thought highly of ourselves.

Denton: Got that from your parents and ain't nothing wrong with it. Beats growing up ashamed. We wanted Mirlee Bee to be proud of her background, just like your mama wanted for you.

Lula Mae: You and Mirlee Bee had enough burdens to bear, her on account of being a coloured girl and you because you had no daddy. We had to make you both strong. I'm glad to see you turned out fine. (Leans forward) So why you want to go and shake things up at this late stage?

Gemma: Not shake things up, Lula Mae. Just take care of unfinished business.

Denton: (Lights pipe) I always believed in minding my own business.

Lula Mae: Not me. (Everyone laughs) Drove your mama crazy. I bet you poking around like this is driving her crazy too.

Gemma: I can't say she's happy about it. But my mother knows that once I've made up my mind, nothing stops me. That trait serves me well in my work.

Denton: (Puffs, smiles) Your mama the same way. Wouldn't even back down when a bunch of rednecks threatened to burn down her house. She tell you about that?

Gemma: No, but I heard a little about it from Mr Tapper. He said white men came out to the farm and then chased you all back home. He said there was a bloody battle in the street.

Lula Mae: Your mama gathered up all the women and children and took us to your house. Then that itty bitty woman scared off them drunken hooligans when they came calling. I bet they didn't admit *that* to their wives. (Hoots)

Denton: You get down to it, coloured and white men ain't so different in front of their womenfolk.

Lula Mae: Some of the women didn't want to go at first, refused to trust your mama. Couldn't figure out why a white woman would choose to live with us or want to help.

Gemma: So how did my mother persuade them to take shelter with us that day?

Lula Mae: (Points) Put you up to it. You told the children there was toys and cookies at your house and they followed you home. Their mamas had no choice but to go along too. Your mama was as poor as the rest of us, but she made sure there was enough to go around. Won them over.

Denton: Lula Mae and me tried to help your mother get along with our neighbours, but in the end, she helped herself more than we helped her.

Gemma: You were already friends with Mama before the white farmers attacked the community?

Denton: Only because my brother Elvan sent her to us. He knew her from the meat packing plant where they worked in Chicago. We wouldn't have taken Tazia in if Elvan hadn't vouched for her.

Lula Mae: Speak for yourself.

Denton: (Abashed) She's right. My wife would take in anyone, she's that good, but I was scared. It wasn't natural, and I was afraid for my family. (Lula Mae gives him the eye) And for myself.

Gemma: E-l-v-a-n? (Denton nods) Do you know which plant?

Denton: Armour.

Gemma: (Writes down this second clue; smiles) I thought so. To this day, Mama won't buy their products. What was her relationship with Elvan?

Lula Mae: Nosy as I am, some things ain't none of my business. Your mother and Elvan be one, your mother and your daddy be another. I'm sure she done got her reasons for not wanting to talk about him. On some accounts, white and coloured women ain't so different neither. (Stands to get more coffee) Mirlee Bee should be coming round about now. She won't eat my dinners, says all that fried food's too fattening, but she ain't above helping herself to my desserts.

Denton: You and her always find something to feud about.

Lula Mae: (Skips Denton's cup) Mirlee Bee and I get along just fine, Mister, and I bet that except for this dustup, Gemma and Tazia ... (Back door opens, Mirlee Bee comes in)

Mirlee Bee: (Hand over mouth) Dear Lord. Gemma?

Gemma: (Overcome) Mirlee Bee. (Long and tearful embrace; step back to look at each other)

Denton: (Red faced, looks down, but smiles) Now, now ladies.

Lula Mae: Here you two. (Hands us each a wad of tissues)

Mirlee Bee: Mama, how come you didn't tell me Gemma was coming? I might have missed her.

Lula Mae: You wouldn't have missed my sweet potato pie. I knew you'd show up. (Points at us to sit; cuts slice of pie for Mirlee Bee and seconds for the rest of us; refills Denton's coffee)

Mirlee Bee: (Waves toward pictures) I'm sure my folks done told you all about my family.

Gemma: I hear you became a teacher.

Mirlee Bee: My mother says it's on account of your mother that I did. (Looks at Lula Mae)

Lula Mae: Tazia paid the farmer's daughter to teach you when she saw you weren't learning nothing at the Negro school. Then she paid extra for Miss Nellie to teach Mirlee Bee too.

Mirlee Bee: School bored me. I might have dropped out if Nellie hadn't hooked me on learning.

Lula Mae: (Eyes drill into me) This visit be worth something if you go back and tell your mama thank you for us.

Mirlee Bee: (Nods in agreement) It made all the difference in my life. So, catch me up on yours.

Gemma: (Changes tape) Your parents can fill you in on the details; no need to repeat myself and bore them. If you're wondering why I came back to Topeka, though, it's because I'm on the trail of my father. Not having much luck, I admit. But with my son getting married in a few weeks, I thought it would make a terrific wedding gift to present him with his grandfather.

Mirlee Bee: I was too young when you lived here to be much help with that. But seeing as how I'm going to become a grandmother in a few months, I think that if you find him, he'll be excited to know he's a grand-daddy. Hopefully, it won't be too long before you're a grandma yourself.

Lula Mae: (Cuts Mirlee Bee another slice of pie) I bet Gemma let Tazia dote on her boy Frankie. Mirlee Bee complained I spoilt her babies rotten. Wouldn't hardly let me look after them.

Mirlee Bee: Mama! How can you say such a mean thing? (Shoves away plate; folds arms) You wait and see if I bring that new great grand baby around after that. Humph.

Denton: (Wags head at me) See what I mean about them two always feuding? Over nonsense.

Gemma: (Laughs) At least Lula Mae speaks her mind. My mother holds it in.

Lula Mae: I'm sure your mama done talk proud about you being a reporter. (Squeezes Mirlee Bee's hand) Just like I'm proud of my daughter teaching.

Mirlee Bee: (Squeezes back) My folks encouraged me, and Nellie Tapper was a mentor. By then, Negro schools weren't as bad as when we went. In fact, of the five districts in the Supreme Court case, Topeka was the only one where conditions were almost equal to the white schools.

Denton: Mirlee Bee knows all about this legal stuff. My girl could have been a lawyer.

Mirlee Bee: Coloured children still had to travel a long way to school though. Topeka argued that the district provided free busing, but they didn't say those poor children got to class too tired to learn. I used to start the day with nap time instead of a reading lesson.

Gemma: I read that Negro parents protested as far back as 1917, when we still lived here.

Lula Mae: Your mama wanted to march with us, but we were afraid seeing a white lady on the line would start a riot. So she stayed in the background and fueled us with coffee and sandwiches.

Gemma: You weren't even asking for the schools to be integrated, just better. All the same, you were forty years ahead of the times.

Mirlee Bee: Brown changed the law seven years ago. It remains to be seen if reality catches up with it. Especially in the suburbs.

Denton: White parents tried to stop us Negroes from buying houses out here in Kiro. Didn't want little coloured children going to their schools.

Lula Mae: Ain't no one ever again gonna tell me where I can live or my grandbabies can learn.

Mirlee Bee: (Shakes head) I'm convinced the testimony that swung the Court to a unanimous decision came from the doll research by those Negro psychologists at Harvard.

Gemma: (Smiles at Denton) She's not only a legal expert; she's a shrink expert too.

Mirlee Bee: Negro kids as young as three preferred white dolls over coloured ones. Thought they were prettier and smarter. That's what finally shot down the idea of separate but equal. Children growing up seeing themselves as dirty and dumb.

Gemma: Did you see yourself as inferior to me?

Mirlee Bee: I envied your hair. It was curly like mine, but not as unruly. And your skin made me think of snow, especially on hot summer days. Did you ever think I was ugly? Or stupid?

Gemma: Gosh, no. From the moment you taught me how to play leap frog, I thought you were smarter. I also wanted dark skin that didn't show dirt, so Mama would stop trying to clean mine all the time. (Everyone laughs) More than anything, I envied your family. From what I saw living in our part of town, all Negro children had fathers.

Denton: (Puzzled) White kids did too.

Gemma: I didn't know any other white kids, except for those two orphan children at our school.

Lula Mae: You knew other white children at church.

Gemma: I didn't make the connection, maybe because church wasn't the same as home.

Lula Mae: For your mother, they were. God lived in your home.

Gemma: Yes, but she didn't bring our home to church. Mama was always wary about priests prying into our lives. I suppose because she felt guilty about my not having a father around.

Lula Mae: So by bringing that man to church for your son's wedding, are you absolving her or making her feel worse?

Gemma: I'm ... Wait a minute. The tape's about to run out. I'll get another.

Lula Mae: No need. We done said enough. (Hugs me) You come by for dinner before you leave on Sunday. You're even welcome to go to church with us beforehand. (Winks) I won't tell your mama if you pray with us Baptists or report you if you skip the Catholic service and sleep late.

The interview ended at 9:45 PM.

part nine
Tazia, San Diego, 1927-1936
chapter 33

"You said we could get a cat when we moved to San Diego." Gemma kicks the leg of the couch like a petulant child. A cloud of dust and upholstery stuffing erupts from the stained cushions.

"Sea Breeze Apartments doesn't allow pets and it's all I can afford." Tazia darns the first of a dozen holes in the arm rests. The repairs are a distraction from her worry about finding a job.

"The rent at Mrs Cerci's house was cheaper and she said we could have a cat." Gemma looks around the apartment and scrunches her face, as if it smells bad. In fact, until they cook their first meal, it smells only of the salt air for which the apartments are named.

"Her place was too small. You would have slept on a couch as bad as this one, instead of having your own room." Tazia hopes this argument will sway her daughter. The real reason she didn't want to live in the part of town called the Italian Colony was that was its own world, full of busy bodies like Mrs Cerci who'd ask about her past: where in Italy she was from, who her parents were, when she came to America, what happened to her daughter's father. They wouldn't hide their disapproval about her not being married and wouldn't take no for an answer when they tried to fix her up with a nice Italian man. In a couple of years, they'd try to marry off Gemma.

"Mrs Cerci's is closer to Our Lady of the Rosary. You could have gone to Mass every morning before work. When you get a job." Gemma puts her hands together in prayer. "You say God is the most important thing in life. I'd give up my own room to be nearer to God."

Tazia starts on the next hole, trying not to smile at her daughter's theatrics. "You'd give it up for a cat. Which you'd stop taking care of once you made friends." Gemma sneers. Tazia changes tactics. "You complain that you only have me for company. At the other apartment, you'd be surrounded by Italian ladies older than I am. Here you can meet people your own age."

"You won't let me make friends any more than Sea Breeze allows cats." Gemma falls on the couch and throws her head back as if appealing to Heaven. But Tazia knows that cats and the church have nothing to do with her misery. She's still heartbroken that Darius broke up with her back in Las Vegas. Tazia aches to confess she put him up to it, but then she'd have to explain her fear that Darius, no paragon of honesty, would accept money to extract information from Gemma which Virgil's bosses could use to help Ayal, now linked to the New York Mafia, and track them down. It would sound even crazier to Gemma's ears than to her own. If her daughter listened. More likely, she'd hear only that her mother was behind the breakup and never forgive her.

"What if I sign you up for swimming lessons? The pool on the corner is advertising ten free sessions." Tazia puts on her brightest smile.

Gemma sighs. "They just do that so you'll join when the free lessons end."

"By then, school will start, and you can take free classes there." It sounds plausible.

"Excuse me, but high school juniors do not swim. At least, not girls. Except at the beach, with boys. And then they only go in the water up to their waist. If I walk around with swimmer's hair, I'll never get another boyfriend."

"Try it," Tazia says. "If you don't like it, you can stop." She appraises her daughter's body. "You have long, beautiful legs. A slim torso. You'll glide like a mermaid in the water."

Gemma walks to her bedroom and looks in the full-length mirror. She returns smiling but quickly frowns when she catches Tazia smiling back. "Will you buy me a new bathing suit?"

They can't afford it but Tazia agrees. Two days later, Gemma takes her first swim class. When Tazia gets back from job hunting, she asks how she enjoyed it.

"It was okay." Gemma, on the couch, doesn't look up from the *Vogue* left behind by the previous tenant.

"I promised that if you didn't like it, you didn't have to go back." Tazia holds her breath.

Gemma hastily puts down the magazine. "I'll go," she says, failing to suppress a smile.

***

The following week, Tazia begins working as a cleaning lady at the San Diego Naval Base. Mrs Cerci, whose husband is a tuna fisherman, had suggested she apply for a job at a canning factory. One way or the other, the tuna industry employs most of the city's Italians. Thinking of her time at the meat packing plant in Chicago, Tazia shudders at the thought of stuffing fish into tins.

Captain Robert Morris, the Commanding Officer, tells her the pay is twelve dollars for a five-day week. It's what she earned in Las Vegas, working an extra day and longer hours, but the cost of living here is higher. However, the base is clean, the air is cool, and the boss seems nice. She'll make the money stretch. Captain Morris hands her a list of duties: empty trash; clean and supply rest rooms; sweep, mop, polish, and/or vacuum floors; clean furniture, fixtures, and equipment; wash windows and mirrors; mix cleaning solutions according to specifications. She turns the page over. On the flip side are the janitors' duties, the same with the sole addition of cleaning heating and cooling vents, only their pay is two dollars more.

"I'd prefer the janitor job if there's an opening," she says.

"There is, but you can't apply for it."

"I can do the extra work. I've even got basic carpentry skills if those are required."

"Sorry. Janitorial positions are reserved for men. Women can only be cleaning ladies."

Tazia discovers what else is and isn't allowed under military rules, but their predictability is soothing, unlike the turmoil at home with her teenage daughter. Not that the men on base are orderly. They pass inspection on the outside, but in the privacy of the bathroom or kitchen galleys, they're slobs. They also complain as much as Gemma—the recruits that they're paid less than enlisted men, and the civilians about earning less than the military. The only creature who performs without complaint is the base cat, Sailor Boy, who Captain Morris says he hired for his unparalleled mousing skills. As happened with cats in her previous jobs, Tazia is the one person to whom Sailor Boy exposes his belly, rewarding her by purring like a ship's engine at full throttle.

Tazia in return rewards the cat with extra tinned goods, purloined from the pantry. On Wednesdays, when the supply officer inventories paper products, he's lax about checking the food. Captain Morris summons

Tazia to his desk one Thursday. "I have a requisition for a larger than usual order of tuna. Either the cook's count isn't accurate or the men are sneaking cans for midnight snacks. Have you seen or smelt telltale signs when you clean their berths?"

"No, sir. I've noticed other things that I don't care to mention, but not food."

The captain clears his throat. "I know it's not easy to support your daughter and yourself on your salary. So, if you ever find you need to supplement ..."

Goodness, he thinks Tazia is taking the tuna to feed herself and Gemma. She quickly dispels that notion. "With your permission, sir, I believe Sailor Boy is the most underpaid civilian here. I propose we redistribute surplus tuna from the kitchen galley to his bowl."

Captain Morris is taken aback. "Won't that lower the number of mice he eats?"

"If that happens, sir, you can rescind the order and I'll cut back accordingly."

The captain smiles. "I believe that complies with regulations."

Having provided for the cat, Tazia remains stressed about her own household. Observing that many officers are unmarried or far from their families, she posts a sign offering her services as a laundress. Captain Morris is the first to respond. He offers to pay her ten cents a shirt.

"Fifteen," Tazia counters.

"Higher pay grades are reserved for those with experience," he jokes.

"I have experience. Ten years. At a Chinese laundry. In Las Vegas. Where winds kick up dust that gets ground into everything." Too late, Tazia bites her tongue. He doesn't need to know where she's worked—or lived—before.

The captain holds up his hands. "Okay, you got me. Fifteen cents a shirt."

"Forget what I said. Ten is fine." Tazia's stomach roils like a ship caught in a storm.

Captain Morris looks puzzled. "What changed your mind?" He waggles a finger and grins. "Are you keeping secrets for the Mafia?"

Just then Sailor Boy saunters by and drops on his back. Tazia, grateful for an excuse not to look at the captain, kneels to pet him. "He was down three mice last week," she says. "I'll cut back his tuna allowance by one tin. Sometimes being overpaid can be as bad as being underpaid."

***

Fall comes and with it, the start of school. When Tazia gets home after the first day, her moody child is bouncing on the couch. "You were right, Mama. I already made a new friend."

"Who is she?" Tazia asks, hoping it is indeed a "she," well-behaved, and a good student.

"Yolanda Soto. She's smart and popular, so she can introduce me around." Tazia would prefer an Italian name, but Spanish is the norm here. "Saturday, we're going to Balboa Park. Sunday, I'm invited for gorditas. Yolanda says her mom's are the best." When Tazia winces, Gemma promises to bring her friend home for ravioli and burbles on, "The Sotos go to church. Yolanda's going to take me to Mission Basilica San Diego de Alcalá. It was built a hundred and fifty years ago."

"A Spanish church?"

Gemma's eyes narrow. "A Catholic church."

"Some Italian churches date back hundreds of years."

Gemma throws up her hands. "Not in this part of the world." She locks herself in her room and turns on the radio. Mexican music leaks out from under the door. When Tazia calls to her that dinner is ready, Gemma says she's not hungry.

Breakfast the next morning is silent. That evening, however, as if the previous twenty-four hours never happened, Gemma announces that she and Yolanda have joined the girls' swim team. Coach Brooks is conducting trials tomorrow and wants Gemma to go out for competitive diving. She has the build for it. Gemma hugs Tazia. "You were right to sign me up for swimming lessons, Mama." She hesitates. "There's no cost to join the team, but we have to buy our own swimsuits. Six to start with." Tazia calculates. She'll have to launder thirty shirts to pay for each one.

Gemma brings up Yolanda's name in every conversation, more than she used to talk about Darius. "We're going to Inspiration Point Sunday," Gemma declares in early December. "You can see the whole valley from there. Yolanda's mom is packing us a picnic lunch."

Tazia's face falls. "What about our dinner after church? We were going to make Christmas biscotti for me to give Captain Morris and for you to give your teachers. And Coach Brooks."

"For goodness sakes, Mama. Only little kids give presents to their teachers."

"Then how about a tour of the base? I've never shown you where I work."

"Just what I want to see. The supply closet, squeegees, and rows of polished desks."

The dismissal stings. "I just thought ..." Tazia stops. If she holds on too tight, Gemma will claw her way free. On Sunday, while her daughter is out, Tazia spends hours making gorditas to surprise her when she comes home. Gemma thanks her but the half-eaten meat pies make it clear they're not as good as Yolanda's mother's. "You haven't asked Yolanda over for ravioli yet," she reminds her. "Next weekend," Gemma promises, then retreats to her room and tunes in the station that plays Mexican ballads. Tazia dumps the leftover gorditas and silently cries herself to sleep.

***

That spring, Tazia and Gemma hear on the radio that Charles Lindbergh will fly from Rockwell Field to New York, where he'll attempt the first solo trans-Atlantic flight. Days later, Gemma comes home gushing. "Guess what? Mr Soto works for Ryan Airlines, the company that built the Spirit of St. Louis. He can bring his family to the takeoff, and since I'm practically Yolanda's sister, they invited me to go with them." Tazia feels excluded but is thrilled for her daughter.

The day of the event, Gemma tries on five outfits before deciding on the green skirt and cardigan that match her eyes. Tazia hands her a green and blue paisley scarf Captain Morris gave her for Christmas. Gemma is so excited she forgets to kiss her goodbye when the Sotos pick her up. So Tazia is puzzled when, that evening, she comes home subdued. "We were at the far end of the viewing stand," Gemma says "with two other Mexican families and one Chinese. There was no rope, but everyone took it for granted that immigrants would sit apart from the white people."

Tazia puts an arm around her daughter's shoulder. "For most of us, life here is better than what we left behind. Still, discrimination hurts."

"That's not what I'm upset about."

"What then? You couldn't see the takeoff from where they made you sit?"

Gemma unties the scarf and twists it in a knot. "Was my father an illegal immigrant? Is that why you're so secretive about him? Was I smuggled into America? Am I not a U.S. citizen?"

Tazia, perplexed, extracts the scarf and smooths it on the table. "I've told you many times you were born in Chicago. You know I don't lie."

"If there's nothing to hide, what's the name of the hospital where you gave birth to me?"

"You were born at home."

"Prove it."

Tazia goes into her bedroom and returns with Gemma's birth certificate. DEPARTMENT OF HEALTH, CITY OF CHICAGO, BUREAU OF RECORDS are the three lines across the top. On the bottom, a stamped name reads Chester A. Walters, Asst. Registrar. In between is the child's name, sex, colour, and date of birth: Gemma Gatti, female, white, August 16, 1911. Below, on the line that asks for the mother's name, her name before marriage, place of birth, age, and number of previous children is written Tazia Gatti, same, Italy, seventeen (17), and none (0). The space to the left for entering the father's name, birthplace, age, and occupation is blank. Gemma reads it, hands it back to Tazia, and retreats to her room. She doesn't turn on her radio.

***

By Monday morning, Gemma remains subdued but no seems longer angry. Tazia can't tell if she's relieved to know she's a citizen or resigned to her mother's reticence. Either way, the mood will pass. Tazia, however, finds herself growing angry that the birth certificate asked for the father's occupation but not the mother's. Maybe American women stay home, but immigrant mothers like her are forced to go to work. And earn less than men who do the same job.

Later that day, polishing the floor in the office adjoining the loading dock, Tazia has an idea. The Navy has a job category for civilians who transport supplies and spare parts around the base. The grade and pay scale are higher than hers, without separate classifications based on sex. For the next four Saturdays, while Gemma is off with Yolanda, Tazia takes driving lessons, the lone woman in the class. On the first day of summer, she presents Captain Morris with her license. "I'd like to apply for a transport job," she says.

He shakes his head, hands back her license.

"Why not?" she asks. "The listing doesn't specify the person's sex."

"Because there are no women with that classification. It's assumed they're all men."

"The regulations don't say women are not eligible, do they?" Tazia points to a dark blue binder on the shelf she dusts weekly. "So, by the rules of Navy protocol, women are eligible."

Captain Morris takes back her license. "I don't suppose I can pass this up the Chain of Command, but I'm willing to give you a try." He hands

Tazia a set of keys and a requisition for towels, toilet paper, and window cleaner. "Distribute them equally to units 7, 12, and 16. Oh, and Tazia." She stops for further orders. "Please don't take up smoking next. It bothers my sinuses."

The following week, another opportunity presents itself. When several janitors contract a stomach flu, Tazia takes over vacuuming air vents, and cleaning and oiling fan blades. As long as she's at it, she replaces loose screws and shims the captain's wobbly desk.

"Where did you learn to use tools like that?" Captain Morris asks, admiring the work.

"On a job where my boss wasn't such a stickler for the rules." Tazia tosses the keys in the air, catches them, and snatches the supply order from his desk. She's giddy on the way to the van.

In mid-July, Tazia reports back for the captain's evaluation. He grimaces. "I'm sorry. I couldn't move the request up the Chain of Command. The rule is that women can only type or clean." Tazia is angry and disappointed. "The best I can do." the captain continues, "is increase your pay fifty cents a week. Also, I'll authorize your access to a base car for personal use. When school starts this fall, you can pick up Gemma after swim practice and take her to diving meets."

Tazia's shoulders slump. It is not the victory she thought she'd earned. "One more thing," the captain says. "I'll keep the tank filled so you don't have to spend your extra pay on gas."

***

At the first meet of the season, Tazia sits with the Sotos. Other than the occasional nod and hello at school assemblies, they have never actually talked. Mr and Mrs Soto are accompanied by Yolanda's older brother, who is leaving next week to study engineering at UCLA. He blushes when his parents speak of their pride at having come so far in just one generation.

"What do you think Yolanda will do when the girls graduate at the end of this year?" Tazia asks. The indoor smell of chlorine is disorienting after the familiarity of fresh salt air.

"She's applying to UCLA too," answers Mrs Soto. "What about Gemma?"

"We haven't talked about it much," Tazia admits, "but I hope she'll go to San Diego State Teachers College. I can't afford to send her out of town."

"Your daughter's smart," says Mr Soto. "Maybe she'll get a scholarship."

A whistle blast gets everyone's attention. "Meet's starting," Mr Soto says. Coach Brooks organizes the team according to sex and event—swimmers by stroke, divers into low and high board—and delivers a pep talk. His words can't be heard in the stands, but he bounces on his feet, waves with abandon, and grins nonstop. The students listen, rapt and unblinking.

Tazia, whose has never met the coach either, is surprised to a see well-muscled, forty-ish man, with graying beach blonde hair. From the way Gemma refers to him, switching from Coach Brooks to Reggie, short for Reginald, Tazia expected someone not much older than his students. But he is a few years older than Tazia, and they regard him with the adoring eyes of children still young enough to worship their fathers. After each event, they look toward him for approval. The loyalty he evokes pays off; their team wins most of the competition.

Gemma scores the highest points for any dive that day. Tazia doesn't know the names of each somersault and twist, but Gemma is like a rare sea creature soaring through the air, slicing into the icy blue pool, and resurfacing a heartbeat before Tazia worries she won't. Only when Gemma runs to the coach for a big towel and an even bigger smile, does Tazia fear for more than her daughter's safety. Coach Brooks, like a benign father, threatens to lure Gemma to his watery lair. Tazia feels like she's the one in danger of drowning.

***

The following spring, Tazia returns home from work to find Gemma waiting for her with a thick envelope and two cups of espresso. Her eyes are lit with excitement, but her fingers drum the table. She slides the letter across its beige Formica surface for Tazia to read.

Dear Gemma Gatti:

The Admissions Committee is pleased to inform you that you have been admitted to attend the University of California at Los Angeles, beginning with the 1929 fall semester. Admission is highly competitive; your acceptance thus reflects the high caliber of your achievements. Our sincere congratulations. We are further pleased to announce that you have been awarded a scholarship from the Athletic Department in the sport of Diving.

The enclosed materials detail the terms of your admission and the amount of this award. Please complete and return all the forms within four weeks of

*receiving this letter. We look forward to hearing from you and welcoming you
to our campus.*
  Sincerely,
  Office of Admissions

Tazia takes a gulp of coffee, then two more, before she speaks. "You
didn't tell me you applied to UCLA. I thought you were going to live at
home and go to school in the city."

Gemma extracts a sheaf of papers from the envelope and shoves them
toward her mother. "They're giving me a full scholarship. Tuition, room
and board, plus a stipend for transportation and books. It won't cost much
more than if I stay here and go to the state teacher's college."

"We already spend every penny I earn. I budgeted so you could continue
your education here. You'll have to tell them no."

"I won't. I'll get a job sweeping classrooms if that's what it takes."

"I'm a cleaning lady. I won't allow my daughter to be one."

"You won't allow your daughter to do anything. It's stifling, but one way
or another, I'm going to escape. If I can't go away to college, I'll ship out
with the Navy as a nurse's aide or radio operator. It's your choice. Either
I go a hundred miles north to Los Angeles or I sail to the other side of
the world." Gemma snatches the papers, dumps her coffee, and leaves for
Yolanda's.

Early the next morning, before going to work and while Gemma gets
ready for school, Tazia knocks on the office door of Coach Brooks. He
ushers her in with a smile as wide as the one he bestows on his students.
"Isn't it wonderful? I'm so proud of Gemma. You must be too."

"She didn't tell me she applied to UCLA. I signed a form for the state
teacher's college. Period." Tazia refuses the coach's offer of coffee.

He frowns. "I assumed you knew. That's why I recommended her for the
scholarship." They let the implication that Gemma falsified the parental
signature hang in the air. Coach Brooks smiles again. "Obviously, she
wants to go very badly. She's a talented diver and will be an asset to their
team. More than that, your daughter is highly intelligent. Whatever she
decides to major in, she'll be a success. And a credit to you."

"I don't need empty compliments," Tazia says. "Nor does my daughter
need someone who acts like a father encouraging her to leave home."

The coach blinks. "I don't blame you for being upset, but the idea wasn't
mine. It was Gemma's. All the kids talk about going to UCLA. At their

age, they want to break free." He hesitates. "I know you two are close. It would be good for her to get a little distance."

Tazia rises. "Don't you dare tell me what's good for my child."

"Forgive me for speaking out of turn. I'm only saying what I think is good for all children. More so for those whose parents came to this country and struggled so their kids could have the opportunities they didn't." He points to himself. "Mine were Irish sheep farmers."

"Being a teacher is an opportunity. Aren't your parents proud that you became one?"

He smiles. "Very proud. But Gemma has the brains and drive to be anything she wants. Would you deny her that chance?"

Tazia sits again. "She *is* smart. And determined to get what she wants." Like Ayal, she muses. The coach looks straight her. She holds his gaze for five seconds. "I'll think about it. Now, I can't be late for work." She stands to go but turns back at the door. "Gemma doesn't know ..."

Coach Brooks nods solemnly. "This conversation is between us. You're Gemma's parent. What you tell her is your business." He smiles and waves Tazia down the hall.

All day, Tazia's tears stain the faucets as fast as she scrubs them. In the afternoon, she picks up Gemma after diving practice. "I've done some figuring. If you get a lifeguard job this summer, and Captain Morris lets me use the car to and from work, instead of taking the bus, we can afford it." Her heart pounds. "I only calculated for one year. We'll see how it goes after that."

Gemma hugs her so hard that Tazia momentarily swerves before regaining control of the car. "Thank you, Mama. You're the best mother ever. I'll visit every chance I get."

"The door's always open." So is Tazia's heart, and it hurts. Yet if she doesn't let Gemma leave, the door will close. When Tazia left home, she never saw her own mother again. Of course, they were separated by an ocean, not a hundred miles of road. Gemma has Ayal's brains, but she's also like Tazia, stubborn and strong willed. She can only hope her daughter makes wiser choices.

chapter 34

Dear Mama:

Third semester, and I still pinch myself to prove I'm really here. My new roommate, Irene, is sweet, rich but not stuck up. The UCLA diving team is top notch. I'm practicing a longer handstand and straighter angle of entry, also a winning smile for the judges. Not too much, though. Overcorrecting a smile can get you marked down as much as overcorrecting a dive.

My favourite class is journalism with Dr Morton Stein. Other professors focus on the boring mechanics of writing, like making the subject and verb agree. He cares more about the content, like making a story newsworthy. He says if we pay attention to how a piece reads, then writing it will flow. Professor Stein's main interest is labour issues. You'd like him.

Are you still taking the bus up for Parents Weekend? If you come Friday morning, you can go to journalism class with me that afternoon. My next assignment is to interview you about why you came to America and ended up in California. I know you hate questions but you don't want me to get a failing grade, do you? So pretty please put your mouth in gear. Too bad you can't drive a base car here, but hopefully Captain Morris will let you take the whole day off.

Amore e baci,

Gemma

Captain Morris would, if he were still Tazia's boss. And let her make up the lost hours. However, he's been replaced by Captain Nimitz, a stickler for rules. Not only must Tazia forfeit wages to visit Gemma, she has to scrimp for bus fare. The new captain's first order was to rescind her pay increase. She's had to cut Sailor Boy's tuna ration and limit use of a base car to official chores.

Dr Stein delivers a lively lecture about employers forcing workers to sign a statement that they will not join a union. "It was a reporter in the *United Mine Workers Journal* who first called them 'yellow-dog contracts.' Why do you think he gave them that name?"

Three hands go up. One boy guesses it's for the colour of the rag paper they're printed on, another jokes that the agreements are as lame as stray mongrels. Dr Stein calls on Gemma. "They reduce employees to the level of dogs that the bosses can kick around. Workers sign away their constitutional right to organize."

The professor beams. "Excellent analysis, as usual, Miss Gatti." He surveys the visiting parents and points a chalk-covered finger at a father. "Did you ever sign that type of contract?" The man squirms and admits he's one of the "bosses" who make employees sign them. Dr Stein singles out another father, who says, "I'm not fond of unions, or FDR, but if it's a constitutional right ..." He looks to his son for support. The boy blushes and stares at his desk.

A beefy man's hand goes up. "I signed one, so I could feed my family. But me and my buddies are organizing." He looks around. "I hope there ain't no spies here to report me."

Amid nervous laughter, Dr Stein turns to Tazia, the only woman there without a husband. She wonders what Gemma said to him about her. "Please tell us what your experience has been." His voice is respectful, not as challenging as when he addressed the men.

"Mostly I've worked for individuals, not companies, so it hasn't come up." Tazia hopes that's the end of the questioning.

"Where?" the professor demands, his voice more aggressive.

"Different places." Tazia glances sideways at Gemma, whose pen is poised over her paper.

"And now?" Dr Stein persists.

"I work for the government."

Dr Stein's face lights up. "Do you think public employees deserve the right to unionize?"

Tazia takes a deep breath. As long as the question is impersonal, she might as well speak her mind. "If conditions are unfair, they should be allowed to organize." She points a finger back at the professor. "But even if men are allowed to form a union, they wouldn't let women join."

To her surprise, Dr Stein roars with laughter. "No doubt you're right. It's obvious where your daughter gets her fire from."

Later, over dinner in the dorm cafeteria, Gemma's spaghetti sits neglected while she raves about Professor Stein. "Isn't he cool? I knew you'd like him. He liked you."

"I can see you're learning a lot in his class." Tazia doesn't eat either.

"I've decided to major in journalism. Dr Stein thinks I'd be a great investigative reporter. I want to focus on labour issues."

"Your letter said that was his specialty." Tazia sees the worship in Gemma's eyes. It seems her daughter is bound to seek out fathers. This one is Jewish to boot, with an unnerving tendency to probe into others' lives, albeit to teach his students a moral lesson.

"I'm doing it for you, Mama. You got kicked around your whole life. It's time workers were treated like people, not dogs." She lifts her water glass. "To stoking the fire of indignation."

Tazia clinks her glass against Gemma's. "To the workers of the world, especially the women." She hopes Gemma's career choice is indeed inspired by her, not by Dr Stein.

Dear Mama:

I'm coming home next week to march with you at the Lemon Grove Grammar School rally. It's outrageous that the San Diego School Board approved building a separate facility for Mexican children. Most of them were born in this country. And for them to claim the new school would be more sanitary, and "Americanize" the children (what does that mean?), plus provide "backward and deficient students" with more appropriate instruction, is downright offensive.

Anticipating a bite of your biscotti is making me salivate. Bake a double batch because I'll be bringing a friend with me. No need to meet us at the bus stop. We're driving down.

Amore e baci,

Gemma

Tazia rereads the last paragraph. On previous visits, Gemma's asked to bring home a girlfriend. No longer threatened by these relationships, Tazia admires how easily her daughter gets to know people. It's a useful skill for a journalist. However, this is the first time Gemma has announced, not asked permission to invite, a guest. One who owns a car. And is missing the word "girl" before "friend." Anxious as this makes her, Tazia looks forward to the visit. She's lonely. Sailor Boy died last week and was buried at sea. Tazia sewed him into a canvas bag with a chunk of concrete and the base chaplain said a nondenominational prayer. Captain Nimitz hasn't issued an order to replace the cat, despite the mounting mouse population.

Monday morning, Gemma and Todd Kane, a pre-law student, pull up in his car. He is tall, red-haired, lightly freckled. Nice looking. Tazia judges his car is neither old nor new, and gently battered, typical for an undergraduate. Over coffee and cookies, they chat about school, today's demonstration, and Todd also being an only child. Not typical for an Irish Catholic family.

Todd drives them to the rally, where they gather under a sign reading *Ningún estudiante en La Caballeriza*. "No students at The Stable," he translates. It's the parents' nickname for the Mexican-only school. During the fiery speeches, Todd again interprets key phrases for Tazia and Gemma. *Nuestros hijos son ciudadanos estadounidenses*—"Our children are U.S. citizens."

"How do you know Spanish?" Tazia studies Todd again. It's unlikely he has anything other than Irish blood in his veins.

"Classes. I want to be a public defender and many of my clients won't speak English." He smiles. "I'm learning Italian too, so I can communicate with Gemma."

Tazia laughs. "But my daughter barely speaks Italian."

"That's not true, Mama," Gemma protests. "*Parlo molto bene italiano.*"

"Espresso, biscotti, ravioli," Tazia snorts. "That's not Italian."

"*Posso avere più soldi?*" Gemma tries.

"No, you may not ask your mother for money." Todd tweaks Gemma's nose. She blushes and looks at Tazia, who laughs. Better her daughter look at him with adoration than at Dr Stein.

Committee members circulate among the crowd, collecting money. Tazia empties all her coins in the donation box. Todd stuffs it with bills. She waits for a sign that he's showing off, but he immediately begins reading a pamphlet. Tazia decides he's genuine and accepts his offer to buy lunch. The sandwich shop isn't fancy, yet she feels guilty at her pleasure in being served.

For the rest of the visit, Gemma's eyes flit between her mother and her boyfriend. "We're staying in L.A. the first half of spring break," she says, giving Tazia a hug before getting into the car, "but we'll come down here the second half." There is no mistaking the double use of "we." Todd says he enjoyed meeting Tazia and thanks her for the cookies she gives them for the road.

Watching them drive off, Tazia feels torn. Pulling her one way is the realization that Todd is a fine young man. He's Catholic, cares for Gemma, and supports the right causes. If Gemma hadn't gone away to college, she might have ended up marrying a sailor with the unsavoury habits Tazia has come to know too well. Todd also has money, not too much and not on display, and his eyes are green, like Gemma's, so they will give her green-eyed grandchildren. Other than his not being Italian, he's ideal. Then what is this doubt tugging Tazia the opposite way? Todd is exactly what she wants for Gemma, someone who can give her daughter a better life. Perhaps therein lies her dissatisfaction. Todd is from another world, one that Gemma is increasingly comfortable in, but one that Tazia is afraid she herself will always feel excluded from.

chapter 35

Graduation Day. Tazia, together with Yolanda's parents, sits in the stadium, craning to see their daughters amid a throng of blue and gold robes. A student dressed as a bear cavorts on the field. The buzz in the air reminds Tazia of the bees that swarmed through the hills of Loro Piceno. Joy mixed with sorrow overcome her. What would her parents make of their grandchild earning a college degree? She lifts her face to the sun and recites a prayer of thanks. "Benedictus Deus, Bless His Holy Name, for today's special gift and the lifetime gift of my daughter. Amen."

"There they are," says Mrs Soto. Over her cap, Yolanda has draped her grandmother's mantilla. Gemma wears a radiant smile. There are too many tall, young men for Tazia to pick out Todd. Thank goodness, in the crush of people, she won't have to meet his parents today. Right after the speeches, the Sotos will drive them back to San Diego. To Tazia's delight, Gemma is excited to return home, where she has a job interview with the *San Diego Union*. She even asked Tazia to help her shop for a dress. "You know well-made clothes, Mama, even if you don't buy anything nice for yourself." Gemma promises that once she earns good money, she will dress her mother in style. A nice thought, but Tazia has no intention of letting her daughter provide for her.

After the ceremony, Tazia makes her way to the library where, Gemma said, other families weren't likely to meet up. Sure enough, only two parents are waiting, the father tall with fading red hair, the mother slim with faint freckles. She has no doubt they belong to Todd. Their clothes are not ostentatious, but Tazia does indeed recognize fine tailoring. When Gemma arrives, they hug her. Tazia has met Todd half a dozen times, but her daughter has spent many weekends with his parents, who live in the hills overlooking Los Angeles. Gemma makes introductions.

"I'm glad our first meeting is on such a happy occasion," says Maura Kane. "We'd love to celebrate by treating you and Gemma to dinner," adds Patrick. "I've taken the liberty of making reservations for five at the Biltmore."

"That's so kind." Tazia notices a spot she missed when she polished her shoes last night. "But we're driving back to San Diego with friends of Gemma's, and we can't miss our ride."

"The Sotos can take my stuff, Mama. Todd will drive us home later. Is that okay, honey?" Gemma squeezes Todd's elbow. He says he's happy to and can spend the night with a fraternity brother. That's where he plans to stay during his future, and frequent, trips to San Diego. He'll work for his father's oil company over the summer, then attend Stanford Law School in the fall. "I think Yolanda's feelings would be hurt," Tazia admonishes, "and it treats her parents like they are ..." She looks at the Kanes, not sure if they will take this the wrong way. "Servants."

Gemma turns red. Tazia fidgets. "Another time," says Maura Kane, with the grace of a woman practiced in smoothing over awkward moments. They chat briefly about graduation until it is time to go. Todd tells Gemma he'll be down at the end of the month. They embrace as if they will be separated for two years, not two weeks. Then Gemma follows Tazia to the Sotos' car.

***

The newspaper assigns Gemma stories about how well San Diego is surviving the Depression. Her first front-page piece describes spinoffs from the government investment in military aviation. "Consolidated Aircraft Corporation of Buffalo to Relocate All 800 Employees to San Diego." At Convair, a photographer takes pictures of the Navy flying boats they're building and she interviews workers about the joys of living in California instead of the snow belt. An infusion of WPA money keeps the Navy base busy too, with 3,000 officers and 50,000 sailors for Tazia to clean up after. But after six years, she's reached the top pay grade and complains that she's hit a "sea wall."

"I'm frustrated, too." Gemma tosses her notebook on the table, a few months into the job. "I write stories about industry with glowing quotes from owners and the Chamber of Commerce, but I know there are disaffected workers. I feel like I'm letting down Dr Stein."

This is the first time Tazia has heard the professor's name since Gemma graduated and it still irks her. "Give it time," she says, slicing a pork roast redolent with garlic. Gemma's salary, modest as it is, means they can afford an occasional splurge on meat.

"I'm letting you down too." Gemma pours them each a glass of Chianti. "I'd rather write about how government money benefits the military and the owners of companies they fund, but not a penny goes civilian workers. Especially women, like you." Gemma picks up her notepad.

"Plenty of us have worse jobs." Tazia thinks of Triangle and Armour. "Besides, I could lose mine. The same goes for others. I don't want my story in the paper."

"Whatever you say would be off the record. Ditto anyone else I interview."

"Don't interfere, Gemma. These days the only ones complaining are on the unemployment line. People with jobs keep their mouths shut."

"I've never known you to keep yours shut." Gemma glares. "I take that back. You open it to protest injustice. You glue it closed when it comes to talking about yourself."

Tazia sighs. "I can't stop you, but I've tried to teach you that speaking out should be to help others, not harm them. Writing about workers at the base could jeopardize their livelihood."

Gemma fiddles with her pen. "You're right. But there's got to be a way to expose bad working conditions that makes heads roll at the top without crippling the people on the bottom."

Tazia smiles. "You do have a way with words." Like your father, she thinks.

Gemma's break comes when she's assigned a series of articles about the tuna industry. After the Navy and aircraft manufacturers, fishing and canning is San Diego's biggest employer, bringing over $30,000,000 a year to the economy. In the first piece, Gemma tours the Van Camp Seafood Company and meets the Italian and Portuguese immigrants who work there.

Tug to Tin to Table: The Story of Tuna by Gemma Gatti, Union Feature Reporter

The plant manager takes us through the process from the moment the fleet arrives at the wharf to cans being trucked to your local store. Large cranes hoist baskets of tuna off the boats and empty them into a flume, where the fish flow a hundred yards into the cannery. After inspection, the tuna is moved on conveyor belts to a room where men gut and wash the fish, then load them into ovens for pre-cooking. After cooling, the tuna are sent to 60-foot cleaning tables, where women remove the bones and skin, and separate out the white meat. The tuna is then conveyed on wooden trays to packing tables, where more women place the meat by hand into cans. Advanced machinery then drops measured amounts of salt and oil in the cans as they move along a conveyor to lidding machines. Once sealed, the cans are steam-cooked, cooled, and readied for shipment.

***

The day the story appears, Gemma calls to say she won't be home for dinner. "You should have seen how exhausted the women looked. When I asked them how long their shift was, the manager tugged me down the line. But I sense they want to talk, so I'm hanging around until they get off."

"They could get fired," Tazia reminds her.

"Don't worry. It will all be anonymous, and I'll interview them blocks from the cannery."

"Be careful," Tazia warns. She sits at the table until Gemma comes home, shy of dawn.

Two days later, when Gemma rushes in with the paper, she crows, "At last, an article I'm proud to attach my byline to." This time, Tazia pours the wine and asks her to read it aloud.

The Sad Ballad Behind Tuna Salad by Gemma Gatti, Union Feature Reporter

Tinned tuna in our stomachs comes to us on the backs of weary workers in San Diego's canneries. Fishing boats arrive at all hours, often three or four at a time, and workers are on call to run to the canneries as soon as the fleet docks at the wharf. "It has to be packed right away," one worker explains, "no matter how flooded the cannery is with fish." "We worked straight through," another tells me after a twenty-hour shift. "No lunch, a ten-minute break for dinner. Tough luck if you have to go to the bathroom." And the women's pay for sacrificing sleep, food, and an empty bladder? Thirty-three cents an hour. "If not for the Depression," they agree, "we'd quit." "Why not protest, unionize?" I ask. "The bosses always find out who the agitators are," they whisper. "We'd be fired. You speak for us." Will you, the readers, speak out too? The next time you put a fork full of tuna in your mouth, think of the cannery workers standing day and night on their feet.

***

Tazia toasts her daughter. Each sip of wine recalls clattering sewing machines, screeching sausage grinders, bloody fingers. At Van Camp, women like herself race to keep pace with the endless sea of fish moving down the line. "No more vitello tonnato," she says, "until conditions improve."

The *San Diego Union* publishes an editorial. The *Sun* picks up the story. Grocers report a drop in sales of tinned fish. A week later, Van Camp announces a half-cent pay raise and quarter-hour break for every ten worked. Two weeks later, it's as if Gemma's article had never appeared.

"It's hopeless," she complains over a plate of plain sliced tomatoes. "Words only go so far. I became a journalist because I thought telling the truth would bring about big changes."

"Without your article, there wouldn't have been any changes. Keep at it. More will come."

"Time hasn't improved your working conditions or pay."

"The military is a man's world, cleaner than a factory, but in other ways, worse. Someday women will have more say in how things are run. Look at Eleanor Roosevelt influencing FDR"

Gemma crashes the salt and pepper shakers together. "The First Lady's power is indirect. I want women at the top, making their own decisions, instead of doing it through men."

Tazia cradles her daughter's angry hands. "Your generation will take that leap forward."

"Only if more mothers like you push us." Gemma purses her lips. "It wouldn't hurt if fathers did too."

part ten

Gemma, Chicago, 1961

chapter 36

This is Gemma Kane, speaking with Miroslav Mucha, who was my mother's foreman at the Armour meat packing plant, at his apartment on Damen Avenue on the near west side of Chicago, Illinois. Today is Monday, May 29, 1961, and the time is 3:30 PM.

Mucha: Can I offer you a beer?

Gemma: No thanks. May I get myself a glass of water? (Rinses coffee mug in sink piled with dirty dishes; shoos away flies; sits opposite Mucha at scarred wooden table)

Mucha: You won't object if I have one? (Crushes empty can of Schlitz; tosses it in trash full of empties; pops open another) American beer tastes like crap, but this brand's the local favourite. The story is that Joseph Schlitz sent kegs of his stuff to Chicago after the great fire of 1871.

Gemma: Interesting. Did Mr Schlitz think beer would help put out the fire?

Mucha: Ha. More likely, he thought we could drown our sorrows in it. (Eyes overflowing trash can, swats at fly, frowns) Some things never change.

Gemma: I'm sorry. Did I call at a bad time? I can come back later this week.

Mucha: Nah. One day ain't no better than another. (Drinks, sighs) It's the money. I worked at Armour forty years before they booted me. Without a pension. Told me there were too many accidents on my watch that cost them thousands in workmen's compensation.

Gemma: (Sympathetic) That sounds like an excuse management would use to cheat you.

Mucha: I blame the union more. If it weren't for them sissy claims, I'd have done alright.

Gemma: (Bites tongue; sips water)

Mucha: (Shrugs) Nothing I can do about it. That was fifteen years ago. I'm eighty now. Thirty-five bucks a month Social Security pays for this lousy place and two meals a day. (Points toward crumbling plaster, cracked linoleum.) Ain't bought new clothes in decades. See this? (Indicates threadbare vest.) Red and white, like the Bohemian flag. Wore it to work every day, proud of where I come from. (Swigs; burps) Can barely make out the colours now.

Gemma: I'm surprised the company didn't treat you better. You were a foreman. They acted much worse toward people on the bottom of the ladder. Like my mother.

Mucha: (Snorts) Yeah. Being shafted almost made me side with them. (Lights chewed-up cigar, coughs phlegm into grimy handkerchief) Ought to give these up (waves cigar, points to empty cans), but I'm too old to change. Health's going to hell (grins), but my memory is still good.

Gemma: (Leans forward) I'm glad to hear that since I came all this way to interview you.

Mucha: (Shakes head) Don't know why you bothered. I can't help you find your father. You're on a fool's errand anyway. I figure your mother buried her secrets fifty years ago. They're rotted in the ground by now, nothing but a useless load of dirt. (Opens another beer)

Gemma: You knew my mother right after she came to Chicago, the most likely time for some clue to slip out. Wherever she moved, the first thing she did was find a place to live and ...

Mucha: (Interrupts) She probably lived in Packingtown, like most everyone at the plant. Even if the dump is still standing, whoever lives there now ain't gonna let you poke around.

Gemma: (Waves away comment) I know. That's not where my question is going. The *second* thing she did was find a job.

Mucha: Ah, then you're in luck. I happen to remember your mother because most of the workers were from Eastern Europe, like me. She was the first Italian I hired. (Closes eyes as if picturing her) Although she wasn't the first pregnant woman without a husband hanging around.

Gemma: Did she say *anything* about my father?

Mucha: Nah. Your mother wasn't a talker. Kept her mouth shut and did her job. Some women never closed their yaps. Drove me crazy. I tried earplugs, but I then couldn't hear when the grinder clogged up or the belt stopped.

Gemma: I suppose you had to fix them right away.

Mucha: Yup. The last thing the plant could afford was a slowdown. Armour had to keep up with Swift. Between them, they must have had thousands of workers.

Gemma: (Checks notes) According to my research, the stockyards employed forty thousand people during the years my mother worked here. The number kept growing until after the war, when it became cheaper to pack and ship meat from closer to where the livestock were raised.

Mucha: (Nods) The Yards shut down a decade ago. Serves the bastards right. Not that it matters to me anymore. (Gets faraway look, refocuses on me) I suppose I should have asked this sooner, but how did you know I used to be your mother's boss? I always figured we were nameless.

Gemma: The company didn't keep records of line workers or slaughterers, but I found a list of foremen from those years. (Smiles) I'm a labour reporter. I'm good at tracking down that stuff.

Mucha: Bully for you, but back up a step. How did you know it was Armour? There were lots of plants back then, before the big companies bought them out.

Gemma: (Laughs) I remembered that my mother never bought Armour products. (Hesitates) I also talked to the brother of one of your employees, Mr Elvan Wright. Do you remember him?

Mucha: Oh, I remember Elvan all right. Not because he was The Yard's biggest nigger. (Rears back) Oops. I should have known, you being your mother's daughter, you wouldn't like that word. (Grins) I hired lots of (emphasizes) niggers. Takes one animal to kill and gut another.

Gemma: (Winces)

Mucha: (Still grinning) Reason Elvan sticks in my mind is cause the grinder ate his hand. Whole damned thing. A woman was so busy jabbering she didn't see her hair had come loose from its net. Grinder caught the tail end and pulled her head after it. For some reason, Elvan was working the line that day, not ripping out in the yard, and he reached in. Grabbed her neck just in time, but his hand ... (Grimaces) Had to shut down the line for two hours to clean up the mess. Woman didn't even thank him. She was pissed a nigger dared to touch her. (Shakes head) I never understood it.

Gemma: (Gags) I can't believe it either. A man saves your life and you're angry he touched you.

Mucha: That's not what puzzles me. It's the sacrifice that nigger made. It's one thing to give a helping hand, it's another to give one up. (Guffaws at own joke, coughs)

Gemma: (Gulps another cup of water, feels nauseous)

Mucha: (Wipes eyes) When your mother suddenly stopped showing up at work, I thought maybe she was pregnant with Elvan's baby. You got a little jigger brother or sister?

Gemma: (Takes a deep breath) Let's just say my mother's reason for leaving is another of her long-buried secrets, so there's no point in *you* trying to dig up that dirt now.

Mucha: (Chuckles) Touché. You got your mother's spunk. (Leans back, regards me) Judging by how you look and talk, I'd guess your mother done all right for herself in the end. (Throws empty beer can at trash, misses, lets can roll around on floor) Better than me.

Gemma: She never felt sorry for herself. And she found *some* kind people along the way. Friends come in all sizes and colours. You never know who's going to reach out and lend a helping hand.

Mucha: (Sneers) I could use some help. I should have asked you to pay me for this interview.

Gemma: Good reporters don't pay their sources.

Mucha: (Grins, self-satisfied) You didn't learn what you came here for anyway.

Gemma: Not about my father, but you helped me see my mother more clearly. So, off the record (hands him a twenty), buy yourself a new vest and a bigger trash can.

The interview ended at 4:15 PM.

chapter 37

This is Gemma Kane, speaking with Elvan Wright, a friend of my mother's, at his apartment on 36th Street on the south side of Chicago, Illinois. Today is Wednesday, May 31, 1961, and the time is 10:00 AM.

Gemma: I'm sorry I'm late. I was rerouted because of construction. (Laughs) I haven't lived in Chicago since I was three, so I can't pretend to know my way around.

Elvan: (Tsks) That new Dan Ryan Expressway is doing worse than making folks late. They say they're building it so it's easier to get downtown, but it just happens to runs smack dab between Bridgeport, the white neighbourhood to the west, and the Black Belt here on the east. Road just makes it easier to segregate us. In my opinion. (Grins, sheepish) Not that you asked.

Gemma: You don't have to stick to answering my questions. Tell me all about life in this town. (Grins back) Well, more about life then than now. Not that I expect things have changed much.

Elvan: Back when I came, there weren't no separate neighbourhoods for Negroes and whites. I lived in Packingtown, same as your mother. I can't think what else to tell you. And you already done told me on the phone about your visit with Denton and Lula Mae.

Gemma: (Nods) They're getting on in years. Taking care of each other. Squabbling.

Elvan: Now there's something that hasn't changed. (Chuckles) I don't get to see them much, but they send pictures of the children and grand babies. (Stares at me, shakes head) I can't believe the little baby I remember is a grown woman, sitting across the table from me. I guess when you live to be near three-quarters of a century old, you get to see everything. Tell me again about your family. I was so flummoxed when you called, whatever you said went plumb out of my mind.

Gemma: I told you about Todd, my husband. He's a public defender. And I'm a labour reporter. (Smiles) On the side of labour, not management. My son Frankie is getting married next month and I'm trying to find his grandfather—my father—as a sort of wedding present.

Elvan: I do recall that part of our phone conversation. Do you think you'll find him?

Gemma: (Grimaces) No real leads so far, but I have the feeling I'm getting closer. In the meantime, I'm learning a lot as I travel back in time to the places my mother lived.

Elvan: Learning about your mother?

Gemma: Yes. But I'm also thinking back on my own life. (Laughs at self) People don't usually do that until they've reached old age.

Elvan: Fact is, some start earlier. Others never do it. Too painful I guess. They prefer to think of the life that comes after death. Folks say that's why Negroes are partial to church.

Gemma: What about you?

Elvan: Humph. I try not to think about much at all. I used to pray, and sing too, but that seems pointless nowadays. (Looks at kitchen clock) Ten thirty is early for me. It's easier to get through the day when I don't wake up until it's half over.

Gemma: I'm sorry I made you get up early. I hope talking with me won't be painful.

Elvan: And I'm sorry I can't offer you a meal or nothing. (Holds up stump of missing right hand) I'm clumsy in the kitchen. Lula Mae keeps badgering me to move to Topeka so she can take care of me along with Denton. She says ain't no difference between babysitting one old man or two.

Gemma: (Smiles) I can just hear her. (Looks around small but tidy apartment) You manage to keep your place neat though.

Elvan: Vacuuming and dusting is things you can do with one hand. Not cooking, though.

Gemma: Mucha told me how you lost your hand, saving a woman who wasn't even grateful.

Elvan: (Looks at stump) Actually, I lost my hand in stages. I was already missing a finger or two when I met Tazia.

Gemma: (Unable to wait any longer) What exactly was your relationship with my mother?

Elvan: I wanted to marry her.

Gemma: (Dumb-founded) Why?

Elvan: Simple. I loved her.

Gemma: What did she say?

Elvan: No.

Gemma: (Takes it in) What could you possibly ...? (Hesitates) I'm sorry. I don't mean to imply any prejudice. It's just that I don't see why you'd want to marry a woman who was having another man's baby. Especially when you knew nothing about him. (Leans forward) Or did you?

Elvan: No. But knowing Tazia, I couldn't believe he was a bad man.

Gemma: Tell me what you "knew" about her. Please, please.

Elvan: (Puts hand and stump in lap; looks directly at me) She was the most unprejudiced person I ever met. Not a bone of judgment in her body. (Jerks head) Not like that woman she lived with.

Gemma: (Swallows) So the vague memories I have of that person are real, not a dream? Do you remember her name?

Elvan: I'll never forget it. (Enunciates) Veronika Nowicki. (Snorts) I expected a man like Mucha to talk down to me, but that woman called me nigger to my face. (Bangs stump on table, winces with pain) People like her are the reason I don't think about the past.

Gemma: (Writes name) There must have been lots of people the same as her.

Elvan: Yes, but none so bent on destroying *my* dreams. Plenty of bigots keep you from working, but she stopped me from loving. She turned me away from your mother and convinced her to have nothing to do with me. I hold her responsible not only for Tazia saying no, but for leaving.

Gemma: I don't know if this will make you feel better or worse, but I never knew my mother to base her life on what other people told her to do. She'd have defied this Veronika if she wanted to. (Searches Elvan's eyes) Nor would I conclude that my mother didn't love you. The only thing that would make her run was the fear that something bad would happen to me.

Elvan: I wouldn't have hurt you! I wanted to be your father.

Gemma: I'm sure she didn't think *you'd* be the one to hurt me. More likely, in the short run, she was afraid my father would look for her in another big city. And in the long run, she fled wherever she thought she could make a better life for me. If we'd stayed, I'd have missed the chances I had in California. (Speaks earnestly) On the other hand, if we hadn't left and you'd been my father, I expect I would have been satisfied and wouldn't feel a need to look for my real father now.

Elvan: (Eyes tear up)

Gemma: (Sees carvings in corner behind dresser, almost obscured by family photos; walks over to small wooden figures; sneezes) It looks like you forgot to dust this shelf.

Elvan: I can't bring myself to touch them. Or to throw them out. After losing my hand, I made a special vise to hold the wood when I carved, but my heart wasn't in it.

Gemma: (Recognizes style of carving) My mother saved a baby rattle that you must have made for me. She gave it to my son Frankie to play with it. I don't know what happened to it after that.

Elvan: (Wipes eyes) People can be cruel. When they take away your love, it robs you of your faith. You and your husband sound like good people. (Walks to shelf, picks up tiny dog, smiles at me) After seeing how well you turned out, I just might take up carving again.

Gemma: When my mother has a great-grandchild, I'll write and ask you to carve a rattle for the baby.

Elvan: (Flexes fingers on remaining hand) I just might do that too. Maybe carve something for your mother as well, if you think she'd accept it.

Gemma: I believe she'd be honoured.

Elvan: What does Tazia need?

Gemma: (Thinks) A different kind of toy. One for her beloved cat, Lucy.

The interview ended at 10:50 AM.

chapter 38

This is Gemma Kane, speaking with Veronika Nowicki, a friend of my mother's and a "second mother" to me as a baby, in the kitchen of Palermo's Italian Restaurant, at 63rd and Maplewood, in Chicago, Illinois. Today is Thursday, June 01, 1961, and the time is 3:15 PM.

Veronika: (Wipes eyes with apron) I never expected to see you again after, what, half a century?

Gemma: Almost. I was three when we left, so it's been forty-seven years.

Veronika: (Stirs huge cast iron pot of tomato sauce on industrial-size stove; wipes brow) I'm sorry, it's hot in the kitchen. (Wipes eyes again) I can't stop crying.

Gemma: The dining room is almost empty at this hour. Would your boss let us talk in there?

Veronika: The Calderones are so kind, they'd let me do anything. But their special sauce must be stirred every ten minutes, exactly, so it's better that we stay here. (Winds small music box in hutch above stove; china ballerina in tattered pink tutu begins to turn)

Gemma: How pretty. It looks old. (Listens) For some reason, the tune sounds familiar. Is it a well-known piece of music?

Veronika: *Sleeping Beauty*. But perhaps you recognize the music box itself?

Gemma: (Shakes head) I don't think so, and yet ...

Veronika: Your mother bought it for you at Marshall Field. I was angry that she spent money we couldn't afford, but later I was thankful. When she took you away, it was the one thing of yours she left behind. (Smiles, wistful) The music takes ten minutes to wind down. For months after you left, I'd allow myself a ten-minute cry in the morning and again at night. Now I use the music box to time when I have to stir the sauce.

Gemma: I'm surprised you cook in an Italian restaurant. Chicago must have lots of Polish ones.

Veronika: Yes. That's where I worked after I quit Armour. But Tazia and I taught each other our favourite dishes from home. Italians thought a Polish woman cooking lasagna would amuse the customers. They hired me to work in the kitchen and say "buona sera" to people in the dining room. I was a hit. Waiters liked me too. They got bigger tips when I came around to their tables.

Gemma: Did they split them with you?

Veronika: A few. But most were supporting families. With you gone, I had only myself to take care of. (Starts crying again) I'm seventy-three. It's time I stopped working. (Points to gray hair, wrinkles) But I have to eat. Besides, what would I do with myself except get bored and lonely?

Gemma: (Hands Veronika a Kleenex) I never thought about how our leaving affected others, but being a mother, I can imagine your pain. If it makes you feel better, now that I'm with you, a few memories are coming back. Smells more than images or sounds. Pie. Dill. Cabbage soup?

Veronika: That's right. We were poor. Soup made a filling meal. Especially if I could add a few shreds of pork. (Music box stops; stirs sauce; rewinds)

Gemma: Maybe that explains why growing up I was the only kid who liked cooked cabbage. I guess it had a pleasant association for me.

Veronika: We made a good family, the three of us. I loved your mother, and I adored you the moment I set eyes on you.

Gemma: My mother said I was born at home. Were you there?

Veronika: Oh yes. It was a difficult birth. You were breach. But your mother was so strong, even the midwife was proud of her. I wanted to call a doctor or go to the hospital, but Tazia refused.

Gemma: Poor people, immigrants especially, didn't trust doctors back then. Even today, most Mexican families in California prefer home remedies. (Laughs) My mother's favourite cure for a sore throat is still hot milk with a spoonful of butter, chopped garlic, and honey.

Veronika: (Grins) That's not Italian. It's Polish. I used to make it for you at the first sign of a sniffle. (Turns serious) I don't think your mother mistrusted doctors. I think she was afraid that if she gave birth in a hospital, there would be a record that your father could use to track you down.

Gemma: And now I'm trying to track him down. Do you know who he was?

Veronika: I wish I could help, but I don't know anything. Your mother was pregnant when she got to Chicago, so I assumed the baby's father lived in New York. Her belly wasn't too big yet. The cast on her leg was more of a problem.

Gemma: Goodness. Why was her leg in a cast?

Veronika: It happened during the fire. That's how she ended up coming here. She and my cousin Olga worked together at Triangle.

Gemma: (Excited; stutters) Your cousin? What's her name? Does she still live in New York?

Veronika: Olga Zabec. That's her married name. (Writes Olga's address and phone number)

Gemma: (Bounces) Oh, Veronika. I can't thank you enough. Tell me everything you know about when they worked at Triangle, and their lives in New York. Maybe my father worked there too.

Veronika: Like I said, I don't know. Your mother never talked about the fire, except she got angry when we heard on the radio how easy the owners got off.

Gemma: To this day, she still won't talk about it. I can understand her need to bury it, although I admit I wasn't always so sympathetic. You're sure she never said anything about the other people she and Olga worked with? Where she lived? What she liked to do on her day off?

Veronika: All I can tell you is what her life was like once she moved to Chicago. (Music box stops; stirs sauce; hands music box to me to rewind)

Gemma: (Nods) I'd like to hear about that too. If it doesn't get me closer to my father, it gets me closer to my mother. (Touches Veronika's hand) Closer to you too.

Veronika: Life was hard. We worked long hours, six days a week. Different shifts, so we could trade off taking care of you. Sundays was for church. Your mother insisted on going to the Italian church across town, even though it meant dragging you on the bus. It hurt me that she wouldn't come to the nearby Polish church with me. Mass was Mass, I thought. It wasn't until my fifties that I understood how holding tight to the rituals we were born with connected us forever to home. Tazia realized that before she turned twenty. Maybe because she had you and was more aware of passing down your Italian heritage. Whatever the reason, your mother was wise before her time.

Gemma: Tell me more. What was our "family" like? Wait a minute. (Changes tape) Okay.

Veronika: Home was special. No matter how dirty and smelly the plant or Packingtown, we made our own little heaven. With you as our angel. You loved music. Every night after supper we sang songs from Italy or Poland and danced around the table. You also loved to count things. We didn't own a lot, but you were happy counting things like the number of potato slices on your plate. (Smiles) Not that you were always well behaved. You could be stubborn and demanding.

Gemma: (Laughs) My mother would say I'm the same today.

Veronika: You knew just how to get one of us to say "yes" if the other said "no." It was like a contest between Tazia and me to see who could be the better mother.

Gemma: My mother could be possessive. Was she jealous of you?

Veronika: I had to respect that I was your "second mother," but I think Tazia was grateful. We both came from large families and missed our younger siblings. It was joy to have a little one in the house and to raise you together. (Stirs; rewinds)

Gemma: I got the feeling in the other places I've visited so far that it wasn't hard for my mother to pick up and leave. It must have been hard for her to leave here though.

Veronika: I'd like to believe that. I still wonder sometimes if I drove her away.

Gemma: How?

Veronika: You told me on the phone that you got my name from ... that nigger man. He was nothing but trouble, and I told your mother so. Tazia wasn't one to take kindly to interference.

Gemma: That's for sure. (Hesitates) I admit that after I spoke to Mr Wright, I wasn't sure what kind of woman I'd find when I met you. You and my mother will never see eye to eye on some things, but now I know what a good person you are. Taking my mother in without any questions, helping to raise me like I was your own. (Feels face getting hot) I guess I'm angry at my mother for taking us away from here. She hurt you, and given how attached we were, she hurt me too.

Veronika: I was also angry at first. I can't count how many times I had to confess that to my priest. But I forgave your mother eventually. I never bore children, but I understand a mother's first instinct is to protect her child. In the end, I think Tazia left because she was afraid for you.

Gemma: Afraid that my father would find me? Try to take me away from her?

Veronika: Possibly, but after three years she must have known the chance of his coming after you was slim. I think Tazia was afraid you'd grow up to have a life as hard as hers. Armour used to bring in kids your age to unclog the grinders. (Shudders at memory) I can't say what your mother thought she'd find when she ran, only that she had faith God would lead her someplace better. (Stirs; rewinds)

Gemma: In the long run, I guess He did. It was a pretty roundabout route, though.

Veronika: Where did you go?

Gemma: (Ticks off on fingers) Topeka to begin with. My mother worked on a farm, which she liked, and we met some wonderful people there. Next was Las Vegas, where she found romance.

Veronika: How lovely. (Suspicious) With who?

Gemma: A dashing Italian man.

Veronika: White! (Sighs with relief)

Gemma: But not the marrying kind. We've been in California the last thirty-four years. I think my mother felt she was doing worthwhile work for the Navy, but the most satisfying part of her life has been seeing a third generation added to the family. If you thought she was a devoted mother, you should see how head over heels in love she is as a grandmother.

Veronika: (Grins) I'm glad Tazia found the good life she wanted.

Gemma: For most of that time, she made a good life for me. Only in the two years since she retired to a little town that reminds her of home, do I think she's found a good life for herself too.

Veronika: Tell me how she looks so I can picture her happy at last.

Gemma: (Thinks how much older Veronika, also Elvan, look by comparison) I can't remember how she looked before, so it's hard to describe what's different now. There aren't any pictures.

Veronika: (Nods) I remember your mother's camera and how fussy she was about the pictures she took. Only of you, and never with something in the background that would give away where.

Gemma: That hasn't changed. Even at my wedding! (Closes eyes) Most of her hair is still dark, which makes her look ten years younger. Her skin is smooth, maybe because she's done worrying about me. Only her hands are a giveaway. The term "manual labour" makes sense when you look at her. And you. And so many other hard-working people I've met on this journey. (Shrugs) I know that description doesn't help much, but I know my son would say his grandmother is beautiful.

Veronika: Tazia always was a beautiful person.

Gemma: So are you. (Hugs, kisses, tears) I came to Chicago with a vague memory of a woman whose name I didn't know. I'll never forget your name now. (Music box stops; is not rewound)

The interview ended at 4:25 PM.

part eleven
Tazia, San Diego, 1936-1951
chapter 39

"Lighten up on the gas pedal," Tazia says, reprimanding the recruit driving her from Administration East to South Unit One. When he flinches, she softens. "Would you drive your mother like that?"

"No, Ma'am," he says, blushing. Like the other young men whose job it is to transport her across the growing base—two new tracts of land and twenty-nine buildings to clean—he likes to speed and swerve when there's no supervisor around to keep him in check.

Tazia told the new C.O. it would be more efficient if she drove herself, without waiting to be picked up, but he dismissed her with a flick of his fingers. She's tempted to report the recruits' recklessness as further justification, but it's the hidebound officers and Navy regulations she's angry at, not these boys. They're just showing off, and without young women around, the forty-two-year-old Tazia is their only audience. She hopes that as the momentum to go to war builds, the C.O. will reconsider the best use of the sailors' time, but she's unlikely to win that battle.

Now, taking the bus home, her annoyance is replaced by anxiety about another upcoming battle. Sure enough, Gemma is sitting at the kitchen table, poring over a sample book of wedding invitations. It's open to the page featuring parchment with gilt lettering.

"Which do you like better, Mama? Cream or heather paper? Gold or silver printing?"

Tazia flips back to the beginning of the book where the cheaper invitations are. "Nice plain white paper. I can splurge on purple ink."

Gemma slams the book shut. "How many times do we have fight about this? Todd's parents are paying."

"The bride's family pays for the wedding, not the groom's." Tazia minces basil.

"In this case, the family with the money pays."

Tazia grips the knife handle and takes a deep breath. "I have money. Not as much as the Kanes, but I work hard for it and I want to pay for my only child's wedding." She begins to slice onions. Usually she does this without tears, but not today.

Gemma takes the knife, finishes the onions, and peels garlic to rub on the bread. "I know Mama, but you have to understand. Just as picking up the tab is important to you, a big to-do matters to Todd's parents. He doesn't care. And neither do I. Well," she says and smiles, "only a little."

"We'll compromise," Tazia says. "The Kanes can cater the meal. I'll bake the cake."

"I want a fancy one, with tiers. You don't know how to make those."

"The wedding cake is cut and gobbled in ten minutes. What does it matter?"

"You wouldn't know. You never had one."

Tazia stiffens. "I'll make an Italian almond cake. In seven tiers. How many people?"

"The ballroom holds two hundred."

Tazia looks at her tiny oven. "You said the guest list would be small, to fit in the Kanes' backyard."

"Maura decided she preferred their country club instead."

Tazia crushes a basil leaf in her trembling hand. "So the Kanes will have all their friends from the club, and on your side, there'll only be me."

Gemma hands her a dish towel. "And friends. You'll sit with the Sotos. They're family."

"Yours, not mine." Tazia tears sprigs of parsley. "I'm paying for your bouquet."

"Maura also wants floral centrepieces on the tables."

Tazia throws up her hands. "I can't."

"Relax, Mama. I'll ask Yolanda to make them. She's artistic."

"Okay, I guess. She's your matron of honour. What did you decide about the ceremony?"

"I already told you. Our priest and the one from the Kanes' church will officiate together."

Tazia puts the food on the table, and plunks down on her chair. "As long as the service is in Latin."

"For goodness sake, Mama. Did you think their priest was going to do it in Irish?"

Two days before the wedding, Gemma tells Tazia the Kanes hired a photographer. "I want good pictures," she insists. Tazia doesn't challenge her but brings her old Brownie and refuses to pose for the professional's shots. "Mama," Gemma pleads, "I want *you* in them too."

"Today is about you and Todd, not me." Tazia touches the beaded lacework she's sewn on her daughter's gown, wishing her own mother were here. "You look beautiful," she whispers. "Now, go smile for the camera."

A month later, when Gemma brings the photo album to Tazia's house, she is not smiling. "My own mother, missing. If my father had walked me down the aisle, he'd have been proud to be photographed with me." Tazia is silent. She wants to comfort Gemma, but the fact is she has no idea how Ayal would have felt. After twenty-five years, she can no longer claim to know him.

***

With help from Todd's parents, the newlyweds buy a small house around the corner from Tazia's apartment. "I'm never going to escape my mother," Gemma half-jokes, but until she and Todd are established in their careers, it's the only neighbourhood they can afford. Tazia sews curtains and helps them choose furniture with durable upholstery. She embroiders a linen tablecloth for when they have guests. Usually it's their friends, but Sunday dinners are reserved for the three parents.

Tazia alone is also invited midweek. Although she does most of the cooking, these relaxed meals are a respite from work. The new Commanding Officer, Commodore Byron McCandless, is stiff and demanding. "One of the recruits got caught saying the C.O. had a mast up his ass," she says over risotto croquettes one night. After two jelly glasses of Chianti, she's a little tipsy.

Gemma giggles. Todd starts to refill their glasses. "Sweetheart," she says, "let's have the good wine." A year into their marriage, earning more, they can splurge. Todd is either indifferent to nice things or self-conscious when his clients can barely afford food, but Gemma's eyes shine with each new vase or fluffy towel they buy. Tazia is happy for her daughter but worried for herself. She doesn't want to be the poor relation whose child belongs to another class of people.

"Your mother prefers the cheaper stuff." Todd winks at Tazia. "Me too." Gemma tosses her head and gets herself a better bottle and a stemmed wine glass from the cabinet. When she returns, Todd proposes a toast. "Here's to the simple life." They laugh and drink.

Gemma is next. "Here's to Todd winning the deportation case and my being assigned the article about the exploitation of civilian aircraft workers." Again, they clink glasses.

"Here's to the growing success of your careers." Tazia takes a gulp, then adds, "Followed by a growing family."

Gemma splutters and lowers her glass.

Todd calmly takes another sip. "Great risotto, *suocera*" he tells Tazia, helping himself to seconds. "Wait until you taste the apple barley pudding Gemma made for dessert."

Tazia pushes away her wineglass. She's had too much. "Did Maura teach you to make the pudding?" she asks Gemma quietly. Her daughter is trying to control her rapid breathing.

"Are you kidding?" Todd rubs his wife's shoulder. "My mother doesn't know pudding from parsnips. It was our cook's specialty. When Gemma found out I missed it, she taught herself to make it." Gemma leans her cheek against Todd's hand. Tazia thinks how much they love each other. Again, she's happy for her daughter, and this time only a little wistful for herself.

Dinner ends smoothly. Todd heads for the living room to review briefs for tomorrow's court case, while Tazia and Gemma wash up. When the last plate is draining, Gemma throws the sponge in the sink. "Stop pushing me, Mama. It's our business when we have kids."

"I know," Tazia says. "I'm sorry." She wrings out the sponge. "It's just that you and Todd can afford to start a family now."

"Money isn't what's stopping me. I want to have a career. It's hard enough for women as it is. It will be harder once I become a mother. My time won't be my own."

"I'm sure Todd's parents will help pay for a babysitter."

"I still want to be home for dinner and on weekends and go to every school play and recital. I refuse to be the kind of mother Maura was and foist off raising my children on others."

"Todd turned out okay."

Gemma looks at him through doorway. "Yes, he's a miracle." She and Tazia sit. "I want to be like you, Mama. No matter how hard you worked, you always had time for me."

"Until you didn't want me around anymore." Mother and daughter grin. "I know you don't want to make my mistake, becoming a mother too young, but I worry you'll get too old."

Gemma rolls her eyes. "I'm only twenty-six. Besides, most of our friends are waiting to get married and start families. The Depression is slowing everyone down."

"All the same," Tazia persists, "you better get started soon if you want a big family."

"Suppose Todd and I only have one? Will you be satisfied?"

Tazia thinks of her sister and brothers, her parents' siblings, the many cousins. Everyone needed to run an olive farm. "One child was enough for me. One grandchild will be too."

Gemma looks at the new refrigerator and pressure cooker in her tidy kitchen. "Sometimes I worry I won't be able to manage even one child and make it as a reporter." Tears slide down her cheeks. "How did you do it all?"

Todd comes into the kitchen, sits between them. "You won't be alone. I'll be there every step, even changing diapers." He folds a dish rag into a lumpy triangle. "I won't vanish. Promise."

Gemma nods, but her forehead wrinkles. Tazia trusts Todd more than her daughter does. A man born rich who chooses to defend the poor isn't self-centred like Ayal, or heartless like Virgil. Todd Kane is a white-Irish Elvan. Tazia smiles. Todd will be a good father.

***

Gemma is twenty-seven when Frankie is born, ten years older than Tazia was when she had her. Although she had Veronika, Tazia had missed her mother during the pregnancy more than at any time before, or since. Gemma peppers Tazia daily with questions. "Is it normal to feel this tired?"

"Yes, at the beginning and the end." Tazia remembers winter days when she wanted to nap inside a packing crate beside Paulie, and summer days when it felt like she was carrying a boulder in her belly. Stolen moments with Elvan were the only time she forgot her discomfort.

Later in the pregnancy, Gemma calls in a panic. "The baby hasn't kicked since yesterday."

"I'm sure it's fine," Tazia calms her. "Like us, babies have active days and quiet ones."

"But what if something's wrong with it?" Gemma persists. "Did my father's family have a history of some disease that could kill babies?"

"Not that I know of," Tazia says cautiously. In fact, she has no idea.

"Don't know or won't tell?"

"He never mentioned any such thing to me, nor did anyone in his family." Technically, this is true, Tazia thinks, and for now it's enough to quiet Gemma, who calls an hour later to complain that the baby's kicking is making it impossible for her to meet a deadline at work.

A week later, Gemma again demands to know more. "Was my father afraid I'd be born a freak? Did he leave while you were pregnant because he couldn't bear to see how I'd turn out?"

"Gemma, no more questions that I can't answer." Tazia is by now as exasperated as her daughter. "I'm healthy. You came out healthy. Your baby will be fine too."

And so he is. Gemma, wrapped up in Frankie's immediate needs, stops being a pest about the past. Todd, true to his word, changes diapers. Patrick and Maura buy a full layette and fancy birth announcements. Tazia fantasizes sending one to Ayal. She studies the baby for any resemblance to him, but she no longer remembers his face, only his cleverness.

Frankie's eyes are deep green, like his parents.' They follow Tazia as she croons Italian lullabies and feeds him bottles so her daughter can return to work. When he is sated, Tazia wraps him in Gemma's baby blanket and, in a rush of love, gives him the rattle Elvan carved long ago.

Gemma strokes the blanket. "It's so beautiful, I hate to use it. Frankie will spit up on it."

Tazia laughs. "Your spit-up made it more beautiful. So will his."

"Did I play with this rattle when I was a baby?" Gemma shakes it gently.

Tazia nods as Frankie turns toward the sound, fingers curling and uncurling in rhythm.

"It looks handmade," Gemma says. "Where did you get it?"

"Someplace in Chicago." Again, Tazia speaks a kind of truth. She worries her face will betray her, but Gemma is looking at her child, not her mother.

Todd's parents also bring gifts, expensive ones, when they come for Sunday dinner. There are toy trucks and airplanes, little blue suits, a tricycle before Frankie can even crawl.

"I wish I could buy him nice things," Tazia says, "but this is the best I can do." She hands the baby a small rag doll she stitched with a goofy face and springy red yarn for hair. Frankie puts it in his mouth and gurgles a happy stream of saliva.

Gemma hugs Tazia. "What you give us is priceless, Mama, cooking us dinner every night and doing our laundry. I couldn't do it without you."

Frankie drops the doll. Tazia picks it up and pretends it is talking. "Hello, *caro uno*. Are you happy to see your nonna?"

The baby babbles back. Gemma laughs. "I wish Todd's parents played with him like that. Especially Patrick. You'll be a real grandmother, but he'll never really get to know a grandfather."

Tazia waits for a burst of recrimination, but there is none. Since becoming a mother, Gemma fusses more over her child's future, less over her own past. "Then I'll have to be both Nonna and Nonno," Tazia says. If she can drive like a man, she can learn to throw a baseball.

***

One Sunday, after the Kanes leave and while Gemma naps, Tazia and Todd play with Frankie, now a year old. He uses the coffee table to pull himself up and stretches a chubby arm toward the shiny teething ring that Patrick and Maura brought earlier. Todd tugs it just out of reach. The baby slides closer, holding tight to the table's edge. Now Tazia moves it two inches. Frankie lunges for it and falls down. They wait for him to cry, but he gets up and sidles toward the toy, still leaning heavily against the table. This time he grasps it and whoops with glee. Todd claps too and Tazia, joining the celebration, knows she was right to think he'd be a wonderful father.

Gemma emerges from the bedroom, cranky from having her sleep interrupted. Her lips open in an exaggerated yawn. Tazia braces herself for a whiny "Pipe down," but before Gemma closes her mouth, Frankie lets go of the table and takes a step toward his mother. They hold their breath. He takes another step before he falls down, at which point the three adults cheer. Frankie, startled, begins to cry. Tazia lets Gemma scoop him up; Todd embraces the two of them.

"It's okay, Sweetie," Gemma soothes Frankie.

"Mommy and Daddy got excited because you walked," says Todd. "Nonna too," he adds.

Tazia smiles, then retreats to the kitchen to finish the dishes. As much as she's thrilled to be included in this moment, she knows that these milestones belong to Gemma and Todd. She allows her heart to ache, a little, that she never got to celebrate Gemma's firsts with Ayal. People say bringing up a child alone must be hard because there is no one to help shoulder the problems. They don't know that the greater grief is not having another parent with whom to share the joys.

chapter 40

A second war comes, not without warning, yet unexpected so soon after the first. Tazia worries about the family she left behind. Do they suffer from hunger? Are her parents still alive? Are there nephews she never met who are fighting? Thoughts roil inside her. She is proud her work for the Navy is helping the Allies achieve victory, but she can't deny that they are battling her homeland.

As the war escalates, the base fixes damaged ships and builds dry docks, the biggest over three thousand tons. It also trains tens of thousands of Air Force pilots. Tazia is exhausted from the increased work load. Some nights, she wishes she could go right to bed instead of helping with Frankie. She puts on a bright face for his sake but allows herself to complain to Gemma.

"The Navy revised its manual for cleaning ladies. More duties, same pay."

"Did you say something to Commodore McCandless?"

Tazia plays chase with Frankie before sinking onto the new carpet, already stained with mashed peas and strained carrots. "I tried. He said I should be grateful for the job security."

Gemma presses her. "Use Rosie the Riveter as an example. Women are taking on men's jobs and getting paid more, even if it's still less than men."

"I did, and it was no help. He said that when the war is over, women will be right back where we started, so there's no point getting used to more."

"How dare that S.O.B." Gemma runs for her notepad. "I'm going to write about this."

"No. I could lose my job."

"You have more clout than you think. The Commodore has been your boss since 1937, longer than any other C.O. on the base. Surely he appreciates you by now."

"He doesn't appreciate being challenged. The answer to your doing an article is still no."

"Stubborn as always." Gemma sighs. "But you're wiped out. If you won't let me write about the problem, at least reconsider our offer to buy you a car. You'd save an hour a day not riding the bus. Plus, it would make it easier to shop on the weekends and go to church."

"And drive down the street to spend more time helping you with Frankie?" Tazia teases.

"Mama," Gemma says and laughs. "He's the one thing that revives your spirits."

Tazia takes several deep breaths. "Okay," she finally agrees. "A *used* car."

The car saves time, but the added work hours accumulate faster. Finally, after a fifty-hour week, Tazia asks Commodore McCandless why she hasn't been paid at the higher overtime rate.

"It's wartime," he tells her. "Overtime is suspended."

"Isn't the Navy supposed to notify civilian employees of a change in policy?"

"It's my personal decision." His words are clipped. "Do you have a personal objection?"

"No, sir." Tazia retreats but doesn't dust his office for the next two weeks. The following month, she works back-to-back sixty-hour weeks. The Commodore calls her into his office, wipes a white-gloved hand across his desk, and holds up a forefinger. Tazia apologizes and under his watchful gaze, gives the room a thorough cleaning. Inside, she seethes.

"You should have scrubbed *him* down," Gemma scolds. "I would have snapped long ago."

"I'm not you." Tazia shrugs, but part of her wishes she were more like her daughter.

What finally tips Tazia over the edge is a late-night strategy session for Washington's top brass. Commodore McCandless, nervous about hosting the meeting, orders her to double clean his office, the conference room, and the officers' bathroom. "I expect you to stay and tidy up afterwards," he says, "in case we have to reconvene tomorrow morning."

"I'll stay if you agree to pay me time and a half." Tazia holds herself as straight as a recruit. "Otherwise, not only will I leave on time today, I won't be back tomorrow."

Commodore McCandless stares at her as if she's joined the enemy. "That's unpatriotic."

She bristles. "Sir, how long have I worked for you?" She waits while he uses the fingers on both hands to count. "In all that time, with no change in status or pay, I've taken on janitor's duties in addition to my cleaning chores." She enumerates: clearing air vents, repairing hot water heater valves, reinforcing shelves to bear the weight of added materiel. "I even shimmed your desk when you complained your signature had begun slanting and no longer met Navy standards."

The Commodore smiles in spite of himself. Squaring his shoulders, he says, "I'll promote you to a level one janitor with commensurate pay." Tazia grins back. "But only until the Axis is defeated. When the war ends, we'll revisit your status. And pay scale. Dismissed."

Tazia heads for the supply room where she mixes a batch of cleaning solvent and straps on a tool belt. To Gemma, this victory may seem small; to Tazia, it's enormous. For once, she defended herself and went after something instead of running away.

***

The boost in confidence revives Tazia's energy with Frankie too. She loves taking him places in the car. One day, Gemma asks her to pick him up at preschool when she and Todd have to work late. "We'll be home for dinner, though, so don't load him up with biscotti and chocolate milk."

Tazia promises and when she walks into Frankie's classroom, he's so excited to see her that he flings himself into her arms and pulls her around the room, pointing out his favourite toys.

"Look, Nonna. I can build the biggest tower in the whole wide world." They take turns stacking blocks. When the pile teeters, Frankie knocks it over, covers his ears, and gives Tazia a sly look. "Mommy gets angry when I make things go bang." Tazia laughs. "I'm not Mommy," she says. Together, they rebuild and knock down the tower twice more.

Next they play with modeling clay, after that cars. One by one, other children are picked up and then it is time to leave. Frankie hurls a car on the floor. "I don't want to go," he whines.

"I brought *my* car," Tazia says, knowing it's a treat for him to ride alone with her. Frankie is out the door so fast she has to run to catch him. He kicks happily against the seat cushion. His legs are growing long, like his mother's. Already he's losing his little boy chubbiness.

"I'm hungry," Frankie says, when they are barely a block from his preschool.

"We're almost home. I'll fix you some crackers and peanut butter."

"I'm hungry right now." Frankie's voice gets louder and higher. His vigourous kicks make the seat bounce.

Tazia passes a place whose sign has intrigued her since it went up a year ago. "Oscar's Drive-In Restaurant." It's the first of its kind and the new recruits love it. She turns the wheel into the lot so sharply that Frankie nearly tumbles into her. Wide-eyed, he watches her roll down the window and order two hamburgers. When they arrive, he regards Tazia as if she's a magician. He gobbles, burps loudly, and sings to the tune of *Twinkle, Twinkle Little Star*, "Yummy, yummy, yummy burger." Tazia eats slowly; she's never had a hamburger before. It is not bad, she thinks, but it would taste better with tomato sauce and served on Italian bread. Like a meatball sandwich.

Back at his house, Frankie takes out the hundred-piece block set the Kanes bought him for Christmas, but before his tower is two feet high, he knocks it down, bored. "Let's paint, Nonna." Tazia spreads newspaper on the table, gets construction paper, and mixes the paint powder with water. Frankie is learning his colours at school, and she's been teaching him their names in Italian. "*Rosso, blu*," he recites, making wide stripes. Not yet able to control the brush, he accidentally smears red and blue paint past the edge of newspaper. "Mommy will get angry."

"You can help me clean it up before she gets home," Tazia says. "How about *giallo*?" Frankie paints a large yellow sun. Excited by the motions of his arms, he makes bolder strokes. He mixes the colours in their containers, smears more paint over the edge of the paper, and wets the newspaper underneath so thoroughly that it soaks through. After he fills half a dozen sheets of construction paper, Tazia looks at her watch and tells him it's time to stop.

"Not yet." Frankie upends a container of paint, making a red river. Tazia runs for a sponge and is almost back at the table when Gemma walks in. She glowers at the scattered blocks and the paint, dripping like blood.

"I asked you to pick him up and bring him home, not to let him destroy the house."

"Calm down." Tazia waves the sponge. "It won't take me long to clean up."

"When I was his age, you made me clean up after myself. You never scold him."

Tazia crumples the soggy paper and starts wiping. "Grandmothers are supposed to indulge their grandchildren."

"I wouldn't know," Gemma shoots back. "I never had one." She hurls her pocketbook at the blocks and several skitter across the floor. Frankie, his head swiveling between his mother and grandmother, begins to cry. Gemma, contrite, kneels and draws him to her. "I'm sorry, Sweetie. You must be hungry. Come into the kitchen, and I'll fix you something to eat."

Frankie, barely sniffling now, says he's not hungry. "Nonna took me to Oscar's."

Gemma's words fly like spit. "On top of everything, his appetite is spoilt. You promised not to stuff him with cookies."

"I didn't. He ate a hamburger." Tazia hesitates. "And fried potatoes."

"Great. As usual, you didn't lie or break your promise—technically." Gemma throws the blocks into their container. The crashing makes Frankie cry again. Soon, he is shaking with sobs.

Tazia and Gemma both rush to him, pressing his body between theirs until he calms down. Then mother and daughter press against each other.

Gemma speaks first. "I'm sorry. I get wrought up trying to do a good job at work and be a good mother at home." She sits cross-legged on the floor; Frankie curls up in her lap. "Todd's wonderful when he's here, but whenever a major case comes up, his job comes before mine. My editor says he understands, it's the same with him and his wife, but I worry he'll assign big stories to the men." Gemma, surveying the mess, gets irritated again. "And then I come home to find ..."

Tazia sits beside them and strokes Frankie's head. "Maybe you expect too much. You and Todd work hard, but you're paid well. Look at everything you give your son. He lives in a nice house, goes to a good school. Be grateful for what you have, instead of missing what you don't."

Gemma sighs. "You're right. Patrick and Maura help too. Financially. In every other way, you do more for us, for Frankie." Frankie's eyes close. "Yolanda says I'm a brat to complain. Her folks do what they can, but they're not as rich as Todd's and they have to help her brother." She hugs Frankie with one arm, Tazia with the other. "How on earth did you manage on your own?"

"I had no choice." Tazia pauses. "No, that's not quite right. I *chose* to make you the most important person in my life. You knew that and it made you strong." She looks at Frankie, asleep in Gemma's arms. "He knows you feel the same way about him. He'll be fine. And so will you."

chapter 41

Three years later, the war ended, Commodore McCandless is as good as his word. One of his final acts before being replaced by Commodore Boak is to demote Tazia to her former position and salary. Gemma is incensed. Once more, she asks her mother's permission to write an exposé.

Tazia again refuses. "You should know me by now," she tells her exasperated daughter.

"Sometimes I feel as if I barely know you at all. Maybe my son will do better than me."

In fact, he might. The older Frankie gets, the more Tazia enjoys spending time with him. He's grown from a temperamental preschooler into a thoughtful boy. They spend hours together at the San Diego Zoo, dwarfed by the biggest bird cage in the world and staring wide-eyed and silent at the lions prowling free on the other side of the moat. Unlike his mother, Frankie doesn't push Tazia to tell him things. On the other hand, he trusts her enough to reveal his own secrets.

"Daniel called my drawing dumb," Frankie says as they walk to the Monkey Yard. "Then Michael grabbed it. The teacher yelled at me to sit down when I tried to snatch it back."

"Which drawing?" Tazia pictures her favourite, taped to Gemma's refrigerator. "The house on the water, with the birdbath and carved door?" Frankie nods. "It's beautiful."

"Did you notice the turret on top, Nonna, so you can climb up and see the ocean?"

"Yes. And a balcony over the garden. I'd love a house like that. Why didn't your friends like it?"

"Because it wasn't a car. That's what other boys draw. Cars, trucks, and tanks." Frankie takes Tazia's hand. "Daniel and Michael say only girls draw houses."

Tazia leads him to a bench overlooking the zoo's arched entrance, winding paths, and stone snake house. "Italy's great architects were men. Their castles and cathedrals have lasted hundreds of years. The things those boys draw will be out of date before you're in high school."

Frankie nods. "Okay. But I still feel bad when my friends tease me."

Tazia puts her arm around his shoulder. "Someday they'll envy your talent. And when you become a great architect yourself, you can design a house for me."

"And live in it with you?"

"You'll have your own family, with children who call your parents *Nonna e Nonno.*"

Frankie jumps up, satisfied, and tugs Tazia's hand. "Let's go see Rubie and Lotus."

"What kind of house do you think hippos like to live in?" she asks.

"A really, really big one!" he sings. "I'll draw it when we get home." Which he does, only when Gemma gets the tape, Frankie insists, "It's for *Nonna's* refrigerator."

Gemma's face falls. Tazia knows she's jealous. Not only is Frankie is closer to her than to his mother, but Tazia, in turn, pays more attention to him than to her daughter. She feels guilty, but Gemma is no longer a child. She can take care of herself. Also, she has a husband to love her.

***

To celebrate Frankie's eleventh birthday, Tazia takes him to Union Depot, where they board the electric street car for its final ride. He presses his nose to the window. "I'm sad the old trolleys won't run any more, Nonna. I'll miss the clanging bells and the tangled wires overhead."

"Not me," Tazia says with vehemence. "When I came to America, I rode the street car for hours between Brooklyn and Greenwich Village and it was no fun at all." She stops. Never before has she talked about that time. "Look." She diverts Frankie's attention to the gigantic Guardian of Water statue. "Remember going there for your birthday last year? It's the same age as you."

"Yeah. You said Italy has even bigger statues." Bragging about Italian artists has become their private joke. Tazia is relieved Frankie is distracted, until he says, "I didn't know you lived in Brooklyn. Tell me more about the old days."

"There's nothing to tell. It was a long time ago, I worked hard, and I was poor."

"What kind of work did you do? Did you live alone? Who were your friends? Mom told me she was born in Chicago. When did you move there? Were you still poor when she was born?"

Tazia fishes in her purse for a roll of Life Savers, takes a red one for herself and offers Frankie green, his favourite. "Today is beautiful. Let's not spoil it talking about the past. When we get off at the last stop, I'll buy us ice cream cones and Cracker Jacks." She tweaks his remaining dimple. "Or are you too old to get excited about the prize inside the box?"

Frankie surrenders, for now. "You're the only prize I need, Nonna."

***

In the six years that follow the war, Tazia works for a succession of Commanding Officers, each with his own quirks. Commodore Boak makes her order pine-scented furniture polish because lemon gives him hives. Captain Womble wants his books rearranged quarterly, first alphabetically, then successively by topic, author's rank, colour, and size. Captain Beattie demands starched towels in the officers' rest room, and Captain Mitchell requires three coats of floor wax, bright enough to reflect the silver garters holding up his socks. Tazia caters to their whims, but each change in command irritates her more. She doesn't see why she is always the one to adjust.

"Growing up, was it hard on you that we moved so many times?" she asks Gemma the day before Frankie begins junior high. He'd gone with Todd to buy shoes for his fast-growing feet.

"I'm forty years old. Why ask now?" Gemma rinses a plate and hands it to Tazia to dry.

"I see how nervous Frankie is about making friends at his new school. I just wondered how you felt, changing cities as well as schools."

"Making friends was easy. Keeping them was the hard part because you wouldn't let me get close to them." It's a sensitive topic, one they haven't discussed since Gemma left for college and could do as she pleased. "What about you? Moving meant changing jobs every time."

"It made no difference. Except for the farm, one job was as bad as another. Except now that I'm older, it's harder to change bosses." Tazia pauses. "Frankie's lucky he's lived in the same city and house since birth." She thinks, but doesn't say, that he also has two parents. Gemma hasn't asked about her father since Frankie was a baby, and Tazia is not about to bring it up.

Gemma takes a deep breath. "I've been waiting to tell you, and now is as good a time as any. Todd and I are buying a new house, about five miles from here. We already have a buyer for this place. If our offer is accepted, we'll move at the end of next month."

Tazia keeps wiping the now-dry plate. "So we won't live around the corner anymore."

"It's only a couple of minutes by car," Gemma says. "You can still visit every day."

"It won't be the same." Tazia puts down the dishtowel. "Three generations, together."

"I know, Mama. But Frankie's growing up. Soon he'll want to spend time with his friends, not his parents." Gemma puts an arm around Tazia's shoulder. "Or even his beloved nonna."

"So Frankie will have to switch schools and start making friends all over again?"

"No. Assuming the deal goes through, I've arranged for him to transfer to the junior high near our new house. Todd or I will drive him until we actually move. Unless you'd like to help?"

"Of course." Tazia smiles, but the pain of losing Frankie gnaws at her. Five miles will soon stretch to longer and longer distances.

***

While Gemma and Todd wait for the moving van, Tazia picks up her grandson. They'll spend the day together, then she'll bring him to his new home in the evening. Frankie stalls.

"All your things will be at the new place," Gemma says, trying to usher him out the door.

"I don't care about my stuff, Mom," Frankie whines. "It's the house I'm gonna miss." He roams through the empty rooms, brushing windowsills, spanning kitchen cabinets with his long arms, and craning his gangly neck to look up at the soffits. Just when Tazia and Gemma think he's done, Frankie heads outside to pace one last time around the small backyard.

Gemma drums her polished fingernails, chipped from packing, on the counter. "My son may be the only thirteen-year-old boy to get sentimental. About a house, of all things."

"Take it as a compliment to you and Todd that he was happy here." As a child, Gemma's never lived in one place long enough to become attached, but Tazia understands. The older she gets, the more she misses her home in Loro Piceno. She need only close her eyes to recall its red stone walls and tiled roofs. Inside, under heavy wooden beams are the three whitewashed rooms, a big kitchen and two bedrooms, one for her parents and the latest baby, the other for the rest of the children. It holds two clothes cupboards, the first for Tazia and Bianca, the second for the twins, Fino and Fredo, and later little Zito, if he'd lived. Behind the house is the garden, where rosemary and lavender scent the air. The two-hundred-year-old farmhouse is part of Tazia's deepest self, in the same way that this modest thirty-year-old house will forever define Frankie.

She and he spend a melancholy day at their favourite haunts. After the zoo, they stroll the El Prado walkway to admire the California Building's renaissance facade, then Mission San Diego de Alcala, the city's first mission. In the nearly quarter-century since moving here, Tazia has finally learnt to appreciate Spanish architecture. Then it's on to the white dome of Palomar Observatory. "Its simplicity is holy," Frankie says. "A direct link to God without the froufrou of convoluted carvings." Tazia smiles at his sophisticated language but cannot feel the same degree of reverence in such plain surroundings. On the other hand, she concedes that the wood and glass used in the modern architecture Frankie has come to love brings the beauty of the outdoors inside.

Frankie, a growing teenager, eats throughout the day, but come six o'clock he's ravenous for dinner. "Where to, Nonna?"

She takes him to the first drive-through, a place the recruits rave about. "Remember when we went to Oscar's drive-in? You thought I performed magic when a tray was brought to the car. At Jack-in-the-Box, you order at a window and they put food in a bag to eat wherever you want."

Frankie, stomach gurgling, chooses Pacific Beach. They park and sit close to the ocean. Most people have gone home for the day. "Nonna," Frankie chews his second hamburger, "you're the only grandmother of all my friends who drives. I like that you're different." He holds out an onion ring. "Try one," he says. "That'll make you the only grandmother I know who eats them."

Tazia takes a bite and reaches into the bag for another. "No ketchup," she says laughing, when Frankie hands her a packet. It's another of their private jokes. He knows she regards ketchup as a poor substitute for marinara sauce. To tease her, he coats his French fry in a blob of the red stuff.

"I'm glad you drive," he says, finally slowing down. "You'll be able to visit us every day."

Tazia gazes at the waves, gently lapping on the sand. The air is growing chilly; she drapes a sweater over her shoulders. "But you won't be able to come alone to my house anymore."

"I will when I get my license," he says.

"By then you'll want to drive other places, not to your old Nonna's."

"I'll always want to see you." Frankie moves closer. "I love Mom and Dad, but most of the time they're too busy to really listen to me. I can tell you anything." He laughs. "Almost."

"Tell me something now." Tazia slips her arms in the sweater's sleeves so she can wrap one around him. She waits patiently, knowing he is searching for something meaningful to share.

"I went to David's bar mitzvah on Saturday." David is in Frankie's new crowd of friends, whom Gemma describes as good students, not yet obsessed with girls. "It was interesting, but also kind of boring."

"Interesting how?"

"The synagogue was plain, no stained glass or statues, but up front was an ornate carved box that held a scroll, the Torah, that David read from. In ancient Hebrew. He said there were no vowels and he had to practice reciting it for months."

"Seeing how other people worship is always interesting," Tazia says, remembering the strange but lively Pentecostal service from years ago. "What was boring?"

"I couldn't understand a word. Except for David's sermon. That was in English."

"What did he talk about?"

Frankie shudders. "Sodom and Gomorrah! Not defiling our bodies. A weird topic for a kid, but David didn't have a choice. Your Torah portion is determined by your birthday." He thinks about what to say next. "We had to wear little hats on our heads. Yarmulkes. I felt silly."

"We cover our heads in church too. It's a way to show respect for God."

"I suppose. But don't you think it *is* silly to say a thirteen-year-old is ready to be a man?"

Tazia looks sideways at her grandson and can't help but think of the baby who loved to play peek-a-boo and squish bananas through his chubby fingers. "It depends on how you define being a man. I don't think the Jewish people believe your friend David is ready to get married and go to work, but he is capable of getting serious about religion and making a commitment to God."

"And studying Torah. That's what David's rabbi says is important."

"Some Catholic churches confirm children at seven, the age of reason, but these days, most do it in their teens. You'll be confirmed next year, so it's similar to what Jewish people do."

"Mmm. I never thought of it that way."

"In the end, even though we do things differently, we all worship the same God."

"But they don't believe in Jesus." Frankie frowns. "Will David go to hell?"

"It's too early to say. It depends on what kind of man he becomes."

"Will I be damned? I don't respect my body." Frankie burps, loudly. "I'm hungry again. Can we stop at Hage's for ice cream?" Tazia claps him on the back and agrees to this final treat.

First, however, they watch the sun go down. Tazia is glad she's taught her grandson about religious tolerance, yet her feelings are complicated knowing that he's one-quarter Jewish. Her old fears about Ayal are reawakened, with a new twist. Not only did she steal his daughter, she's also denying him his grandson. In the Holocaust's aftermath, Jews are driven to repopulate their numbers. Her secrecy deprives Ayal of what rightfully belongs to him, and to his people.

Is she committing a sin? Or being irrational to the point of silliness? Tazia looks at the vast ocean and darkening sky, but they offer no answer. She lets Frankie pull her up. Then, like a man, he gives her his arm and leads her to the car.

part twelve

Gemma, New York, 1961

chapter 42

This is Gemma Kane, speaking with Olga Zabek, a coworker and friend of my mother's at Triangle Waist Company, at her apartment in the Bronx in New York City. Today is Tuesday, June 6, 1961, and the time is 9:00 AM.

Gemma: (Sits on worn couch covered with handmade doilies; accepts tea and cookies) Thank you. Oh my goodness, kolaczki filled with poppy seed paste. (Bites one) They're exactly like the ones my mother makes.

Olga: (Sits at other end of couch) Tazia bakes Polish pastries?

Gemma: Your cousin Veronika must have taught her. That would explain why they taste the same as these. A family recipe?

Olga: Yes. Our mothers were sisters. They learnt it from their mother who learnt it from hers and back who knows how many generations.

Gemma: It must be wonderful to trace your family back that far.

Olga: Forward too. I'm a great-grandmother of five. They all live close by. A big help to me since I'm not well. I wish my husband had lived to see them. (Points to side table full of family photos; sighs) We had a hard life. His heart gave out in his fifties.

Gemma: What kind of work did he do?

Olga: Subway maintenance. Repairing the tracks, crawling under the cars. He would come home as black as a chimney sweep.

Gemma: You must have worked hard too. (Looks ninety but is early-to-mid seventies) What did you do after the Triangle fire?

Olga: More of the same. I started sewing as a little girl and never learnt to do anything else. I did basics, like hems and seams. (Smiles) Not like Tazia. She sewed beautifully. I still remember the layette she made for you, which she kept hidden in the scrap bin. Does she still sew?

Gemma: Not for many years, but she's taking up embroidery again since she retired.

Olga: I'm glad her hands are still nimble enough. (Massages knuckles) Arthritis, even on warm summer days like this.

Gemma: (Nods sympathetically) Why did you and my mother become friends? There must have been scores of girls on the shop floor.

Olga: I'm not sure. (Pauses) We were both Catholic ... although, so were many of the others.

Gemma: Faith was important to my mother. Was that true for you?

Olga: Yes. Especially when times were hard. I lost two children before their first birthday. Some days there was barely enough to feed the rest. Three were still in school when my husband died. Nine births all together.

Gemma: Wow. You had a big family.

Olga: (Smiles) I came from one too. So did Tazia. Loneliness drew us together. I missed my sister Anastasia the most, so your mother having the same name in Italian was a comfort.

Gemma: What did my mother tell you about her childhood?

Olga: Neither of us spoke English well, which made it hard to talk. But we'd pool our lunches to share the smells and tastes of our homes. (Laughs, remembering) Tazia had a good ear for bird calls and she waved her hands like the wind racing through Italy's hills. We were both raised on farms, hers grew olives, mine hops. Sometimes after our shift, she'd rub a spot of grime off the window to watch the pink and orange streaks of the setting sun. I knew from her tears that she was dreaming of a good day's end after planting or harvesting.

Gemma: (Nods) In Loro Piceno. Aguana, the small town where she's retired, sounds just like it.

Olga: (Spreads fingers as if in blessing) I'm happy Tazia got to return home, in a way. (Pensive) Perhaps another reason we became friends is that we were both traditional and old fashioned, although your mother was more adventurous. I was a few years older and not as flighty as the girls her age, who smoked and went out with the young men after work.

Gemma: What about my mother? Did she go out with someone from the plant?

Olga: Oh no. She lived with a couple her parents knew in Italy and went straight home. Campo? Compo? They were very strict. If she dated anyone, it would have been under their supervision.

Gemma: (Writes down both spellings) Probably Campo. It's a common Italian name. (Sighs)

Olga: Are you disappointed it's not much of a clue or (laughs) because I have no naughty stories about your mother? Tazia did like to have fun. She had a knack for imitating Mr Lemke, the meanest foreman I ever had.

She copied his scowl and bow-legged walk when he came down the aisle counting our piece work. It was daring of Tazia. She would have been fired if he caught her.

Gemma: I'm disappointed because I thought maybe one of the men at the plant was my ...

Olga: No dear. I'm sure it was the salesman from the company that printed Triangle's flyers.

Gemma: (Startles) Why didn't you say something ...? (Stops) Sorry. I don't mean to jump on you. Please. Tell me what you know. Take your time.

Olga: (Folds hands in lap) Your mother and I never talked about him. We had no polite words or gestures for that sort of thing, but I knew the assistant manager lent them his office for ... visits.

Gemma: So, you're certain that he was my father?

Olga: Who else could it be? I could tell she was pregnant. I'd seen my own mother enough times to recognize the signs. But we were both private people. Tazia didn't confide in me.

Gemma: I don't think she's ever confided in anyone. Except maybe my son.

Olga: Tazia wasn't being secretive or dishonest. She was ashamed. We were raised to be good Catholics and sent here to help our families back home. Your mother would have felt that she'd betrayed her parents' trust.

Gemma: Did the salesman offer to marry her? Or help to support the baby. (Blinks) I mean me! Please, please, do you know his name?

Olga: (Shakes head) Like I said, I knew nothing about him, except where he worked. (Claps hands) Goodness, silly me. I saved a memento from every place *I* ever worked. I must have one of those flyers from Triangle. (Stands, limps into bedroom, comes back with brochure)

Gemma: (Studies advertisement, on good stock, not yellowed, with pictures of shirtwaist styles) Look. (Hand trembles) Here at the bottom. Allegro Printers. With a Brooklyn address and phone.

Olga: That was fifty years ago. I'm sure the business has long since closed.

Gemma: (Continues reading on the back) It's got the owner's name. Mordecai Da'veed.

Olga: I guess there's a chance he's still alive. Or a member of his family is. It's an unusual name.

Gemma: (Stunned) It's Jewish. Was the salesman—my father—Jewish too?

Olga: Probably. Jews hired other Jews back then. Still do, I suppose. (Closes eyes, pictures him) He didn't have a particularly big nose. His hair *was* kinky, but he was very handsome. A lot of the girls flirted with him but the only sewing machine he ever stopped at was your mother's.

Gemma: (Clutches flyer to chest) Can I keep this?

Olga: Of course. I don't know why I hold onto such things anyway. A spool of thread, a pair of scissors. Maybe to prove I existed at those jobs, although my aches and pains remind me enough. It's not as if my memories are pleasant. (Ponders) Sometimes it's wisest to let go of the past.

Gemma: I'm not ready to do that yet. Not if finding my father gives my son a new perspective on his future.

Olga: (Embraces me) Good luck, dear. Just be sure poking into the past doesn't upset Tazia's future. Your mother worked hard for the family she made in America. (Holds my chin, looks in my eyes) I can see she did a wonderful job. She deserves to enjoy the peace she's finally found.

The interview ended at 9:45 AM.

chapter 43

This is Gemma Kane, speaking with Mordecai Da'veed, the retired owner of Allegro Printing, at his apartment in Brooklyn, New York City. Today is Wednesday, June 7, 1961, and the time is 1:00 PM.

Gemma: Mr Da'veed. Am I saying it correctly?

Mordecai: Yes, it's a phonetic spelling of the way David is pronounced in Hebrew.

Gemma: It's unusual. Thankfully, it made it easy for me to find you in the phone book.

Mordecai: I'm glad. But please dear, you must call me Mordecai.

Gemma: (Nods) I was surprised to see in the phone book that Allegro Printing is still in business.

Mordecai: My son runs the company now. It specializes in Judaica— flyers for the synagogues' holiday events, napkins with the names of the bar mitzvah boy, or the bride and groom, in gold lettering. (Shrugs) It's the American way. Jews today are more American than Jewish. I worry our heritage will end with this generation of parents but *nu*, what can you do? Time marches on.

Gemma: (Notes Jewish calendar on wall, prayer shawl and holy book on corner table) My Italian mother was also big on heritage and she passed it on to me and my son. So, there's hope.

Mordecai: If nothing else, the food will survive. Can I offer you some blintzes? Jewish crepes. (Goes to refrigerator) I'm sorry they're not fresh. We eat these on Shavuot, which was late last month. But my granddaughter Gittel stuffed my freezer with the leftovers, so I shouldn't go hungry.

Gemma: If it's no trouble to heat them up, I'd love to taste one.

Mordecai: Gittel fills hers with chopped nuts, same as my wife Emma, may she rest in peace. The sour cream what you put on top is fresh, Gittel brought it to me this morning. (Shuffles around kitchen, preparing food) You have children, yes? A son who's getting married soon? Mazel tov.

Gemma: Thank you. As I explained on the phone, I'm here because of him.

Mordecai: (Brings two plates with blintzes and sour cream to Formica-topped table)

Gemma: (Tastes) Delicious. You're right. Food will forever connect the generations. (Takes another bite) I'm hoping for something more on this trip, though. You knew the man who I'm pretty sure is my father. He worked for you fifty years ago, but maybe you remember him? He was your sales representative at Triangle Waist Company at the time of the big fire.

Mordecai: (Swallows) Ayal Gabay. I'll never forget him. A-Y-A-L. G-A-B-A-Y.

Gemma: (Catches breath; writes father's name with shaky hand) Please, pronounce it again. (Repeats name after Mordecai) Now, tell me everything you remember about him.

Mordecai: Of course, child. (Stops) Are you all right?

Gemma: (Afraid to move; whispers) Yes. Please, go on.

Mordecai: Ayal was clever with words *and* pictures. He gussied up the flyers that were Allegro's specialty back then. Sales spiked after I hired him. But Ayal was too ambitious to stay with me. He left to open his own greeting card business. I sold him one of our old printing presses to get started. He got the money from his father-in-law, who I knew. I printed flyers for his fur business.

Gemma: (Blanches) My father was married?

Mordecai: (Brings me a glass of water) Sorry, I assumed you knew. Yes, the family was wealthy, by Jewish immigrant standards. Their daughter, Ayal's wife, was a sweet girl. Not a looker, like Ayal, but devout. Never got over his divorcing her, but that was a couple of years after the fire.

Gemma: So my father was still married to her when you sent him to do business with Triangle?

Mordecai: Sure. I used to go myself, but Ayal hit it off with an assistant manager who doubled their order. After that, I let Ayal take over the account. (Shakes head) Terrible what happened to the girls who died there. If I'd known conditions at Triangle were that bad, I never would have taken them on as a customer. I'm not against making a profit, but not with unscrupulous people.

Gemma: (Aloud, but speaking to self too) His being married explains my mother's secrecy about her past. She's a devout Catholic. Adultery *and* pregnancy. That doubles the shame. She'd never consider an abortion. Unless ... How do, or did, Jews feel about it?

Mordecai: It depends. The Orthodox are generally opposed to it.

Reformed Jews accept it. I'm not sure about Conservatives. Mostly we don't talk about it. For us too, it's a *shanda*, a shame.

Gemma: What branch of Judaism—is that the right term—was Ayal?

Mordecai: I don't know. But when he started his own business, he used the name Alan Gordon not to sound Jewish. His company was called Gordon's Greetings. The divorce happened just as it began to take off. I heard that soon afterwards he married a Protestant girl—what we call, you should pardon me, a *shiksa*—from a family much wealthier than his first in-laws. (Tsks) As I see it, after he milked his first wife for her parents' money, he turned his back on her and our people.

Gemma: (Thinks) So my mother not being Jewish wouldn't have bothered Ayal, although maybe marrying a Catholic was considered worse than marrying a Protestant. Her being poor is what would have put him off. Did he have any children with his first wife before he divorced her?

Mordecai: No. He didn't even give the poor woman that much. I heard he had a daughter with his second wife, then I lost touch. The fur company cancelled the account with me. The owner's family wanted to cut off anything that reminded them of Ayal. (Frowns) I'm sorry. This makes your father sound like a bad man. I think he was just young, and eager. Like so many immigrants and their first-generation children. They saw an opportunity to succeed in America, they took it.

Gemma: Thank you for saying that. I'll have to meet him and decide for myself. (Smiles, wobbly) If I had my wish, it's that my son would have a Jewish grandfather as sweet and kind as you.

Mordecai: (Wags finger, grins) Don't get your hopes up. Sweet and kind are not words I would use to describe Ayal. But who knows? The Holocaust changed people, some for the worse and some for the better. Maybe in Mr Gabay's case it was for the better.

Gemma: I don't know how much I'll learn about his past, but maybe it's more important to learn what kind of a person he is now.

Mordecai: Spoken like a Talmudic scholar. (Pulls pocket watch from vest pocket; squints) Gittel will be here soon. My eyes don't work so good anymore, so every afternoon she comes over to read me the *Jewish Forward*. (Squeezes my hand) For you, I wish that your son and daughter-in-law, and their *kinder*, look after you and your mother as good as my family looks after me.

Gemma: (Squeezes back) If I'm successful, I may find another old person for them to look after.

The interview ended at 1:40 PM.

chapter 44

This is Gemma Kane, speaking with Ayal Gabay, my father, at his apartment in Manhattan in New York City. Today is Friday, June 09, 1961, and the time is 4:00 PM.

Ayal: (Stiff; sits in large velvet chair at opposite end of long living room; hair curly and silver at temples; long-legged and slim but with slight paunch; eyes green flecked with orange; wears dark red brocade smoking jacket) I'm still not sure I should have agreed to talk with you.

Gemma: (Nervous; coughs; perches on edge of embroidered chair) I wasn't surprised when you hung up the first time I called. What changed your mind?

Ayal: Curiosity. (Narrows eyes) Frankly, when you claimed to be my daughter, my first thought was that I already have a daughter and I don't need another. You said you had proof?

Gemma: (Pulls out birth certificate) You tell me. Does the date I was born match when you got my mother pregnant?

Ayal: (Stands; walks over; puts on glasses to examine paper; counts the months on his fingers) Yes, exactly.

Gemma: Do you think she was seeing someone else at the same time who could be my father?

Ayal: (Shakes head) No. That's not who Tazia was. (Returns birth certificate; sits in nearby chair; clips tip of cigar and lights it) I believe you're my daughter. You look like Tazia, at least as I remember her. Around the mouth, especially. (Leans forward; stares) You have my eyes though. (Leans back, wary) So what do you want? (Points to antiques, oriental rugs, paintings on wall). Are you here to blackmail me or claim an inheritance? (Removes glasses; clenches right fist in lap)

Gemma: No. That's not who *I* am. As I said on the telephone, I'm just looking for my father, and my son Frankie's grandfather. Like you, I'm driven by curiosity. Fifty years' worth.

Ayal: (Relaxes fist; shakes head as if to clear it) You're real. I can't believe it. Your mother told me she lost the baby in the fire.

Gemma: (Grits teeth) My mother doesn't tell lies.

Ayal: (Raises eyebrows) If she didn't say it, then she implied it.

Gemma: You didn't press her very hard to find out.

Ayal: I wanted to believe what I *thought* she said. But I did try to find her. I walked the streets in Brooklyn's Italian neighbourhoods. I searched other clothing manufacturers after Triangle burnt. (Puts hand over heart) I loved your mother. I intended to keep my promise to marry her.

Gemma: (Flares nostrils) Marry a poor Italian girl? You married the daughter of a wealthy Protestant who could bankroll your ambitions. You changed your name so my mother couldn't find you if she changed her mind. You denied your heritage. Why wouldn't you deny her?

Ayal: (Enunciates) I did not know that you existed. (Returns to normal voice) Look, I understand your being angry. But it's not true that I turned my back on my religion. If someone discovered I was Jewish, I didn't deny it. I just didn't see an advantage in advertising it. Inside, I'm still Jewish.

Gemma: (Looks at ornate furnishings, no symbols of Judaism) You don't strike me as observant. (Sarcastic) Your Sabbath starts soon. I assume we don't need to finish the interview by sundown?

Ayal: (Smirks) We just need to be done before my wife gets home from shopping. She's having a fitting at Bergdorf's, which gives us an hour, unless she gets impatient and cuts it short. (Sobers) It's true I gave up being a religious Jew, but after the Holocaust, I became a stronger cultural one.

Gemma: (Muses) I've heard the same thing from the parents of my son's Jewish friends. Did you, or should I also say "I," lose relatives in the Holocaust?

Ayal: Cousins and their entire families on both sides. Twenty-nine all told. (Frowns) How does that make *you* feel, now that you know you're half-Jewish?

Gemma: I ... uh ... haven't really had time to think about it yet. I always assumed my father was Catholic and probably Italian. We learnt about the Holocaust in school, but I never thought of it as a personal loss. Until now. (Eyes widen) Oh, my. I wonder if my mother's relatives joined the Army or the resistance. It's strange to think of my family fighting on both sides of the war.

Ayal: Tazia never talked about her family, so I have no idea which side they'd have been on thirty years later. But the fact that my Jewishness didn't bother her suggests they weren't prejudiced.

Gemma: (Leans back to study Ayal) Whatever *they* were, *you're* not what I imagined.

Ayal: (Covers nose with hand) Come now, I don't look *that* Jewish.

Gemma: That's not what I mean. Growing up, I had so many ideas about who you could be. As a little girl, I dreamt you were a prince who would carry me and my mother off to a faraway castle. (Blushes) In high school, I pictured you as a rebel running from the law. Also a good dancer and ladies' man. By college, you were the son of a wealthy businessman, a pizza king, forced to abandon my mother or lose his place as future head of the company. Later you took up the cause of your workers and wanted to find my mother, but by then the trail had grown cold.

Ayal: All very touching. And sweet. But remember, it was your mother who left me, not the other way around. And I didn't dream about you because, well, as far as I knew, there was no you to dream about.

Gemma: You could have dreamt about what might have been. *If* a baby had been born, *if* you had married my mother. Your dream to open a business came true, so it's not like you didn't imagine things and make them happen. Of course, once you changed your name, it's as if what you and my mother had never existed at all. She was as good as dead, like your unborn child.

Ayal: She knew where to find me, *if* she wanted to. I didn't change my name or start the business right away. I gather your mother isn't looking for me now, either. But you are, and you found me.

Gemma: (Grudgingly) True, but it wasn't easy. It's taken weeks of working my way backwards to put the pieces together. Something a person without my experience couldn't have pulled off. Actually, I'm surprised I found you listed under your real name.

Ayal: I changed it back a few years ago, although I left the company's name the same. I worried my *shiksa* wife would object, but she says the unusual name makes us stand out when charities list their major donors. It hasn't hurt business either. In fact, my reputation for generosity attracts new customers. Jews and Gentiles alike. (Leans back, stretches legs, rests hands on stomach)

Gemma: Tell me more about Gordon's Greetings. Mr Da'veed said you were very talented.

Ayal: I began with cards but when Hallmark made it impossible to compete, I switched to album covers for record labels and dropped "Greetings" from the name. Now we're simply "Gordon's."

Gemma: (Smiles) So you're agile and adaptable. I can live with that inheritance. (Leans forward) What are you like as an employer?

Ayal: Ethical. I started out doing the design work myself, but as we got bigger, I hired artists and copywriters. I pay well. I spun off a second business just to deal with the actual printing. It's a union shop. (Puffs out chest) Do I pass inspection?

Gemma: (Makes "check mark" in air) I won't write you up in one of my labour exposés. I've been successful in spurring some major investigations, you know, especially in California, and won a couple of journalism awards. (Waits for follow-up question, sign of interest; there is none)

Ayal: (Runs hand over graying hair) Business has been good to me, but I'm ready to wind down and pass along the company. Too bad I never had a son. My son-in-law is itching to take over, but I don't trust his business sense. Too impulsive. And gullible. Worse, he's no artist, so to him it's only about the money.

Gemma: Does your wife trust him?

Ayal: Oh, he's not her son-in-law. I had my daughter with my second wife.

Gemma: And the one who's at Bergdorf's ...?

Ayal: Is my third. She's younger than you. (Reddens) I don't suppose *you're* interested in taking over the business?

Gemma: Like I said, I'm a writer, but for newspapers, not album covers. And I have no artistic talent. (Pauses) My son, your grandson, does. He's an architect. My mother fostered that interest.

Ayal: (Gloats) Dear God, I have a grandson! A male heir. Frankie, right?

Gemma: Yes. Shall I tell you more about him? (Ayal flicks cigar ash into porcelain bowl; leans back to listen) He graduated at the top of his high school class and was captain of the math team. Studied architecture at Stanford. Julia, the girl he's marrying, comes from a good family. Catholic.

Ayal: No need to apologize. He was raised how he was raised. My daughter ... er, my other daughter, has no interest in religion. Not even her mother's Protestantism. I suppose I have no right to complain.

Gemma: They say the apple doesn't fall far from the tree. My mother was always religious and raised me the same way. My husband and I were the same with Frankie. None of us rebelled. I expect Frankie and Julia will raise their children Catholic. Although, if he learns that he's ...

Ayal: Tell me more about what kind of art my boy likes. Traditional? Modern? What music does he listen to? Does he like cars? These days it's all about cars. And young love, of course. We have to run album covers past the censors. Racy but not too racy, or parents won't let their kids buy them.

Gemma: Frankie sowed his wild oats in college, or so I imagine—he told his grandmother, not me—but he's pretty settled these days, After all, he's getting married, holding down a job.

Ayal: Starting a family. The American dream. (Laughs) Worried about supporting them. The *real* American dream, or what keeps people up at night. (Excited) Do you think he'd be interested in inheriting the business? He and his wife, what did you say her name was, would sleep better.

Gemma: (Taken aback) Oh, no. Frankie is really committed to ... (Clock on mantle chimes hour; changes tape)

Ayal: What the company needs right now is someone young enough to be in touch with what's popular these days but old enough to make mature financial decisions. You said my grandson has a good head for math, right? And a person brought up with religion isn't going to do something wild. You did a great job with him. I'm sure your mother helped out too. (Trying to flatter me?)

Gemma: I told you that my son's passion is architecture. He's just starting out and he's very excited about the firm that hired him.

Ayal: (Waves hand in dismissal) If he's just starting out, he's not invested in the firm yet. A smart young man would jump at an opportunity like the one I'm offering. Ask the boy. As soon as you get home. This weekend. Tomorrow in fact. (Licks his lips)

Gemma: Sorry. There's been a change in plans. I'm not ready to go back. (Surprises self)

Ayal: (Stands, paces) Call me right away. Let me know if he's interested, and I can fly out there for the wedding. It's in nine days, right? (Stops) Of course, first I'll need time to tell my ...

Gemma: I said I'm not flying back to California tomorrow. I'm going to Italy.

Ayal: But ... but you came to New York to find me. For your son's sake. Now you have. I'm ready to acknowledge him. Hand over a business bigger than some architectural firm that would hire a kid fresh out of college. (Agitated) I don't understand what's holding you back.

Gemma: You're right that I began this trip to find out who my father was. Except at some point, I realized I was learning more about my mother. There's still a lot I don't know. I have to go back to a time in her life when I wasn't in the picture. That means her family, mine too, in Loro Piceno.

Ayal: What about the wedding?

Gemma: I'll get home with a couple of days to spare. (Smiles) My mother won't be happy, but she can handle it. She's managed worse crises in her life.

Ayal: (Collapses in chair) You know. I really did love your mother. You have my permission to tell her.

Gemma: I'll think about it.

Ayal: (Half rises) And you'll tell my grandson about the business? Or I can do it after you tell him ... you know, all about me. (Sits back; strokes chin) Frankie Kane. I like the sound of it. (Clock chimes the quarter-hour) You better go. My wife will be home any minute. Call me soon, Gemma. (Stands; gives me awkward hug) This time, I won't hang up on you.

Gemma: (Gathers things) I have your number.

The interview ended at 5:15 PM.

part thirteen

Tazia, San Diego, 1951-1959

chapter 45

"I'm usually so decisive, but I can't choose a coffee table for the new house." Gemma, her face pinched, turns to Tazia. The salesman at Marston's Department Store, after praising half a dozen options, has discretely withdrawn behind a nearby credenza. "Which one do you like, Mama?"

"I don't know. I never owned a coffee table. The kitchen table is where you drink coffee."

"I'm leaning toward the old-fashioned maple with chintz upholstery on the chairs. Yolanda agrees. Frankie likes the modern glass-topped table and steel-framed chairs with solid gold cushions." Gemma wanders among the models like a child agonizing over which candy to buy.

While her daughter dithers, Tazia eyes the bedroom displays. If only she could lie down and nap until Gemma makes up her mind. She's overwhelmed by so much furniture. Her living room chairs are Navy cast-offs, draped with shawls. "What does Todd want?"

"He doesn't care, as long as he can put his feet on the table without taking his shoes off. He does have a strong opinion about the price, though."

Tazia turns over a tag. One armchair costs more than she earns in a month. "Things here are expensive."

"We can afford it, but Todd compares how much we have to how little his clients earn, then reminds me they're the same people I write about. He says spending a lot to decorate the house is immoral."

"I'm with him," Tazia says. "The furniture you have is perfectly acceptable. Especially if Todd—and Frankie too I assume—will just put their dirty shoes on it."

"Our new place is nearly twice the size of the old one. Without more furniture, the rooms echo. Don't you hear it when you come over to cook dinner?"

"No. I'm listening for the tomato sauce to bubble so I know when to add the peppers."

Gemma throws up her hands and strides toward the elevator. Tazia follows, shrugging at the sour-faced salesman. "You always take Todd's side." Gemma jabs the sixth-floor button for the Marston Tea Room. "I wish you'd take mine for once."

"I do," says Tazia, angry with herself for spoiling the day. It's not often she and Gemma spend time alone together. "I always take your side when it comes to Frankie."

"That's because you don't have to choose. Todd and I agree when it comes to him. The only way I got Todd to move to a bigger house was because the schools are better."

"My treat," says Tazia, making amends. She takes her daughter's arm as they walk to their table. It's covered with a linen cloth and the silverware looks heavy. "You order for both of us."

"Two Pacific Paragon Salad sandwiches and two slices of coconut cream pie." Unlike her waffling in the furniture department, Gemma has no hesitation about what they should eat. "And coffee." She winks at her mother. "For us to drink at this lovely oak table."

While the food is prepared, they watch models parade through the dining room. There are pleated corduroy skirts and slacks for daytime, taffeta and thin-ribbed crepe for evening. Tazia admires the fabrics and stitching. When their sandwiches arrive, she stares. They're as opulent as the furniture and clothes. She lifts the top piece of perfectly oval rye bread and studies the layers: butter, white turkey meat, bacon, avocado, endive lettuce, hard-boiled egg, tomato, ripe olives, and blue cheese dressing. "How are you supposed to eat this?" she asks, covering it up again.

"Women use a knife and fork," Gemma says. "Men use their hands." She takes a deep breath and picks up her sandwich. Tazia does the same. Her daughter is right. It feels good to treat yourself to nice things. Gemma nods with approval. "When you come over tonight, ask Frankie to show you his latest art project. It's hard to describe, but it has intersecting planes of light and colour. Abstract, yet not cold like so much modern art. His teacher gave him an A+."

"I hope he'll still be home when I get there." Tazia wipes her hands and asks the waitress to wrap the second half of her sandwich. She'll take it to work tomorrow, which will save a little money after today's splurge. "These days, he's off with friends more often than not."

Gemma nods. "Usually at Dan's or Bobby's house. They play math games. I think Frankie applies the formulas to his drawings." She grins. "You groomed him to be an architect. I hope you're not disappointed when his buildings look as formal as his pictures." She sips her coffee, savours a bite of pie, then puts down her fork. "I miss seeing my son, too. I should be happy he's doing something smart and safe, but his mouth is turning as smart as his brain."

"What do you mean?" Tazia nibbles her pie. She would have preferred cannoli.

"Yesterday I told him to put his dirty socks in the laundry hamper. So, he balled them up and shot them from across the room. Of course he missed, but when I got angry, he said it was my choice; I could either have a jock or a nerd for a son."

Tazia laughs. "Such a clever child."

Gemma smiles. "Great. Not only do you side with Todd, now you're defending Frankie."

"I'm just glad he's too young to serve in Korea," Tazia says, turning serious. "The recruits at the base don't look much older than him. I ache for their mothers."

"I can't imagine sending my child off to war. It will be hard enough sending him to college in five years. Now I understand why you didn't want me to go to UCLA. At least, I'll still have Todd when Frankie's gone. And Yolanda says we can find solace redecorating our empty nests."

Tazia folds her napkin. She'll feel even lonelier than her daughter when Frankie is gone. His growing up is already hard on her. Raising Gemma, Tazia was nervous and watchful, but with Frankie, she can finally relax and enjoy herself. She's afraid her days will become empty of joy.

"I know you'll miss him too," Gemma says, reading Tazia's thoughts. "Leaving is harder for the grown-ups left behind than for the children. They're ready for freedom, or think they are."

"You've given Frankie a happy home. He'll want to come back to visit."

"He'll come back to see you more than Todd and me." Gemma pushes away from the table. "You better live a long time so our son will keep visiting us."

"I'm in no hurry to depart. I plan to stick around to see him do his heritage proud."

They board the elevator. To Tazia's surprise, Gemma pushes the button for the furniture floor, not the ground floor exit. "I've decided to go modern," she says. "It will be a reminder of Frankie when he's gone and a sign that he's always welcome to return."

***

On Tazia's sixtieth birthday, Gemma gives Frankie money to treat his grandmother to an all-day celebration. He takes her to Mission Beach Amusement Center where they ride the carousel, whose horses were designed and hand-carved by Italian craftsmen. Next they climb into bumper cars, where Tazia careens around the track faster than a recruit and rams the cars in her way.

Frankie whoops with surprise. "No other old lady does that. Are you daring enough to ride the Giant Dipper roller coaster with me?"

Tazia looks up at the steel tower, hears screams as people hurtle through space. Images of bodies flying off window ledges appear before her eyes. She trembles. "I'll sit this one out."

"Nonna, are you okay?" Frankie leads her to a bench and fans her with his ticket.

"I'm sorry." Tazia's heart races. "When I was only a year older than you … " Her voice trails off.

"You went to an amusement park and something bad happened?"

She presses her eyelids together. When she opens them, Frankie's face is ashen. He asks if he should call his mother, if they should go home. "No, I'm fine now. How about another spin on the carousel and then I'll buy us ice cream?"

"Cotton candy too?" Frankie wrinkles his nose. He knows Tazia regards it as poison.

"If you promise not to tell your mother," she says. Let him think she's referring to the spun sugar. Then, her colour restored, she lets Frankie help her stand. "Let's go enjoy ourselves."

chapter 46

Two years later, with Frankie's acceptance from Stanford's architecture program propped on the mantle, he and Tazia go out again. Todd's parents are throwing a graduation party at their house that weekend, but Tazia wants time alone with Frankie first. The Kanes told her to invite whoever she wanted, but after fourteen commanding officers in twenty-seven years, Tazia has only thought of the first, Captain Morris, as being close to a friend. She doesn't know where he's posted now.

Frankie's parents give him permission to take Tazia to dinner in their car. Gemma wants to pay for the meal too, but Tazia refuses. "It's my treat. I've saved eighteen years for this day."

"You never accept help." Gemma turns to Todd for confirmation, but he says Tazia has earned the pleasure of buying the meal herself. Gemma huffs. Todd tosses his son the car keys.

Winding his way through rush hour traffic, Frankie drives carefully to the Cortez Hotel, where Tazia has made reservations at the rooftop Starlight Restaurant. He parks, comes around to her side of the car, and offers her his arm. Tazia switches her beaded evening bag to her left hand, brushes the lapels of his suit, and looks up into his green eyes. Frankie kisses the top of her head. "I love you, Nonna," he says. "I'll write you all the time from school."

From the lobby, they follow signs to the glass hydraulic elevator, on an outside wall of the hotel that will take them up twelve floors to the restaurant. They wait with six more passengers, but when the door opens and the others get on, Tazia is frozen on her side of the threshold. "I can't," she whispers. Frankie, puzzled, gets off before the door closes.

"What's wrong, Nonna? You can shut your eyes if you don't want to look down."

"It's not that." Tazia is remembering the Triangle elevator hurtling past the floors below hers. She hears people pounding on the gates to be let in, the thud of their bodies landing on the elevator roof as they hurl themselves down the shaft, a crunching noise, and then there's a blank until she awakens in a hospital bed with the kind young doctor staring into her face. "Before your mother was born," she begins, "an elevator in the building where I worked ... "

"You were trapped?" Frankie looks up the shaft at the elevator's smooth ascent. "The fire marshal must check this every day. I'm sure we'll be safe." He looks at Tazia. "Can you tell me what happened?" She shakes her head. "Sometimes talking about it helps," he says.

Again, Tazia shakes her head and purses her lips. Perhaps he's right, but she's too old to change. His face flush, Frankie leads them to the stairwell. Tazia pauses for breath on every floor.

"I'm sorry," she tells him when they're seated and looking at the over-sized menus.

"It's okay, Nonna." He pats her hand. "I'll have other chances to ride glass elevators. It's just that I always feel better after I talk to you and I wanted to return the favour and listen."

"After you graduate, I'll let you do favours for me."

"Promise? I'll hold you to it."

Tazia smiles. "I'm sure you will, but tonight I owe you the favour because I almost spoilt our celebration." She signals the waiter, whispers in his ear, and when an expensive bottle of Chianti is delivered to their table, she pours Frankie a full glass and refills it twice during dinner.

This time it is Frankie who pauses at every floor as they wind their way down to the lobby. Tazia holds out her hand for the car keys when they reach the parking lot. He turns them over. "The wine is one more thing we have to promise not to tell your mother about," she says.

Frankie giggles. "If I tell you things in my letters, will you keep on keeping my secrets?" Tazia nods solemnly. "And someday, will you tell me yours?" He slurs his words.

Tazia starts the car. Frankie is asleep before she can tell him no.

October 15, 1958
Dear Nonna,
I should probably say first off that I miss you, but I'm so busy at school that I almost never think about home. When I do, I miss you more than Mom and Dad, if that makes you feel better (only don't tell them, especially Mom). I have a full class load. Biology is okay (my lab partner Sandra is really cute), philosophy is better than I expected (us Catholic kids will be ahead of the class when we study St. Thomas Aquinas next month), math is fun (I joined

the Math Club), but best of all is architecture. The professor is an expert on Frank Lloyd Wright, and I am in love, love, love with his organic buildings. Next year's sophomore architecture trip is to Fallingwater, near Pittsburgh. Grandpa Patrick and Grandma Maura offered to pay (since they're already footing the rest of my college bill), but you taught me that it will mean more if I pay for the trip myself. I'll earn the money over the summer doing construction work, which is also a good way to learn architecture from the bottom up. When I'm a senior, the trip is supposed to be to New York, to see the Guggenheim Museum, assuming it's finished by then. I'd love to take you along and tour the city where you lived when you first came to America. You never did tell me much about those days, but I bet we'll have more fun than you did! We can even visit an old Italian church, only please, please, please don't be angry that I love modern architecture better.

Love,
Frankie

October 17, 1958
Dear Frankie,

I'd never admit I'm disappointed that you don't miss me because then you might feel so bad you would stop writing me altogether. Your mother misses you a lot. She goes into your room every evening and lies on your bed because the sheets still smell like you. (She hasn't washed them since you left almost two months ago. See, I'm practicing using parentheses like you do.) I take comfort looking at your drawings on my refrigerator. Also, don't worry that I'm angry at you for liking modern architecture. I knew that before you went to school and I still blessed your going. Young people are meant to learn new things, as long as they respect the work of those who came before. From the little I have read about Mr Wright, he respects natural materials (wood and stone, not just glass and steel), and so honours the old Italians. Just remember when you design buildings to include adornment (modern sculptures, if you prefer) and gathering places (like the Renaissance piazzas). Someday I'll sit in one of your places, with you beside me, and lift my face to the sun. Meanwhile, I look down at the floors I continue to polish at the Navy base. Captain Feutsch, the fifth C.O. in as many years, loves the phrase "spit and polish." So that is what I do.

Love,
Your (Naughty) Nonna

March 31, 1959
Dear Nonna,
We staged a panty raid on the girls' dorm last night, although not the one where Dorothy lives. I'm sort of dating her now. We're going to see the new film Some Like It Hot *on Friday. Dorothy is a painter, so she's not as interested in 3-D art as me, but I am learning about adornment from her. She dresses in black with colourful scarves she dyes herself and decorates her face with two-tone lipstick and eyeshadow. She's from Detroit and she isn't Italian or Catholic but don't worry, I'm not going to marry her. Please don't mention Dorothy to my folks. Mom complains that I tell you more than I tell them. From now on, I'll write (OK=Okay) or (DT=Don't Tell) so you know what is (not) copacetic to share. My friends and I went to the beach last Sunday (OK) and I have three pairs of panties hanging from my desk lamp (DT). I'm still waiting for you to reveal your secrets to me. If you won't talk about the past, will you tell me about the future? Do you dream about what you will do when you retire? Are you afraid to die? I aced my last architecture project (OK). I'm enclosing a drawing of the Wright-style house I designed for you, to put on your refrigerator. You'll be pleased to see there's a patio for people to gather, with a fountain in the middle. Is that Italian enough for you?*
Artfully,
Frankie

April 4, 1959
Dear Frankie,
Your secrets are safe with me. I think what set your mother off was when I spoke in detail about your classes. She complains that when she asks about your studies, all you say is that they're "interesting." She's embarrassed she has nothing to report when your father's parents (who are after all paying) ask what you're learning in school. So either tell me what it's OK to say about the marvelous Mr Wright, or send a detailed letter to your other grandparents. And think of a "safe secret" to tell your mother. She loves you. I love you too, and so I will try to answer your questions. To be honest, I've never thought about retirement. The very idea seems strange to me. When you grow up poor, on a farm, like I did, you work until you die. If you can no longer work in the fields, you work inside. Women, especially, can cook, or mend, or watch the little ones. If God is gracious to me, I will live long enough to look after my great-grandchildren. (I am glad to hear that Dorothy will not be their mother!) As to your second question, death does not scare me. Faith takes away*

the fear. My only worry is that I will not recognize my parents when I meet them in heaven. Even now, I no longer remember what they look like. There is no photograph. Will you do me a special favour? Close your eyes and imagine what your great-grandparents look like. Then draw their pictures for me. I will not put them on the refrigerator, but in a special drawer where I keep the few possessions dearest to me. (See, I just revealed another secret.)

    Love,
    Nonna

chapter 47

"Ma'am," Captain Fuetsch says, "the Admiral's inspection is at 700 hours tomorrow. Apply an extra coat of floor polish before you leave today."

"Yes, sir." The first time he called her Ma'am instead of Tazia, like the other C.O.'s, she thought he was being polite. Then she realized he didn't know her name and wasn't interested in learning it. She bends to pick up his nearly empty wastebasket, which he nevertheless insists she clean out five times a day. To her surprise she can barely lift it. She takes it down the hall to the incinerator, but by time she returns to his office, hasn't the energy to carry it back to his desk. She can't remember feeling this tired since the early days of her pregnancy. Or having the same vague sensation of nausea. Without the captain's permission, she sits in a chair by the door.

"Ma'am, are you all right?"

Tazia cannot catch her breath. Pain creeps from her back up to her neck, then around to her jaw. She thinks she smells smoke. Quick, it's important to warn her friend Olga, and also little Paulie. She opens her mouth to yell "Fire!" but no sound comes out. It feels as if her jaw is wired shut. People are pressing against her arm, trapping her in the elevator. Cold sweat pours down her face, soaking her collar. Then the pain travels to her stomach. Dear Lord, she is going into labour.

When Tazia wakes up, a doctor is peering down at her. He is older than she remembers. Her hand goes to her belly. "The baby?" she asks, before her eyes close. Time passes, she comes to again. Where is Ayal with the newspaper? Tazia clutches the bedclothes, wondering why they are so smooth. Did someone rip out the embroidery? Once more, she drifts back to sleep.

"Mama?" Gemma grips Tazia's hand.

"Thank God, you're okay." Tazia sits up, looks around for Veronika and the midwife.

"*I'm* okay?" Gemma gently pushes her mother back down into the starched white hospital pillow. "*You're* the one who had a heart attack."

Tazia swivels her head and focuses. Tubes drip a clear liquid into her left arm, a crucifix hangs high on the wall opposite her bed. Todd sits in a plastic chair beneath it, leaning forward. Tazia's hand feels wet. She looks for the source, perhaps the medicine bag is leaking, then sees that Gemma is crying. She gazes into her daughter's eyes. They glisten like emeralds.

"I thought I was going to lose you," her daughter says and sobs.

"I'm still here." Tazia tries to smile. Her jaw is still sore but breathing comes easily now.

"I don't want you to be gone, ever," Gemma says, dabbing her cheeks with a shredded tissue. Todd brings her a fresh box and plants a gentle kiss on Tazia's forehead.

"You're just afraid I'll die before I tell you about your father," Tazia says.

"Mama, how can you say such an awful thing at a time like this?" Gemma crushes a fistful of tissues in her hand. Todd backs away, but Tazia sees his smile. She manages to return the grin.

Gemma explodes. "You're lucky you didn't die. This time." She says the doctor told her the heart attack was relatively mild, but the next one will be worse. "It's time to retire. Todd and I will help out." She looks to her husband for agreement. He nods, serious now.

"I don't need your help." Tazia pushes herself back up with her elbows. "I'm entitled to a government pension and Social Security. A doctor's note will get me disability benefits too."

"Why are you so stubborn? We can afford it. Let me finally give something back to you."

"How many times must I tell you? I don't want to be repaid for being a mother. If you insist, repay me by letting go of the past and moving ahead with your own life." Suddenly Tazia is very tired again. "Will Frankie be down this weekend?"

Todd is back at the bedside. "Enough Gemma. Let your mother to rest." He takes Tazia's hand. "Frankie doesn't want to wait until the weekend. He's taking the bus home now. You'll see him tomorrow."

"I want him to come alone," Tazia says before closing her eyes. She hears Gemma start to sob again on the way out.

***

Frankie's kiss interrupts Tazia's nightmare of being stuffed into a sausage grinder. Instantly alert, she frets over how tired he looks. "You shouldn't lose sleep worrying about me," she admonishes.

"I'm just wiped out from the bus trip, Nonna. It's ten-hours from Palo

Alto." He pulls up a chair and stretches his long legs across the end of her bed. "Mom grouses you worry so much about everyone else, you brought this on yourself. She grilled your boss because she's convinced you weren't feeling well before the heart attack and didn't let on to her."

"I'll bet the captain relished that interview." Tazia chuckles. "At least he'll remember my name from now on. Not that it matters at this point."

"Mom also asked your doctor so many questions he said it was like being back in medical school. She's listing your diet dos and don'ts." Frankie lifts the lid off the lunch tray, pretends to gag, and puts it back. "She was disappointed when the doctor said you could continue to drive."

"Your mother means well, but I wish she would stay out of my business."

"Yeah, I know what you mean. Being nosy is great for her job, but it's not a trait either of us appreciates." He clasps Tazia's hands. "We have to look out for each other."

"We always do," she says and pulls his head onto her chest, as if he were still the squirmy little boy who was afraid Gemma would get mad when he made a mess. The almost adult Frankie calmly lets Tazia hold him close. After a minute, she releases him.

"Mom's right about taking good care of yourself, though. I want you well enough to go to New York with me and party at my graduation."

"That's over a year away. By then, I'll be so strong I could work on a farm."

"No more work for you, but for my first job, I'm going to design you a house." He pulls two photos from his satchel. "Here's a Prairie house." He waits while Tazia examines the shallow sloping roof and open sky above it. "And this is a Usonian. See the flat roof. It's built on a slab, as basic as it gets." Again, he lets her study the picture. "Which do you want, Nonna?"

"Neither." Her grandson's brow creases. "They're both lovely," she quickly adds. "Simple and natural. No wonder you like them."

"But they're not for you." Frankie folds his arms. "Tell me what *you* want."

"A simple stone house, although wood is fine too. One story." Tazia closes her eyes and, as she has so often lately, sees the home and fields of her childhood. "I think I care more about where the house located. I'm tired of cities. I miss the land around Loro Piceno. Hills and valleys, flowing water, olive farms as far as your eye could see."

Frankie snaps his fingers. "I know just the place. Aguanga." He tells her about an olive-growing town just seventy-five miles to the north. "Mark, a friend on my math team, grew up there. He invited me to go home with him last year when Aguanga celebrated its centennial."

"They really grow olives there?" Tazia heart races, but with excitement, not stress.

"On small family farms, like the one where you grew up." Frankie stretches out his lanky frame again. "My friend hates the place. There's nothing to do." He winks. "You'll love it."

"Yes" is all Tazia needs to say.

"Trust me to find you a plain house there, Nonna. I'll whitewash the walls, fix the roof, and shore up the foundation." Frankie grins. "I'd do the work for free, but I'll let Mom pay me. That way you can tell her that you're finally accepting her help."

Tazia breathes deeply, the hospital unaccountably scented with rosemary and lavender. Her head sinks onto the pillow. This time when she sleeps, she won't be standing in a factory. Instead, she'll be on a ladder, in the trees, tossing olives down to Bianca and the twins, who will fill their baskets with the ripe fruit. Beyond them, she'll just make out what her parents look like.

***

In early spring, when feathery white flowers will soon blossom on Aguanga's olive trees, Tazia surveys Sea Breeze Apartments, where she has lived for thirty-two years. The used Navy furniture will stay behind; she has only to decide what personal items to take. Thinking of Frankie's photos of the cottage he readied for her, the first thing she packs are his drawings, attached with magnets to her refrigerator. The oldest houses he made in preschool; the latest piece is his end-of-semester project. Her untrained eye spots the talent in the clean designs of his new work, yet she prefers the childhood drawings, with their uneven stonework, homely gargoyles, and lush flower gardens.

Moving from kitchen to living room, Tazia chooses a paperweight that Captain Morris gave her when he said goodbye. It's a model of the USS Parsons, the first ship he commanded. He acknowledged that the prospects of a civilian woman working for the Navy were limited but urged Tazia to steer her own course as best she could. She's served thirteen other commanding officers since then, with nary a trinket or word of encouragement to remember them by.

The bookcase below the ship model holds magazines, novels handed off by nameless C.O. wives, and Tazia's Bible. She takes this last item and two more. One is another Bible, a small one Pastor Balter pressed on her the first time she and Gemma visited Lighthouse on the Rock. Tazia never read it, feeling it would be an act of blasphemy, yet she didn't throw it away. The other keeper is a primer Nellie Tapper gave Gemma and Mirlee Bee to practice reading aloud. Tazia would cook dinner while the girls played school, Mirlee Bee the teacher and Gemma her student. The day Tazia and Gemma boarded the train for Las Vegas, Mirlee Bee gave Gemma a red ribbon from her pigtail. It's tucked inside the primer, a bookmark of their final minutes in Topeka.

Beside the bookshelves is the regulation Navy desk where Tazia sat to pay bills. She had no documents to store in it, although since her heart attack Gemma's been urging her to make out a will. Goodness knows what her daughter thinks she has to leave behind, other than the secrets she'll take to the grave. She opens the middle drawer and rummages among pens and notepads until her hand lights upon a cat toy at the back. When Tazia pulls it out, she sees that the price tag is still attached. She'd bought it after Sailor Boy died, intending it for the new base cat, but no succeeding C.O. was interested in keeping up the tradition. She pitches the toy in the wastebasket.

Gemma's room has long since been cleaned out, so Tazia goes into her own bedroom and opens the closet. Inside are the old clothes she wore to scrub sinks and polish floors, rags she no longer needs. She's agreed to let Gemma take her shopping for new clothes, along with dishes and kitchen utensils. She's about to close the door when she sees, scrunched on the far right, a white dress she hasn't worn in decades. It is still spotless, starched, and retains the creases that Jung Lo hand-ironed into its pleats. She carries the dress to the bed and rolls it up so it won't get wrinkled in her suitcase. There's a small lump in the right pocket. Folded inside a piece of tissue paper, Tazia finds a pair of earrings. They must have been from Virgil, although she cannot remember receiving or wearing them. There are tiny glass beads on the pendulums. Or are they diamond chips, with monetary value? If they are, and she'd known it when she moved to San Diego, dead broke, would she have sold the earrings instead of keeping them as a remembrance? Tazia smiles, recalling sweet hours spent lying in bed with Virgil, his lips cooing Mafia hit terms in between long, soft kisses. She rewraps the earrings, then places them and the dress in her bag.

Swiveling to the dresser, Tazia opens the top drawer, salvages a few undergarments, and dislodges a silver diving medal. It must have gotten overlooked when she gave Gemma her other awards. She tosses it in the suitcase; maybe Frankie will want it. In the middle drawer is a pile of blankets she hasn't used since escaping the harsh Midwestern and Prairie winters. Tazia won't need them where she's going now either. She leaves them and wrestles the warped drawer closed.

Tazia hesitates before pulling out the bottom drawer, which holds what she thinks of as her private stash. Folded on top are Gemma's embroidered baby dresses. Her daughter kept the baby blanket after Frankie no longer needed it, hoping to pass it down to her own grandchildren. Tazia smiles to think of these same threads enfolding her great grandchildren as they nestle inside her arms. Beneath the dresses is the picture she'd asked Frankie to draw of the great grandparents he never met. His imagined portrait of her parents is better than having a real photo of them.

Below the drawing is a small enameled jewelry box. Tazia unlocks it and takes out Elvan's rattle. When Frankie outgrew it, she'd reclaimed it. With all the toys from Todd's parents, it was soon forgotten. Underneath the rattle is Ayal's picture poem. Slowly she brings it to the bed, now stripped of linens. He must have written it on the printer's high-quality acid-free paper, because it hasn't yellowed. The words are as bright as the day he'd handed it to her: "Ayal is Hebrew for deer/Anastazia Italian for reborn/ The day I met you my angel/My nighttime brightened to morn." Equally clear are Ayal's whimsical pictures. Only Tazia's memories have faded with time. Would she have been better off leaving the note to burn in the fire? She looks out the window, sees ghostly images of floating bodies. Better to preserve some memories, even if they carry pain.

All that is missing is any trace of Veronika. Tazia wishes she'd saved one of the chipped ceramic bowls from which they had fed a sometimes cranky, more often exuberant, Gemma. She wonders what became of the woman who was like a big sister to her and a second mother to her daughter. Then she relocks the jewelry box and lays it carefully inside her bag.

Returning to the bed, Tazia slides open the drawer of her night stand. Inside is the photo album with pictures of Gemma. As she'd intended, they trace her child's development, beginning at age three, yet always in nondescript settings. Tazia remembers where each was taken, but to the unknowing eye, they could be anywhere. She packs up this final memento and takes one more walk through the apartment, at the last minute retrieving the cat toy from the trash. For the first time, in Aguanga, Tazia will be able to have a cat of her own. Then she carries the suitcase outside and puts it in her car. It's very light, well under the limit of what the doctor said she was allowed to lift. That's not much to show for a life of sixty-five years is her immediate thought as she closes the trunk. Then she reconsiders. Not much of material value, but there's a wealth of memories—work, people, and most important, the three-generation family she created. Not on her own, after all, but with the warmth and wisdom of those who helped her along the way.

She slips behind the wheel, breathes in the fresh salt air and puts her key in the ignition. As the engine fires up, Tazia smiles. Her journey from Italy through America isn't over yet.

part fourteen

Gemma, Loro Piceno, 1961

chapter 48

This is Gemma Kane, speaking with Alba Agnelli, a niece of Anna and Luigi Campo, the couple with whom my mother lived in Brooklyn, at her home in Loro Piceno, Italy. Today is Monday, June 12, 1961, and the time is 7:00 PM. [Note: Alba speaks English, but not well. Her oldest granddaughter, Paloma, who is about Frankie's age and teaches English, translates as needed.]

Gemma: (Sits outside small stone house under trellis of flowering white clematis; sips espresso; smells cookies, still warm from oven) Mmm. My mother doesn't make this kind. What are they?

Alba: Amaretti, almond macaroons. From an old Campo recipe. Each family has its own version. *Mangiare in fretta.* Eat now while it's crisp outside, chewy inside. Later is good too, but crunchy.

Gemma: (Eats two, licks fingers) *Grazie.* Have you gotten over the shock of my call?

Alba: The shock, yes. But not the anger. Not at you, at your mother. My aunt and uncle went to their graves feeling guilty about her death.

Gemma: Why? They weren't to blame for the fire they thought killed her.

Alba: No, but they were responsible for looking after your mother when she came to America. Her parents had been so kind when fire destroyed our family's orchard. You know that's why my aunt and uncle emigrated? They felt they should have helped Tazia find a safer place to work.

Gemma: They were all unsafe back then.

Alba: In a tragedy, who cares about such facts? They suffered, almost as much as the Gattis.

Gemma: (Eyes tear up) I'm so sorry. It must have been awful for them. My mother doesn't talk about it, but I think her secretiveness comes in part from her own guilt. Can you ever forgive her?

Alba: Maybe, but first I'd have to understand why she did it.

Gemma: I believe she was afraid her parents would never forgive her for getting pregnant.

Alba: (Shakes head) The Gattis weren't like that. They were pious but too loving to reject their own daughter ... or their grandchild.

Gemma: And the rest of Loro Piceno? Fifty years ago, people weren't so liberal.

Alba: True. And some are just as conservative today. (Shrugs) Buy regardless of what others thought, it doesn't make what your mother did any less cruel to her family and friends.

Gemma: (Nods slowly) She didn't *intentionally* cause harm.

Alba: (Folds arms; frowns) A sin is a sin.

Gemma: Her guilt *is* undeniable. But the Church teaches us that intention ameliorates judgment. I believe my mother didn't want to shame her family. She was trying to spare them from pain.

Alba: What about my aunt and uncle's pain?

Gemma: My only excuse is that my mother was young and scared. Her judgment wasn't the best, but at seventeen, whose is?

Alba: (Unfolds arms; smiles slightly) Not mine. (Winks at granddaughter; Paloma blushes)

Gemma: My mother wasn't thrilled about my making this journey, but she didn't put up barriers either. At some level, she's letting me be her emissary. If I apologize for her, can you accept it?

Alba: (Purses lips) I need to hear it from Tazia herself. Meantime, as I said, I'm not angry at you. (Embraces me) People here still holds grudges against those who fought on the other side in the war. We have to get over it, for the sake of the younger generation. (Holds Paloma's chin) So, ask me what you crossed an ocean to find out.

Gemma: What my mother was like before she moved to America. *Per favore*, tell me whatever you remember.

Alba: (Breathes deeply, as if to clear the air) I have many good memories. We grew up together. And *oh bontà*, the two of us made mischief! We played tricks on the teacher (grins at Paloma), greasing the chalkboard with olive oil so she couldn't write on it. She was glad when we stopped going to school to help at home. My family teased me when I married. Agnelli means lamb. I grew into my husband's name, but it was more fun being wild, especially with Tazia as my confederate.

Gemma: Did you two find other ways to make trouble after you left school?

Alba: As the oldest in our families, our job was to watch the little ones. Hot summer days, we'd fill their bellies with cookies to make them fall asleep under the trees. Then she and I would race to where the Gatti farm borders the Fiastra stream. (Puts hand over mouth; rocks with laughter)

Gemma: (Laughs too) What? Tell me!

Alba: We went swimming. Naked. We'd make a lot of noise to signal the boys that we were there and then when they came to see, we'd pretend to be surprised and jump out of the water, grab our clothes, and run back to the fields. We were fully dressed again before the little ones woke up.

Gemma: (Grins) I can't imagine my proper mother doing that. Your parents never found out?

Alba: If they suspected we were up to something, they didn't know what. We had to stop though when one of the twins—your uncle Fino or Fredi—told Mrs Gatti he wasn't hungry for dinner because he'd eaten so many biscotti after lunch. Your grandmother must have been tempted to turn over babysitting to your aunt Bianca right then and there. (Pauses to wipe tears of laughter)

Gemma: But she didn't? (Eats another cookie; as Alba said, it is crunchy inside and out)

Alba: No. Bianca was even more *sventata*, I think you say "scatter-brained" in English. But of course, when Tazia left, Bianca had to take over anyway. She learnt faster than me to be a good girl. (Turns sober) Bianca was also a comfort to the whole family after my aunt and uncle wrote.

Gemma: Poor Bianca was speechless when I phoned her over the weekend. I'm seeing her the day after tomorrow. First, I'm meeting my Uncle Zito. He was just a baby when my mother left.

Alba: (Nods) I remember. Zito was so sick and spindly. He was born with bad lungs. The money your mother sent helped her parents pay for the doctor and medicine.

Gemma: And when the money stopped coming?

Alba: The neighbours took up a collection, but by then he was almost all better. The Gattis made a feast—a little one because they were still in mourning for Tazia—when the doctor pronounced Zito cured. (Lifts arms, makes fists) Wait until you see your uncle now. Big and strapping, even at fifty-two. Outworks his grown sons and runs rings around his grandsons.

Gemma: I wonder if my mother knew she helped save his life. She never talks about that either, again, I think, because of her guilt. I hope when I tell her about Uncle Zito, it will smooth out the wrinkles in her brow. (Smiles) Retirement has already subtracted ten years from her face.

Alba: (Pours us more espresso; regards my face) You're as pretty as your mother. She was the handsomest girl in the village. If she hadn't been so nice, I'd have been even more jealous.

Gemma: Tell me what she looked like. Wait a second. (Switches tape) Okay.

Alba: Slim but sturdy. A thicket of red-black curls. Dark eyes, deep as the swirling pools in the stream where we swam. They gleamed when she was naughty and flashed when she got angry.

Gemma: (Closes eyes) I can see that girl in the woman she is today. *Grazie* for this lovely gift.

Alba: *Prego.* (Blinks, twice) The boys in Loro Piceno were crestfallen when Tazia's family sent her to America. She could have had her pick of suitors when it came time to get married.

Gemma: (Looks at setting orange-gold sun) Did she have a sweetheart while she was still here?

Alba: No. Despite teasing the boys, we were good girls. Not that we had a choice. The village nonnas kept their eyes on everyone and reported the first sign of bad behaviour to our parents.

Gemma: So my mother never had a secret romance? Or did anything immoral?

Alba: Nothing worse than flirting. Besides, who had time? Between taking care of our brothers and sisters, helping our mothers cook and clean, and harvesting with the rest of the family, we were too busy to get into trouble. Of course, I suppose, where there's a will, there's a way.

Gemma: And how would you describe my mother's will?

Alba: I never thought about it. Tazia was simply my friend. We shared the same life, until she left. (Ponders) I always assumed her parents sent her because she was the oldest. Now I wonder if they glimpsed something wild and hoped giving her a big responsibility would settle her down.

Gemma: And then they had to live forever after with the thought that they were responsible for her death. (Shivers, despite warm air) I don't know how a parent *can* go on living after that.

Alba: Children died all the time back then. But the land teaches you that every year, with a new crop, comes hope. So, while the Gattis grieved, they looked to the future, and their four remaining children. (Muses)

Interesting, though, that they stopped having babies after Zito. Maybe they saw Tazia's death as a message from God. To be grateful for what they had and not to seek more.

Gemma: That's my mother's philosophy. She said I should be grateful for the life she gave me and shouldn't stir things up by looking for my father.

Alba: And?

Gemma: She was right about the danger of looking for him, although I'm glad I did. Otherwise it would have continued to haunt me. (Smiles) But my mother never warned me against looking for her. I'm grateful for the messages you've given me. No doubt, I'll receive more from the Gattis.

Alba: Who knows? Maybe some from God too.

The interview ended at 8:15 PM.

chapter 49

This is Gemma Kane, speaking with Zito Gatti, my mother's youngest brother, at the Gatti family cemetery on their olive farm in Loro Piceno, Italy. Today is Tuesday, June 13, 1961, and the time is 7:00 AM. [Note: Uncle Zito speaks fluent English, which he learnt in order to export olive oil to the U.S., Great Britain, and South Africa; no translator/interpreter needed.]

Zito: I hope you'll forgive me for suggesting we meet this early in the morning. I wanted to show you around the farm before it got too hot, which it will be in just a couple of hours.

Gemma: No problem. With jet lag, my internal clock registers eleven at night, so I'd be more tired if we met later. (Checks tape recorder) I hope the batteries last.

Zito: You'll only need them in the cemetery and the orchard. Once we get to the *frantoio*, there'll be electricity and you can plug in.

Gemma: Frantoio?

Zito: The olive press, or mill. It's not far. Nothing is, the farm's small, although bigger than when Tazia was a girl. Over the years, I bought three neighbouring properties. So many families gave up. It's hard to compete with the big companies. (Lifts tape recorder) It's heavy. I'll carry it on the way to the fields and mill. Unless you want to take the truck?

Gemma: No. I'd rather walk the land. Soak in every inch, sound, and smell of what my mother's life was like here. (Listens to cicadas humming; feels sirocco wind blowing in from the Sahara, already bringing the day's heat and humidity.)

Zito: Tomorrow, when Bianca prepares a feast for you and our whole family, you'll experience every taste too. (Laughs) Especially anything made with olives. The oil runs in our veins. It's why we Gattis live so long. (Pulls the few weeds off parents' graves)

Gemma: (Reads headstones) My grandfather died ten years ago; my grandmother only five. I wish I hadn't waited so long to come. Imagine if they'd died knowing their daughter was alive.

Zito: They might have felt worse, unable to grasp why Tazia let them think she'd died. This way, their final thoughts were of a dutiful daughter, who helped their youngest child—me—survive.

Gemma: I suppose they would have also been terribly upset to find out she'd gotten pregnant and had a child out of wedlock. I'm sure that's why my mother chose to disappear, to spare them the shame. (Looks at Zito's sun-weathered face) Actually, I expected you to be more shocked about the circumstances of my birth. The Catholic Church hasn't changed its position on that.

Zito: No, but with your own family, standards are looser. (Smiles) I can't speak for everyone, but most of us are happy to meet you. God and your mother willing, we'll see Tazia again too.

Gemma: (Excited) You could all come to the wedding next week. I know it's last minute but ...

Zito: (Holds up hand) Whoa. One big event at a time. Let this news sink in, then we'll see about our making a trip to California or Tazia coming here.

Gemma: You're right. Besides, I can't know how the others feel until I meet them tomorrow. (Chews fingernail; stands)

Zito: (Picks up tape recorder; walks toward fields) If it's our moral judgment that concerns you, don't worry. The Gattis are traditional but also *progressivo* when it comes to accepting people.

Gemma: (Walks alongside) That must be where my mother gets her openness from. (Hesitates) I know this is a sensitive topic, but can I ask which side you were on during the war?

Zito: (Opens shirt with free hand to reveal scar below left shoulder) The twins and I fought with the resistance. Partisans stored guns in the big ceramic vats where we kept olive oil. (Laughs) They never rusted. We also hid two Jewish families in the cellar, scrounging rations to feed them.

Gemma: (Leaps over narrow gully; climbs hill, out of breath) You're in better shape than me.

Zito: The work keeps me in shape. (Slows pace) Funny to think I'm only two years older than you, yet I'm your uncle.

Gemma: Having a brother and a child so close in age must have seemed strange to my mother too.

Zito: Growing up, I heard so much about the big sister who went to America. When I got older, I thought how she died in a fire, unable to breathe, when she'd literally given me the breath of life. (Sets down tape recorder; sits under olive trees)

Gemma: (Sits too; leans against gnarled trunks) These are so stunted and twisted compared to California's giant sequoias. I'll take you to see them when you visit.

Zito: These have been in our family over a century. It takes a few years for them to bear fruit, but then they can live for hundreds more, hopefully until my great-great grandchildren inherit the farm. (Strokes trunk) I wonder how they'll harvest olives then. We still do it by hand. Three people per tree, one at the top of the ladder and two below. A mixture of green and black olives makes the most flavourful oil. You slide the fruit off the branches like beads off a necklace. (Motions) Then you drop the olives into the *brucatura*. (Shows me an empty basket)

Gemma: My mother's patience for slow methodical work still amazes me. She must have learnt that trait in these fields. (Laughs) I'm not like her at all. There must be quicker ways these days?

Zito: Some pick by hand using nets and plastic rakes, which is a little faster, only less careful. Big growers harvest mechanically, but the machines pick unripe olives along with ripe ones and bruise a lot of fruit, which then has to be discarded before it's pressed. It can also damage branches. Of course, large farms can afford the waste, but we coddle every olive we grow. (Runs hand through hair) I'm sorry. I've probably told you more about harvesting olives than you want to know.

Gemma: Not at all. I'm here to learn about my mother and work was a big part of who she was. Beginning here. In some ways, her life was as twisted as these trees, but also as deeply rooted.

Zito: I wish I could tell you more about her, but other than saying she saved my life, our family rarely spoke about Tazia. Italian tradition holds that doing so after the period of mourning invites the dead to return to earth instead of resting in peace. (Tilts head) Actually, since she's not dead, do you mind if I ask *you* about your mother. A sort of reverse interview.

Gemma: (Laughs) Why not? Sometimes the speaker learns as much as the listener.

Zito: You said work was an important part of who Tazia was. After the fire, what did she do?

Gemma: More menial work, most of it awful. America is the land of opportunity, but for my generation, not hers. All the same, my mother kept her sense of pride. (Thinks) You know, in all my years as a labour reporter, I felt I had to defend helpless workers against their bosses, shame management into treating people better. Maybe I didn't give workers enough credit for the dignity they already possessed, without any help from me. (Grins) See? I already learnt something.

Zito: (Looks up at feathery gray-green leaves and tiny fruits) I've always worked for myself and my family. I couldn't stand to work for someone else. I'm too independent.

Gemma: Mama managed to stay independent too. No one controlled her spirit even if the work itself got her down. (Looks at distant hills; smiles) There was one job she enjoyed though, on a wheat farm. The land was as flat as rolled pasta dough, but the work reminded her of home.

Zito: Do you think liking her independence was the reason Tazia never married?

Gemma: Gee. I never thought of that. She's not against marriage. She approves of mine so much she often gets along better with my husband than me. (Laughs) If I had to explain why my mother stayed single, I'd say it was because she devoted her life to me. I like to think it was enough for her, but now I wonder if my existence held her back. God, that's an awful thought.

Zito: I'm guessing Tazia was fulfilled raising you and helping raise your son. It was her choice. From what you said, no one, including you, could make her do what she didn't want to.

Gemma: (Smiles) *Grazie*, Uncle Zito. You make me feel better.

Zito: That's what families are for. (Pats my hand) Now, tell me more. Did Tazia have hobbies?

Gemma: She was interested in anything Italian! Art and architecture. Cooking. The last two years she's taken up embroidery again. Frankly, though, my mother was too tired most of her life to have what you'd call hobbies. Leisure was a foreign concept to her. (Hands Zito tape recorder)

Zito: (Walks toward frantoio) It's the same when you grow olives. Never a break. As soon as one season ends, the next begins, although harvest time is the busiest. The olives should be at the mill within twenty-four hours of picking. (Points to small frame house on far right) Mine. (Points to large stone house at the other end of field) The original farmhouse, where Tazia grew up. Bianca lives there now. It's also the family gathering place. The twins live in town. Fino owns a grocery store, Fredi's a tailor, but they come home each fall to help with the harvest. (Mops brow) Here we are.

Gemma: (Enters cool stone building; dwarfed by equipment; shivers) It's freezing in here.

Zito: So the oil won't go rancid. (Plugs in tape recorder) The press isn't running now. Harvest is late fall, just before cold weather sets in. But I can show you how the frantoio works if you like?

Gemma: (Nods; changes tape)

Zito: If the press were running, it would be so loud you couldn't hear me talk. (Demonstrates) First the olives are washed, then this wooden shoot drops them into the shallow stone trough.

Gemma: It's huge! (Estimates twelve feet in diameter)

Zito: These two stone wheels (each six feet across, turned on edge, yoked together) roll across the olives to grind them, pits and all, into a paste. The oil is pressed out, then a vertical centrifuge separates the oil from the vegetable water and *sansa*—pomace, in English. Finally, the pure oil is drained into basins.

Gemma: What does this do? (Points to large blade jutting out from centre of yoke)

Zito: It keeps the olives moving. Men, machinery, nothing stands still.

Gemma: Maybe that accounts for my mother's restlessness.

Zito: It *is* nice to flip a switch, though, so motors turn the presses instead of donkeys, like back in Tazia's day. (Flexes muscles) We do one pressing, but cheaper brands do several.

Gemma: Is that what's meant by extra virgin?

Zito: For that classification, the acidity must be under eight percent. We still bottle by hand too and attach our own labels. The bigger farms mechanize all those steps from the mill, where they use steel drums instead of stone, to the final product they ship to market.

Gemma: It sounds like the meat packing plant where my mother worked when I was very young. People got horribly hurt all the time. Does that happen with the machines here?

Zito: Rarely. People are safe, but mechanization oxidizes the fruits' enzymes which means the oil has less aroma and taste.

Gemma: Better bruised fruit than bruised men.

Zito: And your mother?

Gemma: A survivor. Intact. And she made sure I stayed safe too.

Zito: *Buona* or I'd never have met you or heard you talk about your mother.

Gemma: Five weeks ago, I couldn't have told you as much about her as I did today.

Zito: I always felt bad that the older children knew Tazia better than me. Now I know more than they do. (Laughs) At least until tomorrow evening, when they interrogate you at Bianca's house. (Hugs me) Meanwhile *nipotina, addio e amore.*

The interview ended at 8:30 AM.

chapter 50

This is Gemma Kane, speaking with Bianca Lagorio, my mother's next-oldest sibling, at the Gatti family farmhouse in Loro Piceno, Italy. Today is Thursday, June 15, 1961, and the time is 4:30 PM. [Note: Aunt Bianca, like Alba, speaks English, but not well. Paloma, Alba's granddaughter, sits in on the interview to translate or interpret as needed.]

Bianca: (Brings coffee and biscotti to long wooden table in kitchen with fireplace, beams, white-washed walls; wipes eyes with apron) See this stitching. (Flowers and birds are like those on baby clothes and blanket back home) Your mother embroidered this apron more than fifty years ago.

Gemma: It looks new.

Bianca: I only wear it on special occasions. Weddings, confirmations, funerals. And whatever you call today. (Grimaces) *Lode a Dio*, I can't believe you're here. Or that my sister is alive.

Gemma: As the next oldest, news of her death must have hit you almost as hard as your parents.

Bianca: (Nostrils flare) I'll never forget my mother collapsing on the cold tiles of this very room when my father read the letter from the Campos. I had an image of Papa hurling it in the fireplace, but five years ago, after Mama died, I found it among her keepsakes. Do you want to see it?

Gemma: (Nods)

Bianca: (Carefully unfolds yellowed paper with deep creases and spidery handwriting in faded ink; hands it to Paloma to translate) *Dearest Friends, We are heartsick to tell you the tragic news that Anastazia died in a fire at the factory where she sewed. Many other young girls were killed too. Their bodies were too badly burnt to be identified, so we cannot even send you her remains. We promised to look after her and now we live with our guilt. The priest says to forgive ourselves, it is not our fault, but we have let you down. May God have mercy on Anastazia's innocent soul. We cry for her and for you, until the day you are reunited in heaven. In prayer, Luigi and Anna*

Gemma: (Thinks of Frankie) I can't imagine ... a letter, from so far away, not even a body to bury.

Bianca: If only my parents had lived long enough to hear that Tazia hadn't died after all.

Gemma: Zito says the news might have been harder to live with than thinking she was dead.

Bianca: My little brother. So smart. (Taps forehead) But sometimes he is wrong. (Touches chest) My heart pounds just thinking of my sister's betrayal. And the peace it would have brought Papa and Mama to know she was alive. How can I not be angry at Tazia for them?

Gemma: You have every right to be. Are you also angry on behalf of yourself, being forced to take her place?

Bianca: (Stiffens) Don't I have that right too?

Gemma: You do. *I'm* angry at my mother. She kept me from my father and your entire family.

Bianca: (Studies my face) You don't look angry.

Gemma: You should have seen me six weeks ago. Not to mention when I was a teenager. If I'm less angry now, it's because I have a better idea why she acted the way she did. At first I thought she was afraid your parents would reject her. Now I think she was afraid of hurting them.

Bianca: (Raises eyebrows) You mean she wasn't worried for herself, but for them?

Gemma: You said it better than I could.

Bianca: (Snorts) I learn quickly. But understanding and forgiving don't happen at the same time. You've had six weeks, but I've barely begun to absorb the news. Meanwhile I ricochet between sorrow, relief, and rage. Who knows when, or if, I'll understand, let alone forgive Tazia.

Gemma: It's easier for me because I've also lived with half a century of my mother's goodness. You've never known that part of her.

Bianca: (Slides finger along groove in old table) I pray my own children will forgive the wrongs I committed against them. We do our best, but we make mistakes.

Gemma: Like my mother.

Bianca: Yes. Except that I've never done anything as cruel as Tazia. (Straightens shoulders) All the same, the Church tells us that if God can forgive, we should too.

Gemma: So you'll forgive my mother?

Bianca: (Smiles ruefully) I'll work on it. (Caresses my hands) Seeing you is a good beginning. (Refolds letter; slips it inside apron pocket) My sister wrote us too, once a month, but her letters stopped about three months before the Campos told us she'd died.

Gemma: (Calculates) Around the time she knew for sure she was pregnant.

Bianca: Shame can silence a woman's voice. (Pushes cookies toward me) *Mangiare.* I don't know what became of Tazia's letters, but I remember one where she talked about a little girl named Paulie who she said reminded her of me. Mischievous. Defiant. (Grins) But charming.

Gemma: I heard that after my mother set sail, your parents worried you'd be irresponsible.

Bianca: I daydreamt. While my body did chores, my head soared above the hills. (Looks out window) I was jealous of Tazia. I wanted to be the one on that boat. I wouldn't have minded so much if she'd promised to send for me, but (smiles), typical big sister, she lorded it over me that I was stuck here. (Sobers) Later, after we got the letter, I felt lucky. And guilty about envying her. I resolved to *reforma*, how you say, change my ways? *Essere buono*, be very, very good.

Gemma: (Pats Bianca's hand) Alba reassured me that you became the family's rock. Even Zito praised you. And this time, I'm sure he was right.

Bianca: *Grazie.* (Puts hands to cheeks in mock alarm) Now that Tazia is the oldest again, I hope my brothers don't stop listening to me. (Laughs) I can be very bossy.

Gemma: Don't worry. My mother never wanted to be the boss. (Grins) Except of me. (Muses) Nor did she want to be bossed. What she's craves is to be left alone. Who's this? (Pets gray cat with large green eyes twining itself around chair legs)

Bianca: Prezzmolo. (Picks up cat) She's nursing a litter. (Nods toward barn, next door; coos) Does mama cat need a break? (Fetches bowl of milk) See those eyes? Her name means parsley.

Gemma: Thank goodness my mother didn't name me that!

Bianca: (Looks at my green eyes) You didn't get those from the Gattis. Unless Tazia mated with one of our cats. (Nuzzles Prezzmolo) Between my brothers and me, we have over a dozen.

Gemma: Trust me. My father is no pussycat. But a love of cats runs in the family. You should see how my mother dotes on Lucy. I take back what I just said about my mother not liking to be bossed. That cat rules her household.

Bianca: (Laughs) Lucy aside, what you say fits my memory of Tazia. A free spirit, not controlled or controlling. Unguarded. (Sweeps arms toward windows) As open as the hills of Loro Piceno.

Gemma: (Shakes head) That sounds nothing like the woman who raised me. In all honesty, my mother was closed and secretive. It infuriated me growing up. It still does. (Feels anger well up)

Bianca: (Leans close; intense) Now it's my turn to help you understand. Trauma changes people. What happened to your mother in America changed her. But in the end, God has a way of making things work out, *non è vero*? (Leans back; smiles) If your mother had told you more, you might not be sitting here. And I wouldn't have had a reason to wear this beautiful apron.

Gemma: I guess I'm not as ready to forgive as I thought. (Lets the anger ride for now; studies apron's feathery flowers and dark leaves) Do you embroider too?

Bianca: Our nonna tried to teach me, but I lacked Tazia's patience. (Spreads fingers) My clumsy hands are better suited to kneading dough and rolling pasta.

Gemma: (Smiles) Cooking, sewing. Mama's always been so proud of her Italian heritage. She passed along her love of the arts to my son Frankie.

Bianca: Her what?

Gemma: Her fascination with art and architecture.

Bianca: (Frowns) Are we talking about the same person? All Loro Piceno has in the way of old architecture is Roman ruins and *Castello Brunforte*, a medieval castle. The only time Tazia would have actually seen Renaissance buildings was in Ancona, when she boarded the boat for America.

Gemma: (Stunned) It's almost laughable. Yet, it's also touching that seeing those great edifices during her last hours in Italy made such an impression that my mother carried it with her for life.

Bianca: Just because Tazia was a country girl doesn't mean she didn't appreciate the big world.

Gemma: Just the opposite. She didn't take it for granted. Was she sad to leave home?

Bianca: I remember lots of tears, but Tazia had ... what's the word? Wanderlust?

Gemma: (Nods) Maybe that's another reason we moved so much. All the same, my mother often spoke of Loro Piceno with longing.

Bianca: It's easy to romanticize a place after you're gone. But her life demanded a larger canvas.

Gemma: And America was a huge continent with an infinite palette of colours. (Ponders) Suppose she *had* come home when she got pregnant. How do you think your parents would have reacted?

Bianca: (Considers) I don't believe they would have condemned her or looked down on you. You've met the people here, seen our way of life. What do you think?

Gemma: That for the most part, she, we, would have been welcomed. It was her own guilt that kept my mother away. (Amazed) Just think, if she'd had more trust, I could have grown up here.

Bianca: (Smiles) And what do you think about that?

Gemma: This is the most beautiful place I've ever seen. But, no offense, I can't imagine spending my whole life in this village. (Changes tape)

Bianca: (Folds hands in lap) So perhaps when your mother chose not to return here, she was thinking of you, not just herself. (Corners of mouth turn up) Did you bring any pictures?

Gemma: Believe it or not, there are none of my mother. And since I wasn't planning on coming to Italy when I set out, I didn't bring any of my family. Oh wait. I always carry one. (Pulls from purse photo of Todd, self, and Frankie at college graduation). I promise to send pictures from the wedding. I wish I'd brought a camera. I'd love to take home a picture of you for my mother.

Bianca: (Leaves; brings back photo of entire family) From last Christmas. I have lots of copies. You give this one to Tazia. (Looks at watch) Oh my. Everyone in this picture will be here soon. I'm sure the twins will have cameras. They always argue over who has the latest equipment.

Gemma: (Laughs) I never had brothers or sisters to fight with. Only my mother. (Studies photo for family resemblances) Frankie looks just like Fino and Fredi. Roman nose, bushy eyebrows.

Bianca: And you look like my daughters. They'll be here any minute to help set up. It's cooling off enough to eat outside. I hope you like olive oil. (Laughs) We use it in everything. There'll be plenty of wine too. From Zito, homemade. Do you want to rest a while before the party starts?

Gemma: No, thank you. I'll walk around the farm. To imprint it on my memory. (Hesitates) Do you think after we eat that everyone would be willing to record a short message for my mother?

Bianca: They'd be thrilled. (Points to tape) Do you have enough of those for everyone?

Gemma: Don't worry. A reporter learns never to run out of tapes. Still, I'm a bit overwhelmed. I left home looking to expand my family by one— my father. Instead I'm about to meet dozens.

Bianca: So the journey was worth it?

Gemma: Yes. But the best part was discovering the family I started out with—my mother.

The interview ended at 5:30 PM.

Tazia paces around her cottage, waiting for Gemma to arrive. They'd talked on the phone for hours yesterday, after Gemma returned from Italy. She'd gone over where she'd been, who she'd interviewed, and the trail that led her to her father, but she wanted to tell Tazia in person about meeting Ayal and her trip to Loro Piceno. Tazia had tried to gauge her daughter's reaction from the tone of her voice, but Gemma had spoken in her reporter's "just the facts" manner.

When the car pulls into the gravel driveway, Tazia sets espresso cups and wine glasses on the table. She'd like a shot of both. Gemma enters, throws her suitcase on the pullout bed, and wraps Tazia in a big hug. It's been six weeks since they've seen each other, the longest separation since Gemma was in college. Tazia steps back to study her. She expects her daughter to be tired, but she looks as if she's just awakened from a long, refreshing sleep, eager to recount her dreams.

"Todd will bring the rest of our bags when he drives up later," Gemma says. The two families, Frankie's and Julia's, with their parents and grand-parents, are having dinner together tonight at a fancy restaurant that the Kanes insisted on paying for. The wedding is tomorrow.

They sit at the table. Gemma shakes her head no to the coffee cup, wine-glass, and biscotti. "I'm saving my appetite for tonight." She accepts water with lime. "Mama, you should have seen the feast Bianca prepared the day I met everyone. Pasta, sausages, plain olives, marinated olives, skewered olives, bread dipped in olive oil, almond olive oil cake, iced lemon olive oil cake."

Tazia remembers her nonna baking those cakes for big family gather-ings, and imagines Bianca, a half-century older than when she left, in the farmhouse kitchen. Had Tazia stayed, that role would now be hers. Instead, she's rarely cooked for more than four. She prefers it that way.

"But I don't want to get ahead of myself. First let me tell you about my father." Gemma drinks half her water, then eats a cookie after all. Tazia takes this as a good sign, her daughter's way of saying she still belongs to her mother. "Before I start, though, is there anything I should do to help get ready for tomorrow? Last minute shopping? Food? Decorations?"

"Now you ask?" Tazia waves her hand. "You were supposed to be home a week ago."

"I know, I know. But that extra week turned out to be even more important than finding," she makes air quotes, "Mr Ayal Gabay."

Tazia has not heard his name in fifty years. She waits for her heart to pound, but feels only a mild flutter, like a bird settling in its nest after a long flight. The name has lost its power.

"Besides," Gemma cajoles, "I knew you could handle the preparations without me."

"And so, I did," Tazia says. "Together with Mrs Lonski and the Benedettis. Everything is set." She crosses her arms and glares at her daughter.

Gemma glares back, but soon breaks the silence. "Do you want to hear about the meeting with my father?"

Tazia unfolds her arms, pours a glass of wine. "Of course," she says softly.

The contentment Gemma radiated when she arrived has disappeared. She looks grim. "I'm not sure what to say" she begins, suddenly uncertain. "I mean, obviously you know who he is."

"Not any longer. People change."

"Well, if he's changed, it's for the worse. Although I'll concede he looks good and must have been quite handsome." Gemma sneers. "Still, I'd like to think he was nicer when you and he ... made me. But maybe he wasn't, even then, and that's why you ran away without telling him."

Tazia pinches her bottom lip, choosing her words carefully. She will *not* tell Gemma that her father urged her to have an abortion. No child should hear that. "I honestly don't know why I ran. I suppose I didn't trust Ayal to marry me." She sips her wine. "I assume you found out that he was Jewish and already married, to the daughter of a well-to-do fur merchant?"

"Yes. I also learnt he married twice more, to wealthier women, who weren't Jewish."

This time, Tazia waits to feel jealousy or resentment. She feels neither, only mild curiosity.

"He's rich himself now." Gemma describes the antique-filled apartment and explains how her father opened a successful greeting card business, which now makes record album covers.

Tazia pictures Ayal in his opulent surroundings, like a Medici in his palace. "Your father was a talented artist with a gift for words. He was ambitious, even greedy, but also charming."

"That's what drew you to him?"

"Yes. My life was drab. Living with friends of my parents, working six or seven days a week. Not even a cat to call my own." As if summoned, Lucy jumps into Tazia's lap. She smiles. "When I was with Ayal, that colourless world vanished. I dreamt of a brighter future, with him."

"But you knew it was only a dream, so you left?"

"By then, my dream had changed. You were at its centre, and the only way I could see to make it come true was to go somewhere new. I didn't have a plan, only a hope." Tazia scratches beneath the cat's chin until it begins to purr. "I suppose I was foolish."

"You weren't." Gemma wags her head. "If I dared think so when I started out, everyone I met these past weeks changed my mind. You were nobody's fool. You stood up for yourself."

"I stood up for you."

"In your mind it was the same thing." Gemma pauses. "No. That makes it sound like I was the only one who mattered. You did it for yourself too. Your pride. Your dignity."

Tazia has always told herself that Gemma was the reason behind everything she did.

Gemma pushes on, trying to persuade her. "Your dreams started in Italy, when you were still a girl. You wanted to know what was beyond those hills. You were born an adventuress."

A memory of wanting to follow the sun westward to where it set fills Tazia's mind. "You may be right," she concedes. "It *has* been an adventure, although not like I imagined." She holds Lucy close, letting the cat's vibrations penetrate her chest. "I wonder, if I'd stayed in New York, whether it would have worked out with Ayal after all. Instead of stuffing sausages and swabbing toilets, I'd have eaten dainties and had a maid. We'd have been rich." The thought amuses her.

"You know, my father has another daughter, with his second wife. He's not happy about his son-in-law taking over the business." Gemma frowns. "He has this cockamamie idea that he can hand it over to Frankie, his male heir. He begged me to tell him. If not, he'll spring the news."

Tazia's scalp tingles. "Did you invite Ayal to the wedding?"

"He invited himself."

Tazia bends forward.

"God, I hope he doesn't come," Gemma spits out.

Tazia sits back. She rather hopes he does, whether to satisfy her curiosity or test her immunity, she's not sure. "How has Frankie reacted to the news about his grandfather?"

"To be honest, he hasn't said much, certainly nothing about wanting to meet the man." Gemma grimaces. "Not that I've encouraged him." She swirls what's left of her water. "On the other hand, he seems taken with the idea that he's one-quarter Jewish. Maybe because he's about to become a married man, he's intrigued by the thought of adding a new religious identity too."

"And you?"

"I don't know if I can think of myself as anything other than Catholic this late in life." Gemma touches the small silver cross she wears around her neck. "How would you feel if Frankie and I chose to embrace that part of ourselves?"

Tazia regards her bible on the sideboard, where that morning she'd marked the passage in Matthew about a man and wife becoming one flesh. When Gemma got married, Tazia regretted that it was a sacrament denied to her. But anticipating Frankie's marriage, joy alone had filled her when she read Matthew's words. She takes Gemma's hand. "Up until a few years ago, I would have felt threatened. Now, it wouldn't bother me. I've learnt that your gain is not my loss."

***

The women lock eyes and know, without speaking, that they're ready for a break. Gemma hangs up the dress she brought to wear to dinner. Tazia admires its deep red colour and delicate beadwork at the neck and hem. "The groom's mother will sparkle tonight," she tells her daughter.

"I wish you'd wear something brighter than your old navy dress," Gemma says when she sees Tazia's outfit laid out on the bed. "Grandmothers deserve to shine too."

"I'm happier in the background, basking in the glow of my child and grandchild."

"Well, if you insist on being a reflection," Gemma says, pulling a faceted crystal pendant from her suitcase, "wear this." It was Todd's present to her on their twentieth anniversary. She fastens it around her mother's neck and beams when Tazia looks in the mirror, smiles, and leaves it on. The necklace glints in the mid-afternoon sunlight as they sit down to resume talking.

Gemma pours a glass of wine. Tazia switches to coffee. Gemma sets the photograph of the Gattis from last Christmas in front of her mother. Tazia's gaze alternates between the picture and Gemma's face. "You look like Bianca," is all she says. Then she fetches a picture of Frankie from her bedside table. "Like Zito," she nods. Gemma waits but Tazia makes no further remarks about her siblings, their children, or the other assorted family members in the photo. Then Gemma pulls out her tape recorder. "Everyone sent you a greeting," she says and hits play, handing Tazia a list of the order in which they speak. Tazia sips her espresso, her face impassive as she listens.

Only when Zito's booming voice come on does she smile and wipe her eyes. "For a baby born with weak lungs, he grew up strong."

Gemma pauses the tape. "You saved his life." She lets Tazia savour the moment, before pressing the play button again. After the last message ends, she studies her mother's composed face. "I'm surprised, Mama. I thought you'd be more interested. Everyone was so excited and full of questions about you. It was ... well, other than getting married and giving birth, meeting them was the most emotional experience of my life. In some ways, more meaningful than meeting my father. I expected a bigger reaction from you. This is your family." She shoves the picture closer.

Tazia gently slides it back. "They *were* my family. You and Frankie are my family now."

"So when you ran away from my father, were you also running away from them?"

"I don't think so. My memories of Italy are happy. Although..." Tazia hesitates. "Perhaps I was hurt that my parents sent me away. My head knew they did it reluctantly, for the sake of the others, but my heart must have been wounded." She sighs, suddenly tired. "It's so long ago. How can I know for sure what I felt then? All I can be certain of is what's in my heart now."

Gemma moves the photograph and tape recorder aside so she can reach across the table and take Tazia's hands in hers. "Perhaps all the years of your moving from place to place weren't about running *from* or *to*, but simply travelling *with*. With *me*. Lovers, like jobs, come and go, but a mother and her child are forever."

Tazia nods. This sounds right. Her smart daughter has grown wise on this journey.

"And when we got to California, and opportunities opened up for me, you were able to stop." Gemma frowns. "All the same, Mama, I have to ask, did you ever feel that I held you back? That your life would have been fuller, or more successful, if you hadn't had me to take care of?"

"No, *cara*. You were my reason for living. A source of worry, but a bigger source of joy."

Gemma reaches for the photo. "I'm happy you're fulfilled, but your disappearance left the family with a hole. Some are angry but in time they'll forgive and want to see you. We can invite them here, or you can go there. Late fall or early winter, when they're less busy on the farm."

"Invite them here."

"You don't want to visit Loro Piceno?"

"No. My travelling days are over."

"Once again, you surprise me Mama." Gemma smiles. "Although, I must say I'm relieved."

"Why?" It is Tazia's turn to be surprised.

"Despite what you say, I'm afraid that if you went home, you wouldn't come back."

Tazia looks around her kitchen. "This is home. I started my life in Italy, but America is where I'll end it. Like you said, it's *who* I'm with, not *where* I am. And the people you met—Veronika, Elvan, Denton and Lula Mae, Ju-Long, Virgil, most of all, Ayal—made my life here."

Gemma sighs, satisfied. An old mantle clock, a gift from Frankie when Tazia moved into the cottage, chimes the hour. "Darn," says Gemma. "Todd will be here soon, and we have to dress for dinner." She carries the dishes to the sink. "There's so much more I want to say. I don't even know what it is yet." She runs the water but stops to wipe her eyes.

Tazia envelops her daughter in an embrace and rocks her as if she were still a child. "I'm not running away. We have the rest of my life to talk."

chapter 52

Early the next morning, Tazia sits outside, facing east, drinking coffee. Lucy lies at her feet. Todd and Gemma are already next door at the Benedettis, waiting for the caterer and florist. After they left, Tazia had rummaged in her dresser until she found the jewelry box with Ayal's note, printed on Allegro stationery. She lifts it from her lap now, rereading his poem and admiring his drawings. A shiver like the one she felt fifty years ago courses through her body. She was right to hide the card all these years. The company name would have been a clue for Gemma to trace her father a long time ago. It is better that she found her way to him on her own, when she was ready.

She hears the sound of hammering. That would be Frankie, putting up a *chuppah*, the traditional canopy used at Jewish weddings. He'd told Tazia at dinner last night that he planned to erect one with posts and a web of olive branches on top. After consulting with his best friend David, whose bar mitzvah he'd attended in junior high school, Frankie had also decided that he and Julia would stomp on a glass, signifying breaking old family ties to start a new one. Only they'd substitute an olive oil cruet for a wine glass. Julia had been enamored of both ideas. Tazia isn't sure what else Frankie has told her about his grandfather, or what the rest of her family has heard. They looked at her aslant over drinks, but since they barely knew her anyway, everyone was too polite to ask whatever questions were on their mind. She expects religion will emerge as an issue when Frankie and Julia are ready to have children, but that is between them to work out.

Slipping Ayal's note in her apron pocket, Tazia lifts her face to the rising sun. It is already getting warm. Normal highs in June are in the low seventies but they are having a heat wave. Four days ago, the temperature was almost one hundred and ten degrees. It's good there will be tents to shade the guests, although Tazia would prefer to stroll through the Benedettis' olive orchard. She grows drowsy, thinking of her family farm in Italy, and through half-lidded eyes, sees a young man in shirt sleeves approaching. For a minute, lost in reverie, she thinks it is one of her brothers, before remembering they are all old now. It is, of course, Frankie.

He hands her a small plate of salmon canapés, intended for the wedding reception.

"You're bringing *me* food?" she asks, patting the chair beside her. "Now that's a switch."

Frankie kisses her and sits. "I'm here to get a cloth to drape over the *chuppah*, Nonna."

"What's traditionally used?"

"David says a prayer shawl, a *tallit*, if possible one that belonged to an ancestor."

Tazia goes into her house and brings out an embroidered shawl. "*My nonna made this and it's what I wear to pray in church.*" Frankie holds it in his hands as if it might blow away, although the day is windless. Tazia expects him to hurry off, but he remains seated. "So," she asks, "beside adding these Jewish rituals, what do you think about discovering who your grandfather is?"

"Funny, but it's not a big deal to me. I only care about him to the extent that he's part of *your* life, which I always want to hear more about." Frankie grins. "Now I know your big, dark secret. How wild you were in your younger days." He studies her as if she's become a different person. Tazia thinks back to last night, how Julia too had regarded her as something other than Frankie's grandmother. In fact, everyone around the table had taken surreptitious glances, seeing her as something more exotic than the old woman she'd been the day before. Only in Lucy's gold eyes is Tazia exactly the same. She smiles to herself and feeds the cat a salmon canapé.

Frankie stirs. "There's so much I want to ask you about that time, but if I don't hurry back to the Benedettis, Mom will have a cow."

Tazia walks him down the driveway. "Like I told your mother yesterday, I'm not going anywhere. There's plenty of time to talk, until I die." Frankie pecks her cheek and saunters off. Tazia stares at the muscles rippling beneath his cotton shirt. Her daughter worries Ayal will try to lure him away, just as she once worried he'd come for Gemma. Tazia has learnt there's no cause for alarm. Children don't let themselves be stolen. They know where, and to whom, they belong.

***

Three hours later, at the Benedettis', Tazia stands to the side, under a grove of trees, as guests begin to arrive. In the clearing where the service will take place, Father O'Brien, a young priest, sets out the items of a traditional

Catholic wedding, gifts of bread and wine which will be brought to the altar once the couple has said their vows and exchanged rings. He looks unfazed about performing a ceremony to unite a Polish bride with an Italian-Irish and now Jewish groom. Tazia smiles at the flexibility of youth.

Nearby, the wedding party conducts a last-minute rehearsal, lining up in the order of the processional and arranging themselves around the *chuppah* beneath which the bride and groom will stand. Earlier there was a debate about whether to smash the cruet after the Rite of Marriage or post Communion. The Lonskis were afraid that done wrong, it would invalidate the marriage, but Father O'Brien had reassured them it didn't matter. God was eager to bless this union.

From her off-centre post, Tazia observes Gemma flit around, straightening tablecloths, misting flowers, moving centre pieces a quarter of an inch and then moving them back. Twice Todd waltzes her around to calm her down. The third time, however, Gemma stays agitated. She glances over her husband's shoulder toward the area where guests are parking, anxiously scanning the approaching faces. She is looking for Ayal. Her lips move in silent prayer. Tazia imagines her daughter imploring the Holy Father not to let her own father come.

Once again, Tazia considers where she stands on this issue. Given a choice, she wants to see him. It's an interesting, and unexpected, reversal of positions. Her family would be happier if Ayal didn't show his face and, of course, she wants the day to go well for them. Yet, a selfish part of her is curious about what a reunion with him would be like. The possibility of this moment has followed her for half a century. Now that she's stopped running, Ayal can catch up to her. She smiles, ready for him. Deeply rooted, like a hundred-year-old olive tree, she can stand her ground.

The photographer arrives. Gemma looks toward Tazia, frowns at her son, and shakes her head. Frankie laughs and, ignoring his mother, strides to where Tazia observes the proceedings. He extends his hand and Tazia takes it, following him to a spot midway between the altar and the *chuppah*. Frankie makes her stand next to him, with Gemma, Todd, and Patrick and Maura Kane to her left. Julia is on Frankie's right, with her parents and four grandparents completing their half of the picture. Thirteen people, a lucky number after all. Tazia smiles for the camera.

acknowledgements

Pinpointing where the idea for a book germinates is elusive. Likewise is knowing where to begin thanking those who helped nurse it from conception to production. To start with essentials, I extend my gratitude to everyone connected with Vine Leaves Press. First, I send a rousing thank you to Peter Snell who recommended the book for publication and whose unflagging enthusiasm for good books reassures writers everywhere that we will always find an audience. Second, I express both awe and gratitude toward the multi-talented Jessica Bell, whose literary and creative abilities make every VLP publication a work of art. If I could sing as well as her, I'd warble my appreciation. Third, my heartfelt thanks go to my fairy godmother Dawn Ius, who stepped in to once again wow me with her development edits. Our dialogues and digressions merit a book in themselves. Fourth, fifth, sixth, et. al, I have such admiration and gratitude for the remaining cast on the production team. VLP is a truly global endeavor, and its publications reflect the staff's collective sophistication and dedication to the art of the word and its ability to unite the world.

The next people to acknowledge are my fellow writers. I began with a short story that later became the opening chapter in the book. My "Saturday" writers group was the first to set eyes on Tazia's opening story and helped shape the narrative that gave birth to Gemma and the novel. Special thanks to group members Lori Eaton, Amy Gustine, Marni Hoffman, Keith Hood, Danielle Lavaque-Manti, Paul Many, Cathy Mellett, Polly Rosenwaike, and Sonja Srinivasan. Once I embarked on the book, my "Sunday" writers group sustained me as I debated the best way to handle structure (narrative plus interviews), character development, and the balance between historical detail and dramatic momentum. For their unflagging encouragement, I thank Janet Gilsdorf, Marty Calvert, Danielle Lavaque-Manti (again), Cynthia Jalynski, and Jane Johnson.

I'm lucky to have a stalwart set of friends who read my work. Chief among them are Gerald Gardner, Terry Alexander, Lynn Liben, Benedette Palazzola, Jennifer Burd, and Sue Terdan. I'm also blessed with supportive relatives, notably my brother Joel Savishinsky and cousins Pam Alson and

Joy Bader. I don't ask them for feedback, only the reward of a guaranteed fan base to cheer me on. My son-in-law Milton Dixon validates my delight in the research I do. He shares my joy in learning for its own sake. Milton is also half responsible for my grandsons Oscar and Emmett Dixon-Epstein. My play dates with them refresh me at the end of each writing day, and their love of books delivers the comfort of knowing that literature will endure.

Last, and always most important in my life, is my daughter Rebecca Epstein. *Tazia and Gemma* is ultimately a story about a single mother raising her daughter, teaching her about self-respect, justice, and familial love. If the person my daughter has grown into is a measure of my achievement in this central endeavor of my creative life, then I am thrilled to have succeeded.

vine leaves press

Enjoyed this book?
Go to *vineleavespress.com* to find more.